DEEP INTO THE DARK

ALSO BY P. J. TRACY

THE MONKEEWRENCH SERIES

Ice Cold Heart
The Guilty Dead
Nothing Stays Buried
The Sixth Idea
Off the Grid
Shoot to Thrill
Snow Blind
Dead Run
Live Bait
Monkeewrench

The Return of the Magi

DEEP INTO THE DARK

P. J. TRACY

MINOTAUR BOOKS
NEW YORK

This is a work of fiction. All of the characters, organizations, and events portrayed in this novel are either products of the author's imagination or are used fictitiously.

First published in the United States by Minotaur Books, an imprint of St. Martin's Publishing Group

www.minotaurbooks.com

Designed by Devan Norman

Library of Congress Cataloging-in-Publication Data

Names: Tracy, P. J., author.
Title: Deep into the dark / P.J. Tracy.
Description: First edition. | New York : Minotaur Books, 2021.
Identifiers: LCCN 2020035305 | ISBN 9781250754943 (hardcover) |
ISBN 9781250783578 (ebook)
Subjects: GSAFD: Mystery fiction.
Classification: LCC PS3620.R33 D44 2021 | DDC 813/.6—dc23
LC record available at https://lccn.loc.gov/2020035305

First Edition: 2021

10 9 8 7 6 5 4 3 2 1

To PJ

LA is a jungle

—JACK KEROUAC

DEEP INTO THE DARK

Prologue

LOS ANGELES, THE CITY OF ANGELS. The sobriquet promised the divine and its golden façade radiated celestial perfection, but peel back the fragile veneer and the deception was revealed. There were very few angels here, and even less perfection, a testament to how torpid the human race had become.

He understood *true* perfection and knew it was extremely difficult to achieve. The correct psychological approach was paramount to actualizing it. You had to eschew insecurity and disregard the internal voices that would stifle your creativity. External obstacles must be confronted with confidence and determination. Your self-dialogue could not be negative or influenced in any way by the recollection of past setbacks or failures. Chronic remorse, Aldous Huxley had written, was a most undesirable sentiment.

Don't wait for opportunity, make opportunity. And perhaps the most important tenet of all: never allow yourself to think the next body of work *has* to be perfect; instead, have faith that it *will* be perfect. Conviction, experience, patience and discipline, planning: all critical components to the execution of a worthy creation.

He was finally prepared. When the time was right, it would be flawless. "Three's a charm," he whispered, watching the woman he knew so well, a rare angel, enter the bar, envisioning what she would look like dead. The next body of work to be executed. That was funny.

Chapter One

HOT. HOT AS HELL. RELENTLESS SUN warped by thermals rising in sluggish, syrupy pillars above the dull landscape of rock and sand. The Shamal wind blasting his exposed cheeks with grit. The soft, steady rumble of the Humvee in front of him, fumes from the exhaust, and then a sudden, deafening sound as the unrelieved beige transformed into unthinkable things. Pink mist, a fireball—shining, twisted metal kiting awkwardly in the air and slashing down on him along with body parts. An arm, white bone with stringers of sinew and bloody, shredded muscle trailing from it. A leg, half a face, a hand . . . were those fingers? Disembodied phalanges snatching at the air in an attempt to break their fall?

What did you see? What do you remember?

A child screaming. And then total deafness, total blackness.

Sam Easton woke up shouting on the floor next to his bed, legs tangled and thrashing against the damp sheets he'd dragged to the floor during his somnambulant dive to safety. It had been three days since the last dream. He was getting better.

It took five minutes for his heart to subside into normal sinus rhythm, another five for his mind to firmly settle back into the present. He'd reluctantly given up the tranquilizers two months ago because they made him tired and fuzzy. They were also highly addictive and he'd felt that dragon growing inside him like a demonic fetus, so he'd slayed it to forestall any more dysfunction in his life. Those early days without the cute little oval crutches were bad, so bad that desperation had driven him to entertain more holistic options. The vast, dubious landscape of alternative medicine had frustrated him enough to consider voodoo, satanism, or anything else that didn't entail a regimen of bark tea, yoga, or colonics. Whoever had come up with the notion that bowel-purging was equivalent to soul-cleansing was a masochistic idiot.

But it hadn't been all bad because he'd learned a little about meditation, and lately, he found that if he took deep breaths and focused on the Maneki Neko lucky cat statue on the dresser—two paws raised for protection—he could cleanse his memory without pharmaceuticals or violating any orifices. Not entirely, but enough to function during the day without slipping back in time. That used to happen at the most unpredictable and inconvenient times—during job interviews, dinner out, while he was making love to his wife, Yukiko. She was the one who had given him the lucky cat. It was ridiculous, but it helped, and he had a very Machiavellian outlook on wellness.

The new antipsychotic Dr. Frolich had given him also helped, and the booze did, too, at least on a temporary basis. But that was expressly verboten, at least from a clinical perspective. Besides, he'd promised Yuki he'd stop drinking, although that promise remained woefully unfulfilled.

Not that she was here to keep tabs on him. Everything that was broken about him had finally chased her away three months ago. She'd been brave and loyal and patient, but everybody had a tipping point. He didn't blame her for wanting some distance. For needing it. If he could leave himself, he would. He still regretted bringing that up in therapy.

Are you having suicidal ideations, Sam?

If, by that, you mean do I want to kill myself, then no.

He hadn't exactly been lying to Dr. Frolich. He'd had enough death for a lifetime and he certainly had no plans to enact his own, but the thought did cross his mind on occasion. That was something he'd never confess to her because the repercussions would be endless and intolerable. And really, how many people in times of despair or hardship hypothetically pondered the idea of leaving this world prematurely by their own hand with no intention of acting on it? A lot, he was certain of that. Nihilistic thoughts were a dark, human indulgence, specifically a First World phenomenon by his estimation. Nobody who genuinely feared for their life thought about killing themselves; they just thought about survival.

Once he could trust his legs to carry him, he went into the bathroom, turned on the shower, and brushed his teeth without looking in the mirror. It hadn't taken him long to break that very normal, knee-jerk human habit—just a simple check to see how you looked. Did you have crazy hair? Clear eyes or bloodshot ones? Dried drool at the corner of your mouth? But mirrors made you see things through another's eyes, and nobody, including him, and maybe especially him, wanted to look at a bifurcated face.

Viewed from the good side, it was handsome, with sharp planes and a strong, straight nose inherited from his father. But the other half had been seared into waxen rubble that seemed to ooze over reconstructed bone. The plastic surgeons claimed they weren't finished with him yet; but in his opinion, some things just couldn't be repaired and he was beginning to accept that. Maybe one day he'd look at himself in the mirror again and see what was there, not what wasn't.

A randy, neglected wife of a movie producer had told him his face was sexy and mysterious, like a half-finished picture of Dorian Gray. This literate cougar had been drunk and probably coked up at the time, putting her education to use in a way she'd probably never imagined back in college. He'd escaped her wandering hands and the awkward encounter easily enough, but the memory hadn't left his mind. There was something profoundly sad and bent about it.

His rear side was a different story. Without his face staring back at him, he was just observing somebody else's misfortune, and it was morbidly fascinating to him. Every morning when he got into the shower, he glanced in the mirror at the strong, ropy muscles of his back and buttocks, and the scars that crisscrossed them. A chunk of flesh missing here, a little piece missing there. Whole but not.

At least you made it back.

That day nobody else had, not Kev or Shaggy or Wilson, who had left behind widows and children—and not Rondo, a colonel's son whose greatest fear wasn't death but disappointing his father.

Sam wasn't entirely sure he'd made it back, either. He didn't need a shrink to tell him that, just like he didn't need a shrink to tell him why he could look at his ass but not his face.

He stood under the hot water for a long time, watching the suds from a bar of Irish Spring foam from his skin and swirl down the drain. The foam was always white, and he wondered what reaction caused the green variegations in the bar of soap to disappear when they hit water. His degree was in electrical engineering, not chemical, so he was content to let it remain a mystery.

He shaved the good half of his face blindly, then dried off and dressed in jeans and the requisite logo T-shirt for his lunch shift. Was Pearl Club the only cocktail lounge in Los Angeles that could boast a bar back with an engineering degree? Sadly, probably not.

Chapter Two

MARGARET NOLAN WASN'T ANTISOCIAL; SHE JUST didn't like human beings as a general rule. She especially didn't like them in her private space, which was sanctuary from the world at large and especially from her work. The irony wasn't lost on her that the only two people outside of family she'd invited to see her new house also happened to be colleagues: Detective Al Crawford, her partner in Los Angeles PD's Homicide Special Section; and Detective Remy Beaudreau, also of Homicide Special Section, and a man she was probably going to sleep with soon, against her better judgment. So much for balance in life.

It wasn't a housewarming party—to call two guests a party was pitiable. But whatever it was, it had been a stupid idea from conception, and in a moment of weakness, she'd allowed herself to be bullied into it by Al.

Come on, Mags, it's not like donating a kidney.

How the hell did he know? He still had all his organs.

With the imminent arrival of Al and Remy, she was suddenly seeing her Woodland Hills rental from a different, hypercritical perspective, which really pissed her off. It didn't seem so enchanting now; it just seemed like an outdated cube perched on a tuft of crab grass. There was no back yard, just a skinny strip of concrete walkway, shadowed by a vaulting, scrubby hillside that provided superior habitat for pet-devouring coyotes. The front yard wasn't much better, the prominent feature being an overgrown clump of bird of paradise. The agent had told her it was the official flower of Los Angeles, which was news to her, but this one didn't have any flowers. From the dismal appearance of the foliage, she doubted it ever would. Maybe she should fertilize it.

It's really lovely, honey, so much better than that tiny apartment in Echo Park. Let me help you unpack the rest of these boxes and then I'll take you to lunch.

Mom had seemed to approve in her usual reticent way. When she liked something, or pretended to, there was always a qualifier, always a reminder of something negative that killed some of the joy. Even so, it had been a nice morning spent together, drinking coffee and assembling a house. Until Mom had excavated photos of Max.

After ten minutes of crying in the bathroom, she'd declared a migraine and fled the scene like Satan himself was chasing her. Two days later, she'd dragged Daddy to Hawaii for an extended stay. Everybody dealt with grief in their own way, but she hadn't realized until that day her mother chose not to deal with it at all.

She sighed and kept an eye on the front window as she fussed with the placement of the cocktail napkins, stemware, and plates on the dining room table—the vase of freesias in the middle. She shouldn't have gone with the freesias. They were too small to be a proper centerpiece, and their aggressive fragrance competed with the funk of the cheese board she'd spent a fortune on at the Beverly Hills Cheese Store.

Why do you care? What is your problem?

The problem was, Nolan was an unrelenting perfectionist, even if she was doing something contrary to her misanthropic nature. She had no skills in this milieu, couldn't even comprehend the desire to acquire them. Her transient military family, always exhausted from ricocheting from country to country, had never developed any yen to entertain, so she had no example to emulate or work from. Her former, hateful apartment in Echo Park certainly hadn't been inspiration to start exploring the art of hosting, and her job didn't allow her much time to even consider it because people were constantly killing one another in this city.

The throaty rumble of a Porsche engine announced the first arrival.

Remy pulled into the driveway and climbed out of his sleek, sapphire-blue car carrying an obscenely large bouquet of white lilies and a bottle of champagne in a silver bucket. He was wearing casual linen instead of a suit, and it was disconcerting to see him out of his work clothes for the first time, one step closer to nudity.

Maybe it would be equally jarring to him, seeing her one step closer to nudity in a dress, her arms and legs exposed. But she didn't think so. Aside from the fact that he was probably accustomed to imagining her naked, nothing seemed to faze him, not even the most horrific crime scene. He was either a sociopath or had a titanium shell protecting his soft spots.

She held the door open for him, noticing its clunky paint job for the first time. "Wow. Is this all for me?"

"It's a housewarming, right? Or am I at the wrong place?"

She smirked and took the flowers and champagne. "Not a house-warming, but thanks, this is really nice of you."

He was tall and thin, with black, indecipherable eyes, a terrific head of curly hair, a sauntering walk. She'd never been able to ascertain if his gait was out of arrogance or a result of his physique.

He looked around and nodded his approval. "This is a great place, Maggie."

"It's better than where I was."

"Your enthusiasm is infectious."

It suddenly struck her that she knew very little about this man on her threshold, this man bearing lavish gifts. The extent of her knowledge was that he came from a wealthy Louisiana family and had graduated from Tulane before signing up for the police academy in Los Angeles. He was affable enough, but there was a secretive, chilling darkness surrounding him that precluded the usual small talk that was a normal part of getting to know someone. It was definitely a factor in the attraction, maybe the sole source of it. How disappointing it would be to learn mundane details of Remy's life, like he brushed his teeth in the morning along with everybody else.

She frowned, discomfited by the realization that she was hot for a human version of a redacted document, which said more about her than him. The fact that he hadn't commented on her dress or how great she looked in it said more about him than her. She appreciated a grown-up who didn't slobber for sex. Gratuitous flattery was repellent.

"Something wrong?"

"No. Yeah. I'm a terrible hostess because we're still standing in the foyer. Come in." She gestured him into the dining room and stuffed his flowers into the vase along with the freesia. "They're beautiful, Remy."

"White is a representation of death in some cultures, so it seemed particularly appropriate given our mutual vocation."

"I'm truly touched by the macabre symbolism. Interesting that brides wear white in Western culture, isn't it? Or maybe it's appropriate."

He raised a brow at her. "You're wearing a lovely shade of pessimism this evening. If it makes you feel any better, when I asked you out for a drink, I wasn't talking about marriage."

Her cheeks flared and Remy noticed. It was the bane of the fair complexion that accompanied strawberry blond hair. She'd been avoiding The Drink for weeks because she didn't trust herself or Remy. They were both on the summit of the same hormonal slippery slope that led to regret and ruin. Life was dangerous in so many ways.

His flat, obsidian eyes were on her, eyes that seemed to follow her and see everything, like in those spooky portraits of Jesus her grandmother had hanging all over her house. "Open that champagne and tell me how you like living in the Valley. You were in Echo Park before, right?"

"Right." She peeled the foil from the top of the bottle and wasn't sure what to do about the metal cage around the cork. How pathetic. She was in her third decade and didn't know how to open a bottle of champagne. He graciously spared her further humiliation by taking the bottle and deftly freeing the cork. Not with a dramatic pop but with the faintest hiss of escaping gas.

When you open a bottle of champagne, it should sound like a Frenchman's fart.

Where the hell had she heard that?

He poured, then lifted his glass to hers. "Cheers to a change of venue."

She gulped down half the glass, then reminded herself of the virtue of temperance. "I guess we're finally having that drink."

"This is coercion, it doesn't count. You didn't tell me how you like the Valley."

"It's nice. Quiet." Another sip. The bubbles were entering her bloodstream and it felt fantastic. "Any breaks on your cases?"

"Unfortunately not."

"I'm sorry. Have some cheese," she said, as if cheese was an antidote to a serial killer.

Remy broke off a piece of Roquefort and wandered back to the living room. "It's got a good vibe, very global."

"I'm a very global person from a very global family."

"There's a story behind everything, then." Like a raptor eyeing a rodent, Remy picked out the most hidden, vulnerable thing: the far corner table that held her brother's memorial. Silver urn with her share of his ashes; a photo of them together before his final deployment to Afghanistan; another vase of freesias, a flower he loved and the reason she always kept them around.

"This is much better than visiting a tombstone and leaving flowers to die on a grave. People we've loved should always be honored like this." His eyes lifted to the window. "Al's here."

She followed Remy's gaze and saw Al trundling up the front walk with a cellophane-wrapped basket. He wasn't wearing a suit either. The blue polo shirt was a little tight around his soft, middle-aged gut, and his khaki slacks were slung low on his waist, a woven belt holding them up. Even though she adored him, she definitely wasn't thinking about him naked. She'd leave that to his lovely, devoted wife, Corinne. He smiled and waved at her, then fumbled in his pants pocket for his phone.

She knew the look. Dispatch. Another dead body, and they were next on the roster. She slammed the rest of her champagne and bolted a large bite of Burgundian cheese with a name she couldn't pronounce.

Party over.

Chapter Three

NOLAN STOOD JUST INSIDE THE MOTEL room's doorway. She always liked to take things in at a distance first; but in this case, she had no choice. The blood splatters radiated so far from the victim on the sagging bed that they created a biohazard crime scene boundary. The walls were splashed with it, and the filthy carpet looked like it had been sprinkled with reddish brown confetti. The aftermath of a butcher, a madman. Jackson Pollock couldn't have done any better.

She was sickened. Enraged. And very, very sad. The environment where a homicide took place said volumes about the killer and the victim. It also determined how depressed she would be for the next several days. When they took place in lovely settings, she attempted self-succor by rationalizing that as atrocious as any murder was, the victim had at least enjoyed some comfort or pleasure in life.

But this poor woman, a resident of Aqua Travel Lodge—a rancid boil in the most squalid part of central Los Angeles—certainly hadn't enjoyed much comfort before death. According to Ray Lovell, the vacuous motel clerk with meth teeth who had found her, she'd been a junkie who sometimes turned tricks, sometimes tended bar at the Kitty Corral, a topless dive across the street that catered to the very bottom layer of human sediment. It all cheapened her violent, sorry demise.

The additional insult was the fact that nobody in this piece of shit, room-by-the-hour flophouse knew her name, not even Ray, who was apprised of a few things about her personal habits, probably because they'd had a sex and drugs association. He wouldn't be shedding any tears tonight.

She desperately wanted to burn the Aqua down, along with everybody in it, because it would certainly be a charitable act for the betterment of humankind. She would never confide to anybody, not even her partner, how she viewed crime scenes or how they sometimes made her feel homicidal, so she endured the anger and depressions in stony, bleak silence.

Al was standing next to her, taking shallow breaths through his mouth to fend against the reek of ripening death. "It's him. It's got to be. Same MO, same hunting ground."

"No question. This is Remy's game, the task force's game. If we'd known this an hour ago, we'd still be at my place drinking his champagne."

"Trust me, the champagne would be gone by now. So this freak mutilates women in public places and keeps walking away without any witnesses. Even if he was wearing a space suit, he'd still be covered in blood just from stripping down, so what's his magic?"

"No magic, he picks motel rooms so he can wash up. Motels like this, where nobody cares what goes on, and where there's probably a decade's worth of blood and hair and body fluid everywhere. It hides the trace."

"You're thinking like a smart killer."

"I'm thinking like a smart detective."

"Maybe the killer is a smart detective."

"Not the right time for stupid syllogisms or jokes, Al."

"It was a partially serious comment. This guy is savvy and slippery."

"He's a shadow dweller, all serials are. Nobody notices them, just like nobody notices their victims until they're dead. If there's any magic, that's it."

"LAPD better figure it out soon. He's got us by the balls right now, and the press is going to go ballistic. Just wait for the morning paper. They're going to make us look like a bunch of diddling troglodytes who can't put their pants on in the morning."

"Since when do you worry about the press?"

"Never, but Remy is heading up the task force, and he's a good guy and a great detective who's going to get smeared unless he has somebody in shackles soon."

"Remy can take care of himself and his task force." She turned away and breathed into the collar of her shirt, hoping the enthusiastically touted "spring fresh scent!" of her laundry detergent would mitigate the rank miasma hanging in the room. More likely, she would always associate clean clothes with a ravaged woman and the stench of death. That's why the coroner warned you never to put mentholated ointment under your nose when you entered the morgue like the cops on TV. If you did, Vicks VapoRub would never soothe a cold or clear your sinuses again; it would just fill them with olfactory memories of decomposition.

Nolan focused on the victim's jeans: bloody, torn at the knees, frayed at the cuffs, but still buttoned and zipped. "He doesn't rape them," she finally said. "Why? Serial killers are almost always psychosexual."

"It's all about control, whatever form it takes. He's getting his rocks off somehow, you can be sure of that." Crawford shook his head and looked away. "This sick fuck is going to make a mistake. They all do eventually."

"Let's hope the Aqua is his last stand."

He retrieved his phone from his suit coat pocket. "Amen to that. I'm going to let Remy know. I'll meet you outside."

While he ducked out to make the call, Nolan took as many steps into the room as she could without contaminating the scene. The nameless woman had been brutalized with a knife, her torso flayed open in a badly botched dissection, just like the previous two victims in the Miracle Mile neighborhood. The only things left of her that resembled anything human were above the neck and below the waist. He never touched their faces, and there wasn't an obvious sexual angle. All of this had significance to an incomprehensibly warped mind, but it wasn't her case to solve.

She offered a silent apology to Jane Doe, then turned away and walked down the dark, garbage-strewn hall to the exit. Outside the smudged glass door, the street was crawling with police cruisers, the night awash with strobing red and blue emergency lights. Garlands of crime scene tape fluttered in the warm night breeze. Radios crackled and voices droned. Beyond the street barricades, the news satellite vans were gathering. Like all predators, they had sharp noses for the scent of blood.

Predators, prey, parasites—that was Los Angeles in three words, and more often than not, it was hard to make a distinction between them.

Remy showed up ten minutes later, wearing a navy blue suit that looked far too expensive for the job he was about to embark upon. She'd thrown away a few suits after particularly gruesome crime scenes, knowing she could never wear them again, so what was the point in spending more than the bare minimum? Maybe he didn't own any cheap suits.

His steady black eyes grazed over both of them and he tipped his head toward the Aqua's blurry front door. "Show me."

Chapter Four

ALL THE STOOLS AT PEARL CLUB'S polished zinc bar were occupied, and the dense crowd of posh, hip Angelenos waiting for vacancies was overwhelming the front of the house. They shifted and jostled to a numbing techno soundtrack under dreamy, cinematic lighting, a combination far more trance-inducing than the liquor they were planning to imbibe.

Melody Traeger hustled to keep up with drink orders because the faster she dispensed alcohol, the bigger the tips got. It was bartender logic at its most basic. She'd also developed a more specific consumer behavior model based on customer types to optimize remuneration for her services.

Statistically speaking, struggling actors left generous tips because they were still in the service industry themselves. Movie biz heavyweights also tipped well because they had large studio expense accounts, but the juniors sometimes didn't tip at all. Music industry people were unpredictable, which skewed her statistics, but anecdotally they were poor tippers unless they were hitting on her, and about fifty percent of them fell into that category. She'd chosen a psychology major purely for the self-help aspect, but it definitely had other practical applications. When she finally got her degree next year, she would be unstoppable.

Tonight had been a long but lucrative shift, and she was counting the minutes until ten, when she could turn the bar over to the relief crew and get on with the rest of the night. Ryan had come here straight from the airport and was waiting for her at the end of the bar, sipping a beer.

One of her smitten regulars, a venerated session drummer and producer named Markus Ellenbeck, flagged her over. He was an unabashed anachronism, with his dyed black mullet and chunky, clunky rock 'n' roll jewelry. There was no pretense or posturing about it; he was simply wearing the skin that made him comfortable, uncaring that the skin was outdated by a few decades. You couldn't fault anybody for authenticity. It was an admirable trait.

He smiled and laid a fifty on the bar. "Can I get another martini, Mel?"

"Sure, same gin?"

"Yeah, and a couple extra olives for dinner." He leaned forward and winked conspiratorially. "Hey. I think I finally figured out why you look so familiar."

"I keep telling you why. It's LA, I'm blond, and I have one of those faces."

He looked victorious, as if he'd just solved the mystery of the universe. "Poke."

"Poke what?"

"It was an all-girl punk band."

"Never heard of them."

"Not many people have. They weren't around long, but they were good." His eyes probed her, looking for signs of deception. "You played guitar. Actually, you shredded guitar. Your stage name was Roxy Codone."

"You're hilarious. I've never touched a guitar in my life and I hate punk rock."

He deflated a little, and then his uncertainty turned to full-blown disappointment as he studied her face more carefully. "I guess I'm off base, you're way too pretty to be Roxy. She was a fucking mess."

"Keep trying, sweetie. Maybe one day you'll remember the first time you saw me was here," she said, and whisked away his empty glass.

She stole a quick glimpse of herself in the mirror behind the bar as she reached for the expensive gin Markus liked to drink. Between the colorful bottles, she saw a smooth, young face that didn't betray what she'd been a few years ago, the very least of which had been a guitarist for Poke. In fact, aside from the tattoos, she looked downright fresh and innocent in contrast to the slinking, hyper-coiffed flowers of both sexes that flourished here like an invasive species.

It wouldn't be difficult for Markus to confirm his suspicion. She wasn't living in anonymity, just going by her middle name now instead of Antoinette. But he wouldn't bother. Poke was ancient history, four years gone, and nobody cared what had happened to Roxy Codone. Once you ditched your Twitter account and disappeared from the stage, you were as good as dead.

Ryan knew who she was and what she had been and he liked her anyway. That's why she thought they might have a future together. He was also handsome in a dark, brooding way, very successful, and worked in the music industry—all very alluring attributes.

She served Markus his martini with extra olives, started working on margaritas for table twenty-seven, and glanced at Ryan. He turned his hands over in a questioning gesture—almost ready?—then went back to his disapproving scrutiny of the crowd, keeping a watchful eye on the men clamoring for her attention or another drink, especially Markus.

His jealousy bothered her sometimes, but it was an imperfection she could live with. Everybody had a green streak. It was human nature, and men could be territorial Neanderthals. She and Ryan fought sometimes, they broke up and made up, but wasn't that the way it was with every relationship?

She passed him a smile and held up five fingers for five minutes. He shrugged and drained the rest of his beer.

"You know that guy at the end of the bar?" Markus asked.

"Not really your business, is it?"

"I suppose it isn't, but I like you a lot, Mel. Steer clear of him. He's a flaming asshole."

•

Ryan filled two wine glasses with an excellent California cabernet and brought them to the living room where Melody was luxuriating in the splendor of his apartment. She loved the vast, open space and the oversized leather sofa with down-filled pillows that were as soft and yielding as marshmallows. She was enthralled by the gleaming chrome and glass and granite, the lacquered cabinet with its dizzying array of high-end electronics. There was a grand piano in a corner by the bank of windows that looked down on cacophonous Sunset Boulevard. She could get used to living in a place like this.

He sat down next to her, put an arm over her shoulder, and clinked her glass in a silent toast. He seemed sullen and preoccupied, which puzzled her.

"How was Vegas?"

"Fine."

She took a delicate sip and let the expensive wine loll on her tongue before swallowing, just like the wine reps did when they hosted staff tastings at Pearl Club. "That's it, it was fine?"

"Just business. Boring compared to you." He brushed her cheek with the back of his hand. "I've been thinking."

Melody sensed a subtle shift between them and felt a wisp of anticipation stirring through her body. She'd suspected for a while that he might ask her to move in with him, and now might be the time. And how would she react? Not too enthusiastically, she decided. "About what?"

"Pearl Club. I want you to quit."

She blinked at him, confounded. He might as well have dumped a bucket of ice water over her. "What are you talking about?"

He glowered into his wine, then got up and started pacing. "You heard me. It's not a good place for you, for us. Shitheads like Markus Ellenbeck drooling over you all night—hitting on you—it's embarrassing and makes me sick. I don't want you around him, and I don't want you at Pearl. I can't take it anymore."

"You're kidding, right?"

"No, I'm not. Quit."

She felt her mouth slip open in astonishment. How could this even be a topic of conversation, let alone a serious one? "I can't quit. I make great money and I have rent and tuition to pay."

"I'm sure you can find something else that pays just as well where they don't make you dress like a . . ." He eyed her abbreviated tank top and shorts disdainfully. "Like *that*."

Melody's stomach knotted and her heart was pounding so hard that she could feel the throb in her temples. Ryan was being outrageous, ridiculous, and so viciously cold. She felt brittle all over, on the verge of shattering. But she couldn't find any words. She would be like millions of other people who tossed and turned in their beds tonight, imagining what clever, cutting things they might have said.

"Guys hit on me, big deal," she finally said, hating how feeble her voice sounded. "Pearl Club isn't unique in that regard."

He stopped pacing and sipped his wine thoughtfully. "Maybe you like it."

"And maybe, since you haven't offered any alternatives, this conversation is over." She stood abruptly and grabbed her jacket. "I'm not fighting about this, it's ludicrous."

"Come on, Mel, don't ruin things over a stupid job. We have fun together, and you want to keep having fun, don't you? I know I do."

Fury and heartbreak didn't seem to go together, yet those were the two overwhelming emotions she felt. "That sounds like an ultimatum."

He shrugged apathetically. "It's just a choice. I'm surprised you're finding it such a difficult one to make."

Stand up for yourself.

"I'm not quitting," she said with resolve. "Pearl Club helped me pull my life together and it's paying for my education, which should be more important to you than your fragile ego."

His speed startled her and she couldn't duck fast enough. Suddenly, she was fifteen again, semiconscious on the filthy floor of her father's trailer in eastern Coachella Valley. Bright, spiky stars floated behind her closed eyes and his hateful voice was remote, thick and garbled, like it was coming from someplace far away. But not far enough.

One day you're gonna learn to keep your mouth shut, you stupid little bitch.

Chapter Five

SAM WAS SITTING IN THE HOT sand, playing poker with Kev, Shaggy, and Wilson. Old-school, five-card stud because they were all sick of Texas Hold'em. They were drinking Cokes they wished were beers, trash-talking each other, laughing. Planning the next prank that would keep everybody from hanging themselves.

The landscape was desolate, except for a free-standing Pizza Hut guarded by two goats with bells shaped like guns hanging from their skinny necks. More goats materialized, coming down from the distant mountains, followed by military personnel from enlisted to generals. They swirled around them, oblivious to their presence and their poker game.

Except for Captain Greer, who approached them carrying a tower of pizza boxes. "I'm in for the next hand with pepperoni and extra cheese." He tossed the boxes on top of the kitty, made up of the dog tags of dead service members.

Sam searched the crowd of humans and goats. "Where's Rondo?"

"Who cares?" Kev said.

"Probably off by himself, unraveling somewhere," Shaggy snorted. "Dude's not cut out for this shit."

Wilson was flicking his fingers against his cards impatiently. "Weak of the herd. Guy like that could get us all killed."

Sam couldn't understand why his friends were being such assholes.

"He's still got our backs, cut him some slack." He looked to Captain Greer, who was busy feeding a slice of pizza to a goat.

"We won't leave anyone behind," he finally said. "Not even Rondo."

Wilson called the hand and Sam threw down a full house. Black aces and eights. The dead man's hand.

"Lucky fucker!" Shaggy howled, throwing his cards in the air.

Kev smiled. He didn't have any teeth, and there were dark holes where his eyes should have been. "Not so lucky." He slapped down four of a kind, made up of decapitated queens.

A scowling Afghan air force officer appeared, wearing a powdered wig and a shredded, black judge's robe over his uniform. "It doesn't count if the queens don't have heads. Off with their heads!"

Everyone but Sam started laughing. Even the goats were laughing. He started to panic. "Where's Rondo?" he asked again.

"Rondo's gone," Wilson said solemnly. "We're all gone. Go home, Sam."

"I don't know where that is anymore."

"Sure you do. For fuck's sake, don't stay here."

Everything flashed white, then red. In the distance, a child screamed as a set of bloody dog tags flew through the air and landed on his lap. They seared his hands when he turned them over to read the name: Ronald Doerr. Rondo.

Sam didn't wake up on the floor this time, but his throat was raw, so he knew he'd been shouting, maybe screaming. Yuki wasn't here to wake him up anymore, so the dreams went on for as long as his subconscious allowed it, which was always too long. His zero-three record was perilously close to being nullified. Still, it was true he hadn't had a dream for three nights. That was something to hang onto.

He lay on his back, steeping in sweat as he stared at the ceiling. Supposedly, remembering was the only way to forget. But dreams like this one weren't memories, they were ghoulish, torturous mosaics of guilt and fear, sorrow and regret.

When he was fairly certain his heart wasn't going to explode, he went to the shower to find comfort in a familiar ritual: avoid the face, look at the backside, watch the magic white leprechaun foam swirl down the drain. He pulled on running shorts and an Army T-shirt and headed for the kitchen to make coffee.

There was a woman on his sofa, snoring softly. Not his wife. Melody, a slender, tattooed arm hanging out from beneath a throw his mom had crocheted for him before his first tour in Afghanistan. A piece of home, she'd said proudly as she'd presented it to him. He would never tell her the truth, that he hadn't taken it with him on either tour because he didn't want it despoiled by war, and it had been the right decision.

Apparently, the early morning thud of the *Los Angeles Times* hitting the front stoop had stirred Melody awake because it was lying on her chest, opened to a headline that read: "Third Woman Found Mutilated—Is There a Monster in Miracle Mile?"

A really stupid article because of course there was a monster in Miracle Mile; he'd butchered two women since April, and today's grisly discovery on June tenth made it three. One a month. There had been a low-level frisson in the city, people on edge, waiting to see if there would be another. *When* there would be another. And now, in their incalculable idiocy, the press had granted him a moniker, further motivation to keep up the great work.

Sam squinted against the sunlight coming through the partially opened living room blinds, felt a wicked headache start to gnaw at the fringes of his scrambled brain. He noticed the black Jeep Rubicon parked across the street again, morning dew pearling on all the tinted windows except for the driver's side that faced his house. He'd been seeing it intermittently for the past few months, and as stupid and irrational as it was, its presence agitated him. Then again, a lot of things agitated him lately; topping the list were his uncertainty about his mental stability and his ambivalence toward his future.

Sam closed the shade and gathered twelve empty beer bottles from the coffee table. It had been a long night. More for Melody than for him. He'd had five beers, the rest were hers. No wonder his screaming hadn't wakened her.

Chapter Six

VIVIAN EASTON SERVED COFFEE FROM HER great grandmother's Tiffany sterling service, pouring into delicate Limoges cups. The pieces were such beautiful relics of a bygone era, a part of her inheritance she rarely used. It was so nice to finally have an occasion to open the glass-front hutch and revisit her family history, as ignominious as it was.

Their association with William Mulholland and the Los Angeles Aqueduct project at the turn of the twentieth century had made fortunes for all involved by desiccating and destroying entire towns through chicanery and propaganda. She wasn't particularly proud of that legacy, and her mother had rebelled violently against it, joining the 60s counterculture and never leaving, even when it was long dead. Quite an overreaction in her opinion.

In spite of some personal misgivings about her family wealth, it still frosted her that Mulholland had a famous road named after him when it was her great-grandfather who'd really made the aqueduct a reality. He'd done so much for the city, helped make Los Angeles what it was today. He'd also made golf courses in the former desert of Southern California possible, which in her mind was redemption of a sort for past sins.

"Do you take cream or sugar these days, Lee?"

"No, but thank you, Vivian." General Leland Varney was a broad and effusive man, and his florid cheeks impressed on people the appearance of perpetual anger. But Vivian had always found him to be a magnanimous and jolly soul despite his rank and the political maneuvering it had undoubtedly taken to get there.

He took a sip from his flowered china cup and gestured expansively, as if bestowing upon the world the graces of her lovely Pasadena yard. "This is such a beautiful place. The gardens are glorious. I always remembered you had quite a green thumb, but I don't recall the pool."

"Jack and I put it in the year before he died. It was his favorite thing in the world. I couldn't keep him out of the water."

"I don't doubt that Jack loved it. Water was in his soul. I always wondered why he chose the Army instead of the Navy. Whenever I asked, he was vague about it."

Vivian raised a brow circumspectly. "That surprises me. I never considered Jack to be vague about anything. He never mentioned his father?"

"Oh, he did, but always in passing. Colonel Dean Easton, very decorated, a Vietnam war hero."

"And an intransigent Army man. Dean's influence was encompassing, and he wouldn't hear of the Navy. It was West Point or nothing."

Lee shook his head ruefully and let his gaze drift to the pergola, riotous with lush pendulums of lavender wisteria. "God, I miss Jack. Horribly unfair, him being taken from us so young."

Vivian nodded solemnly. It *was* unfair, a fit and vibrant man taken down by a faulty heart. Humans were all just ticking genetic time bombs, waiting to explode. Jack had told her that in the hospital in the presence of his doctors, who'd given bland smiles and uneasy nods. They knew. Life was short, and if the capricious lottery of DNA didn't favor you, it was much shorter. "I thought it would get easier with time, that's what they tell you, but sometimes I think it gets harder. Is it the same for you with Katherine?"

"It's been ten years, and I still wake up every morning expecting her to be there. And in a way, I guess she still is. What do you do to fill your time now, Vivian?"

She pushed a silver tray of pastel macarons toward her guest. "I've been trying my hand at baking. And of course, I golf quite a bit."

Lee chuckled. "Jack was never a fan."

"He thought it was dreadfully boring. But of course, anything would be boring after combat, he was a bit of an adrenaline junkie."

"Yes, he was." Lee shook his head in disapproval. "I can't believe we're still in the goddamn sand after all these years. Sorry for the language."

"No need to apologize. I feel the same."

His eyes shifted from the wisteria to a grouping of agapanthus. "Jack and I started our careers over there in the first Gulf War. That's almost thirty years ago."

"A long time. Too long."

He rubbed his chin thoughtfully and recaptured her gaze. "I've always believed that peace is a utopian delusion, an anomaly and antithetical to human nature. Somebody always has something worth killing over, and any serious student of history will tell you that."

"Put that way, peace does seem naïve."

"But I still pray for it even though it would put my kind out of a job. But I'm not here to discuss world affairs or philosophy. I want to know about Sam, I think of him every day. How is he faring?"

Vivian allowed herself a distressed sigh. "He seems to be doing much better, at least he tells me so. But I'm his mother, so of course I worry about him constantly."

"A tragedy and a hell of a thing to recover from, but Sam's got it in him. When I visited him at Walter Reed, I saw a fine, brave young man with a fighting spirit, just like his father. His docs there agreed with me."

"He was grateful for your visits. Being hospitalized for that long was extremely difficult for him."

"No gratitude necessary. You're both family to me. Is Sam still having trouble with his memory? I know it was frustrating for him, but things like that have a tendency to resolve as the brain heals."

"I think that aspect is improving, but unfortunately he keeps his struggles from me. I don't know if he really believes he's fooling me or if he's trying to protect me."

"A bit of both, I imagine. I've been looking into some excellent engineering opportunities with the government. When he's ready to start talking jobs, I'll set him up."

"That's another thing that troubles me. He's only interned as an engineer and went straight into the Army after college. He loved soldiering more than anything, and it's really all he's known."

"A good soldier adapts, and Sam was a great one. Believe me, he's going to excel in whatever he chooses. I'll make sure he lands in the right place for him."

"Thank you, Lee."

"Is Yukiko still being supportive?"

Vivian felt her face turn into a stiff, emotionless mask, like it was entombed by wax or frozen by an overly aggressive Botox session, two beauty treatments she indulged herself on occasion. But this was free of charge—her facial muscles simply froze whenever unpleasant things came up. "They recently separated."

"I'm very disappointed to hear that."

"I was as well, but Sam tells me it's temporary, and I'm certainly hoping for that. He needs stability in his life right now."

Lee nodded commiseratively. "It takes a certain temperament to be a military spouse. There is tremendous sacrifice required in the very best of circumstances, not to mention the worst, and some people just aren't up for the job."

Vivian thought about her own rebellion against her mother, marrying a military man, which had galled her to no end. There had been plenty of sacrifices along the way; but Lee was right, some people just weren't up for the job. But when you truly loved someone, you stood by them no matter what. "I just want Sam to be happy. I try not to judge Yukiko, but it's difficult in my position."

"Understandable. What can I do to help?"

"I'm sure he'd love to see you while you're in town." Vivian's facial muscles re-engaged as a plan suddenly formed in her mind. "I was going to invite him to dinner this Sunday. Won't you join us if you're still in town?"

"I will be in town, and I'd be honored."

"Wonderful!" She plucked a pink macaron from the tray. "It's so good to see you, Lee, but I have to ask what brings you to Los Angeles. We're a long way from D.C."

He smiled and his tanned face crinkled into an intricate web of wrinkles. "I'll tell you a little secret if you promise to keep it to yourself for now."

Vivian clasped her hands together. There was nothing she loved more than secrets. They allayed the tedium of life after children were grown and husbands were dead. "You have my word. I won't tell a soul."

"Of course you know Captain Andrew Greer, Sam's commanding officer."

"Certainly. Sam has always thought the world of him."

"I assure you, the feeling is mutual."

"I'm glad to hear that, I thought it might be. He was very attentive after the accident whenever he was stateside. I understand he received a Bronze Star."

"He did, and it was well deserved. He's an excellent man and a natural leader."

"Sam said as much, so I was quite surprised to learn he'd left the Army with such a promising future in service."

"I was initially, too, until I heard his vision for service of another kind. Andy is quietly forming an exploratory committee and aims to run for Congress next election if the tea leaves read right. I think he's the man for the job, so I'm lending a hand where I can, introducing him to some top people I know here on the West Coast. He flies in tonight."

"That's such exciting news!"

"I think so. Andy has also mentioned Sam on several occasions. We both think he would be an outstanding asset to the team in any capacity, whatever he might be ready for. If you have an extra place setting, I'm certain he'd cancel anything to join us on Sunday. I know he wants to tell Sam personally while he's in town."

Chapter Seven

SAM POPPED TWO SLICES OF BREAD in the toaster and started a pot of coffee. While he considered poaching some eggs, he heard soft, apologetic footsteps as Melody made her way into the kitchen, his mother's crocheted throw draped over her shoulders. A drinker's sleep had mussed her hair into tangled strands of blond, and her pretty face was marred by an ugly black eye.

She sagged wearily into a chair at the cheap dinette table he'd picked up at a garage sale two weeks ago. Yuki had taken the Stickley that used to sit on the braided rug to furnish the rental bungalow she now called home. For some reason, she hadn't taken the rug.

"Thanks for letting me stay last night, Sam."

"Anytime," he said, setting a plate of buttered toast down in front of her. "You can stay whenever you want, just as long as you get rid of that Ryan asshole who likes to hit girls."

She touched her black eye gingerly, then winced. "I don't want you messed up in this—"

"Too late for that. It was too late when you rang my doorbell at midnight." He passed her a bottle of water while the coffee maker grunted and burbled and did its work.

"He seemed like a good guy," she said without bitterness, just defeat.

"He's obviously not. You weren't talking much last night, so tell me the whole story. Who is he?"

"He's a promoter."

"Typical LA line of bullshit. So what does he supposedly promote besides violence against women?"

She tried for a sour look, but there wasn't enough energy behind it to give the expression any real impact. "Rock bands. Concerts."

"Not that it matters, but does he make any money or is he a poser?"

"He has a new BMW and a nice place off Sunset. And a condo in Vegas."

"You know that doesn't mean anything, especially in this town. Who does he work for?"

"Jesus, you're nosy. You sound like a cop."

He waited patiently.

"He owns Salamander Productions."

Sam had heard of it. They were a midrange outfit that repped regionally, mostly bread-and-butter acts that could fill Los Angeles and off-strip Vegas clubs but not premiere venues or stadiums. "Appropriate that he named his company after a reptile."

Melody sighed anxiously. "We've been seeing each other on and off for a year. He never hit me before."

Sam felt a stark anger unfurl inside—anger at the bastard who'd given her a black eye, anger at the people in her life who'd abused her to the point of reticence, anger that things like this happened every day all over the world. "But he'll hit you again. Press charges and get out. You know how this shit ends once it starts, and it's never good. Ditch his ass."

Melody nodded, but it wasn't a committed nod. "I will."

"I'm not convinced."

Her mouth twitched in irritation. "It's complicated, Sam."

"There's nothing complicated about violence. That's the one thing I know."

She looked down and started picking at the label on her water bottle. Self-consciously? Or was she simply considering her options? Her situation might be straight-forward, but Melody herself was Byzantine. On one hand, there were a lot of hard edges to her. He didn't know a lot of details about her past, but he knew some. Substantial drug problems—first Oxy, then heroin. She'd lived on the streets for a while. But she was intelligent and strong and optimistic, and she found a way to climb the steep mountain out.

"Don't let Ryan diminish you."

"I won't. He didn't."

It was the right answer, but Sam knew all too well that it was impossible to entirely escape a dark past or prevent it from affecting your decisions. It was insecurity and fear, he supposed, lying just beneath the surface like cancer, waiting for the right moment to come out of remission. That's probably why he and Melody had gravitated toward each other, had learned to trust one another during his past six months working the glamorous job of bar back at Pearl Club. They could talk to each other about things they couldn't share with anybody else, especially when they were drunk.

Melody wanted a happy ending. Right now, it was some promoter and his BMW, nice place off Sunset, and condo in Vegas—and she didn't want to let it go.

"I know what you're thinking," she finally said.

"I'm pretty sure you don't."

She scowled and took a sip of water. "After what I've been through, how could I be so stupid?"

"Melody, you're not stupid. But things won't get any better. You were afraid to go back to your own apartment last night, for Christ's sake, what does that tell you? It tells me you think Ryan might end up killing you if you don't walk away now. I'm being serious."

"And he might kill me if I do."

"That's specious logic for staying with an abuser."

She looked at him with bleary eyes, made a startling green by her bloodshot whites. A trick of contrasting colors. "Is 'specious' my vocabulary word for the day?"

"It's an underused word." Sam knew she was conflicted, running a threat assessment, reframing things in her mind as she tried to make sense of her predicament and make it more palatable to whatever idealism still confused her heart and mind.

"I didn't mean that. Ryan isn't a killer, he just gets jealous sometimes."

Ryan, owner of Salamander Productions. He wouldn't be hard to track down if he needed to. *If* he really owned the company or even worked there. LA was full of lies and hyperbole because there were plenty of victims who could be deceived or manipulated by them. "Stop making excuses for him. You know better and you can do better. Way better. You're not a victim anymore, so don't act like one."

She recoiled in her chair. "You're harsh this morning."

"Tough love."

"Has a lecture ever changed *your* mind?"

"Am I lecturing you?"

"Yeah. You did last night and you're doing it again now."

"Huh. Well, for the record, every time I got a lecture, I did just the opposite."

She folded her arms across her chest in vindication. "Exactly."

"So think of it as a pep talk."

"Semantics," she muttered under her breath as the coffee maker crackled a final wheeze, announcing the brew cycle was finished. Sam filled two mugs and dosed them both generously with milk and sugar.

"Drink some coffee, eat some toast. You'll feel better."

She took an exploratory bite, then another before abandoning the idea of eating. "Ryan's a coward. He won't kill me."

She was nothing if not persistent in her defense of the scumbag. Ryan had gotten his hooks into her. Were BMWs really that great? "It's the cowards who kill, you know."

"You're not a coward and you killed."

"In battle. Normal life isn't war. At least it shouldn't be."

Melody toyed with her mug, processed that, scraped a bright pink fingernail along the auto shop logo emblazoned on white ceramic. Sam couldn't remember how it had come into his possession. It didn't really matter, but he hated the holes in his memory. Especially hated that some of the things he didn't want to remember played loud and clear in his mind while the innocuous details of regular life sometimes escaped him.

"How are things with Yukiko?" she finally asked, initiating an official change of subject.

Sam sighed and rubbed the left side of his face, the side still intact. "I don't know how it'll turn out."

"Is that up to you or to her?"

"I guess it's up to both of us. Whether she wants to participate is her decision."

"She loves you, right?"

"She does. But I'm not the same guy she fell in love with. There's a difference. Besides, I'm not really that loveable."

"I think you are. And you're cute, too. Do you know the waitresses all think you're on-fire hot?"

"Then they're all fetishists."

"Everybody has scars, yours are just on the outside. But it's not the scars. You're kind. Respectful. Or maybe it's the combination." She tipped her head and studied him for a moment. "The scars, they make you look dangerous. Are you?"

"I'm incredibly dangerous."

"See? On fire. I'm not hitting on you, by the way, just sharing my perspective."

"You're entitled to an opinion, even if it's wrong."

"Maybe I am wrong. According to you, I'm a terrible judge of character."

"You just made my point for me."

"You're also a smart ass." Melody sipped her coffee delicately, a pinky finger raised. A former junkie with a debutante demeanor, as discomfiting as it was charming.

The throw slid off her shoulder, fully exposing her inked arms, the phases of her life, her various rebellions and hardships. They were all etched there in vivid color as an invite, a challenge to interpret if you dared get close enough. There was a shamrock on her right bicep that reminded him of his soap. Irish Spring. Magic leprechauns who turned green into white.

She noticed him scrutinizing it and she flexed her muscle with a sad smile. "I got this for luck."

"Is it working?"

"It's just a charm, a talisman, whatever. We make our own luck. But it can't hurt, right?"

"I get it. I have a lucky cat."

She looked around hopefully. "You have a cat?"

"No, I have a lucky cat. Maneki Neko. The ones you see when you walk into an Asian restaurant or business."

She gave him an unexpected smile. "No way. You mean those cat statues that wave at you?"

"Not all of them wave, but yeah."

"Cute. So you have your own talisman."

"Yep, one with absolutely no mystical properties I believe in, just like your shamrock. But like you said, it can't hurt."

"Everybody needs a symbol of hope. Mind if I use your bathroom?"

"Go ahead, you know where it is."

"I should after last night. I don't know how many beers I had, but they went through my kidneys before my liver had anything to say about it."

"That might be a good thing."

Melody retrieved her purse from the living room floor and disappeared into the bathroom while Sam gulped coffee and helped himself to her uneaten, second piece of toast, which had turned into a cold, limp, butter-soaked sponge. He went to the front window and lifted the shade. The black Jeep was gone. He briefly wondered if it had ever been there to begin with.

Chapter Eight

MELODY CAME OUT OF THE BATHROOM ten minutes later looking transformed. Crisp, put together, and almost innocent if you didn't look too deeply into her eyes. Her blond hair was brushed and tied into a neat ponytail. She'd managed to conceal her black eye with some skillful makeup application.

She was still wearing her work clothes—the tight tank with the Pearl Club logo stretched across her breasts, the shorts that gave an enticing hint of firm buttock—the *"tip multiplier,"* he called the uniform. A genius piece of marketing that shamelessly capitalized on the weakness of men.

She caught his eye and plucked the front of her tank top before sitting down and draining her coffee mug. "I read an editorial in the paper a couple days ago. This pisses some people off. They call these uniforms exploitative, a shameful example of flagrant sexism. Legitimate businesses walking a fine line between entertainment and prostitution. As if Pearl Club was a low-rent strip club selling their employees through the back door. As if I need a civic babysitter."

"Some people have too much time and sanctimony on their hands. But it is sexist, you have to admit."

"Sure it is, but I have a good-paying, honest job in a skimpy costume. Big deal. Nobody's telling me to get on my back or on my knees. Anybody who says there's a fine line between this uniform and selling your body for real doesn't know what the fuck they're talking about."

The tough Melody, the one he knew best, was back. "You're absolutely right."

She narrowed her eyes. "You're wondering about me."

"It's none of my business. Besides, it doesn't matter."

She traced a finger around a rectangle of light the sun painted on the table. "On the streets, you don't do it for money, you do it for protection or drugs. *That's* a fine line."

"Maybe you should write your own editorial."

"Maybe I will."

"Can I ask you something that doesn't have anything to do with Pearl Club or skimpy clothes?"

"Sure."

"You won't like it."

She shrugged. "Whatever. Shoot."

"What's the difference between being treated like shit by Ryan and being treated like shit on the street?"

He braced himself for a cyclonic onslaught, but she surprised him by letting her eyes roam thoughtfully around the kitchen for a moment. "Nothing, I guess. Nothing at all. Maybe that's just what I got used to."

"You can get used to anything bad if you deal with it every day."

"Like war?"

"Like war. But it doesn't have to be like that. It shouldn't be like that."

"Is that what you're working on figuring out?"

"I'm trying. Does Ryan have a black Jeep?"

"No, he drives a Beemer, I told you. Why?"

"Nothing."

"That was a pretty specific question for nothing."

He shrugged. "I'm not only dangerous, I'm paranoid."

She didn't smile, but her single dimple on the left side of her mouth made a brief appearance. "At least you're not an asshole."

"Now that's something I'd like on my headstone."

Melody finally laughed, then tossed a twenty on the table. "For the beer. I cleaned out your refrigerator last night."

He pushed the money across the table. "I quit drinking."

She didn't pick up the bill. "As of this morning?"

"Yeah."

"When I was in treatment, they said I could never drink again or I'd relapse."

"I guess they were wrong."

"They wanted me to believe that addiction is an essential part of my identity, but it's not. Addiction is complicated, humans are dynamic—and there are no absolutes. But it's probably a good thing for you to do, quit drinking. With the meds and all."

"That's what the doc says."

She fussed with her purse, checked her phone, pushed the money toward him. "For the crash pad then. It's hard to find lodging this good on short notice."

"The toast won you over?"

"The coffee was better, but that's not saying much. What time do you start?"

"Four. The easy shift."

"Me, too. See you then." She got up to leave, made it to the door, then paused, hand on the knob. "What's the worst thing, Sam?"

"What do you mean?"

She looked over her shoulder, then walked back into the kitchen. "You know. I heard you shouting this morning."

A good question, and one nobody had ever asked him outright. What *was* the worst thing? Waking up screaming after a combat dream or some seriously fucked up version of life on the base? Losing a wife? Traumatic brain injury that came with blinding headaches; memory loss; partial hallucinations when the world went unexpectedly blurry and you saw strange shapes, strange colors? Working as a bar back when you had an engineering degree and a Purple Heart? "I don't know. I guess that's the worst thing."

"I wanted to help . . . I just didn't . . . I didn't know if I could. I wasn't sure what the right thing to do was. I'm sorry."

"I don't know what the right thing is either, Mel. But thanks."

She nodded, then let herself out quietly, leaving Sam to ponder the twenty dollar bill sitting next to the plate of languishing, butter-sponge toast. For some reason, the whole tableau seemed absurd, just sitting there like an ironic piece of pop art. Even more bizarre was his sudden thought that if you were a starving refugee in a war-gutted country, maybe this toast and this money would be *your* symbol of hope—something you might tattoo on your bicep or put on a national flag if you ever won the toast and the money from the enemy.

And that pretty much closed the circle on absurd for the day. At least he hoped so.

Chapter Nine

NOLAN HATED PARKING GARAGES. EVEN IF they were above ground, they seemed subterranean and stifling, places where trolls of all kinds could lurk unseen. There were so many opportunities for concealment: behind cars, pylons, elevator vestibules, in stairwells. One of the most important skills a cop could possess was identifying potential hiding places because clues and criminals were reluctant to be found.

It was the same with her car keys, which was why she was late for work this morning; but traffic on the Hollywood Freeway would be the official explanation, one nobody would question. It was her belief that people in LA were unremittingly apathetic about being late to any engagement because no effort was required to come up with an excuse. And if you were socially awkward, it was a great icebreaker at parties.

I'm so sorry I'm late, the 101 was an absolute nightmare!

Oh my God, you're lucky you weren't on the 405!

Don't even get me started on the 210, I can't believe people actually live on that side of town . . .

She stepped out of the car and felt the promise of a beautiful warm day on her skin, forgetting about lost keys and traffic and serial killers. But it was hard to forget her aversion to parking garages when she heard footsteps echoing strangely behind her, glancing off the concrete surfaces, folding into an eerie frequency. Even though this was a police garage, she put her hand on her weapon before turning around.

"Don't shoot me, Maggie." Remy was walking toward her with a weary smile. His unruly black hair was starting to corkscrew, even in the dry LA air, and she wondered what it looked like in the humidity of Louisiana. His dark, inkblot eyes were cupped with purplish pouches. The fine blue suit he'd been wearing last night was a rumpled mess, and he hadn't bothered to shave.

"From the looks of you, it might put you out of your misery. Did you catch any sleep?"

"An hour standing up, maybe."

"What's the news from last night, anything good?"

He shrugged his ambivalence. "Uncooperative witnesses. A million different fingerprints to sort through and run, maybe one of them will pop this time around. And the field unit actually found fibers in that shithole that match some from the crime scene in April."

A fresh flow of darkness began seeping into Nolan's soul as unbidden images from last night unrolled in a gruesome, mental cinema. "That's something."

"It might be, if we can find the source."

"Did you ID her?"

"Stella Clary. Twenty-seven, from Lodi, no next of kin."

Alone in a world of suffering. At least she had a name now. Stella Clary wouldn't be totally forgotten; she would always exist in the sad, dark place in her heart reserved for victims. "Nobody saw anything?"

"Are you kidding?" he scoffed. "You were there. Nobody at the Aqua was sober enough to see their own reflection in a roomful of mirrors."

"Any clues he was operating somewhere else before LA?"

"The MO doesn't match anything in the violent crime databases."

"Three victims in three months is a brisk pace for a serial that's just starting out. And these killings are high risk, in public spaces. It's like this guy is at the end of his run, can't control his urges anymore. Or he's anxious to get noticed."

"He's getting plenty of notice. The press gave him a name this morning, did you see that?"

"Yes."

"At first I was pissed as hell, but maybe it's not a bad thing. It'll feed his ego and maybe he'll get cockier than he already is. Sloppy."

"One a month. Do you think he'll keep to his schedule?"

Remy sighed. "Serials are creatures of habit. He might not be capable of deviating. But I don't plan to wait and find out. The task force is on this around the clock now."

"What about the feds?"

"They're sniffing around, offering their support, but the captain hasn't officially brought them on board yet. I have no problem with it, but the decision is up to him."

"Al and I are here for you if you need some extra eyes."

"I appreciate that. I hope you drank the rest of the champagne when you got home."

She had, and quickly because it had fuzzed the images of Stella Clary's butchered body for a little while. Long enough to get to sleep. "I felt obliged."

"Good. When you open champagne, you always throw away the cork." His expression softened. "I didn't have a chance to ask yesterday."

"About what?"

"How you're doing. I haven't seen you around much since the visitation."

Her thoughts rewound to that dreadful, surreal day at the funeral home in Reseda. She remembered the countless faces of colleagues and strangers, friends and family, all swirling in and out of her field of vision like images in a carnival funhouse mirror; her mother blotting her eyes with a mangled tissue while her grim and steadfast father greeted mourners in the receiving line; Max's fiancée weeping as she sat in a large carved chair, looking small and defeated. The furniture had outraged her. It was too dark, too oversized, like ponderous wooden weights specifically designed to further drag down wounded spirits.

"I'm okay. Thanks for being there, Remy." She felt his eyes but didn't meet them.

His phone chirruped a text alert and he stared at his phone for what seemed like a long time. "We just got a hit on prints from a vodka bottle we found in Clary's room," he finally said.

"Good. Go."

He pocketed his phone. "The drink offer is always open, Maggie. No pressure."

Not a good idea, getting tangled up with Remy Beaudreau of Homicide Special Section. A horrible idea. "Catch your killer, and we'll celebrate."

Chapter Ten

MELODY SLID HER GREEN VW BEETLE into her designated slot in the empty communal carport of her apartment building. There were only six units here, and all of her neighbors had day jobs, although she had no idea what those jobs were. She rarely ran into any of them except sometimes on weekends. It was perfect—most days, she could almost imagine it was her place alone.

She checked her rearview mirror before she got out, a precautionary measure that was hardwired into her as much as breathing was. Nobody there. Not her potentially homicidal boyfriend; not some freak from her past or the Monster of Miracle Mile; not some homeless man taking up temporary residence beneath the lemon trees by the breezeway, which happened on occasion. It was safe, safe for now, but she still clutched her pepper spray as she got out of the car.

A little dose of selective fear is a good thing, a necessary thing. You just have to decide when it's important to be afraid of something, dear girl.

Great advice from Aunt Netta, who'd been a veritable font of axioms. She hadn't been afraid of much, certainly not her cherished '57 Thunderbird convertible that had ultimately ended up being her coffin in a bad accident on the 405 on a lovely spring night. As gruesome as it all was, Melody thought that Netta would have been pleased by the way she'd left this world, in her precious, cherry-red buggy, top down, radio blasting, her gray hair flying in the wind right up until the time the semitruck had crashed through the median into oncoming traffic and onto her. Even if the '57 had been outfitted with airbags and roll bars and every other modern safety feature, it wouldn't have changed Aunt Netta's outcome.

Another of her maxims came to mind, that there were two ways out of every trouble, and the right way sometimes isn't the one you think of first. But there had been no way out of that kind of trouble.

Melody often wondered what her world would look like now if she'd been able to live out her adolescence happily with Aunt Netta instead of getting shunted off to her last known living relative, the sack of shit who Social Services called her father. There was no question it would be much better. She'd definitely be a college graduate by now, a music major; that had been Netta's dream for her. Maybe she'd even be happily married with a kid or two. That semi hadn't just taken one life. But at least she still had one, and she wasn't going to squander it feeling sorry for herself.

Teddy, the caretaker and dilettante gardener, was hacking away at an unruly rosemary hedge in the courtyard. It filled the air with a heady menthol smell that somewhat neutralized the skunkiness of marijuana that perpetually emanated from him. He wore his hair in ratty dreadlocks and was wiry and sun-cured, a piece of human jerky. He could have been as young as thirty or as old as fifty, but Melody suspected he fell somewhere in between. "Hey, Teddy."

He did a graceful pirouette, shears still held aloft, and gave her a beneficent stoner smile. His eyes were fixed in a permanent squint, but slices of glacial blue peeked out through a brown terrain of wrinkles. "Mellie! What do you know?"

"I know the hedge is looking good."

"You think so?"

"I do." She had always wondered how he was able to prune things to perfect symmetry time after time considering his enthusiasm for cannabis, but asking the question would have been unforgivably rude.

"Thanks. I've been reading online about this guy who calls himself The Plant Whisperer. He says if you empty your mind and listen closely, the plant tells you what to do. I think there might be something to it. It's the same with the waves. They tell me what to do, too."

"That's a nice philosophy. I have a hard enough time getting animate objects to be honest with me. The wind's picking up—are you going out?"

"Most definitely. Surf's supposed to be going off at Zuma."

"That's good?"

"It's great. Hey, if you ever want to try it, they call me the Dalai Lama. I can get a quimby charging in a day or two, no lie."

Whatever that meant. "Thanks, but I'm a landlubber. I hate sand and the ocean freaks me out. You can't see what's underneath you."

He scratched his jaw thoughtfully. "The men in gray suits, they freak a lot of people out. If it makes you feel any better, I only know one dude who got lunched by one. But he lived, just lost an arm, and he still surfs. The sharks were here first, we have to share."

Melody gave him a pained smile. She had no intention of sharing a body part with a prehistoric fish. "Yeah, I think I'll stick to dry land."

"That's cool, no pressure."

She stooped to gather a few fragrant rosemary clippings. "Can I take these?"

"Help yourself. Put some in your tea. It's good for your liver."

"My liver could probably use the help. Thanks, Teddy." She waved goodbye and unlocked her apartment. It wasn't much, but it was hers. There were polished hardwood floors and fresh paint, and in her humble opinion she'd done a decent job pulling it together on the cheap with flea market bargains and one very long day at the colossal IKEA in Burbank, where she'd spent most of her first paycheck and all her tips from Pearl Club. It was a step in the right direction. Progress.

But for all the progress she'd made in her accommodations and her life, Sam had forced her to acknowledge all the confusing white noise clamoring in her brain. He'd done an excellent job reminding her to listen to that finely tuned inner voice that warned of danger and could sometimes save your life. It was why she'd finally run away from Coachella Valley, why she carried pepper spray, why she had a little snub-nose gun stashed beneath her mattress.

But Ryan had muted that voice with his illusive charm, and now she had a black eye and a decision to make. How could you tell when a dream might become a nightmare?

A little dose of selective fear . . .

But weren't there mitigating factors to every risk, even dangerous ones like dating a man of means with an inconsistent temper? Why else would people helicopter ski and base jump and free dive if they didn't ignore that voice in the interest of something that improved their life?

Her phone kept squawking at her—texts from Ryan, none of which she read—so she turned it off, along with the fierce temptation to see what he had to say. He could stew for a while longer. Maybe he could stew forever, she wasn't sure.

She went to the kitchen, put the rosemary clippings in a vase, and decided to brew a pot of proper coffee. Not that Sam's offering hadn't been kind, but it had tasted awful. As she was filling the carafe at the sink, she noticed her curtains fluttering over the kitchen table like gauzy butterfly wings, taking flight on the breeze. Had she left the window open? She didn't think so.

She felt the hairs on the back of her neck rise and sting like tiny, gnawing teeth. If somebody had been in her apartment, were they still here? Would she even know since she'd done such a good job of silencing that voice in her head?

"Goddammit," she hissed, gathering strength and then stalking through the apartment, armed only with pepper spray, refusing to be a prisoner in the only sanctuary she'd ever had.

Her pulse pounded in her ears as she made an exhaustive search of each room, looking for anything out of place—the kitchen, the living room, the bathroom, and finally the bedroom. Her nervous, heavy breath stopped up her throat when she saw the vase of long-stemmed red roses sitting on her dresser, two dozen of them. No note, just the roses, but she knew they were from Ryan, an offering on the altar of absolution.

She felt a brief flush of happiness, then guilt for being such a malleable mark, then all of that was usurped by a creeping anger. Ryan didn't have a key; her door had been locked, so that meant he'd pried open her kitchen window and climbed in to leave his apology bouquet. There was nothing charming or sweet about that. It was an unforgivable breach of her previously inviolate space. She could never leave her windows unlocked again. He was taking things away one at a time. That was the way it worked.

Abusers are controllers. Abusers are manipulators. Prince Charming gives you a black eye, then breaks into your apartment and leaves you roses. You forgive him, capitulate, and the next time it will be worse.

Her warning system had been reawakened and it growled in the back of her brain, but she decided to keep suppressing it, at least for now. The roses were just too pretty. Live in the moment, appreciate what you have.

And she did, marveling at the twenty-four perfect blooms. She fingered a few of the soft, velvety petals, then shoved her face in the bouquet and sniffed deeply. They didn't smell like much—she'd read somewhere that you had to sacrifice certain characteristics to hybridize for beauty and durability and get long-stemmed roses like these, and the first to go was fragrance. But she didn't mind that they were Frankenstein flowers with no scent—she'd never gotten roses from a boyfriend before, not even a single, cheap stem from a kiosk or a convenience store.

A rap on her front door dispelled the thrall of the roses and her grip tightened on the pepper spray. Fear and paranoia were bedfellows. Once they had you in their command, they didn't relinquish their dominion easily.

"Mellie, it's Teddy."

She sighed in relief, let her shoulders unbunch, then went to the door. A split second before opening it, she pushed down her sunglasses from their perch on her head and covered her black eye.

Teddy was holding an enormous handful of rosemary clippings. "Extras, if you want them. I don't know how much tea you drink, but it's good for the bath, too."

"That's sweet, Teddy, thank you."

He swept into a dramatic bow. "At your service."

She hesitated. "Did you see anybody come into my apartment last night or this morning? Or leave?"

He frowned, creating a rugged corrugation of creases on his forehead. "No way, definitely not. You've got a problem?"

"No. Not really."

"If you have a problem, I'll help you."

"It's nothing, somebody just brought me flowers when I wasn't home. I'm the only one with a key, so I think they came in through the window."

His eyes widened in alarm. "You call that nothing? I say that's some bad juju, girl, and you're nervous. I can tell. And you should be. I'll keep a lookout, and you keep that gun of yours loaded. There's some fucking maniac they're calling the Monster running around the city. You can't be too careful."

"No, you really can't be too careful." Melody felt a sudden emptiness in her stomach. Not hunger or hangover but a vague, painful void originating from someplace else. It was the feeling of being alone. "Thanks. Do you want some coffee? Rosemary tea?"

"I'm good, thanks. Hey, do you know somebody with a black Jeep?"

"No. Why?"

"I see one around sometimes. Parks outside. Maybe you have a secret admirer and he brought the flowers."

Melody's thoughts stuttered, then stopped. Sam had asked her if Ryan drove a black Jeep. "I don't know anyone with a black Jeep. Maybe he lives around here." *Or maybe he's watching you.*

Teddy puffed up his narrow chest. "I told you, I'll keep an eye out. If you need anything, give me a shout, I'm always here unless I'm surfing."

"Thanks. Stay safe, watch out for the men in gray suits."

"For sure. And you watch out, too." He swept into another theatrical bow and went back to the courtyard, his gait swaying a little.

She watched Teddy start on the lemon trees with his pruning saw and clippers, then retreated to her bedroom, turned her phone back on, and picked up the texts from Ryan, which had started early this morning.

I'm so sorry about last night, Mel. Give me a shout.

Mel, call me.

Mel? I'm really sorry, please call me.

Meet me? My place 2 nite?

Mel? I'm SORRY.

There were more, but she didn't bother reading them. She took a deep breath, then composed a short text back to him.

Thx for the roses. Don't ever break into my apartment again or I'll kill you.

She almost pressed send, her finger poised on the key, just a few millimeters away from taking a stand. Time dragged as she stared at the face of her phone and the text bubble that contained all her fury in a few simple words. She knew where the anger came from, but she'd never seen it in print and it was strangely liberating. To hell with it. He'd scared her more than once, he'd hit her, and now it was payback time—even if it was an idle threat made in the heat of the moment. It would probably make him laugh, which humiliated her and made her angrier all at the same time.

Jim the Scrub Jay suddenly appeared at her bedroom window and tapped insistently with his stout beak. He was looking for his morning peanuts. She pressed Send, hoped she wouldn't regret it, and went to the kitchen to get Jim his breakfast. He was such a funny, resourceful bird—he stuffed his mouth full of peanuts, flew to the sweet gum tree, stashed them in the hollow where the trunk split, and came back for more.

Her phone blatted out a text alert, startling her and Jim, who dropped a big mouthful of peanuts and flew away.

What roses? What are you talking about?

Chapter Eleven

AFTER MELODY LEFT, SAM FINISHED HIS coffee over the obituaries, a ghoulish habit he'd acquired recently, then swallowed some aspirin and walked through the house he and Yuki had purchased with a VA loan. They'd furnished it nicely with a joint account bolstered by her job as a graphic designer and made grand plans for their life together. The den, now a weight room, would become a nursery when they decided to have kids. The unremarkable backyard would be reimagined with plantings and a tiled patio. There would be a grill station, a firepit, and seating for all the guests they'd have over on the weekends. Maybe a pool one day.

There wasn't an ocean view in this part of Mar Vista, but the house was close enough that you could smell the sea and feel its dampness, especially at night. It was a damn good starter home for West LA and a fine place for a young couple to build a future. That was all before he'd signed up for his second tour.

Yuki had insisted he stay in the house because it was familiar, it was home, and it would help his recovery. But it wasn't home without her, it was just a house. A roof over his head with an empty refrigerator and a half-empty bed.

He slipped into his running shoes and did a few stretches against a wall, trying not to think of his future, as remote and uncertain as it was.

Dr. Frolich had suggested that he might find solace in imagining better things in the coming days and months, but he couldn't muster a positive vision. He couldn't muster any vision at all. He wasn't sure if that was from lack of imagination or fear of it.

At least he could still run. He could run forever. He would take his usual jagged route, side streets off Bundy Drive to Brentwood, then down San Vicente Boulevard to Santa Monica and the ocean, roughly eight miles each way.

The Los Angeles morning was bright and warm, the sky cerulean, smudged with a few streaky clouds. The sun hadn't quite burned off the marine layer yet—that damp, ocean-borne haze tourists always mistook for smog—and he could feel its weight, its presence as he eased into a jog. He blocked out the sounds of traffic, construction, car alarms, and leaf blowers and focused on the sound of his feet slapping asphalt, his breath echoing in his head. After four miles, his pores opened up and he started sweating, flushing out the toxins from the night before. For the last time. At least that was the plan.

When he got to Brentwood, he cut through the grounds of the West Side Veterans Affairs campus, which seemed appropriate. The lush, three-hundred-plus-acre grounds were home to empty, derelict buildings that ironically hadn't served veterans in decades. It did serve lots of other interests by leasing storage facilities to movie studios, a baseball stadium to UCLA, an athletic complex to Brentwood School, and a laundry service for hotels. There were vague plans to renovate part of it into housing for the multitude of homeless veterans in LA and eventually provide other services. What a great idea, using VA property to help veterans. Why hadn't anybody thought of that before?

On San Vicente, he paused to drink some water and catch his breath under the exotic umbrella of a coral tree, a subtropical transplant in a city filled with transplants, both botanical and human. Sweat was now coursing freely down his face, painting dark splatters on his Army shirt. He was almost to the ocean. He did have a future after all—make it to the ocean.

Several joggers bobbed in place at the crosswalk, waiting for the light to change. An underweight young brunette in hip, expensive workout wear glanced at him, then did a double take. He got that a lot. There weren't many people walking around with two faces.

Then again, she might not have even noticed. She could simply be aghast at his comparatively ghetto running attire and the unseemly amount of perspiration he was producing. He occasionally saw a fair athlete on his runs, but the majority of them were dabblers who didn't work hard enough to sweat much because they weren't conditioning for survival, they were conditioning for vanity. The real agenda here transcended physical fitness, and the superficial mattered most. San Vicente Boulevard and adjoining Adelaide Drive were picturesque meat markets abundantly stocked with prime cuts. And in their world, he was probably offal.

The woman looked vaguely familiar, but that didn't mean anything. Sometimes every stranger looked familiar to him, and sometimes everybody he knew looked like a stranger. And it was Los Angeles—she could easily be an actress he'd seen on TV.

She gave him a tentative smile, then her aggressively groomed brows furrowed in concern. "Are you okay?"

Sam suddenly felt his strong legs start to wobble and weaken and he let himself sag to the base of the tree as squiggly red lines started to dance in front of his eyes and across the woman's forehead.

It's important not to panic when these things manifest, Sam. Try to breathe through it. Brains heal, but it's a process.

Easy for you to say, Dr. Frolich. "I'm fine, thanks. Overdid it is all," he lied.

"Are you sure?"

"I'm sure . . ." his peripheral vision started to blur as the red lines morphed, writhing into letters. That had never happened before. He watched in fascination as a word formed on her smooth forehead, like it had been seared there with a branding iron: *Accident.*

"Katy, come on!" The impatient voice of one of her running pals.

"I'm okay, go," he reassured her, then closed his eyes, focused on the rhythm of his heart. The red word eventually pixilated and disappeared into a fine, sparkling dust. When he opened his eyes again, Katy and her fit, fashionable, impatient friends were gone, replaced by a lone male jogger who was glancing at him warily. Just another crazy, freaking out under a tree in a Brentwood median—it happens every day, his expression said.

Sam's vision was normal. No colors, no words. And miraculously, no headache. Up ahead, he saw a cluster of flashing police lights. He hadn't heard any sirens, which meant he'd blacked out. For how long, he didn't know. He never knew.

What did you see? What do you remember?

"Nothing," he said, startling the nervous jogger and propelling him forward against the traffic light.

He wouldn't make it to the ocean today. He'd be lucky to make it home.

Chapter Twelve

REMY STEPPED INTO THE GLOOM OF the Kitty Corral and was hit by the sour smells of spilled beer and unhygienic humans. A substandard sound system was blasting a thirty-year-old EMF song, a staple of strip clubs still. Behind smeared Plexiglas, a wasted, topless woman wobbled on spike heels, trying unsuccessfully to keep time to the music. It was painful to imagine that she'd been a child once, with an unwritten future. The author of her life was a sadist.

Four ragged denizens were scattered around the bar and in unison swiveled their heads laconically to look at him. It wasn't noon yet, but they were all drunk or high or both and didn't seem to care that there was obviously a cop in their midst. They didn't seem to care about anything—not themselves, not the drinks in front of them, not the woman trying to dance. He recognized all the men from last night, when he'd come in to canvass. Maybe they'd never left.

The man behind the bar hadn't been here last night. Impossibly, he looked even more dissolute and slovenly than his mug shot. He was missing a front tooth and his bloated face looked like a greasy, overinflated balloon. He squinted, then scowled as Remy approached.

"You're a cop."

"And you're Thom Rangel." He showed his shield. "Detective Remy Beaudreau."

He let out a rattling cough and spit on the floor. "You want something to drink, Detective?"

"I want to know about Stella Clary. She worked here."

His rheumy eyes narrowed. "On and off. I haven't seen her for a while."

"Yeah? Well, I just talked to Ray Lovell and he says different. He had amnesia last night, but I just jogged his memory."

"I don't know no Ray Lovell."

"Sure you do. He works across the street. At the Aqua."

"I heard there were tons of cops there last night. Is that what this is about?"

Rangel was really bad at playing dumb, which was incredibly ironic. He was a natural. "You didn't hear?"

"Hear what?"

"Stella Clary is dead. Murdered." No reaction. "But you already knew that, your buddies here probably couldn't wait to tell you." He looked around the bar—all the customers were studying their drinks.

"Ray Lovell says you were at the Aqua with her yesterday, and I've got your prints on a vodka bottle we found in her room."

His eyes were suddenly busy, scoping the room, presumably for potential avenues of escape. "No surprise, we partied sometimes."

"Yesterday?" When he didn't answer, Remy leaned across the bar. "Don't fuck with me, Thom."

"We may have had a drink or two."

"And then you killed her?"

"No! Hell, no! I liked her."

"I took a look at your rap sheet. You're a violent guy. You like to get rough with women. You used a knife on the last one."

"Bitch attacked me with it first. It was self-defense."

"The jury had a different opinion."

"Look, I served my time and I'm off probation, so stop harassing me."

"I haven't even started. Do you know Holly Churak?"

"No."

"Olivia Riemers?"

"Never heard of either of them."

"Not even from the paper?"

"I don't read the paper."

"They're dead, too. They hung around this neighborhood."

"Whatever."

"I'll be showing your mug shot around."

"Go for it, I'm not a killer."

Remy considered the waste of human flesh in front of him. Serial killer? It was possible. Ted Bundy had created an unrealistic perception that they were charming and intelligent, but statistically they were average or below and typically socially isolated. They were all incapable of remorse, all pathological liars, and Rangel wasn't remorseful or forthcoming. He nodded at the bulge at his waist, a gift from God that made things even easier. "Felons aren't allowed to possess firearms, you know that."

Rangel's face flushed red and he started to back away. "This is a dangerous place. We get trouble in here sometimes."

"Raise your hands and step out from behind the bar. And don't even think about running."

The bar flies watched Rangel get cuffed with bovine indolence. Remy wondered how long it would take them to figure out the drinks were on the house.

•

"Look, man. *Detective.* I told you, I partied with Stella for a little bit yesterday, then went home around two and slept it off. Ask my landlady, she saw me come in."

"From where I'm standing, you're the last person who saw her alive."

"That's bullshit! She partied with a lot of people. I stopped at two o'clock, but she didn't."

"Give me some names."

"Don't know any names. We just drank together sometimes, that's it. It was always just me and her, that's the way we both liked it. I'm clean except for the booze. She never did drugs around me."

"Considerate."

His expression became oddly pensive, extraordinary for somebody with the intellect of an annelid. "Before I left, she said she was going downtown to score."

"Where?"

"I don't know, where the drugs are. That should narrow it down. Can I get some more coffee?"

"We're tossing your apartment right now, Thom. Does that worry you?"

He shook his head. "You won't find nothing. I didn't kill her. If I had to bet, it was the guy she thought was following her."

Chapter Thirteen

RYAN GALLAGHER TOSSED HIS PHONE ON the sofa in disgust. Roses. Somebody had sent her roses. Probably that son of a bitch Markus Ellenbeck. He was a liar and a cheat and an arrogant asshole, way past his sell-by date, but he still thought he was hot property just because he'd drummed for some *important* bands on some *important* albums twenty years ago. Big fucking deal. He probably still had slut groupies throwing themselves at him, but Melody had never been impressed, which made her an irresistible target for conquest. Goddammit.

Or maybe she'd just been playing hard to get. She had a coy, conniving side to her. All women did. She still hadn't responded to his last text, which made him wonder if the roses hadn't hit the mark and she was with him right now. *Thanking* him.

He clenched his fists and ground his teeth, trying to banish the hot burn in his throbbing brain, the vision of Markus Ellenbeck's smug face as he humped Melody.

He leapt off the sofa and stalked to the guest bathroom, rummaging through the drawer for his blow. He felt a fresh surge of anger when he saw that the vial was half-empty. No wonder he had such a searing headache, Melody's bitchiness had set him off on a binge last night, and there was only one cure for that.

He dug into the bottle with the tiny spoon attached to the cap and got two good nosefuls, and the headache went away instantly. But what was left wouldn't get him through the day, let alone the night. Time to reorder.

He sat down on the toilet and made the call. "Hey man, can you make a delivery today?"

"What do you need?"

"An eight ball."

"Give me an hour."

"Fine. Thanks."

He hung up and closed his eyes for a moment, relishing the numbness in his nostrils and the euphoria of the high-quality dust working through his system. He felt better now, calmer. An eight ball would last a while, get him through this bullshit.

Now he had to figure out what to do about Melody. She was a pretty good girl, although she'd been high maintenance lately. He wasn't quite ready to cut her loose, but maybe he should reconsider. Her mention of a break-in puzzled him. What did that have to do with anything? And the death threat had been truly bizarre, beyond the pale, and that really infuriated him. She wasn't making sense and she was starting to get defiant, two warning signs she was creeping into psycho bitch territory. Maybe more trouble than she was worth.

It occurred to him that she might be making everything up to piss him off because of last night. Admittedly, he probably shouldn't have hit her, at least not so hard, but the rage had flared so suddenly and white-hot that he hadn't been able to contain it. That's how much he liked her, crazy or not.

He dug out another spoonful and snorted it with gusto, enjoying the burn, the pain with the gain. He'd get his supply replenished, then he'd go see Melody and get some answers.

Chapter Fourteen

AS THE UBER DRIVER PULLED UP to his house, Sam saw Yuki's blue Honda parked in the driveway. She was sitting on the front step like a little kid, her yellow sundress pulled down to cover her knees. A breeze ruffled her straight black hair, shorter than it was when he'd seen her last week, just grazing her shoulders now.

Her sunglasses were too big for her small face, but she loved them anyhow. He'd bought them for her on Venice Beach, cheap knockoffs of some designer. He had a pair just like them somewhere, but it hurt too much to wear them because they reminded him of the last good day they'd had together—the day before he'd left for Afghanistan for the second and last time.

He hastily pushed a cash tip into the driver's hand and muttered a thanks as he jumped out. "What a great surprise. You should have let yourself in, Yuki. It's still your house, too."

"I would have in another five minutes. You didn't answer my calls. I was starting to get worried."

"I was jogging," he stated the obvious, plucking at his sweat-drenched shirt. "Cardinal rule of exercise—turn off the phone."

"Couldn't make the return trip?"

"One-way ticket today. I almost made it to Ocean Avenue, but I started getting a headache and thought I'd better take it easy." The headache was a little white lie, but he had no intention of telling her about the thrilling appearance of a new symptom. That was something to be sorted out with his shrink and possibly his neurologist first.

Her mouth turned down in an inverted crescent of distress. "It must have been bad for you to take a cab home."

"It wasn't so bad that I had to take a cab, just bad enough to take an Uber."

She rolled her eyes fondly, then stood up, revealing a Whole Foods bag that had been sitting on the step behind her as if she'd been guarding it. "I brought some lunch. I hope you don't mind."

"I'm thrilled. Thanks." It was awkward, walking up to greet her in front of their house as if she was an out-of-town guest who had arrived too early. Did you kiss your estranged wife or just peck her on the cheek? A hug, perhaps? No, that was out of the question. He was too disgusting to hug. He settled for a chaste kiss on the mouth.

"I'm happy to see you, Sam. You look good. Sweaty, but good."

"Thanks. And you look terrific. Let me take a quick shower before we eat, otherwise I won't be a very pleasant dining companion."

She lifted her chin, assessing him. "I would be grateful."

The house seemed to regain a natural rhythm when they walked in together. It was like she'd never left. Sam knew it was all a fantasy, but he was fine with fantasy for now. She took over the kitchen effortlessly, getting plates, silverware, napkins, while he excused himself.

Five minutes later, he reentered the kitchen, smelling much better and dressed in jeans and a poor, defenseless button-down he'd found suffocating in a dry cleaning bag at the back of the closet. It was something he'd wear on a date, and this was sort of a date. Wasn't it?

The table was set, and plastic containers from Whole Foods were neatly arranged on the table, each with their own spoon. If Yuki had still been living here, the salads would have been dumped into Japanese pottery bowls and sprinkled with different garnishes, like tiny ribbons of scallion and carrot or toasted sesame seeds. The old Yuki would die before she'd serve any meal out of plastic deli containers or without a personal touch. Her uncharacteristic lack of care didn't bode well for the encounter; but she *had* brought lunch, so maybe he was overthinking things.

She nodded her approval at his transformation and sat down but didn't comment on the dinette table, out of kindness he assumed. She also didn't comment on the two dirty coffee mugs on the counter, if she'd even noticed them at all.

"I ran into your mother today. Grocery shopping."

Always *your mother*, never Vivian. It annoyed him, it always had, but the two had never been great friends. "You were in Pasadena?"

"I had an early client meeting there. I'm in between appointments now, so I thought it would be nice to catch up over lunch."

"It's very nice. How is Vivian?"

"Worried about her golf handicap, worried about you."

"In that order?"

Yuki scoffed. "She said you don't call her enough."

"Whenever I call her, she's on the golf course. And I'm sick of hearing about her handicap."

"It's twenty."

"Did she tell you about the neighbor's Shih Tzu? That's her latest fallback obsession when she exhausts the topic of golf."

She gave him a weary smile, letting him know she wasn't in the lightest of moods. It also telegraphed a dolorous shift to things more weighty than outdoor recreation and overly coiffed pets. "How are you, Sam?"

There was genuine concern in her tone and on her face. The question was a bit generic, but that made answering easier. "Better. I think the new meds are helping."

"You should tell your mother that."

"I do every time I talk to her, which apparently isn't often, but she doesn't believe anything I tell her."

"Should I believe you?"

Sam eyed a container of kale salad and felt his stomach churn. It was too green, too filled with things humans weren't meant to eat in his opinion. "You should, but that doesn't mean you will."

"Talk to me."

Yuki was direct, impatient, and often abrupt. She never bothered with finessing a conversational segue because in her opinion it was time wasted that could be applied to more productive discussion, like problem-solving or decision-making. Her rigidly practical world view was decidedly masculine, one people often mistook for rudeness or self-absorption, but she was neither of those things.

She blamed her Japanese mother for that particular trait, but Sam had never seen it echoed in his mother-in-law, who was the very embodiment of charm, a skilled mistress of the silver tongue. Maybe she had a different personality when she was speaking Japanese, but he didn't think so. Yuki's abrasiveness read pure LA to him, nothing to do with her mother's homeland.

"I went three nights without a dream."

She gave him a nod of encouragement. "That's good, Sam."

"I think so. We'll see what Dr. Frolich says about it today." He helped himself to a potato salad without too much green, just pale mezzalunas of celery. "What about you?"

"I miss you."

"I miss you, too."

"But the separation's been good for me."

Just what he didn't want to hear.

"Has it been good for you?" Yuki, always looking for quick, clear, incontrovertible answers to her questions, even if there weren't any.

"If it's good for you, it's good for me."

Her tiny shoulders slumped. "That's a nonanswer."

"I mean it. You needed space. You needed a break. And I can work on things without feeling guilty. Bad. For what I'm putting you through." He spoke the words without much thought, but once they'd come out of his mouth, he realized there was truth to them.

Her eyes suddenly filled with tears. "That's so stupid, Sam. I'm here for you. I didn't leave because I wanted you to be alone to work on things."

"I understand why you left, Yuki." He reached out and covered her hand in his. "I think it's good for you to have time off. And I love you. I always will."

She sniffled and looked up. "I love you, too. You seem better. Dr. Frolich is working out?"

"So far."

"You were so dead set against seeing a psychiatrist in the beginning. What changed?"

"I was sick of being sick." That was the truth, but he really didn't know if he was getting better or worse. That was another thing he wouldn't tell her, another torment to add to his list. Secrets, lies, put on a brave face and maybe it will stick. Counterproductive maybe, but desperation had a way of constructing brilliant artifices. The only problem was they were built in quicksand and there was no way to know if they'd collapse, or when.

A single tear slid down her cheek, tracing a crooked, wet path on her skin. "I feel so guilty. I feel like I betrayed you, deserted you when you needed me most."

Sam had never known her to ask for amnesty, which was essentially what she was doing, so he didn't know how to respond. And if he was painfully honest with himself, he wasn't feeling the generosity of spirit to lie and tell her what she wanted to hear.

When she finally realized he wasn't going to assuage her guilt, she continued. "But it got to the point where I felt like staying would do more harm than good, that I couldn't be any help to you without some time away. To rest, regroup, get strong again. Does that make sense?"

"You don't have to justify yourself," he finally said. "And stop feeling guilty. It's a worthless emotion."

"But it's a powerful one. You know that. And you know how hard it is to escape it."

He did know, and now he was feeding that same demon again, feeling guilty about her feeling guilty, which was exactly what he wasn't supposed to be doing at this juncture in his life. "Let's just take this one day at a time, okay? Twelve-step it to success, just like Bill and his friends."

"Who's Bill?"

"He's one of the guys who founded Alcoholics Anonymous."

"Are you going?"

"I stopped drinking. I'm in spontaneous remission." *For a whole ten hours, give our brave veteran a Medal of Honor!* "Did you know that seventy-five percent of people who recover from alcohol dependence do it without any help, including treatment or AA?"

"I take it that's a no."

"You can apply the philosophy to other things. One day at a time, Yuki. Keep telling yourself that."

"Okay. But I suck at that."

He smiled and squeezed her hand. "Yeah, you do."

And she did suck at that. Aside from being a stringent pragmatist, Yuki was a highly regimented person, meticulously organized in every aspect of her life, and her mind was always a light-year beyond the present. On Sunday nights, she knew exactly what she would wear to work for the entire week, knew what meals she would prepare on what day. She kept a journal that outlined her six-month plan, her one-year plan, her five-year plan, her ten-year plan. She probably knew what date she would retire.

Unlike him, she knew exactly what her future would be, at least before a husband with PTSD had screwed it all up. He wondered if she knew whether he was in her future as she saw it now. He wanted to ask, but he didn't want to hear the answer. Her unexpected visit was a bright spot of joy, but he could also sense a dark, implicit tenor to it, a dismantling of something important at the core of it. Her manner was suddenly strange and desperate and seemed cold to him instead of familiar. She said she missed him, but maybe she missed the idea of him, missed what he had been before. And maybe the separation had been more than just good for Yuki—maybe it had set her free and that's why she was here—to tell him that.

It shouldn't have surprised him that their impromptu lunch ended in the bedroom, but it did—a sweaty, apocalyptic nirvana, the greatest farewell fuck ever before Yuki told him she had accepted a once-in-a-lifetime job offer in Seattle. It wasn't the end, she promised. Please think about moving to Seattle, she implored, as if changing locale would fix everything. But he hadn't been a part of her decision, and that said it all.

She was crying when she left. Sam wanted to, wished he could, but the deadness inside him squelched any tears, any emotion he had left.

He went to the front window and watched her drive off in a blue Honda hearse that was carrying away their marriage. He looked down the street and saw that the black Jeep was back, parked a half a block away. His grief turned to groundless fury in a blinding flash. The next time he was cognizant of his surroundings, he was standing on the front porch with his Colt Anaconda in his hand. His second blackout of the day. Jesus Christ.

Shaking, he shoved the gun in the waistband of his jeans and looked down the street. The Jeep was gone, along with any recollection of what had happened between the time Yuki had driven off until now. Whenever now was. He was afraid to look at his watch.

Chapter Fifteen

MELODY WAS TRYING TO KEEP HERSELF busy, doing laundry, cleaning the apartment, making hummus and a fruit salad to have on hand. But no matter how much she moved or how fast, her nerves continued to fray, and every strange sound made her heart flail.

She kept checking her phone every few minutes, but Ryan hadn't sent a text since *What roses?* and hadn't responded to her answer: *The roses you left in my bedroom.* He hadn't been on social media, hadn't called either; so eventually she'd called him—several times—but his phone went straight to voicemail.

She wanted to nurture her anger, but fear had slithered into her mind like a dark, poisonous snake. Jealousy was Ryan's trigger, and now he knew she had a secret admirer. He wasn't responding because he was going to confront her in person, accuse her of having somebody on the side. He might be on his way over right now.

Sam had been right about him, but she hadn't let herself see it because abuse had been so normal in her life since Netta's death. The abused sought out abusers, it was right there in all of her psychology textbooks.

Even more frightening was the fact that someone other than Ryan had crawled through her window to leave her a special gift, and she had no idea who or why. But maybe Teddy was right and it had something to do with the black Jeep. And Sam knew something about that, although she couldn't imagine how. She called him, but his phone went to voicemail, too, leaving that same empty hollowness of isolation she'd felt earlier. She wanted to seek out Teddy's company, maybe even his advice, but he'd left to go surfing. It was just her, hummus, fruit salad, and a gun, which was on the kitchen counter next to her phone.

She didn't drink during the day, never during the day, and never before a shift, but she found herself sitting on the sofa, clutching her phone and gun, gulping down a Sierra Nevada. Booze and firearms, a fantastic combination.

The soft, soothing buzz of the first beer sent her to the fridge for another, and when she'd finished that she ran to the bathroom to pee, thinking about all the mistakes she'd made in her life and *how would she stop making them*?

She suddenly hated herself for clinging desperately to the idea of Ryan as a knight in shining armor; to the kindness of Sam, who had much bigger things to worry about than a fucked up coworker; and to the consideration and protectiveness of Teddy. Any man who showed her compassion instead of horror became a crutch for her, which made her weak and pathetic, a revolting emotional vampire who was never going to entirely climb out of the darkness unless she learned to handle the past demons on her own. No time like the present to take charge. Kick ass. Take names. Call the cops.

She considered that option for a moment. It wasn't a bad one—she could file a report, get her fears on the record in case Ryan or the black Jeep guy killed her or she ended up in a position to have to kill them in self-defense. But the idea quickly fizzled away when she imagined how the conversation might go.

A stranger broke into my apartment and left two dozen roses in my bedroom and I want him arrested. My boyfriend didn't leave them, but now he knows I have a secret admirer and I'm afraid he might kill me because it turns out he's jealous and violent. Oh yeah, and I think there's a black Jeep following me. No, I've never seen it, but I heard about it from two people, a stoner surfer who thinks he can communicate with plants and waves and a really nice guy who's suffering from serious PTSD and has hallucinations sometimes. Booze on my breath? I had a couple beers because I was so stressed out . . . yes, I do have a record because I used to be an addict, but I'm over all that now, a good and productive citizen, honest.

Good luck with that.

Chapter Sixteen

DR. FROLICH WAS HANDSOME IN THE way old movies and books characterized "women of a certain age," as if there was a point in life when you were no longer worthy of feminine adjectives. She'd let her hair go gray and kept it wrapped in a messy bun at the nape of her neck. She wore a suit, but it was wildly colorful and deconstructed and nothing she'd bought off a rack anywhere.

She reminded Sam of his maternal grandmother, a long-time Berkeley resident who had been the very embodiment of that mien while she was still alive—a trust funder-turned-hippie bent on pissing off her parents in retaliation for their wealth, which she'd considered unethical or something to that effect. Everything she'd ever worn had been purchased at some art fair, and everything that had passed her lips or her guest's lips was organic and green and often liquefied, which Sam blamed for his aversion to things like kale salad. The green hadn't saved her from breast cancer, but he didn't fault her for trying. DNA was cooked into you from conception, and lucky cats, shamrocks, and vegetable smoothies were symbolic forces against the omnipotency of both genetics and fate. Dr. Frolich was busy at her computer when he walked into her office, probably entering notes on her previous patient's chart, but Sam preferred to imagine she was surreptitiously shopping online for outré clothing between appointments. She looked up and seemed genuinely happy to see him. "Hi, Sam. I'm pleased to see you looking exceedingly healthy today."

"Fresh air and exercise."

"Where did you find fresh air in LA?"

Sam smiled at her joke in spite of the monumentally shitty day he was having.

"How are you?"

"Honestly? I've been a lot better."

Her bright blue eyes disappeared in an elaborate mesh of crow's feet that advertised her scorn for cosmetic surgical intervention. "Sit down." She gestured to the cozy seating arrangement by a window that looked out on busy Wilshire Boulevard. There were a couple leather chairs, the requisite sofa, and a coffee table with a box of tissues, handy for mopping up the consequences of any crying jags.

A vase of white calla lilies adorned a credenza filled with psych textbooks, some that Dr. Frolich herself had written. He scanned the spines of her work, which bore grim titles like *Deep into the Dark: Methodology in Treating Posttraumatic Stress Disorder* and *The Long Road to Trauma Healing.*

She gathered a notebook and pen and sat across from him, her face very serious now. "Tell me what's happening, Sam."

This was the moment that always confounded him. Where did you start? At the beginning? At the end? Somewhere in the middle? "Yukiko stopped by today," he finally said. "Unexpectedly."

"How did that go?"

"It was good for a while. Except she brought kale salad."

Dr. Frolich raised an unpruned eyebrow. "Classic passive-aggressive behavior. You're clearly being punished."

"That's what I think. Even worse, she served everything out of the plastic deli containers. It was horrific."

"You said it was good for a while. What changed?"

"She said she missed me but the separation has been good for her."

Dr. Frolich scrawled a few notes but didn't say anything. Psychiatrists were very much like cops, allowing lags in the conversation that would hopefully become so awkward, the subject would be compelled to babble on to fill the uncomfortable silence. Just like he'd done with Melody this morning while pressing her about Ryan. Maybe he was learning some unexpected life skills in therapy.

"Yuki's feeling guilty. About the separation."

"That was a very difficult decision for both of you. Do you think her absence has been helpful to you in any way?"

"I didn't think so."

"But?"

"But today I realized that with her gone, I wasn't feeling guilty anymore about putting her through my hell. So we swapped—she left and took my guilt with her. But then I started to feel guilty again because she feels guilty. Funny how that works."

"Do you remember when we talked about guilt being a kind of drug? A coping mechanism?"

"A destructive, negative coping mechanism. A way of life, if you succumb to it."

"You're a good patient with a good memory."

"Only for psychiatric sessions and baseball trivia. I don't remember where I got my Auto World coffee mug, and stuff like that drives me nuts."

"Baseball? You've never talked about that."

"I played in college. USC. My true skills were bench warming and random, odd facts about the game."

She gave him a challenging smile. "No-hitter, Yanks versus Cleveland, 1993."

"September fourth, Jim Abbott pitching. Born without a right hand, but he still had a ten-season career."

"I am duly impressed."

"You never talked about baseball either, Doc."

"That's because it's my job to listen. But I guess my secret's out now—baseball is a minor passion of mine. Sam, you're dealing with things better than you know. I don't often see a sense of irony or a sense of humor come through these doors. Certainly not self-effacement. And none of those things come without intelligence and strength. You're going to get through this."

"That's my plan. Is Jim Abbott supposed to be an allegory? Overcoming hardship and all that?"

"I was actually just testing you on your baseball trivia. It's a diagnostic tool. For instance, if I had a patient who tells me he's a physicist and says e equals mc squared represents the dimensions of his living room, I have a baseline for treatment."

"That's pretty specific. You had a patient like that, didn't you?"

She gave him a demure look. "It was a purely hypothetical example."

"I'm not as crazy as your hypothetical example. That should make you happy."

"It does. And you're not crazy."

She might change her opinion if he told her about his obsession with the black Jeep or the episode that had culminated with him standing on the front porch with his gun. They smacked of paranoia and impending psychosis, so he decided to add them to his growing list of secrets. Pretty soon he'd have to start writing it all down—who knew what, who didn't.

"Is there anything else about Yukiko's visit you'd like to talk about?"

He focused on the vase of lilies, and words tumbled out of his mouth before he could stop them. "Yuki took a job in Seattle. She leaves next month. We fucked like bunnies, then she told me. If you're interested, I don't feel anything. Just numb."

Dr. Frolich leaned back in her chair. She was gifted in the fine art of the impassive expression, but this news seemed to take her by surprise. "You must be in shock."

"That's one way to put it."

"Are you angry?"

"I don't have the energy to be angry. And why should I be? I'm the reason she left. I'm the reason she's moving to Seattle."

She closed her notebook and placed it on her lap. "The things that have happened to you, the things happening now, none of it is your fault, Sam. It's important to understand that."

"Then who should I blame?"

"Nobody. There's a difference between being a victim and having a victim mentality. Victims move on and improve their situation. People with a victim mentality never do. It's the easy way out, blaming somebody or something else for your misfortune, nothing but mental gymnastics that exonerate you from taking personal responsibility and doing something to rectify your situation. Life isn't fair, and it never has been. The expectation that it should be, without any effort, is the very definition of insanity in my opinion."

Sam thought about Melody and the harsh words he'd said to her about being a victim. She used to be one, but she didn't blame anybody, and she'd climbed out of her hole on her own. "That's a good point."

"You've had a lot of devastating losses in your life."

"And now I have one more to add to the list."

"Did Yuki say she wanted to end the marriage?"

"She didn't have to."

"If she didn't specifically mention it, I'd like to encourage you not to get ahead of things. Just because she took a job in Seattle doesn't necessarily mean it's the end."

"I think it is. I know it is."

"Is that a husband's intuition or fatalism?"

"Does it matter?"

"Yes, because neither of those things is grounded in reality. They're merely projections. Right now, you're not seeing anything but a single path to a bad outcome."

"I don't see any other paths."

"That's because you've already finished the journey in your mind." She folded her hands together and leaned forward. "This is a fresh wound. Give yourself some time to process everything. And keep an open mind to other possibilities, a new perspective."

Sam shrugged, suddenly feeling exhausted. "So don't jump straight to divorce court, is that what you're saying?"

"Something like that. Let's take a short break, I'll get us something to drink. Coffee or water today?"

"Water, thanks."

The break ended the first half hour of talk therapy and commenced the second, which was usually devoted to pharmacological discussion. It gave him time to regroup after walking the hot coals of psychotherapy, and he appreciated it.

•

"I'd like to ask you about the new drug, Sam. You've been on it long enough to be seeing some results if it's something that will work for you."

"I think I am. I didn't have a dream for three nights in a row. That seems like progress."

"It is progress. Have you noticed any side effects?"

If you read the two pages of disclaimer notes included in the pharmacy bag when you filled any given prescription, you would be tempted to throw the pills away and live out your natural life as God intended. If you actually started the medication, you would become fixated on the endless roster of potential discomforts and life-threatening maladies, anything from dizziness to nausea, headaches, blurred vision, and organ failure—and of course the worst, which was sudden death. Most everything he had was preexisting, so he couldn't blame the new drug. But he did have something to say on the matter.

"Actually, I have. Just this morning, when I was jogging." Sam told her about his incident on San Vicente, about the red, writhing word that had formed on Katy's forehead while he was sitting beneath a coral tree. It took ten minutes to tell the story because Dr. Frolich kept interrupting with questions.

"You must have witnessed the accident and then blacked out, transposing the timeline in your mind."

"No, it was all pretty clear . . . what accident?"

She took a deep breath and retrieved her laptop from the desk. She tapped on the keyboard for a few seconds, then turned the monitor to face him. "Is this her?"

Sam stared at a picture of Katy from a newsfeed. "Yes, that's her."

"Katy Villa. The mayor's daughter. She was killed in a hit-and-run on San Vicente at eleven-thirty this morning. Right around the time you said you were jogging."

Sam thought about all the flashing emergency lights he'd seen when he'd regained consciousness and felt his throat close up. He barely registered Dr. Frolich talking about a follow-up neurology consult.

"Sam? Sam?" she was saying.

"Sorry. So . . . are premonitions a side effect of the new drug? Because I didn't see that on the accompanying list of horrors when I filled my prescription."

She gave him a sympathetic smile. "It wasn't a premonition, Sam, and I don't think it's related to the drug. There are a lot of variables, and at this point I won't rule out a pharmacological or psychological component, but my guess is you experienced a new neurological phenomenon of some kind."

"Like an enhanced hallucination, something like that?"

"You've described similar episodes in the past, blackouts and brief hallucinations with colors and shapes, something like synesthesia. Seeing a word is a derivative of that. I'm going to speak with Dr. Guzman and I'd like you to see him as soon as possible."

"But I didn't see the accident, I'm sure of that. When I came to, I was still under the coral tree. I saw emergency lights in the distance, but I wasn't there. I was never there, so the hallucination was kind of a massive coincidence, don't you think?"

"You have no *memory* of being there."

Just like you have no memory of getting your gun and going to the front porch. You're mobile and functioning when you're blacked out, which should really scare the shit out of you. You're not getting better, you're getting worse.

That inescapable conclusion summoned a spirit-crushing despondency that didn't go unnoticed by Dr. Frolich.

"There are multiple explanations for this event, Sam, and I want to cover it in every way so we can find out what's behind it."

And fix it. That was the express implication in all discussions with medical professionals about troubling symptoms or tragic test results. His plastic surgeons had inferred the same thing, but in the end even they would have to admit defeat. And what if his brain was like his face? Something that couldn't be repaired?

"Can you lay out one of these multiple explanations? Because right now, I'm just seeing two. Either my brain is scrambled beyond salvation or my psyche is an unmitigated disaster. Wait, I'm seeing three—I'm suddenly psychic."

"I can't speak to the neurological possibilities, but from a psychiatric point of view it's quite simple. Katy noticed that you were in distress. She was empathetic and asked you if you were feeling all right. You two connected in some small way. During the time you were blacked out, you heard the sirens and either went to the scene or learned of the accident from someone else. This prompted your subconscious to craft a false memory of a hallucination to go with the tragic storyline because you liked her."

"Why the hell would my subconscious do that?"

"Because you're allowing it to punish you. If you had foreknowledge of her death and did nothing to stop it, that makes you culpable. You think you've failed before, back in Afghanistan. You're living survivor's guilt over and over again, and with survivor's guilt comes fixation on death and what you should have done to stop it. Neurological aspects could be an exacerbating factor or a symptom."

"So I'm a total wreck in all ways, but I'm not psychic? I'm looking for a new career, you know."

"I wish there was the possibility of being psychic, but I'm afraid we all have to trudge through each day, not knowing what to expect."

"I guess you're absolutely right about that, otherwise I wouldn't have signed up for a second tour."

"Sam, in your dreams, you mention a voice."

What did you see? What do you remember?

"Right. My subconscious is trying to torture me and apparently finding new ways all the time. I believe you mentioned internal conflict resolution."

"In PTSD, it's not unusual to feel like you have unfinished business. Many patients even rewrite events to serve that narrative and we don't want you to go there. It would be a setback."

"Setback? You mean it could get worse from here?"

She ignored his question, which he didn't take as a positive sign. "Has anything about the voice changed?"

"No. Well, yes, kind of. I'm hearing a child now."

"Saying something?"

Sam shook his head and looked down. "Screaming."

"It could be a repressed memory or it could be a fabrication, a false narrative, as I just mentioned. At this point, I encourage you not to attach significance to these things. Real or imagined, they are part of a nightmare. Have you been able to remember anything new about that day?"

"I remember too much about the blast, but nothing that happened before it, not for several days. And nothing after it, until I was at Walter Reed. Will this ever go away, Dr. Frolich?"

"That's what we're working on, and you're making some progress, Sam, don't be discouraged. This is a long journey." She steepled her fingers and gazed out the window. "There is some new research on the effects of high explosive blast waves on the brain. They've found a previously unidentified injury pattern, something they don't see in victims of other traumatic brain injuries such as repeated concussions or car accidents. I'll discuss it with Dr. Guzman when I set up your neuro consult."

"And it can cause symptoms like mine?"

"The research is in the very early stages, but perhaps there are some palliative approaches they're considering."

"Maybe Dr. Guzman can send the researchers my MRIs and I can sign up for a trial or something."

She shook her head. "No, Sam. This isn't something they found with MRIs. They discovered it examining thin slices of brain tissue under a special microscope that's a thousand times more powerful than an MRI."

"So I'd have to be dead before they could find a way to help me."

Apparently, the circle of irony and the absurd hadn't been closed after all.

Chapter Seventeen

CONSEULA ORTIZ LET HERSELF INTO THE apartment and frowned. All the shades were open and that wasn't right. Señor Gallagher always closed them before he went to work. There was also a faint scent of trash that hadn't been taken out. Maybe he was home sick today. Or out of town again and had forgotten or hadn't had time to close the shades or take out the trash.

She set down her cleaning caddies and took a few steps inside, then shut the door and looked around. "Señor? Señor Gallagher, you home?"

No answer.

"Señor?"

Out of town, she decided, then got to work tidying the kitchen. There really wasn't much to do—the sinks were empty and still polished from her visit last week, the granite countertops dust-free and uncluttered. The only things in the dishwasher were two dirty wine glasses; maybe he'd had a date. Señor Gallagher had money and he was good-looking, too. He probably got a lot of dates.

Two glasses were certainly not enough to run a load, so she washed and dried them by hand, then carefully slid them into place in the rack above the center island where dozens of other wine glasses of different shapes and sizes hung. Who needed so many glasses? Especially somebody who was never home.

The kitchen trash was empty and didn't seem to be the source of the off-smell, but she sprayed disinfectant in it for good measure. Sometimes rotting fruit or vegetables or meat juices seeped through the liner and got into the bin. Nothing a good bleach and scour wouldn't take care of if it came to that.

Satisfied with the kitchen, she went through the apartment room by room, dusting and polishing and vacuuming. The powder room was as tidy as the rest of the apartment, except for a vial of cocaine sitting on the vanity. Maybe that's why Americans called them powder rooms, she chuckled to herself, pleased that her English was getting good enough to make jokes.

It wasn't the first time Señor Gallagher had forgotten to put away his drugs, but at least he never left used condoms on his bedside table, and for that she was grateful. Some people left embarrassing messes to clean, messes that made her blush or made her sick to her stomach. And she'd caught people in . . . situations. But they didn't care what she saw or what she thought. She was as good as invisible, no more important than a picture hanging on the wall. Much less important than some pictures hanging in the houses she cleaned, she was sure.

But she was discreet, which was why she had a salary and a nice place to live with enough free time to take on other good-paying clients who valued her silence. No matter how loco they were, she kept her head down, didn't touch anything that shouldn't be touched, and did the job she was paid to do.

The guest room hadn't ever been slept in as far as she could tell, so she left the bed made, dusted, then walked down the hall to his office. The door was open just a crack. She paused, thought about knocking, and then it hit her nose. That smell. Trash that hadn't been taken out.

She fingered the cross around her neck, pushed open the door, and started screaming.

•

Nolan and Crawford stood over the body of Ryan Gallagher, laying faceup on the floor of his home office, lodged between a Herman Miller chair and a chrome and glass desk. One flat, sightless eye was fixed on the ceiling, the other obliterated by a close-range bullet. There wasn't much blood. Small caliber, minimal gore; the slug probably hadn't made it out of his skull. His nose was pulped and it wasn't from the gunshot.

"He pissed off the wrong guy," Crawford commented. "Argument, broken nose, the gun comes out and Gallagher's dead. Someone had to have heard something. Even if he got shot with a silenced .22, that still makes some noise. So does an argument."

"Not enough noise. He's been dead a while and nobody called it in. If you live anywhere central in this city, you stop hearing things." Nolan knew this from her own experience living in loud, scruffy Echo Park. Even as a cop, she'd learned to block out the voices raised in anger and the pops that might be the discharge of a weapon. More often than not, the arguments didn't go anywhere, and the pops were either vehicular backfire or asshole kids with cherry bombs or Black Cats.

She looked around the tidy, organized office. No cameras, but not a big surprise. This was a high-dollar security building where most people owned their units. There was a gate and a guard and if you got past those obstacles, there was a twenty-four-hour desk attended by another guard. The guest log, the guards, and the lobby cameras might tell them everything they needed to know, at least if the killer had been stupid enough to run the security gauntlet as a registered guest. Highly unlikely.

On the walls, there were framed posters of bands and several photos of the deceased in a tuxedo on a red carpet somewhere, looking chummy with rockers she didn't recognize, and old men, also in tuxedoes—the widely varied fauna omnipresent at all award ceremonies. "His phone and computer are still here. No signs of robbery, struggle, or B and E. He knew his killer."

Crawford tipped his head and nodded. "Seems to me he knew his killer well enough that he or she had a key. The housekeeper said the deadbolt was locked when she arrived, and the only way you can engage one of those is either from inside or from the outside with a key. Gallagher sure as hell didn't lock it, and the killer sure as hell didn't jump out a fourteenth-floor window."

"They could have stolen his keys."

Crawford slipped on gloves, patted down the corpse, and withdrew a loaded BMW key chain from the pocket of his cargo shorts. "Nope."

Nolan sighed. "If the killer came with a silenced weapon, it was premeditated."

"Maybe a music industry beef. Not to sound cynical about the entertainment biz, but in the photos he's wearing a tux, so he's an exec, which means he's probably screwed a lot of people over."

"I wouldn't give somebody I'd screwed over the key to my apartment."

"Girlfriend could make sense. Sometimes guys are too dense to know they've screwed over their girlfriends." Crawford gestured to the brown vial filled with powder that sat on the glass desktop. "Or maybe he just had some unpaid bills."

"I wouldn't give a drug dealer a key to my apartment, either."

"Girlfriend or relative makes the most sense. The housekeeper has a key, but I'm going to go out on a limb here and say she didn't do it. We've got another problem, Mags. She cleaned most of the place before she got to the office and found him. She could have vacuumed up a shitload of evidence."

"We've got the bag."

"Crime Scene's going to love that."

"They've dealt with worse."

"I know they have, but they're going to throw an epic tantrum and so is the lab. Take my advice. Drop it off, turn, and run like hell, especially if you see Sweet Genevieve. They'll get the job done, but they won't ever forget it."

"Then I'll let you drop it off."

"Sorry, sweet pea, but you're on your own. Continuing education and all that. You won't be a real detective until you piss off the lab."

Nolan gave the body wide berth and walked to the other side of the desk where there was a thin stack of papers. It was a collection of bills, contracts, and what appeared to be gig lists with cities and dates. And at the bottom, a complaint and summons. "He was being sued."

Crawford scratched at a missed patch of whiskers on his jaw. "Huh. If this guy was the one doing the suing, we'd have a slam dunk."

Chapter Eighteen

CONSUELA ORTIZ WAS STILL WEEPING AT the dining room table, attended by a young female uniform who awkwardly stood beside her uttering occasional words of consolation in Spanish.

Nolan sat down across from her. "Ms. Ortiz, do you think you could answer some more questions?"

She blotted her eyes and nodded.

"Are you absolutely positive the door and deadbolt were locked when you arrived today?"

"Yes, absolutely positive."

"Did you notice anything out of the ordinary when you were cleaning, maybe things missing or out of place, disturbed?"

"No, ma'am. Señor Gallagher, very neat. Today it was very neat like always. Everything looked normal, except the shades weren't down."

"The window shades?"

"*Si*. He always puts them down when he leave. But he didn't leave today . . ." Fresh tears started dribbling down her cheeks and she crossed herself.

"Was it unusual that he didn't leave today?"

"I guess so, I never see him. I only met him once, when he interviewed me."

"And he gave you a key at that time?"

"*Si*."

"Could anybody have taken your key?"

She looked puzzled. "No, I have it, I use it today."

"I mean in the past. Could somebody have taken it at some point and made a copy?"

Her puzzlement transformed to incredulity. "No, never, ma'am! My keys, all very important, my clients, they trust me with them."

Nolan understood. Her story was one of thousands like it in the city, invisible people entrusted with keys to literal kingdoms in some cases. A big part of their jobs was keeping them safe. It wasn't a burden she'd ever want to take on. "How long have you been cleaning for Mr. Gallagher?"

"A year, I think."

"Have you ever encountered any of his friends or associates during that time? Maybe they showed up here while you were cleaning?"

"No ma'am, I never see anyone."

"Was there any sign that he'd had a visitor? A guest?"

Her eyes drifted toward the kitchen and she nodded. "Wine glasses. Two, in the dishwasher."

"Are they still there?"

"No, ma'am, it wasn't enough to run a load. I washed them by hand and put away."

Nolan looked up at Crawford. More evidence potentially destroyed if Consuela Ortiz was as diligent as she seemed to be. "Would you show me where?"

She sniffled and rose from her chair, pointing to two sparkling glasses hanging from the ceiling-mounted lattice. Nolan felt a sting of disappointment. Any DNA they may have held was down the drain and polished away. "Thank you, Ms. Ortiz."

She started to wring her hands in distress. "I have another job, can I go now?"

"Please write down your contact information first, then you're free to go."

And then came the next steps: the canvass, the interviews, the forensic disassembling of somebody's life after death as you tried to figure out who might have wanted them dead and why. Sometimes things were obvious, sometimes they weren't. It was a puzzle to be put together piece by piece. Nolan relished the work but hated the disappointment of finding some banal reason for a death, which was what usually happened. Ryan Gallagher had pissed somebody off and got shot because of it. Most murders ended up being sorry, prosaic events; but they mattered, every single one of them.

Chapter Nineteen

SAM HAD A DISMAL REVELATION AS he walked down Wilshire Boulevard toward Pearl Club. Life didn't offer a predetermined depth to which you could sink before you started floating back up to the top. As long as you were still breathing, you could hit basement level and the elevator might still keep going down. You could suffer interminably and then suffer some more.

Death, on the other hand, was the definitive last stop, and in spite of everything, he was one lucky son of a bitch. Fucked up beyond any repair, all recognition, maybe—*FUBAR,* as they said in the military—but lucky. His men hadn't lived to suffer or to thrive and neither had Katy. He had to remember that.

His initial instinct was to try to scour his mind of Katy because there simply wasn't enough room for another ghost. But maybe the ghosts were what would keep him company now that he was alone. It was a disturbing thought but one that was also oddly consoling. Maybe if he made friends with the ghosts, they'd stop tormenting him.

He was almost to Pearl Club and still had nearly an hour to kill before work, so he ducked into The Coffee Bean and Tea Leaf on La Cienega, his recent home away from home, equidistant between his shrink and his job—sadly, the two places where he spent most of his time these days.

The space was filled with people on their devices—*'vices,* he called them, because there was hardly a more addictive substance out there than any piece of cheap plastic with a microprocessor. There was the usual mélange of LA coffee shop denizens, all present and accounted for—nascent talent of all stripes, wannabes, flat-out losers wasting time while they waited to win the Hollywood lottery, all of them believing on some level that their time spent here would somehow generate the next hit movie or the next Big Thing.

This city more than any other was still all about face-to-face networking, but you'd never know it in a place like this—none of the people here seemed interested in anything beyond the myopic scope of their electronic deities, and his guess was their interactions had nothing to do with business. They were here to be seen, noticed, just like on the beauty gauntlet of San Vicente and Adelaide Drive, desperate and on full display, looking for a taker.

He ordered a double espresso, downed it at the counter, and then ordered another double, pretending they were shots of high-octane whiskey because that's what he really wanted, what he craved. He found a seat in the back and united with the rest of the zombies around him by digging his phone out of his backpack, simply for a distraction from the deeply disturbing day.

It had been a bad idea—far from being a mindless diversion, it only served as a reminder of what had happened since he'd gotten out of bed this morning. There were two texts from his mother, one telling him what he already knew, that she'd run into Yuki at Whole Foods; and a second one inviting him to Sunday dinner at four—*surprise guest!*—double smiley face sticker—and a less enthusiastic *Yukiko is welcome to join us.*

Yuki obviously hadn't shared her new life plan with Mama Bear Easton, which had been wise on her part; otherwise, she wouldn't have made it out of the store alive. She'd never entirely trusted Yuki's prickly personality or her commitment to her son. She'd never said as much, but she didn't have to. The separation had galvanized her suspicion, and if his marriage somehow managed to survive, holidays were going to be tense.

It was tempting to think that she'd been right all along, but Mama Bear had no idea what Yuki had gone through and the sacrifices she'd made to help him after he'd come back wounded. Destroyed. That was another secret he was keeping from another person. Christ, the list was getting long and confusing.

After some consideration, he accepted on the condition she reveal the identity of the mystery guest, said he was looking forward to the drive to Pasadena (which he wasn't) and Yuki was so sorry but couldn't make it (total lie). He toyed with the idea of asking about her golf handicap, then decided she might take his gentle riposte seriously and pick up the thread in earnest on Sunday.

The remaining three texts were from Yuki, all of them containing less than five syllables, in keeping with her fondness for brevity. I'm sorry. I love you. Talk later?

He didn't know how to respond, so he didn't and checked his other alerts instead. There was a ping from Pacific Gas and Electric and a couple credit cards reminding him bills were due mid-month, and his bank letting him know that his mortgage had been automatically withdrawn from his joint account with Yuki. There were two missed calls from the VA, probably trying to square up medical coverage for his last facial surgery, and one from Melody. She hadn't left a message, so he didn't call her back. He'd be seeing her soon enough.

Once he'd exhausted the nominal distractions of personal business, he did a search on Katy Villa. There were several articles about her tragic death posted by various online news outlets, but the one he fixated on reported that police were still looking for the vehicle and driver responsible for her hit-and-run death. Several witnesses had described a black Jeep.

How many black Jeeps are there in LA? A thousand? Twenty-thousand? More?

"Goddamnit, get a grip," he muttered to himself, attracting unwanted attention from the twitchy, malnourished retro-punk who'd taken the table next to him. He was just a kid, with pale, wiry arms and a sunken chest. His mop of dull brown hair looked like the pile on a worn stuffed animal. He had the regulation piercings and tattoos of a young societal mutineer, the most prominent being a blurry, blue portrait of Sid Vicious on his right forearm, an ignominious idol who had died of a heroin overdose a couple decades before this one had even been born. Hopefully he would regret it someday.

"Are you talking to me?" the kid asked, almost politely, although Sam wondered if he wasn't going for menace. If he was an aspiring actor, he had a lot of work to do.

"No, I'm talking to myself."

The kid found that amusing for some reason. "Awesome. I talk to myself, too. Not something you want to admit to everybody." He twirled his finger in a circle around his ear and whistled. "Think you're crazy."

"Actually, I might be crazy." Sam figured that was the perfect strategy to abbreviate any further discussion. But on the contrary, it only seemed to serve as some sort of deranged icebreaker.

His eyes flared and glittered with excitement, as if he'd just encountered some exotic species of man-eating animal. Or worse yet, a soulmate. "Dude, for real?"

"Sometimes I think so. My psychiatrist doesn't."

He gave him a lopsided smile, showing perfect white teeth that countermanded his cultivated look of degeneracy. "I'm a filmmaker," he said apropos of nothing.

Of course he was a filmmaker. Along with everybody else here.

"Well, not yet, but I'm in school. UCLA film school. I'm working on my final, my student film."

"Good luck with that."

"My script is about a nutter who steals a car and drives out to the Imperial Valley to either kill himself or somebody else. You'd make a *rad* lead." He leaned back in his chair and closed his eyes, framing a scene with his hands. "I can see you standing on the edge of the Salton Sea, trying to make a choice, and there's garbage swirling around your feet as you walk into the water—beer cans and syringes and dirty diapers, a dead dog, and maybe a toupée. That's when you finally make your decision."

"A toupée. That's an interesting detail."

His eyes sprung open. "I thought so. You wondered about it, so the audience will, too."

Assuming he'd have an audience. "What's my decision?"

"I don't know anymore. With you as the lead, I think it would flow to a perfect and different conclusion on its own. What do you say?"

"That's really tempting, but I'm booked. Shooting in Croatia next month. Or maybe Crimea, I'm not really sure. I get the two mixed up."

"Yeah? I knew you were an actor. You've got that look going on. Dangerous."

"I've heard that before."

"Yeah, I'll bet. You'll carve out a real niche for yourself."

"That's what I'm hoping." Sam pocketed his phone and stood up. "Gotta go. Can't be late for work."

"So you're SAG, right? I can pay Guild scale if you change your mind. I'm scouting locations and shooting some stock footage in the desert this weekend."

"Great time of year for a trip to the desert."

"Hey, why don't you come with me? We can shoot some test scenes, see if you like the whole vibe."

"I'm busy, but thanks for the invite. Have fun. See you around."

"What happened to your face? Not to be rude, but it's pretty dope, like a tragedy and comedy mask. The duality of the human condition, right out there for everybody to see."

Jesus, this kid wouldn't shut up. "You noticed?"

Sam's sarcasm went undetected, or at least unacknowledged. "Of course I noticed, but I wasn't going to open up a conversation like that. That would be rude. So what happened?"

"Farm accident."

"Yeah? That's harsh. You don't look like a farmer." He scrabbled through his battered canvas bag and held out a card. "My name's Rolf. Rolf Hesse. That's my real name, if you were wondering."

Sam took the card out of sympathy. "Actually, I wasn't."

"Yeah, well a lot of people ask. Everybody here has a stage name. They think mine's made up, too, but my dad's German. Maybe you know him. He wrote and directed the *Dead to Rights* movies."

Sam knew the *Dead to Rights* movies, actually liked them. It was a trilogy of contemporary, sexy murder flicks with a nostalgic nod to old noir: great cinematography, ham-fisted acting, and dark, sometimes clichéd scripts. None of them had been blockbusters at first, but they had become cult classics with an avid, global following. Rolf might have a future in film after all if the right pieces of DNA had been attached to his daddy's victorious sperm. "Hans Hesse."

"Yeah, that's my dad."

"Good movies. I'll always remember the raindrops on the dusty windshield before Magda got stabbed in her Jaguar."

Rolf beamed at him. "That was my favorite scene in the whole trilogy. I'll tell Pops you said so, that will make him happy. I've been trying to get him to do another one, but he says it would ruin the magic of three. It's his lucky number, so I guess there's something to that."

Sam thought about lucky charms again. Shamrocks, waving cats, numbers. Apparently, a lot of people had them, regardless of background or socioeconomic status. It was suddenly emerging as a fascinating anthropological subject. "Superstition."

"Yeah, man, it's all over, wherever you look. I'm not superstitious, but if people want to believe in it, that's their gig. I'm not going to harsh on it." He dipped back into his bag, pulled out a bound script, and handed it to him. "This is my baby. Take a look, maybe you'll change your mind about being a part of it."

"You wrote it?"

"Yeah, of course. If you can't write, you can't direct."

Sam took it reluctantly. The cover page read: *Deep into the Dark*. A decent noir title but probably a terrible script. Still, it hit him in the gut. "Where did you get this title?"

Rolf shrugged a bony shoulder. "I don't know, it just came to me and seemed right for the material. Do you like it?"

"It's a book title."

"Oh, yeah? Who wrote it?"

"My shrink."

"What? That's cray! What's it about?"

"Never read it. It's nonfiction. Boring."

Rolf rubbed his jaw in what Sam supposed was meant to be a pensively intellectual gesture. "Pops has tons of psych textbooks in his library. Research for his films. Maybe I saw it and it planted a bug in my brain. It's a cool title. Wow, man. If that's not a sign you were meant to be a part of this, I don't know what is."

"I thought you weren't superstitious."

"I'm not, but there's a big difference between superstitions and signs."

Sam didn't ask for further elucidation on the distinction between the two. "The script is mine to keep?"

"Yeah, definitely. And bear in mind, it's fluid. I would definitely make some changes if you came on board."

Sam shoved it into his backpack, along with his scant emergency supplies—a bottle of water and a baggie with aspirin and a couple tranquilizers, just in case. "Your dad doesn't want to produce it?"

"He hasn't read it, he's busy working on a film in Berlin. Besides, I need to do this on my own, get out from under his shadow and make my own name, you know? That's why I'm in film school."

"Makes sense." Sam wasn't surprised that Rolf hadn't even asked for his name, even though he was hustling him to be a part of his stupid student film. There was a special brand of narcissism that existed in Hollywood and nowhere else on the planet. "Thanks."

"I hope you read it. If you do and decide you want to be my lead, call me anytime."

"I'll put you on speed dial . . ." and then red lines started squirming like bloody worms on the kid's forehead and Sam sank back down into his chair.

"Dude? Dude, are you okay? Are you having some kind of a seizure? Are you freaking out?"

Rolf's voice was distant, echoing in his mind in a slow, distorted cadence as a word started to form. Sam pinched his eyes shut, willing the hallucination to go away, but it wouldn't. Even with his eyes closed, a word eventually appeared, just like it had with Katy: *Overdose.*

But very different from Katy, the word on Rolf's forehead quickly morphed into a YouTube-esque clip of a needle plunging into a collapsed, infected vein on a skeletal arm, followed by a close-up shot of saliva bubbling from the lifeless lips of a slack, graying face.

When Sam became aware again, there was a lot of black in the matrix of his memory, the blank spaces he was used to, and he was gripping

Rolf's arm. There were alarmed shouts, the squeal of metal chair legs scraping the floor, a siren in the distance.

"Dude, just relax," Rolf was saying in a shaky voice. "It's gonna be okay, there's an ambulance on the way."

Sam released his arm and saw the angry, white print of his hand on the kid's sallow flesh. "I'm sorry." Then he got to his feet and started running.

Chapter Twenty

SAM STOOD BY THE DUMPSTER BEHIND Pearl Club and tried to catch his breath, tried to find a better head space without pharmaceutical intervention before his shift started in fifteen minutes. He couldn't go in until he did, and he couldn't not go in and lose another job. Pearl was a record for him, six months. That looked okay on a résumé, but a year looked better if he was ever going to get a real job in his field.

No, Sam hasn't freaked out once since he's been working with us. He's totally stable. In fact, he's probably one of the most reliable employees we have.

Sam analyzed his circumstances in the context of mental health. He'd experienced two similar hallucinations and three blackouts today. There was no question his PTSD was escalating, his sanity was deteriorating. The hallucinations were triggered by stress. The blackouts were self-preservation, a psychological analog to the fight-or-flight response.

He thought about calling Dr. Frolich, then decided against it. He knew what she would say. He was in crisis. The episode with Katy on top of Yuki's unexpected news had generated extreme anxiety, and anxiety was like the space around a black hole. The event horizon. Once you crossed it, you never came back.

And black holes were voracious. The hallucination he'd had with Katy fed the hallucination he'd had with Rolf, who looked like a reasonable candidate for a drug overdose. The kid's incessant babbling about his film had created the YouTube video in his mind. He'd also made a reluctant connection with him and consequently tailored a tragic storyline that might serve his survivor's guilt in the future. There were no such things as premonitions or supernatural phenomena, just brain problems, and he had plenty to go around. And if he didn't drag himself out of his black hole and get over his obsession with death, it would keep happening.

"Dude, are you okay?"

Sam jerked his head up and saw Rolf standing a few meters away. He looked scared, frail. Fucking Rolf. "You followed me?"

"Hell, yes, I followed you. Fuck, man, I wasn't going to let you run around Hollywood freaking out or whatever's going on with you. It's not safe. In your condition, you'll get your ass rolled in a heartbeat." He took a few cautious steps forward. "Can I give you a lift somewhere? That's my ride." He pointed to a black Mercedes AMG convertible. Monster engine, almost two hundred grand off the showroom floor.

Sam briefly let his mind drift into fantasy territory, imagining himself behind the wheel, then shook it off. "Thanks, but I'm already here. At work."

Rolf looked up at the back façade of the club. "You work at Pearl?"

"Yeah."

"Sweet place. Best tapas in town. Staff isn't hard to look at, either. What do you do here?"

"Bar back."

Rolf shrugged. "You could do worse."

And I could do a hell of a lot better, Sam thought, briefly indulging self-pity. "Go on, Rolf. Enjoy your life, I'll get through mine."

"What's your name?"

"You're finally asking?"

"I should have before. I was just so stoked about the movie and you maybe being in it."

"Will you go away if I tell you?"

"Maybe. Probably."

"Why do you care?"

"I'm just asking for a name. I don't want to think of you as the crazy guy from The Leaf because I don't think you're crazy."

"Sam," he finally relinquished.

He passed a wistful smile to the dumpster. "Telegram Sam."

"What?"

"It's an old T. Rex song, 'Telegram Sam.' Bauhaus did a bomb cover in 1980, way better than the original. Check it out on YouTube."

YouTube. God, you couldn't get away from it. "Yeah, I'll do that." Rolf's unexpected, unwelcome appearance had done one thing—irritated him enough to make him forget about everything else and propel his ass into work just to escape. "Gotta go, take care."

"Take care of yourself, Telegram Sam." He started to turn around, then changed his mind, planted his feet. "What did you see back there?"

What did you see? What do you remember?

"In The Leaf. You were looking at me like I was Satan or something."

Sam smiled, seizing an opportunity. Telling him he might be crazy hadn't worked earlier but might now. Christ, he never should have engaged. It had only encouraged him. Stupid. "I have hallucinations sometimes, Rolf. Kind of like premonitions. One came true this morning—I'm not sure what to think about that."

"What kind of premonitions?" he asked, undeterred.

"How people will die."

Rolf's eyes expanded until they were so laughably disproportionate in his lank face, he looked like an owl. "No . . . no way."

"It was just a hallucination. It doesn't mean anything. Necessarily," he said, bending the word for maximum impact. "Just a coincidence, if you believe in them. Or a projection, maybe a neurological condition. Crazy, if you believe in that."

His troubled brow furrowed. "You're shitting me."

"I wish I was."

"So you saw something when you were looking at me?"

"I saw the word 'overdose' on your forehead."

His jaw went slack, then his big eyes jittered down to his arms involuntarily. It was the first time Sam noticed the scars there. Track marks. Or maybe his subconscious had picked them up earlier and that, combined with the Sid Vicious tattoo, is where his hallucination had germinated.

Rolf was finally speechless.

"Finish your film, Rolf Hesse. Do something good. Live to tell about it. I'll be really fucking pissed off if I see your name in the obituaries, and if you're there I'll see it. I read them every morning and I won't forget your name."

Rolf started backing away, then it was his turn to bolt, but to the safety of his AMG and his student film and possibly his room or wing in Daddy's mansion. Unless he really hit rock bottom, he wouldn't be standing by a dumpster losing his marbles tonight.

Sam watched him roar away in his beautiful piece of automotive glory. Mission accomplished. He'd gotten rid of Rolf. And maybe he'd think twice before he stuck another needle in his arm, although he doubted it.

When his phone rang and he saw his mother's number on the caller ID, he thought about ignoring it because her parental radar could pick up the faintest shift in tone or timbre in his voice and she would obsess over it. But a dose of Mom right now might be good medicine. She had plenty of idiosyncrasies, but she was the closest thing to normal in his life at the moment. "Hey, Mom."

"Sam. You sound out of breath, are you all right?"

"I'm just finishing up a run." Maybe a minor misrepresentation but definitely not a lie.

"Oh. Well, I'm calling to tell you how happy I am you're coming to dinner Sunday. Four o'clock sharp."

"Thanks for the invite. Who's the mystery guest? The neighbor's Shih Tzu?"

"Pfft, you're ridiculous, but I'm glad to hear you're in good spirits."

If she only knew.

"Are you sure you don't want to be surprised, dear?"

"I definitely don't want to be surprised. You remember what happened at my tenth birthday party."

"You are just full of spit and vinegar today." Her voice was full of mirth and it made Sam inordinately happy.

"Cough it up, Mom."

"Sam, you won't believe it," she gushed. "Lee Varney came for coffee this morning. He's in town for some meetings. He'll be joining us, and possibly Captain Greer, too!"

A lot of military memories came flooding back—actually, it was more like a memory tsunami washing over him—but it was all positive for a change. "Lee *and* Andy?"

"Their paths crossed on the West Coast and they both want to see you."

"You just made my night."

"I thought I might," she said, purring with satisfaction. "See you Sunday, dear. Call if you need anything."

When he hung up, he pondered the dumpster. It suddenly felt ridiculous to be communing with a trash receptacle, whereas a few minutes ago it had seemed appropriate. He was always reluctant to acknowledge affirmative feelings, as if that would instantly dispel them, but he welcomed this buoyancy of spirit without reservation. It wouldn't last long, but he'd enjoy it while he could.

He dry-swallowed two aspirin to preemptively fend off the headache that was making a sinuous creep into his brain, ignored the tranqs, then finally took the plunge and stepped into the boisterous Pearl Club kitchen. It was the only world that seemed to make any sense to him these days.

Chapter Twenty-one

LANGDON, THE NIGHT MANAGER OF PEARL Club, was chewing out a new, largely disliked waiter while the line cooks snickered softly at their stations. Luis, a sous chef and former Marine, gave Sam a salute, then went back to the octopus he was charring on the plancha. Ashley, who ran the front of the house, was at the computer in the adjacent office, checking reservations for the night and documenting shift changes while she sneaked puffs off an e-cig and sipped coffee. White coffee, code for white wine disguised in a coffee cup. Langdon didn't know about it, but everybody else did.

Sam relaxed. This felt like home, every bit as dysfunctional as his own. He didn't know if that was good or bad, but it was comfortable. He poked his head into the office and said hi to Ashley.

"Hi, Sam!" She shoved the coffee cup behind the computer monitor. "Busy night on the books, are you ready?"

"I was born ready."

She tittered. "You're clocked in, so you'd best get your ass into work before I have to fire you."

"I could really use a drink of your coffee first."

She regarded him shrewdly.

"Everybody knows about the white coffee except Langdon. And we'll all keep it that way."

Ashley nodded and passed him the cup. "Whatever it takes to get through the night, right?"

"Right. Next time, let's do whiskey."

"Not a bad idea. It looks more like coffee, too. But it reeks to high heaven. Maybe vodka."

"Clear coffee, the next big thing. Our little secret." The wine felt good on his palate, felt even better once it started to enter his bloodstream. Maybe the day wasn't a total loss, although his hope for dry dock wasn't shaping up so well.

Tomorrow. The classic mantra of a drinker uncommitted to sobriety. He wondered if Rolf was confronting a similar existential crisis right now.

When he made his way to the lounge area, Melody was already behind the bar, chatting up a handful of lingering, late-afternoon customers. They were finishing their tapas and drinks before they headed somewhere else and made room for the next shift of happy hour drinkers and diners. She engaged them effortlessly as she prepped her bartender's mise en place as meticulously as any chef would before service, but there was something off-kilter about her manner tonight. She seemed disjointed, distracted, like she was just going through the motions instead of genuinely enjoying her role.

He assumed it had everything to do with Ryan, but he wouldn't press the issue. Besides, she wouldn't have much time to dwell on it because the dinner rush was imminent, the second bar rush after that. Pearl Club was open fourteen hours a day, every day, and there were rarely empty bar stools or tables whatever the time. It was an intense environment, but Sam liked it because he never had time to think about anything except doing his job, and Melody probably liked it for the same reason.

Her deftly concealed black eye was almost impossible to see in the low light, especially if you weren't looking for it; but if somebody noticed, he knew she'd come up with an elaborate, entertaining cover story.

I was riding out in Temescal Canyon and the horse they gave me tossed his head while I was putting on his bridle and smacked me good in the face. Tripped on my nephew's toy while I was babysitting and hit the stair railing. Got rear-ended on Melrose by some coked up junior agent from ICM and hit my head on the steering wheel.

She had a quick, creative mind and unlimited possibilities for her future, just like Pearl Club's motto promised on nicely embossed cocktail napkins: The World Is Your Oyster. Corny and equally incongruous because Pearl Club didn't serve oysters. They really should; it was weird that they didn't.

Meanwhile, Ryan was still trolling around somewhere, a boundless loser and predator with angry, clenched fists—just waiting to assert his manhood by whacking his woman and excising her future prospects—undoubtedly to compensate for an inadequate penis and shriveled balls.

He met Melody's eyes. She tried for a smile, but it never fully formed on her lips. "Hi, Sam. I was just telling these nice people to visit the La Brea Tar Pits if they have time."

They were a hip, pretty couple in their thirties, and looked like the clientele that usually inhabited Pearl Club. They fit in here, but Melody had obviously ascertained they were *Ausländers*. "The La Brea Tar Pits are definitely worth seeing," he said. "Think of *Jurassic Park* while you're there and you'll have a whole different experience."

They chuckled, paid their bill with a card, then tossed thirty bucks on the bar before they left.

"They're from Chicago," she said, stuffing the thirty in the tip kitty below the rail as she watched the husband or boyfriend steer his tipsy companion to the valet stand out front.

"What's wrong?"

"What do you mean?"

"Something's bothering you, and you called me earlier but didn't leave a message. What's going on?"

She looked defeated. "Not such a great actress, huh?" She looked up as a large group of young men in suits walked through the door. "It's no big deal, I'll tell you after work. Would you get me two cases of Heineken?"

"You got it, boss."

Chapter Twenty-two

REMY SIPPED TEPID COFFEE WHILE HE watched Froggy devour the "world-famous" French dip. Philippe's was almost empty near closing time and was an ideal meeting spot. It was in the vicinity of Froggy's place of employment, but an unlikely establishment to run into his colleagues. He'd been a useful snitch for LAPD for two years and he seemed to enjoy the role. At least he enjoyed the free food and extra compensation. It was a perfect symbiosis of parasite and host.

Remy pushed the photo of Thom Rangel next to his plate to regain his attention.

"You're sure you've never seen this guy?"

He gave it another cursory examination with his bulging, amphibian eyes. "Hundred percent positive."

He tossed Stella Clary's most current driver's license photo on top of Rangel's. "But you know this woman."

"I wouldn't say I know her, but she's around sometimes." Au jus dribbled down into his sparse goatee and he wiped it away daintily with a napkin. Froggy had the remnants of table manners. "She comes downtown when she has cash money, and sometimes even if she doesn't, if you catch my meaning." He waggled his eyebrows.

Remy tamped down his disgust. "When was the last time you saw her?"

"About a month ago. She came to me for some Xanny."

"You didn't see her yesterday?"

"No, man. Stella's candy of choice is ice and the amigos mostly handle meth. I'm strictly pills. Commerce down here is pretty segregated, we stick to our grids."

"So she came to you a month ago looking for tranqs."

"Yeah, she said she was stressing, like I was a doctor and she needed an excuse." He swirled his finger into the plastic cup of horseradish sauce, the only thing left on his plate. Froggy's table manners had left the building.

"Did she say what was bothering her?"

He leaned back in his chair and put a hand on his stomach, looking content as a cat in the sun. "I don't figure the cost of therapy into my prices, but she was paranoid as hell, either jonesing or tweaked. Same effect."

"So she told you she was stressing, you exchanged goods, that's it?"

He was still licking the horseradish off his finger. "Yeah. Well, actually, thinking back on it now, she did ask me if there was word out about a creeper around here, following women."

Remy's pulse rate doubled. He'd been positive Rangel had invented that part of his story on the spot. "And is there?"

He laughed. "Ain't nobody normal down here, but specifically, no. Like I said, she was paranoid."

"Did she describe him?"

"No, she just asked me about it, took her stuff, and left. What do you want with Stella, anyhow?"

"I want to find her killer."

He blinked quickly, a frog in a hailstorm. "Oh, man. You think there's actually something to her creeper?"

"She's dead, what do you think?" Remy tucked a fifty under his plate. "Put the word out and if you hear of anything, you let me know first thing, got it?"

•

On the way home, Remy considered that there were roughly seven miles between Miracle Mile and the downtown drug district. If there really was a creeper and he was the Monster, that was his territory. All of his victims were heavy users, all had been killed in Miracle Mile. He hunted downtown and killed away from his backyard. Animals didn't soil their dens.

Finally, a new lead, a new focus, something to move on. He called Bill Turner, who was heading up the task force's overnight shift, and briefed him. While Remy caught a few hours, they would be working it.

After his call with Bill, he made an impulsive, last-minute turn onto Stone Canyon Road and pulled up to the valet stand at the Hotel Bel-Air. He needed a few drinks in a civilized atmosphere to wash the foul taste of the past twenty-four hours out of his mouth. Like Froggy at Philippe's, he was unlikely to run into any colleagues here.

Chapter Twenty-three

THE FOUR O'CLOCK SHIFT AT PEARL ended at ten, and Sam was grateful. He felt physically and emotionally gutted. The clientele had shifted from serious diners to the party crowd. Most of them were impaired, milling by the entrance while they waited for a table or a spot at the bar, and all of them were obnoxious to varying degrees. It was the same situation as when he'd had the unfortunate encounter with the producer's wife.

"Let me give you a lift home," Melody said, twirling her keychain around her finger.

"In your beautiful pea-green boat?"

A genuine smile lifted her face for the first time that night. "'The Owl and the Pussycat.' That was my favorite lullaby."

"It's a nursery rhyme."

"And a song. My car's not pea green."

"Not fresh pea green, it's split pea green."

"Whatever, at least I have a car."

"I have a car, I just don't drive it."

"Why?"

"It's too valuable."

"Show me?"

"Sure."

"Got anything to drink at your house?"

"No. You cleaned me out, remember?"

"We'll stop on the way. I'll just stay for a couple, if that's okay."

"That's okay."

On the drive to Mar Vista, Melody was quiet, jittery, unsettled. She kept her hands tight on the wheel, and her eyes kept flicking from her rearview mirror to her side mirrors. Her posture was stiff, her breathing shallow, like she was fighting off an anxiety attack. Sam knew all the tells because he dealt with them every day. But he wouldn't push her. She'd talk to him in her own time, or not at all. It was her choice.

She pulled up to a liquor store on Centinela, a few blocks from her apartment. "What can I get you?"

He unclipped his seatbelt. "I'll come in with you, pick out a vintage bottle of sparkling water."

Melody bought a case of beer and a bottle of chardonnay. Sam caved and picked up a bottle of small batch rye from Kentucky to go with his sparkling water. He would probably drink half the rye and none of the water. He didn't have anything to celebrate, but he certainly had reasons to drink.

"Do you mind if we stop by my place for a minute? There's something I want to show you."

"Go ahead."

Sam had been to her apartment once before, briefly. From what little he'd glimpsed from her kitchen, she'd done a fine job furnishing it and making it welcoming. A work in progress, she'd said, but wasn't everything and everybody? He noticed a big bunch of rosemary in a vase by the kitchen sink and two empty bottles of Sierra Nevada. "What do you want to show me?"

She led him into her bedroom, something he hadn't been expecting, but thankfully she just pointed to a bouquet of roses on her dresser. "Somebody crawled through my window and left these for me while I was at your house. It wasn't Ryan."

"Are you sure?"

"He said he didn't."

"You talked to him?"

"No, just texted. But now he's not responding to me."

"He's pissed off, that's why."

"That's what I'm worried about."

"You should be. You should also be worried about who did leave the roses. Did you call the cops?"

"And tell them what?"

"Gee, I don't know. That you have a violent, angry boyfriend and possibly a stalker?"

She gave him a sharp look. "They can't do anything."

"Call them, Mel, I'll wait with you. And pack a bag. You're staying with me until this gets sorted out."

"I can't . . ."

"Yes, you can."

She twisted her fingers together, picked at her pink nail polish nervously. "Tell me about the black Jeep."

Sam felt something unformulated and dark uncoil inside him. "What about it?"

"Teddy, he lives here. He's the caretaker—said he's seen a black Jeep around. Parked in front of the building."

He shrugged, going for indifference and not sure if he'd pulled it off. "I've seen one around my place, too. It was parked outside my house this morning, but cars park on residential streets. There's nowhere else to park." *And then the black Jeep followed me while I was jogging and ran over a woman I talked to.* Add Melody to the list of people he was keeping secrets from. Maybe it would be easier to keep a list of people he was honest with because there was nobody on that list right now, zero, a cinch to remember.

"You thought it might belong to Ryan. Maybe it does, I wouldn't know if he has another car."

"Let's get you out of here, Mel. Pack your bag. We'll go to my house and then we'll deal with the cops."

Sam left her to pack and sank into the living room sofa, so stiff and redolent with new furniture smell, he wondered if it had ever been sat on before. There were no dings in the wooden legs, no wear and tear on the fabric, no hollows from TV-watching butts denting the cushions. Actually, there were no signs of a real life in the room at all. It had all the bells and whistles of a home but was totally impersonal, like a display at a furniture store.

It made sense. She was just starting out from scratch, building a new life, a new space, and she didn't have family heirlooms or tchotchkes to display because she'd never had a real family. And living on the streets didn't afford the opportunity to gather meaningful possessions of your own.

A work in progress, the apartment and the woman.

He noticed an electric guitar on a stand, tucked in a dark corner. An authentic part of Melody or a flea market prop meant to make the space seem less anonymous? There was no amp, so he leaned toward the latter explanation.

He tensed when he saw a shadow pass by the front window, reached for a sidearm that wasn't there. Paranoia, like guilt, was highly communicable and hard to shake, and he was suddenly being smothered by both of them. He had to move, had to leave. "Almost ready?"

"Yep." She emerged from the bedroom with a small roll-aboard, wearing an oversized Los Angeles Lakers T-shirt, jeans, and a troubled expression. Her makeup had faded, and the black eye was clearly visible now.

"Do you play guitar?"

Her eyes darted to the corner. "No, I just thought it looked cool."

"It does."

"I found it at a pawn shop. I like to wonder about its history and what kind of music it played. It has a story, but I'll never know what it is, which is why I like it."

"You can make up a new story whenever you want."

She smiled wistfully. "Exactly. Let's get the hell out of here, Sam."

They both jumped at the knock on the door.

"Who is it?" Sam shouted, all the anxiety transferring to his voice, making it sound confrontational and probably scary, at least if you were on the other side of the door.

"Mellie?"

Melody hurried to the door and opened it with a backward glance of reassurance. "It's Teddy. Come in, Teddy, meet my friend Sam."

He stepped inside, gaped at her black eye, then gave Sam a wary once-over. "What the hell, are you okay, girl?"

"I'm fine. Sam didn't do this. He's helping me. I'm going to stay with him until . . . I'm going to stay with him for a day or two."

Teddy relaxed and nodded at Sam. "Nice to meet you, man."

"You, too." Teddy was dread-locked, wore a surf poncho, floral board shorts, and flip-flops. He was clearly baked out of his mind and moved like an overcooked noodle. Sam felt like he'd just stepped onto the set of a surfing flick.

"Mellie, the cops were here earlier looking for you."

She blanched. "For me?"

"I told them I didn't know where you were." He reached into the pocket of his poncho and pulled out a card. "They left this, said to call them right away. Are you in some kind of trouble?"

She shook her head. "I haven't done anything wrong."

He cocked his head at Sam. "You're worried."

Oh, hell, yes, he was worried, worried about a lot of things. "Mel said you've seen a black Jeep around."

"Yeah, it was here this morning, but I haven't seen it since."

"Do you know what model? What kind of Jeep?"

"Rubicon. So you think it's bad news?"

"It could be. Keep an eye out. Do you have a pen and paper, Mel?"

She gave him a bewildered expression.

"We'll give Teddy our numbers. Please call us if you see it again."

"You got it, man." Teddy stared at Sam's face through bleary eyes, as if he'd just noticed the scars. "You want me to confront the dude?"

An outlandish image of skinny, stoned Teddy bludgeoning somebody with a flip-flop flashed through his mind. "No, it's probably nothing. But try to get a plate number."

Chapter Twenty-four

MELODY PULLED INTO SAM'S DRIVEWAY AND turned off the ignition. She draped her arms over the steering wheel and gazed out the windshield but made no move to get out. "Teddy's a character, isn't he?"

"Actually, he's more of a caricature, like he's laying it on a little too thick. I think he's got more going on up top than he plays."

She nodded. "I think so, too. I was in his apartment once and there's nothing in there but surfboards and floor-to-ceiling bookshelves. Science stuff, marine biology."

"He's the caretaker. Does he have keys to all the apartments?"

"I don't know. He didn't leave the roses, Sam, if that's what you're thinking. Somebody climbed through my window. If you had a key, why would you go to the trouble?"

"To deflect attention from the obvious. And it just seems like he's trying too hard to be the insouciant stoner surfer."

"This is California, he is one for real. And he's not creepy or weird. I know creepy and weird."

Sam wasn't convinced, and besides, he knew she was avoiding the real issue. "You have to call the cops, Mel. If you don't, they'll think you're avoiding them."

"Why should I talk to them? I didn't do anything."

Her voice was petulant, indignant, like a rebellious teenager's. Sam summoned all the patience in his soul, which wasn't very much at the moment. "You know why. When cops want to talk to you, you cooperate. If you don't, they'll find you anyhow, and if they have to waste time hunting you down, they'll be pissed off. You're not the least bit curious?"

"No," she said unconvincingly.

"And anyway, you need to tell them about Ryan and the break-in."

"I wasn't robbed and someone left roses. They'll think I'm crazy."

She had no idea about crazy. She was concerned about appearing that way to strangers; Sam was worried he genuinely was. He looked out the passenger window at his house, something familiar, something that had positive associations, even though bad things had happened there, too. Today, in particular. The windows were dark, but he'd left the front porch light on. Yuki had been sitting directly under it this morning, and if she'd been here now, in the same place, the light would be dancing in her black hair, limning it with blue.

"You're connected to Ryan. Maybe he beat somebody else up. Maybe he killed somebody."

"Come on, Sam, be real."

"What? You don't think he's capable?"

Melody scowled, the young skin of her brow barely puckering. "I know I have to call them. I'm sorry I'm being a brat, I just needed to vent. It's been a shitty day that just keeps getting shittier."

No kidding. "Don't be sorry."

"Will you take me for a ride in your car first?"

"Seriously?"

"Yes." She got out and walked to the garage, stood there with her arms crossed. Her posture said she'd stand out there and wait forever. Christ, he wanted this day to be over, wanted to feel the burn of rye in his stomach, the cocoon of his bed, smell the scent of Yuki's expensive shampoo on his pillow. But maybe he needed a ride in his car. It was the best part of his life right now.

She let out a startled gasp when the garage door opened. Sam always felt the same way whenever he saw it. The sheen of the sleek Nightmist Blue body, voluptuous in all the right places like a beautiful woman, sharp and feral and masculine in other ways; the glitter of chrome under the fluorescent overheads; the power he knew lay beneath the hood, it all took his breath away every time. And then there were the memories. All excellent ones.

"It's beautiful, Sam. What is it?"

"A Shelby Mustang. A sixty-seven."

"I guess that's supposed to mean something."

"If you're a car person."

"It looks more like a panther ready to pounce than a horse. I've never seen a car like this." She pointed to the lettering on the white racing stripe that ran along the lower part of the chassis. "What does GT 500 mean?"

"It means it's really fast."

"Where did you get it?"

"It was my grandfather's. He loved this more than his wife and kids combined. At least that's what my dad told me, but that could have just been sour grapes. They never got along."

"Your grandfather gave it to you?"

"To my dad. Mom gave it to me when he died."

Melody frowned. "I'm sorry about your dad."

"Me, too. He was a good man with a bad heart."

"Your mom?"

"Alive and kicking and obsessed with golf."

"I feel bad that I never asked you about your family," she said glumly. "Some friend I am, all I do is talk about my problems."

Sam thought about her asking him this morning what the worst part of PTSD was. She was the only one who ever had, besides Dr. Frolich, and she was getting paid to ask questions. "You're a great friend."

She looked away, embarrassed, then started to circle the car with wondering eyes. "Did your grandpa give you rides in it when you were a kid?"

Time rolled back slowly, and Sam remembered his first ride—Grandpa Dean at the wheel, his broad, craggy face lit up with the biggest smile he'd ever seen. The cold, reticent man he'd known for the first ten years of his life had magically been transformed on that day, the scars of a war Sam had yet to learn about erased by a machine.

Do you like to go fast, Sammy?

Yeah! Yeah!

Then hang onto your knickers, young man.

"He did. Grandpa would tear up Mulholland Drive until I was ready to puke. Then he'd take me to Pink's for a hotdog, the sadistic old bastard." He felt his lips inch upward into a pure and joyful smile that reflected Grandpa Dean's from so many years back.

"Did you?"

"Are you kidding, puke in his baby? He would have strangled me and thrown me off a cliff. Puking wasn't acceptable, and I passed the test every time."

"You liked him."

"Yeah, I did. Loved him, too. He was career military, hard on everybody, but I have a lot of good memories of the times I spent with him."

Melody's face softened and her eyes suddenly filled with tears. She turned and wiped them away.

"What's wrong?"

"Nothing. There's just a lot of history here. No wonder you don't drive it, it's like a precious jewel."

"Cars need to be driven or they die. You can't keep a racehorse locked up in a stall its whole life."

"Let's not take it out tonight."

"Why?"

"When you take me for a ride, I want us both to be happy. This is a happy car."

"The car could make us happy. At least for a little while."

She turned back to him, a little mascara smeared beneath her eyes. "Maybe, but all the baggage we're carrying won't fit in that little trunk."

"You might be right about that."

"I think I should call the cops now."

"I think you're right about that, too."

Chapter Twenty-five

SAM HADN'T BEEN EXPECTING THE COPS to pay a visit at midnight, but then he'd looked at the card Teddy had given Melody. Detective Margaret Nolan, Robbery-Homicide, a division that never slept. That's when he knew the night wasn't going to end well. Against his better judgment, while they waited, he poured himself a shot of rye, poured Melody a glass of chardonnay. Eventually the knock came.

Margaret Nolan looked young for a detective, and she was tall, almost as tall as he was. He didn't doubt that she was strong beneath the boxy suit she wore, and her gray eyes and strawberry blond hair, pulled back in a mercilessly tight bun, suggested northern European lineage. So did the sharp angles of her face, attractive but severe. A woman from an old, storied warrior clan was his first, fanciful thought, and that would be a good pedigree to have in her situation. RHD was still an old boy's club, and if you didn't have the right equipment between your legs you had to have the guts to stand your ground.

Her partner was an older gent with a softening gut, wispy hair going gray around the ears, and probing, hound dog eyes. An old timer, probably all of forty-five. The picture filled out: she'd been paired with a division veteran, one who could help her navigate complicated waters, knew people, knew the politics, knew all the dance moves on a crowded, rancorous floor. He introduced himself as Detective Crawford and hung back, letting his protégé take lead.

Of course, this was all a fabrication. Sam crafted stories around everyone he met or even saw if they seemed interesting enough. Trying to read people was a habit, sometimes a hobby when he was bored. *Situational awareness,* they called it in the military.

After the introductions had been made, he invited them to sit. He really wanted to offer them a cocktail because they both looked like they could use one, but he didn't think they'd appreciate the drollness. Besides, there was nothing humorous about the situation. They declined the more appropriate offer of coffee and took seats in two club chairs. Just like the braided rug in the kitchen, Yuki hadn't been interested in taking them.

Since they'd arrived, Detective Crawford had feigned mild boredom, his eyes busy taking in details of the house, but he was paying close attention. Detective Nolan's interest was less subtle and had been split between his scarred face and Melody's black eye; but once they were all settled, she focused solely on Melody, which was appropriate. This was about her. "How did you get the black eye, Ms. Traeger?"

"Not from Sam, if that's what you're thinking."

Detective Nolan waited patiently and let the silence grate on Melody as expertly as Dr. Frolich employed the technique. Sam briefly wondered if shrinks or cops had come up with it first.

"A guy I was dating," she finally said. "Sam is helping me, that's why I'm here. Why are you here?"

"Ryan Gallagher. Is he the one who gave you the black eye?"

Melody's eyes widened.

"I'll take that as a yes. So you and Ryan are a couple?"

"No, like I said, we dated. It was casual, but it's over now."

"When was the last time you saw him?"

"Last night."

"Is that when he hit you?"

She lowered her eyes and nodded.

"Where did this happen?"

"At his apartment."

"On Alta Loma?"

"Yes."

"What happened after he assaulted you?"

"I don't know if I would call it assault."

"That's exactly what I'd call it, Ms. Traeger," Crawford finally spoke. "Tell us what happened next."

"I came here. Sam is my friend and coworker and I was afraid. Why are you asking me questions about Ryan?"

Crawford delivered the news dispassionately. "I'm sorry, Ms. Traeger, but he was murdered in his apartment sometime this morning. We're wondering if you know who may have done it."

Melody's mouth moved, but it took a while for her to find words. Sam knew exactly how she felt. He'd had some very uncharitable thoughts about Ryan Gallagher over the past twenty-four hours, but even a cowardly piece of human rot like him didn't deserve this. A good beating to even the scales, maybe, but a life was a life.

Maybe he did deserve it. Did your victims of war deserve it?

The claws of a fresh headache started an exploratory rake of Sam's brain, and he crossed his arms and tucked his hands in his armpits so nobody would see his clenched fists. It wasn't a good time to have some kind of an episode, especially since they were getting more unpredictable lately. He didn't ever want to see portents of doom wriggling across any foreheads ever again; and he most definitely didn't want to melt down in front of the detectives, stumble into his bedroom, and come out waving his Colt.

"He was murdered?" Melody finally asked in a tremulous voice.

"Yes. He was shot."

Melody covered her mouth, a strange but instinctive gesture for most people who received unexpected and shocking news. "Are you sure? Jesus, of course you're sure, otherwise you wouldn't be here. Oh my God." She curled into a protective ball on the sofa.

"Did he ever mention any problems he might have been having with friends, colleagues? Enemies?"

She shook her head and looked down at her hands, lifeless in her lap. "We didn't talk about things like that. It wasn't that kind of relationship."

Sam cringed inwardly. She'd just admitted the guy she'd pinned some hope on thought of her as a booty call and punching bag, nothing more. Fantasy shattered. He was less sorry Ryan was dead than he had been a few minutes ago.

"So you didn't know he was being sued?"

Melody jerked up her head abruptly. "I had no idea. Who was suing him?"

"Golden West Studios, for unpaid recording time. A hundred grand worth."

Sam watched her mouth form a perfect 'O'. "Markus Ellenbeck's company?"

"Yes, do you know him?"

"He comes into Pearl Club all the time. God, no wonder," she mumbled.

Nolan leaned forward in her chair. "No wonder what?"

"Ryan and Markus hated each other. I thought it was just jealousy."

"What do you mean?"

"Markus is a huge flirt." She gestured to her black eye. "That's what this was about. They were both at Pearl last night, and Markus told me to steer clear of Ryan because he was a 'flaming asshole.' I wasn't sure why until now."

"Was there a confrontation?"

"No. They were at opposite ends of the bar and ignored each other."

Sam processed this new information. Melody was very selective about the things she shared. He hadn't known about Ryan until last night, and now another drama he'd been ignorant of was unfolding in front of him.

Nolan flipped a page in her notebook. "Did Mr. Ellenbeck ever make any threats against Mr. Gallagher?"

"No, of course not. Markus isn't like that."

"How do you know? Do you have a relationship with him?"

Melody looked horrified. "No."

Nolan glanced at Crawford and there was some silent, implicit exchange between them. "Ms. Traeger, you were in contact with Mr. Gallagher this morning before he was killed."

"He'd been texting me. I texted him back."

"You threatened him. Listen, I can understand how angry you must have been, but a death threat is very serious. And it doesn't look good."

"You don't think . . . I didn't kill him!"

"There was no forced entry and no signs of struggle in the apartment, so it's likely he knew his assailant. We also believe they had a key. You own a small caliber gun, the same kind that killed Mr. Gallagher; and as we mentioned, he was shot. You also have a rap sheet. None of those things look good, either."

Melody sat up stiffly, and her posture, her expression, both seethed indignation. "Yes, I have a gun, I'm a woman living alone in Los Angeles. And I also have a rap sheet. Misdemeanor drug charges, not murder, and there's a lot of daylight between the two."

Sam wasn't privy to the death threat piece of the puzzle, or the gun or rap sheet, and he felt disassociated, like a spectator watching some fabulous disaster unfold. Markus Ellenbeck was a suspect, but Melody was, too. And by extension, he was as well. An angry, abused woman with a record and a firearm making death threats, and her unstable protector, one who'd killed in war—and once you killed, it got easier. They'd gotten together and decided to exact the ultimate revenge for a black eye. Case solved, grab some beers, call it a day.

"Do you have a key or keycard to Mr. Gallagher's building or his apartment?" Crawford asked.

"No, I don't. I didn't kill Ryan. Check my gun, it hasn't been fired since the last time I went to the range four months ago. And Sam and my neighbor Teddy will alibi me for this morning."

Sam nodded. "Melody was here until about ten, then she went home."

"Your neighbor Teddy said he spoke with you this morning, but then went surfing for a few hours. Can anyone else alibi you during that time?"

"No, but I didn't leave the apartment."

"You mentioned roses and a break-in in your threatening text," Nolan consulted her notebook. "Ms. Traeger, let's walk through things from the beginning, starting with last night."

Sam watched the two detectives as unobtrusively as possible while Melody told her story. They had good poker faces, but you could see almost imperceptible shifts in their expressions as they listened. Suspicion, empathy, ambivalence, possibly even disappointment—she wasn't making an outright confession and holding out her wrists for the bracelets.

When Melody got to the part of the story about the black Jeep, Nolan and Crawford both reacted with subdued alarm, as they should have because it was spooky. Sam wondered if either of them were thinking about the black Jeep that had run over Katy Villa. Probably not, there was nothing to connect the two incidents, at least not in their minds, and they were arguably the sanest people in the room at the moment.

Nolan closed the cover of her notebook. "But you've never seen this black Jeep yourself?"

"No. Just Teddy and Sam have noticed it."

She looked at Sam. "You didn't happen to get a plate number?"

"No. But it's a Rubicon, the same model Teddy mentioned."

"There are a lot of those in Los Angeles. If you see it again, try to get the plate. Ms. Traeger, is it possible Markus Ellenbeck was jealous of your relationship with Mr. Gallagher?"

"He didn't know we were in a relationship."

"Can you think of anyone else who might have been?"

"No one knew about it."

"Somebody entered your apartment through a window and left you roses, and your neighbor has seen a black Jeep outside your building on multiple occasions. And there was one here this morning when you were. Think hard about acquaintances, coworkers, past associates, any customers at Pearl Club who may have made you uncomfortable."

"You think I'm being stalked," she said flatly. "Stupid question, sorry."

"There's nothing we can do without a direct threat, so be careful. You too, Mr. Easton. If this really is a problem, you're on their radar as well."

Sam nodded and the detectives shifted their focus to him. It was his turn.

"Did you know Ryan Gallagher?"

"I didn't even know he existed until Melody showed up here last night with a black eye."

"Markus Ellenbeck?"

"I know who he is, everybody at Pearl Club does, he's famous. But I'm a bar back, I don't spend time at the front of the house."

"Can you tell us about your morning after Ms. Traeger left?"

"I went jogging, then ate lunch here with my wife. After that, I had a doctor's appointment, then went to work at Pearl Club."

"Busy day," Crawford commented.

Definitely too busy to kill, but Sam decided to keep the remark to himself. "Very."

"We'd like to speak with your wife. Is she here?"

"No, we're separated."

"Who is your doctor?"

"Dr. Lynette Frolich."

"Where does she work?"

"She has a private practice on Wilshire Boulevard, and she'll confirm I was at my appointment. For the record, I didn't kill Ryan Gallagher and neither did Melody."

Nolan cocked a brow at him, then stood. "Thank you both for your time. We'll be in touch."

And that was it. The hot seat for both of them, then a bland dismissal meant to assuage any fear in case they needed to circle back and initiate a surprise offensive in the absence of better suspects.

Sam walked them to the door, anticipating the very precious moment when he could close the door behind them and try to forget he'd gotten out of bed this morning. It was amazing how cops could make you feel like a criminal even if you'd done nothing wrong. Or maybe that feeling was a product of the guilt Dr. Frolich was always talking about. It was depressing how his world view had become so very egocentric lately, and unhealthy by any accounting.

Crawford was halfway to the car by the time Nolan stepped off the porch. Sam knew she was intentionally lagging behind, so it didn't surprise him when she turned around, postponing his happy moment.

"I know who you are, Mr. Easton."

"Right. You did your research on the way over when Melody gave you my address. Military service, no criminal record, a speeding ticket last March, and owner of three registered guns—including a Colt Anaconda—which you didn't mention. Must not be the right caliber. You probably don't see a lot of homicides committed with a gun that size, too loud."

"I'm speaking about your military service. I'm an Army brat. My family sent a lot of prayers your way when you got back."

Sam braced his hand on the doorjamb so he didn't tip over. He hadn't expected that from Margaret Nolan. An official pronunciation of his arrest for the murder of Ryan Gallagher would have made more sense to him. "Oh. Thank you. Did you serve?"

"No, but my brother Max did. He was killed in Nangarhar a few months ago."

"I'm very sorry." It was odd to learn that you had a shared experience with a potentially hostile person in your life. It certainly made them seem less antagonistic. And when it came right down to it, they'd both seen a lot of death. Homicide cops weren't immune to PTSD, but their struggles didn't get the same coverage.

"I'm glad you made it back, Mr. Easton."

"Some days I don't know if I am," he said, instantly regretting his strange outburst of candor.

If she'd found his statement remarkable, she expertly kept her emotions shielded behind eyes the color of tombstone granite that didn't seem to fit with her strawberry blond hair. "I believe you. But I'd like to think we're all here for a reason. Have a good night."

He watched her walk away, a woman from a warrior clan after all, wounded in a different way than he was but wounded all the same. He'd made a connection with her, just like he'd made connections with Katy and Rolf, and yet the red letters hadn't appeared on her forehead. He knew it was pointless to wonder why.

Chapter Twenty-six

SOMETIMES NOLAN PRETENDED SHE HAD A parallel existence that wasn't entrenched in death. In her fantasy, she was never lectured about making the ultimate sacrifice for her country or her multigenerational history of fallen servicemen and women that dated back to the Civil War. There, she was never a disappointment for not embracing the family calling, even though she was putting her life on the line in service to others, too, just in a different way. But in reality they just didn't see it quite that way. Insufferable, ignorant military snobbery, that's what Max had always said. He'd been her only familial advocate.

It really pissed her off that they didn't consider her vocation worthy of even an honorable mention in the scrolls of the hallowed halls of dead relatives—that would only happen if she became a dead relative herself—still, she'd probably only be a footnote, acknowledged but never fully respected.

Max featured prominently in her alternate reality, too, where he was enjoying the most amazing life. He hadn't made the ultimate sacrifice for his country; he was a small business owner in Tarzana or maybe Thousand Oaks, married to his high school sweetheart, with his first child on the way. And she wasn't a homicide cop, she was . . .

What?

That's where the fantasy always ground to a halt. No matter how many twists and turns her musings took, she always had a detective's shield. Death followed her, even in her imagination. She knew it followed Sam Easton, too. He'd put things in perspective for her tonight and made her bitterness seem petty. And in a strange way, he'd made Max seem more present. Or maybe it wasn't so strange.

Her nose twitched as the car filled with the pungent scent of teriyaki. Crawford had unwrapped a beef stick and was gnawing on it with the zeal of a starving Serengeti predator. The smell was nauseating, but it also reminded her she hadn't eaten anything since a bruised, overripe banana for lunch.

"You want one, Mags?"

"Hell, no, I want a slab of prime rib from Lawry's, but that's not going to happen."

"If you're buying, I'll make it happen. That's not sexual harassment, by the way."

"Damn, I was so hopeful."

Crawford let out a snuffle of amusement. Or maybe it was his allergies, they'd been acting up. "How do you know Sam Easton?"

"Know of him. He's a decorated war hero. I thought I recognized the name but I didn't put it together until we got there."

"I'm assuming that has something to do with his face."

"Roadside bomb. He was the only one who survived."

"He must be going through some bad shit, poor bastard."

"At least he made it home. It could have been worse."

"You're right. I'm sorry, Mags."

She thought about Max's visitation again—Remy had been one of many from the department who'd come to pay their respects, but Al and Corinne had been the first ones there and the last to leave. He was a good colleague, a better friend, and they were both family to her. She'd blurted out the truth, but the delivery had been harsh.

And what did she really know about what was worse anyhow? She'd never been in combat, had never been maimed and almost killed, so for her it was automatic to assume life was always better. But was it?

Sam Easton had his doubts. He'd just said as much, which sent her brain racing through the grim statistics of the suicide rate of veterans. What if Max had come back with Sam's experience, in his condition?

Would he be the same laughing, loving brother who'd always stood by her side no matter what, or would he be wondering if he was glad to be back, too?

"I didn't mean it like that, Al. No apology necessary."

He changed topics and drew her out of the past. "The Ellenbeck angle just got more interesting. Money, a beautiful woman, and mutual hatred. With that trio, things can go south in a hurry. Gallagher was punched in the nose before he got shot, that's personal."

"But why kill somebody you're trying to get money out of? It doesn't make sense."

"People lose control. What's your take on Traeger and Easton?"

"Gut? Neither of them are good for it."

Crawford uttered a noncommittal grunt. "Melody Traeger looked pretty surprised when Easton brought up lunch with his estranged wife. She's not around, his coworker is sleeping at his house, so if something's going on between the two of them, that could be motive."

Nolan merged onto the Hollywood Freeway, which was relatively empty at this hour of the night. Clear pavement in LA was so magical it was eerie, like you'd suddenly been transported to a postapocalyptic world. "I didn't see it, and their alibis seem pretty tight. When we check them out, I'm guessing they'll hold. We need to keep the focus on the vic. He was a scumbag with sketchy business associates, a lawsuit climbing up his ass, and coke in his office and bathroom. It's a matter of which one of those things caught up with him."

"Maybe Traeger's stalker caught up with him."

"If she really has one."

Crawford chewed noisily, pulverizing his beef stick. "Somebody broke into her apartment and left roses. That's eerie."

"I'm betting it was Gallagher. He was jerking her around, trying to scare her, you know that brand of controlling asshole. Hell, he may have been the guy in the black Jeep. He doesn't own one, but maybe he was borrowing one, renting one. Or hired a PI to follow her. Something to look at, anyhow."

Crawford tucked his empty wrapper in his pocket instead of throwing it on the floor. Corinne had trained him well, bless her heart. "We need to keep the third-party option on the table. Stalker sees her come out of Gallagher's building last night with a black eye. He's furious. He brings her roses to let her know not all men are dogs, then kills the piece of shit who hurt her. And Traeger works in Miracle Mile and tends bar, just like Stella Clary did. That worries me a little bit."

"If you're thinking the Monster, you're way off base. His victims are vulnerables, and Traeger's not one anymore. He's opportunistic, not obsessive. And he doesn't deliver roses."

"He could have a different kind of fixation on her. I think it's worth bringing to the task force. Maybe they have a black Jeep in their book."

"Go ahead, I'll keep tearing apart Gallagher's life. I'm thinking there might be a whole roster of people who wanted him dead."

Chapter Twenty-seven

OF ALL THE THINGS THAT SHOULD have been occupying Sam's mind, he was thinking of Rolf. Couldn't stop thinking about Rolf. Where was he now? At home planning his trip to the desert? Shooting up? On a slab in the morgue? He supposed it wasn't that strange—Rolf factored heavily into his owns concerns, as did Katy. His new hallucinatory symptoms were all the proof he needed that something else was wrong with his brain. If it was neurological, meds and talk therapy weren't going to cut it anymore, and as insurmountable as recovery had seemed before, his prospects had just gotten worse.

Neither of them had said anything since the detectives had left, but Melody finally spoke as she poured the rest of the chardonnay into her glass. "My aunt had a fifty-seven Thunderbird. A red convertible. Your car reminded me of her, that's why I got a little weepy in the garage."

"Where is she now?"

"I hope in heaven. She was killed in a car crash when I was thirteen. Aunt Netta and the T-Bird were both dead at the scene."

"I'm sorry, Mel."

"I am, too."

"You were close?"

"She raised me from the time I was a toddler, after my mom split."

Sam tried to imagine Vivian walking out on him as a child. It was inconceivable. "You never knew your mom."

"I don't even remember her."

"Do you know where she is now?"

"Probably dead. I was eight the last time Netta heard from her. She was in Europe somewhere, singing in clubs. Alexandra Traeger was a musician, not a mother. Her sister Netta was both."

"Music. That's where your name came from."

"My middle name. Antoinette is my real first name, after Netta."

"She sang 'The Owl and the Pussycat' to you at bedtime."

She took a gulp of wine and nodded.

"So the guitar isn't just a pawn shop find?"

"It is. Another talisman, I guess."

And a symbolic link to family, Sam thought. "What happened after Netta died?"

A barrier suddenly went up, he could feel it, a palpable presence in the room. Do not trespass.

"We're suspects," she said dully.

"They were asking the questions they had to ask. What's with the death threat?"

"I texted Ryan and told him if he ever broke into my apartment again, I'd kill him. It was stupid."

"I would have done the same thing." He reached out and touched her hand. "I know I didn't kill him, and I know you didn't, so we don't have anything to worry about. Are you okay?"

"I'm freaked out and getting drunk seems like a great idea. Pour me a glass of that rye, Sam."

Sam did, and poured himself another, too. The last one, he promised himself. He watched Melody wince as she took a sip, but she didn't make eye contact. She had a lot to process.

"You had lunch with Yuki today?" she finally asked.

"She was waiting on the porch when I got home from my run."

"That must have been a nice surprise."

"It was, until she told me she was moving to Seattle for a job."

Melody stared down into her rye. "That sucks."

"Yeah, it does. But maybe I should have seen it coming."

She reached over and clinked his glass with hers. "Here's to better days ahead, when things aren't so fucked up."

"If that's all we have to toast to, then maybe I should get the razor blades."

"Can you think of a better toast?"

"We're not dead and we're not in jail."

"I'll drink to that, too."

They sat in companionable silence for a while, both of them salving their private wounds with fermented grain, but it wasn't making Sam feel any better, in fact it was making him feel worse. He felt a deep, paralyzing exhaustion settle into his bones at the same time the prodromes of another headache announced plans for a full-on assault of his brain. "I need to go to bed. Are you going to be okay?"

"I'll be fine." She pushed away her glass, an impressive act of restraint for a woman who'd vowed to get drunk. "We both need to sleep."

Sam got up and closed the shades once he was sure there wasn't a black Jeep outside, then checked the windows, doors, and the alarm. "All locked up. Do you need an extra blanket? Pillows?"

"I'm good, thanks."

"Night, Mel."

"Good night, Sam. See you in the morning."

After Sam had gone to bed, Melody remained at the kitchen table, listening to the wall clock tick away the night. It was the only audible sound. Roughly fifty thousand of Los Angeles County's ten million residents called the quiet Mar Vista neighborhood home, and apparently, they were all sleeping. It was a good bet that none of them had been visited by homicide detectives tonight, and Sam wouldn't have garnered that distinction either if she hadn't been here.

Silence didn't offer her mind distraction, so thoughts began to bounce around inside her head. Ryan was dead. Murdered. She knew how, but she didn't know why. She'd known a lot of bad people in her life, but none of them had been killed and they were more deserving, in her opinion. There was no question that Ryan had been flawed, and she had no idea what company he kept when he wasn't with her, but getting shot to death seemed like a steep price to pay for having an imperfect character.

But she hadn't known him. Not at all. One straightforward question from the cops had made that abundantly clear. He could have been a mobster for all she knew. The sum total of her knowledge of Ryan Gallagher was that he took her to dinners in restaurants she could never afford, and if she saw something in a shop window she liked, he'd buy it for her. He'd never invited her to Las Vegas, but he had taken her on one weekend getaway to Palm Springs where there was wine and fruit and cheese waiting for them in the room. But it had all been in exchange for sex, she understood that now. Money never changed hands, it was more insidious than that, and so she'd gotten lost in a fantasy.

But Ryan was out of the picture now, replaced by a stalker. It seemed impossible.

Think hard about acquaintances, coworkers, past associates, any customers at the Pearl Club who may have made you uncomfortable.

Melody *was* thinking hard, but nothing sparked. The people she'd associated with during the drug years were either dead by now or just trying to stay alive. Addicts were too concerned about the next fix to do anything but drug seek.

She considered Poke fans, but that was a nonstarter. She'd burned out like a supernova, as if she'd never existed, instantly replaced by the next new thing. Besides, a Poke fan would throw roses at her like they used to when Roxy Codone was on stage, not sneak them into her apartment. And Markus? The thought of him as a stalker was laughable. If he wanted her, he'd ask.

Her coworkers were the only family she had, and there had been no sketchy figures lurking in the shadows at Pearl Club. They all kept an eye out for that; it was a bullet point in the employee manual.

Maybe Ryan had lied about the roses, another cruel manipulation. It was entirely believable, and although a disturbing thought, it was a more comforting one than the possibility of a stalker.

Melody looked at her glass of rye, half-full or half-empty, depending on your perspective, and downed the rest in one burning gulp. Booze wasn't instructive, but it let you forget, and that's what she wanted to do.

She found her way to the sofa, curled up beneath the throw she was becoming fond of, and closed her eyes. Aunt Netta was in the room, strumming the guitar softly, putting melody to "The Owl and the Pussycat."

Chapter Twenty-eight

SAM WAS LYING ON HIS BUNK in the barracks. Rondo was sitting next to him, dangling his dog tags like a hypnotist's bauble.

"You gotta help me, Sam my man."

"What's wrong?"

"They're after us."

"The Taliban?"

"They're not the only ones."

"I don't understand. What are you talking about?"

"You know." He smiled and blood leaked from the corners of his mouth. He wiped it away and looked down at his hand in surprise. "Shit. I guess it doesn't matter anymore, does it?"

Sam tried to sit up, but there was an invisible weight pressing down on him, suffocating him. "I can't . . ."

"What? You can't talk? You can't get up? Join the club."

"I'm sorry."

"Nothing you could do. You were good to me, Sam, I'm glad you made it." Rondo's flesh started suppurating, dropping glistening chunks of gore down the front of his camo and onto Sam's chest. "Too late for me."

Sam jolted upright, choking, still suffocating. He clawed at his throat, gasping, until finally a rush of air entered his lungs, feeding his oxygen-starved brain. His heart was a heavy metal double-bass drum, and Sam genuinely feared it was finally going to blow this time.

He reached to the nightstand for his water bottle, but his hand was shaking so badly, he couldn't grasp it.

"About time you woke up, Sam my man."

He bolted out of bed and grabbed his gun. "Jesus Christ!"

Rondo emerged from the shadows, whole again, but his camo was bloody. "Bad dreams, huh?"

His Anaconda bobbled in front of him and his teeth started chattering. "Y-you're not real. Go away."

"Some greeting for an old pal. Ty, Shaggy, and Wilson send their regards, by the way. You should put that thing away before you hurt somebody." He started to laugh, a high-pitched trill.

"Leave me alone!"

"That gun's not going to do you a whole lot of good. I'm dead, remember?"

There was a frantic knock on the door. "Sam! Sam, wake up!"

Rondo shrugged. "I guess it's time for me to skedaddle. See you around." And then he dissolved into translucency and disappeared.

"Sam!" Melody pushed open the door and a slice of light landed on him, igniting his brain. "Oh my god, you're drenched."

He placed the gun on the nightstand, sagged onto the bed, and pressed his hands against his temples. The mother of all migraines was moving in for the kill. "It's okay, Mel. I'm awake now."

"Jesus, Sam," her voice was trembling. "Are you alright?"

Her face was paper white, her eyes huge and wet and fixed on the gun. She looked ready to take flight. He didn't blame her. "I will be."

"I thought there was a break-in. You were yelling at somebody."

"A ghost."

"Can I do something? Get you something? Rye?"

"I'm sorry I scared you. Go back to sleep."

"Are you sure you're okay?"

No. "Yeah. I'll see you in the morning."

The door closed and Sam sat in the dark, his blood still hot with fresh inoculations of adrenaline; he wasn't confident Rondo was finished with him yet. Was it a psychotic break when dreams encroached into reality? Had he just crossed the Rubicon of insanity? Or was it the River Styx? Old Charon, a pole in one hand, a straitjacket in the other. Don't pay the ferryman until he gets you to the other side.

Chapter Twenty-nine

REMY ROLLED OVER AND GROPED BLINDLY for his bleating phone. When had it seemed like a good idea to choose a ringtone that sounded like a distressed sheep? While he'd been sleeping, the vodka fairy had stuffed his mouth with cotton, his head with broken glass. The last martini had been a mistake.

"Remy Beaudreau." The vodka fairy had put gravel in his throat, too.

"Hey man, it's Froggy. I might have something for you."

It was three-thirty in the morning, but drug dealing was a twenty-four seven vocation. Criminals were devoted to their craft and had a strong work ethic. He clicked on the lamp and found a notebook and pen. "Go."

"This is worth something."

"We'll see."

"Come on . . ."

"I like you, Froggy. Let's keep it that way."

Grumble, snuffle, snuffle, grumble. "I just asked some of the working ladies down here about the creeper. They gotta keep their eyes open, right? Figured it would be a good place to start. You wouldn't believe the shit they see, I mean just last night . . ."

"Froggy, I'm not paying you by the word."

"Okay, okay. You know that abandoned building on Broadway?"

"Which one?"

"The one where pincushions are OD'ing all the time. The shooting gallery."

"The Rehbein Building, what about it?"

"The ladies tell me they heard about some trouble there. Some skel hanging around. Someone who don't belong."

"Did any of these ladies get a close look at him?"

"Nah, this is just word of mouth from a gal named Wanda. She took a paying customer in there and this dude shows up and starts flashing a knife around."

Remy slid to the edge of the bed and tried to pull on jeans with one hand. "Can you get me to Wanda?"

"Nobody's seen her around for a while. This was a couple weeks ago. That's all I got. So what's it worth?"

"Maybe a French dip."

"Don't shit me, man, this is good stuff. You want me to check it out, make it worth taxpayer dollars?"

"Absolutely not. Stay away from the Rehbein Building and keep your mouth shut. I'm on my way."

Remy hung up and finished dressing. The Monster was meticulous and stealthy, and his survival depended on invisibility; the creeper's actions had been impulsive, too sloppy for an accomplished killer. It didn't dovetail. He gave it a ten-percent chance that they were one and the same, but it was a thread that had to be followed to its terminus, because sometimes, killers went off script.

•

Froggy looked across the street at the graffiti-tagged Rehbein Building. Who knew it had a name? He stepped off the curb and walked toward it casually, like he was just out for a stroll. Things were slowing down on the street, so why not take a look? Maybe do the criminal justice system a favor while he was at it and get a nice payday. The pincushions wouldn't mind, shooting galleries were the most peaceful places he knew because everybody was usually unconscious.

He jimmied a loose board off a broken window, slithered through, and dropped down into the lower level. It was dark, but he recognized the potent reek of drugs, vomit, shit, decay. The aromatherapy of his life, nothing shocking or new to him.

He turned on his flashlight app, but his phone was almost dead and the light was weak, giving him a view of his feet and not much else. Froggy hated the dark and the things it could conceal, but he didn't sense any human presence. It figured—the pincushions would choose the upper floors, away from street level, like sick pigeons roosting in the rafters.

He shuffled slowly, kicking away dead rats, spent syringes, piles of garbage and moldering detritus. Then his phone gave up the ghost, and he was submerged in total darkness. Time to get the hell out of here.

As he backtracked, feeling his way along the wall, his nose picked up a particularly foul smell, which sent him scrambling in the opposite direction. When his foot came in contact with a large, unyielding lump, he froze, and that's when the pain came, blinding and searing, right between his shoulders.

Froggy dropped on top of something squishy and putrid and closed his eyes, absolutely certain he was dead and had gone straight to hell. A moment later, he realized he was still alive and wished he wasn't.

Chapter Thirty

AFTER A DOUBLE-DOSE OF MELATONIN, SLEEP came fast and hard for Sam. Dreamless for a while, but at some point death crept in as it always did. But it was a different kind of dream—this time he was an observer, not a participant.

He saw Melody stepping into a black Jeep Rubicon and getting beaten, saw Yuki being strangled by a faceless man, saw Rolf nodding off in heroin rapture and turning stiff and pale. Magda from *Dead to Rights III* made an appearance, too, sitting in her Jaguar in the rain with bloody stab wounds in her chest, and so did Dr. Frolich, standing on Wilshire Boulevard, waving a Colt Anaconda.

There was also an anonymous phantom hovering offscreen, an invisible puppeteer silently manipulating the dream cast of helpless marionettes. The specter materialized for a moment. She had gray eyes, eyes the color of tombstone granite that didn't seem to match her strawberry blond hair. *What did you see? What do you remember?* she asked, then disappeared.

He didn't wake up in full-blown panic, but his body was reacting the way it did after a combat dream, heart hammering against the wall of his chest, sweat drenching his body, muscles taut as piano wire, ready to strike or flee. Most of the details of this night terror were already dissipating, thankfully almost forgotten, but the image of hands squeezing Yuki's throat was still vivid. He cringed, imagining the choking sounds that would accompany the horrific scene because his dreams sometimes had dialogue, but they never had sound effects. Did anybody's?

Were the hands choking Yuki yours?

He shook his head, trying to scatter the appalling contemplation. Where had it even come from? She'd wounded him, and sure, he was angry, but even his subconscious couldn't be so damaged as to be capable of conjuring such an unimaginable vision. Could it?

No, it had just been another bad dream, a warped amalgamation of fear and anxiety his waking mind couldn't process, and little wonder, considering the way the day had rolled out. But the image was stubborn, insistent, and he would never get back to sleep until he knew she was okay, as irrational as it seemed.

Sam dressed in the dark and crept toward the kitchen. Melody was curled into fetal position on the sofa, her breathing deep and even. He wrote her a note, letting her know he'd be back soon. The digital display on the microwave read 5:17.

He grabbed the keys to the Mustang and let himself into the garage, careful to pull the door closed quietly behind him. By the time he made the drive to Marina del Rey, Yuki would be getting up for work.

Chapter Thirty-one

REMY SQUINTED AGAINST THE BLINDING WORK lights as he watched the crime scene techs collect trace around Froggy and the badly decomposed mound that had been human once. Not Wanda—this person had been dead far longer than two weeks. It was impossible to know if this was an old overdose or the work of the Monster; only an autopsy would tell. He hacked and cut with a heavy, serrated knife, and the bones wouldn't lie.

Froggy had been stabbed multiple times, but it wasn't signature work. A necessity, not pleasure. It was possible this was the site of the Monster's first kill, before he'd established a hunting pattern and perfected his technique, and he'd been defending his handiwork against Froggy. The only problem with that scenario was that serials usually didn't dwell where they killed.

But there were exceptions to that rule, and maybe the Monster was one of them. If he was, they'd chased him away and he was never going to come back.

One of the techs looked up at him. "How far do you want us to take this, Detective?"

"Wall to wall, bag and print everything." The tech didn't roll his eyes or sigh or swear, he just went back to work. Remy didn't know if he would have the capacity for such restraint, it was a big space.

Bill Turner walked the cleared path and came up beside him, the smell of coffee and cigarettes slightly mitigating the other, more offensive smells in the room. "You think we've got something?"

"I'm leaning in that direction. How's the canvass going?"

"We chased all the cockroaches back into their hidey-holes, so we're clearing buildings and hitting every fleabag from here to Miracle Mile. If this is the Monster, he wasn't prepared for Froggy, and he made a damn mess of him, so he's either covered in blood or naked somewhere."

"That's what gets me. Every kill the Monster makes, he's covered in blood, no way around it, so where is he getting rid of his clothes? We've been dumpster-diving for the past three months."

Bill pushed a square of Nicorette gum from a foil pack and began chewing noisily. "He's got a stash place we haven't found, maybe someplace he burns them. Shit, he could be doing collages with them and selling them on Venice Beach."

"Miracle Mile to here. He has range. What's his transportation?"

"If he cleans up in the motels like we figure, he could stuff his clothes in a bag and take a bus."

"Check all the routes."

"We will." Turner had bushy brows, and they came together over his flat nose like a pair of mating caterpillars. "Crawford called me a couple hours ago, asking if we had a black Jeep in our coverage."

"They pulled Katy Villa?"

"No, he and Maggie are working a homicide with a possible stalking element."

"We don't have a black Jeep in our coverage. Using a personal vehicle would be risky, there are cameras everywhere in this city. And we've checked all the footage."

"Yeah. I'm sticking with the bus theory. It's anonymous. One more thing to throw in the pile, though."

Chapter Thirty-two

YUKI WAS WELL CONNECTED, AND ONE of her friends was a multiple Oscar-winning costume designer who was always abroad somewhere, either on location or doing research. Sam had only met her a few times, but she seemed to have a good head on her shoulders, at least for costumes and real estate because she owned a lot of it. The Craftsman bungalow in Marina del Rey was a peach, and Yuki was renting it by the month for far below market value.

By the time he parked across the street, the adrenaline buzz and the panicked, singular sense of purpose had worn off, leaving him feeling depleted and possibly still a little drunk. It was like he'd been sleepwalking and someone had thrown cold water in his face to bring him back to reality. And the reality was, he had no idea what he was going to do now—or what he was even doing here in the first place. To make sure Yuki was safe from his nightmare?

He turned off the car and looked at the dark bungalow. She was still in bed. Even though the sun wasn't up yet, there were some people on the sidewalks already, getting in an early jog before work or taking Fifi out for her morning constitutional. All of them noticed the Mustang, and one man tripped over the curb ogling it. He and the car made a good pair: both of them got gawked at wherever they went, just for different reasons.

While he waited for a light to flick on, he slowly came to the realization that there was no reason for him to be here except that he was becoming unmoored. If he kept fixating on prophesying death, it would keep happening and he would keep getting more paranoid, keep doing unreasonable things, like rushing off at five a.m. to check on Yuki instead of doing the sensible thing, like texting or calling; or even more sensibly, take a bad dream at face value, a simple manifestation of a troubled subconscious, not a cosmic map of the future.

What are you going to do if Yuki notices your car outside her house?

Son of a bitch, that was a great question and another problem. If she saw him, there would be the obvious question: what was he doing here? Then he would be faced with a profound dilemma: either confess his burgeoning madness or allow her to believe he was stalking her. There would be no bullshitting his way out of this one, and the only solution that immediately presented itself was to get the hell out of here.

He started the car, which sounded like a jet engine in the predawn calm, drawing more attention. Before he could put it into gear, a light went on in Yuki's living room, the door opened, and he froze. There was still a possibility she wouldn't notice him, it was dark and she was a zombie in the morning before her coffee. He held his breath and waited for her to emerge, get the paper, and either bust him or retreat back inside.

Instead of Yuki, a muscular, shirtless man wearing pajama bottoms stepped out and retrieved the paper, then went inside without looking up. It was long after he'd closed the door that Sam remembered to breathe.

•

Mulholland Drive, the road that should have been named after his great-great-grandfather, according to Vivian. It was a suicide route if you were in the right vehicle and the wrong frame of mind. But at the moment, it was Sam's road to salvation, a road that led back in time. He was still a kid, Grandpa Dean was behind the wheel, and the biggest problem in his life was trying not to puke as the Mustang roared around the serpentine twists and turns and up to the best view in the world.

But he couldn't sustain the fantasy, so he pulled over at a scenic overlook and turned off the engine, listening to the soft tick as it cooled. He tried to admire the spectacular view of the sun coming up over Los Angeles, but he didn't find it remotely inspiring, not this morning.

There was a perfectly logical explanation for a half-naked man to be getting Yuki's morning paper that didn't involve her screwing somebody else. He couldn't wait to hear what it was. But she wasn't answering her phone, which left his imagination free to traverse all kinds of sordid scenarios, like her en flagrante at this very moment while the phone buzzed on the nightstand, an uncooperative witness to her infidelity and betrayal.

Then again, maybe she was just peeved that he hadn't responded to her texts yesterday, or wasn't prepared to continue the dialogue about her move to Seattle, and the man on her porch this morning was a gay friend visiting from out of town. It was all just one big misunderstanding.

After leaving three messages, he sent her a text asking for a callback as soon as possible. What he would say to her when she finally returned his call was unclear, but he decided it would be potentially disastrous if he confronted her over the phone, especially in his current frame of mind.

So he sat and he waited while the sun rose higher, streaking the sky with ombré shades of tangerine, lavender, and rose. He stepped outside and took a few photos to commemorate this moment in time when his future hung as nebulously as the haze over the city.

It was still and quiet, as peaceful as Los Angeles ever got; but peace was a rare and fleeting thing here, and proving his point, he heard the low, impressive growl of an engine approaching, then slowing, an engine to rival or even surpass the Mustang's. He got back in the car, not wanting to be seen or bothered.

A couple minutes later, a yellow Ferrari pulled up on the other side of the overlook and parked cockeyed, almost parallel to the guard rail. A disheveled couple got out, still wearing evening attire. They'd had a long night, and the party was still in full swing.

The woman was beautiful, young, laughing, and teetering unsteadily on stiletto heels. Her companion was much older, dressed as conservatively as she was provocatively, a common sight in LA, as common as hemp oil and thousand dollar sushi dinners. They kissed passionately in front of the sunrise, then she pulled off her shoes and started prancing around, swishing her ruffled skirt coquettishly.

This was exactly the type of human theater that would normally inspire Sam to craft an elaborate backstory, but he wasn't interested in his fanciful fiction this morning. Besides, he knew this story wouldn't have a happy ending, and happy endings were a sore topic at the moment.

After fifteen minutes of flirtation, groping, coke-snorting, and multiple selfies in front of the sunrise, the May–September couple charged away in the yellow Italian stallion, oblivious to Sam's presence, or more likely, uncaring.

The city was coming to life now. He could feel it more than see it. Yuki still hadn't responded, so he fired up Grandpa's Mustang and headed for home, wishing Pink's was open so he could get a hotdog.

Nothing like a tube of processed meat to soothe a ravaged soul.

Chapter Thirty-three

GOLDEN WEST STUDIOS WAS ON THE lower level of an ultra-hip hotel on Sunset Boulevard. Nolan had never been inside a recording studio, but she couldn't imagine that all of them were as opulent as Markus Ellenbeck's, or as rife with clichés.

He was dressed in tight leather pants and laden with heavy, skull-themed jewelry, at ease in a chair behind the soundboard. Nolan's overall impression was that of a beneficent nobleman of the rock world, graciously giving audience to his serfs.

On the other side of the soundproof glass, two young beauties with falls of wavy, auburn hair and sea blue eyes sat on a leather banquette, sipping champagne for breakfast. Irish twins with talent that wouldn't quit, according to Sir Ellenbeck.

"I didn't kill Ryan Gallagher. His well-being directly correlated with my ability to recoup a hundred grand worth of studio time he refused to pay for. I'll never see a dime from the estate."

Not remotely troubled by the death of another human. In fact, he seemed bored. "Then you'll be able to account for your whereabouts the last twenty-four hours."

He gestured fondly to the twins, his rings and bracelets jangling. They waved. "Siobhán and Sinéad will confirm that I've been here with them. For the past twenty-four hours."

The alibi would be easy enough to corroborate with hotel and studio staff. Ellenbeck wasn't a guy who could slip away unnoticed—Nolan suspected his ego wouldn't ever let that happen. She decided to change tack. "You were at Pearl Club two nights ago. And so was Ryan Gallagher."

He seemed mildly surprised. "I was, Pearl Club is my home away from home. I left at about ten to pick up the ladies from the airport. We started recording immediately."

"Do you know Melody Traeger?"

He smiled fondly. "She's a doll."

"Did you know she was in a relationship with Mr. Gallagher?"

"No. The poor thing, what a nightmare that must have been. She's better off without that prick. She'll realize that eventually."

Cold, Nolan thought. Extremely cold. "Do you have a relationship with her?"

"I have a bartender–client relationship with her. She's a doll," he repeated.

"Nothing more?"

"Unfortunately, no."

"Did you bring her roses yesterday?"

Ellenbeck laughed with genuine mirth. "I don't do jewelry or flowers, Detective. They're too full of symbolism that can be misconstrued. Fine dining, handbags, cashmere, trips—now those are things that can never be mistaken for love. At least not in LA."

•

Nolan shoveled pancakes into her mouth as if she hadn't eaten in a month. She felt like she hadn't slept in a month, too, but Crawford had quite a few years on her, and he wasn't complaining, so she wouldn't either. They both looked like hell and their collective table manners were suffering under the stress of hunger and sleep deprivation, but the other denizens of The Original Pantry Café this morning weren't the types to judge. Not that she cared.

Crawford wiped egg yolk from his chin and his tie and slurped his coffee so loudly that even the strung-out rock and rollers at the table next to them noticed. "Ellenbeck is arrogant and misogynistic, but is he capable of murder?"

"His type doesn't like to lose, and Gallagher had his money and the girl."

"I like the crime of passion angle, but Ellenbeck didn't seem too het up about either one. And he's got an alibi. We need to keep looking."

Nolan sighed. "We've talked to every sleazebag in the music promotion industry who ever laid eyes on Gallagher and we got nothing. Nobody liked him, but he was a gnat, annoying but not important enough to kill."

"The last phone call he made was to a burner phone, I'm guessing it was to his dealer. Maybe something went sideways. He's a confirmed deadbeat."

"Yeah, but he was only holding a few grams. Not worth killing over."

"That depends on who the dealer is."

Nolan dragged her fork through the leftover syrup on her plate and licked it. She needed the extra glucose. Fast energy that would turn to carbohydrates and go straight to her hips. "He was an industry bottom-feeder. He could be dirty. Maybe we should head to Vegas."

"Vegas PD is solid, and he wasn't on their radar. His apartment there is clean. Only thing left is to wade through his computers, and that's going to take some time. But if he is dirty, that's a cash business, and he's going to keep his ledgers clean."

"If he's smart, but he doesn't sound smart to me."

Crawford crumpled his napkin and tossed it on the table. "That's all too complicated and homicides rarely are, you know that. I think he was an everyday arrogant prick and something more mundane caught up with him. Like he slept with the wrong guy's wife or cheated on the wrong woman, something we haven't uncovered yet. We need to keep this close to home, where his killer is."

Nolan knew he was right, and the fact that Gallagher was an abuser was coloring her objectivity. He was an asshole by all accounts, but he wasn't some arch villain and there was probably no grand conspiracy here. "Easton and Traeger are really close to home, but I still don't see it."

Crawford leaned back in his chair. "They're not off the hook yet."

"Neither one of them showed up on his building's lobby surveillance the morning of his murder. Everyone else who did checked out."

"Which means the killer didn't come in through the lobby, he or she used one of the entrances that doesn't have cameras, which implies knowledge of the building. There are four fire doors and the parking garage door with key card entry for residents only. Once we get the log, we need to question everybody who used that door."

"It might not make a difference, someone could have slipped in with a group."

Crawford scratched the grizzled whiskers that were sprouting on his jaw faster than a well-watered Chia Pet. "Traeger doesn't have any witnesses that can place her at her apartment between noon and two. And we haven't talked to Easton's wife yet about their lunch together, or confirmed he had a doctor's appointment, so he's not clear, either."

Nolan sighed and poured more sugar into her coffee. "They really rubbed you the wrong way, tell me why, Al."

"It's not a personal thing, I just see potential motive. Sam Easton and Melody Traeger have some kind of an attachment. Gallagher tossed her around, hurt her. She's pissed, Sam's pissed. And they're not the most stable individuals."

Nolan felt her face flush. "Because she was an addict and he's a wounded warrior?"

"Look, Mags, don't take this the wrong way. But Easton is a war hero with an engineering degree who's working as a bar back, and his wife's renting a place in Marina del Rey, so things obviously aren't good for him back on the home front. He's got some major scars on the outside, so what kind of scars does he have on the inside? If he doesn't have PTSD, then he's not human. I see him as unpredictable, and he probably sees himself that way, so I don't think he'd hold it against me. Traeger has some scars, too. And we've still got the stalker and the black Jeep to think about. The Miracle Mile Task Force doesn't have one in their coverage, but it's still out there, floating around in the ether. And here's another thought: Katy Villa was killed by a black Jeep."

Nolan rolled her eyes. "Anything else you want to throw into the pot?"

"No, I think I'm done."

"You just reminded me that homicides aren't complicated. Backed yourself into a corner, didn't you?"

"I said they were *rarely* complicated."

Nolan tossed some cash on the table irritably. "Christ, you're a pain in the ass, Al. If you ever get shot in the head, I'll be the prime suspect. I'll even confess."

"If that's the way God wants me to go out, it would be an honor if you pulled the trigger."

The rock and rollers next to them were giving them nervous looks now. Nolan leered at them, and they turned away quickly. "Come on, old man, let's go. The sun is up and so are we. Chop-chop, we've got a lot of legwork to do."

He gave her a feisty smile. "Where to, boss?"

"You've got such a hard-on for Easton, let's go talk to the wife and see if your pecker's flying straight."

Chapter Thirty-four

DISAPPOINTMENT WAS AN UNAVOIDABLE ASPECT OF life, but with patience and resolve even the greatest adversity could be parlayed into an inspired result. When facing hardship, you had to redouble your efforts, and success would follow.

Disappointment: his modest fame wasn't commanding the appropriate attention or respect. It shouldn't have come as a surprise. Notoriety was so common now, especially in Los Angeles, and equally fleeting: just a moronic blip on twenty-four-hour news channels, in the bottomless cesspool of social media, within simple, jaded minds that lacked any semblance of vision or imagination.

Solution: a larger presence was required to excite his uninspired audience, and he must pursue this relentlessly.

He glanced down at the newspaper on his lap, an offering left on a bench in Griffith Park by some archaic soul. This sheaf of useless kindling substantiated his hypothesis. On page three, below the fold, was a small article speculating about a monster in Miracle Mile. Yesterday's headline had already been relegated to journalistic backwater. The placement was a sorry reflection on the state of the world and the attention span of its inhabitants. When a serial killer could no longer compete with the licentious behavior of a spoiled, untalented starlet, it was difficult not to abandon hope.

The Monster of Miracle Mile had a lot of work to do if he wanted to secure his place in history.

Chapter Thirty-five

MELODY WAS AWAKE AND IN THE kitchen when Sam got home. She'd exchanged her Lakers T-shirt and jeans for a sleeveless blue dress that showed off her curves and all the ink on her arms to great effect. She was humming as she stirred something on the stove, swaying her hips in time to the tune. It was a very different woman from the despondent one whose life mission had been to drink herself into oblivion last night.

The air was aromatic with the smell of dark, rich coffee, something far more elevated than the low-end grocery store dreck he kept around, and there was a plate of pastries on the table. It made his heart hurt, having a woman who wasn't Yuki in the house humming and cooking breakfast; imagining that she was cooking breakfast for somebody else right now made it hurt worse. But his empty stomach was howling and he was grateful for the distraction from his unresponsive phone and his battered spirit.

"We didn't eat anything last night. I hope you don't mind, I was starving, plus I thought I should pull some weight around here for the free hotel." She put down her spatula, turned to look at him, and froze. "Oh my God. You're pissed. I shouldn't be in your kitchen, taking over like I own the place."

"No, this is really nice."

She shrank into herself in apology. An abused woman anticipating a backhand. That broke his heart, too. "Are you sure?"

"It's fine, Mel. Actually, it's great. I'm starving, too."

"Then why are you pissed?"

"I'm not pissed at you."

"Are you . . . okay? I mean, that must have been a pretty bad dream last night."

"It was, but I'm okay. Honest. Thanks for asking." He plucked a pastry off the plate, a bear claw. "These look amazing, where did you get them?"

She relaxed a little, but there was still some trepidation in her posture and movements. "The bakery on the corner. They even roast their own beans, so I got some real coffee."

"My coffee isn't real?"

Apparently, the question didn't dignify a response. "Do you want some eggs? Nothing fancy, just scrambled."

Sam thought of the leftover salads Yuki had left. "You didn't put kale in them, did you?"

"God, no, why would I do that? No one likes kale, there are only people who don't hate it."

"Then I'd love some eggs. What were you humming?"

"'The Owl and the Pussycat.'"

"You're weirdly cheerful this morning."

She flushed and looked down guiltily. "I know it's weird, and totally inappropriate. I did a lot of thinking last night, I couldn't stop, and what I came up with at three a.m. is that I'm sad for Ryan. I'm sorry he's dead. But I'm not afraid of his jealousy or his temper anymore. I forgot what that felt like."

There was no need for further justification. Ryan was dead and she wasn't afraid. It seemed like such a simple thing, to live without fear. He envied her the place she was at now but was happy she'd made it there and hoped it lasted. "I get it," he said, picking up the morning paper from the table and paging to the obituaries. He was profoundly relieved that Rolf wasn't among the lucky octogenarians who'd died peacefully, surrounded by family. Nope, he definitely wasn't psychic, just barking mad.

"There's an article on Ryan in there. It's small, buried. They quoted Detective Nolan."

"What did she say?"

"You don't want to read it?"

"Not really."

"She said they're pursuing multiple leads and all the usual bullshit they always march out to the press. At least we weren't named." She tried to laugh, but it came out as a weak grunt.

"Anything about the Katy Villa hit-and-run?"

"I didn't see anything, but I didn't read the whole paper. Why?"

"She was killed by a black Jeep."

Melody blinked at him. "How do you know that?"

"I saw it on a news feed yesterday."

"You didn't mention it to the detectives last night."

Sam tossed the paper on a chair. "Didn't need to. Everybody in law enforcement knows about it, she was the mayor's daughter. If there's a connection, they'll find it, but I doubt there is."

"Still, that's kind of freaky, isn't it?"

Sam made some quick mental calculations. Dr. Frolich was the only one who knew about his episode with Katy on San Vicente, but she didn't know about the black Jeep he'd been seeing. Melody knew about the black Jeep but not about his connection to Katy Villa. In the spirit of keeping everyone partially in the dark, he brushed off her question cavalierly, hoping his secrets weren't somehow obstructing justice. "I'm not sure. Part of me thinks so, but like I told you, I'm paranoid. And dangerous."

"And hyperbolic. That's *your* vocabulary word for the day. Sit down, breakfast is ready."

Sam let her serve him scrambled eggs, toast, and coffee. He helped himself to another pastry, devouring almost everything on his plate before she'd even taken her place at the table.

"I thought maybe you went jogging, then I heard the car."

"It was a good morning for a drive. I went up Mulholland. The sunrise was pretty great."

"Too early for Pink's, though."

"Yeah. Maybe I'll go later, it's my day off. Join me?"

"I work from two to eight."

"I figured you'd call in a personal day. You have every reason to."

"I know. I thought about it, but I decided the distraction would be good. Helpful. Stick with a routine and pretend life is normal, you know?"

Sam understood. He also understood that pretending life was normal when it wasn't didn't help anything. But it was her choice, and she'd made it clear she didn't appreciate lectures. "Whatever seems right for you, Mel."

She toyed with her eggs, pushing them around her plate with a fork. "Any plans besides maybe going to Pink's?"

"Lift some weights, get a run, then possibly read a script."

"Like a movie script?"

"Yeah. I ran into a guy yesterday and he gave it to me."

"Does he think you're a producer or something?"

"No, he wants me to act in it."

Her face lit up with a crooked, full-beam smile. It was the first time he'd ever seen all her front teeth. And they were nice teeth, white and even for the most part, but the left incisor was pegged just enough to advertise they were real. A genuine rarity in LA. "That's so cool. You should do it, Sam."

"I don't know shit about acting. Besides, he's just a kid, working on a student film."

"So what? Steven Spielberg was just a kid once, working on a student film. Besides, if you don't know shit about acting, you can't really be choosy, can you?"

"Good point, but I'm not interested."

"You don't think it would be fun?"

"It would be a nightmare. He's annoying and weird and his script probably is, too."

"I suppose that's why you're going to read it, you want to see just how annoying and weird it is. An irresistible temptation." She refilled their coffees and finally tucked into her scrambled eggs. She finished them and her coffee before broaching another dark topic. "Do you think we'll hear from the detectives again?"

"They'll give you a courtesy call when they find Ryan's killer. And they will."

"You're not worried we're suspects?"

"No."

She pushed her plate away, her jolly mood eclipsed by reality now. It was bound to set in eventually. "I still can't believe somebody killed Ryan. It's so surreal."

"It hasn't hit you yet."

"It's starting to. God, who knows somebody who got killed?"

"Most people don't."

She pinched her eyes shut. "I'm sorry, that came out wrong."

"It's okay, Mel. I've never known anyone who got killed in civilian life either. You expect it in war. And I'm sorry about Ryan. Sorry for you. I know you had feelings for him."

She sighed miserably. "I'm not sure what kind. I haven't seen the Jeep this morning, have you?"

"No."

"But you'd tell me."

"Of course I'd tell you."

"I'll ask Teddy about it when I go home, but he would have called if he'd seen it."

"It's probably nothing. Like the detectives said, there are a lot of them in LA. Are you staying here tonight?"

She shrugged uncertainly. "I don't think I need to. But thanks."

"What about the roses? You still don't know who brought them."

"I've been thinking about that, and now I'm sure Ryan did. It had to be him. He was just yanking me around, trying to scare me."

It made sense. It fit with the control freak/sadist personality profile Sam had created from what little he knew about him. But he was getting used to another body in the house, having someone to talk to who didn't interrogate him about his innermost thoughts or progress in recovery.

If there was any progress. "Probably, but my door is open anytime. Even at midnight."

"I know that and I'm really grateful." She looked around anxiously, Sam thought, as if suddenly realizing this domestic scene was as surreal as a boyfriend getting murdered, then stood and started clearing dishes. "I should get out of your hair."

Sam took over and gestured to her chair. "Sit, relax, I'll take care of this. You did all the heavy lifting." He filled the sink with hot water and squirted in the last of Yuki's bottle of organic dishwashing liquid that smelled like grass clippings. He'd been losing pieces of her every day, but this morning, he may have lost everything. He no longer clung to the pathetically feeble belief that there was a logical explanation for the man in her house that didn't involve intercourse. She was gone. She had been for a while, he just hadn't let himself see it.

"If you want to talk about why you're pissed, I'll listen," she finally said. "Otherwise you can just tell me to shut up."

Sam wouldn't see Dr. Frolich until tomorrow. No reason to discuss it now. He still had to absorb things, and talk to Yuki. "It's nothing, I just had another dream this morning on top of the one that woke you up last night. It's frustrating."

"I like to drive when I'm frustrated, too. Otherwise I just feel trapped inside my own head. It makes me panic."

"You don't seem like somebody prone to panic."

"I am sometimes and it makes me hyperventilate. Do you ever feel trapped by this city? Like it's a bad relationship?"

Sam placed the last plate in the drying rack and turned around. "I never really thought about it."

"I grew up here, so did you, but I've been thinking of leaving. Get a fresh start somewhere else where I don't feel like I'm sitting on a powder keg. LA feels different than it did five years ago. I feel different."

"Then it's not a bad idea."

"Do you ever think of leaving?"

"No. Not until this morning."

Melody sat there patiently, looking at him with her big green eyes. They were questioning, but she didn't ask the obvious. "Who knows, maybe a change of scenery would be good for both of us," she finally said.

"Do you want some more coffee?"

She held out her mug. "Thanks."

Sam almost dropped the carafe when his phone chimed. "Sorry, I have to get this," he said, hurrying to his bedroom and closing the door.

Chapter Thirty-six

"HI, YUKI."

"Sam, is everything okay? You didn't answer my texts yesterday, and you sounded really upset this morning in your messages."

He closed his eyes and took a deep breath. Her voice was so concerned, and he'd never known her to be disingenuous with her emotions on the rare occasions she showed any. And she'd never lied to him, at least that he knew of, so it was once again tempting for him to imagine that there was a benign explanation for the man on her front stoop. "We need to get together and talk. Are you at work?"

"No, I took the morning off, I'm going in at noon. Listen, I didn't handle the whole Seattle thing well, and I'm sorry. We do need to talk."

No lies yet. "I can come over right now. I can be there in fifteen minutes."

"I'm busy this morning."

Servicing a guy with six-pack abs? he almost blurted. "I thought you had the morning off."

She let out an impatient sigh. "So I could catch up on things. How about an early dinner? If you're not working."

"I'm not. Yuki, you cried when you told me about Seattle. I've never seen you cry like that. Is there something you're not telling me?"

She was silent for a very long time. The only thing he could hear was her breathing. "No, I'm just sad. We'll talk later. Five o'clock at Taiko?"

Taiko—home of silken shrimp dumplings and luscious black cod, dishes that made him question his agnosticism with every bite. He loved that restaurant, and if things went horribly wrong there this evening, he'd never be able to return to further explore the possibility of a religious conversion. "How about Sushi Roku? I'm in the mood for an ocean view."

"Fine." He heard background noise, the shuffling of papers, a drawer closing. Either her head wasn't in the conversation and she was multitasking, or she was exhibiting displacement behavior—like a cat licking itself to defuse a potentially dangerous confrontation.

"Were you here early this morning, Sam?" she finally asked. "I thought I heard your car."

"There are a lot of loud cars in LA."

"The Mustang has its own sound."

Yuki discerning the audible difference between a big block Ford and another engine? It was inexplicable. "I confess. I had a dream that you were being strangled and I couldn't get back to sleep. I drove by to make sure you were all right." Sam clenched his jaw, keeping the rest inside.

"How did you know I was all right?"

"A light went on, so I left."

"It could have been the strangler who turned the light on. You didn't even wait for me to get the paper, just to make sure?"

Sam felt like he'd swallowed a hot rock that was now burning a hole in his stomach. Yuki was trolling for information so she knew where she stood at dinner tonight. He could ruin her day, like she'd ruined his, and part of him relished the thought. But he would approach this like a special ops mission, where the element of surprise gave you the greatest advantage. "The dream didn't seem so real anymore, so I decided to get out of there before you got the paper and potentially spotted your crazy husband parked outside your house," he lied. "At the time, it seemed like it would be hard to explain my presence without sounding unhinged or stalkerish."

"You just told me, and it didn't sound either unhinged or stalkerish."

"The light of day and all that."

"Dreams are powerful. I thought hearing the Mustang was a dream, too, but I still looked for you when I got the paper."

And there it was, the big lie. She'd been fairly strategic up until this point, but she'd overplayed her last card by volunteering too much information in an effort to sound casual. Yep, business as usual, got out of bed, fetched the paper, went to make coffee. If you saw a shirtless man on the porch, you had the wrong house.

Sam suddenly felt hollow, like a mammoth void encased in a pouch of flesh. "I was gone by then."

"I guess you were. See you tonight, Sam, Sushi Roku at five. Goodbye."

Goodbye. One simple word people said to one another all the time. Context was everything.

He stared at his lucky cat for a while, trying to empty his mind. The cat stared back with flat, unfeeling black eyes.

•

Melody was subdued when he finally came out of the bedroom. She'd tidied things even more, washed their coffee mugs, put plastic wrap over the plate of pastry, and his mother's throw was folded neatly and draped on the arm of the sofa. The countertops sparkled and the cheap table was crumb-free. She looked at him expectantly and gestured to the empty wine bottle sitting by the sink. "I wasn't sure where your recycling was, I didn't want to snoop around."

"I'll take care of it. Thanks for cleaning up."

"I'll get going, then. Jim is probably hungry."

"Who's Jim?"

"My scrub jay. I feed him peanuts. He's pretty tame now. If I leave the window open, he'll hop in and grab the peanuts out of the basket on the kitchen counter. Maybe he left me the roses."

Sam was stunned when he felt a chuckle rising up his throat. It never made it all the way, but it had gotten close. Apparently you could still think about laughing when you were standing on the edge of a cliff, gazing down at the end of the world as you knew it. Or maybe he'd just given up on feeling shitty and was entering some kind of manic phase in an attempt to retain or reclaim his sanity.

"Want to take a drive first? Pink's opens in half an hour."

"A hotdog at nine-thirty in the morning after we just ate breakfast?"

"Reckless, I know. But you're dealing with the fact that your boyfriend was murdered and I just found out I have a cheating wife."

Melody's face changed very little, but it was enough to intimate sorrow and disappointment that was genuine, familiar to her. She'd been betrayed in life, too. Maybe in different ways, but when a cornerstone of your existence crumbles, you recognize the same malady in others and feel the pain all over again.

"Oh, no. Are you sure, Sam?"

Was he? "I'll tell you about it over a bacon chili cheese dog. You said we should wait until we're both happy before we take a ride in the Mustang, but the way things are going, we'll both be dead before then."

Chapter Thirty-seven

SAM AND MELODY SAT AT ONE of the tables outside, eating their dogs and observing the eclectic assortment of people gathered at Pink's so early in the morning. There were the disheveled partiers coming off benders, none of them looking nearly as good as the couple at the scenic overlook had; tourists checking off an LA landmark before the line got too crazy; a truckload of landscape workers; and a TV host and his crew filming a live segment.

He and Melody stood out most of all, though, a lovely young woman in a dress with fully inked arms and a black bruise under her eye that makeup and sunglasses couldn't entirely conceal; and her dubious companion, a man with half a face who drove an iconic piece of American automotive history.

Melody slurped orange soda through a straw angrily, as if she was punishing the soda and the straw. "What a bitch. I want to strangle her myself."

"There are two sides to every story. Yuki's been through a lot."

"And you haven't? Don't make excuses for her. You said that exact thing to me about Ryan yesterday and you were right."

"I guess I did."

"You don't fuck over people you love ever, especially when they're hurting. Bitch."

Melody was taking the news of Yuki's infidelity badly, as if it was a personal effrontery. "No, but I have to listen to what she has to say, so I'm not going to pass judgment until I talk to her tonight."

"It seems pretty cut and dried to me. Why are you so calm?"

"I'm not, but losing my head isn't going to help anything."

She let out a disgusted snort. "I don't know what your shrink would say about it, but in my opinion, if that's the kind of person she is, then you're better off without her."

Were things really so cut and dried? Betrayal seemed simple, all or nothing. But eight years of marriage and sacrifice and extraordinary struggle wasn't simple, and it changed you, changed your perspective. Melody didn't have that type of relationship experience, couldn't understand it, so there was no reason to argue the point. But her outrage made him feel good, even though it didn't alleviate the pain. He couldn't be furious with Yuki, at least not right now, so she was his surrogate. "Let's get out of here, Mel. I'm worried about Jim starving to death without his peanuts."

"If you saw how fat he was, you wouldn't worry. Thanks for the dog. And especially for the drive. I won't forget it."

"Thanks for not puking."

"Just take it easy on the way back, I've got a full stomach."

As Sam hopped into the Mustang, a white Range Rover with a lot of aftermarket bling pulled into the spot next to it. Melody, lagging slightly behind, was detained by the driver, who had rolled down his window and was delivering an impassioned monologue about the splendor of the car. Whoever he was, he was a Shelby devotee who wanted it and seemed ready to throw cash out the window for it.

"Sorry, it's not for sale. Have a good day," she said pleasantly.

The driver jumped out, gesturing at the Mustang worshipfully as he circled it, importuning for just a peek at the interior, the engine.

Jesus H. Christ. It was Rolf. Sam closed his eyes, actually hoping for a hallucination this time around, but when he opened them, Rolf was still there. He sank down in his seat and smashed a baseball cap on his head, hoping he'd give up and leave before recognizing him. But he didn't leave. His fervor was unrelenting, and Melody was getting flustered, so Sam finally opened his door and stepped out. "You looking for some hot wheels, Rolf?"

His head rolled back and his eyes bugged. "Telegram Sam? No fucking way. What are you doing here?"

"Same as you I suspect, getting an early lunch."

Rolf's wide eyes jittered back to the Mustang. "Are you shitting me? This is your ride?"

"Yeah."

He sucked in his hollow cheeks. "Damn. Damn, what's the story?"

"Family heirloom."

"So you probably don't want to sell it."

"It's definitely not for sale. Besides, it doesn't look like you're short on cars."

"I'm not, but I don't have a drop-dead Shelby GT 500. It's my dream car and this thing is mint. All original?"

"One hundred percent."

He gave it a long, wistful look, then returned his attention to Sam, his expression earnest. "Hey, are you doing okay, man? I'm sorry I ran off yesterday, you just rattled me."

"I'm fine, thanks, Rolf. Glad to see you're doing okay, too."

He took a few awkward steps back and showed him the insides of his arms. "You got me wrong, Telegram Sam, I'm not a high-baller anymore. Quit that shit a while ago, but I'll never get rid of the scars." He turned and gave Melody a charming smile, as if heroin addiction was an ordinary topic of conversation. Ironically, it was for her, she'd been there herself after the prescriptions ran out. "Sam and I met yesterday. I'm Rolf, nice to meet you, what's your name?"

"Melody."

"Pretty name." He gestured to her tattoos, far more focused on them than any of her other attributes. "Nice. Who does yours?"

"Kjell, he's in the Valley, just off Ventura."

"Oh yeah, the Norwegian heavy metal dude. I know him, good guy, he's done a couple of mine. Are you an actress?"

"No."

"You should be." He cocked his head inquisitively. "You work at Pearl Club, don't you?"

"I tend bar there."

"I thought I recognized you! I go there sometimes. Great place, love the octopus. I just found out yesterday that Telegram Sam worked there." He glanced in his direction hopefully. "Have you read the script yet?"

"Haven't had time."

"Running into you here is another sign, you can't deny it. Pops and I come to Pink's every Friday when they open, it's the German sausage thing. He's out of town now, but I always keep up the ritual, even when he's not around. You being here . . . we were *obviously* meant to go deep into the dark together."

Sam was already very deep into the dark, but he wasn't going to share that with Rolf. "Right. We've got to go, see you around."

"Hey, wait. Have you had any more of those visions?"

"No."

"So you don't see anything on my forehead right now?"

"No, Rolf."

"I'd like to work that into the script. Call me. Nice to meet you, Melody. Make sure Sam reads it. There's a part in there for you, too. You'd be perfect as Sam's leading lady. Actually, standing here right now, I don't think I can make the movie without either of you. You don't ignore the signs when things align like this." He gave a backward wave as he sauntered up to the stand.

"So that's your scriptwriter?" Melody asked when he was out of earshot.

"Yeah."

"Telegram Sam?"

"I told you he was weird and annoying. And maybe nuts."

She glanced at the Range Rover. "Pretty deep pockets for a film student."

"He's Hans Hesse's son."

"*The* Hans Hesse? The *Dead to Rights* guy?"

"Yeah."

"So Rolf is kind of Hollywood royalty. Wow. That's a trip."

"So is he." He thought she frowned, but he couldn't really tell with the sunglasses. Frowns weren't smiles turned upside down. The tells resided almost solely in the eyes and brows, and her sunglasses were covering them.

"What did he mean about the visions?" she finally asked.

"Just something I made up yesterday to try and shake him off me. He's nothing if not persistent."

"Yeah, I figured that out. Are you going to read his script?"

"Probably. Eventually."

"You like him."

"I don't even know him."

"He's like a sad pound puppy, waiting for you to adopt him."

"What's the opposite of 'anthropomorphize?'"

"'Zoomorphisize.' Did I pass my vocabulary test today?"

"I just wanted to know. I had no clue."

Melody hemmed in a smile and gave him a nudge on the arm. "Oh my God, who doesn't know that word?"

Chapter Thirty-eight

NOLAN RAPPED HARDER ON THE DOOR of Yukiko Easton's Marina del Rey rental. It was a gorgeous little bungalow a few blocks from the water and fueled her latent misgivings about her own choice of rental. But a property like this would be far more expensive, so every year she lived in the Valley, she would be putting money in the bank that would eventually accrue into a down payment for a house of her own. With LA's exorbitant real estate prices, she might be able to afford one the year she retired.

"Ms. Easton? LAPD, please open up."

Crawford sucked in his cheeks and maneuvered his tongue around his mouth. She tried hard to chase away the image of him coaxing shreds of his breakfast bacon out of his molars. "She's not home, Mags."

"And she's not at work, and not answering her phone."

"Not everybody is connected to their phone with an umbilical cord. We'll come back later."

Nolan crossed the porch and looked through the front window, hoping for a glimpse between the slats of the wooden shade. It was closed tight. "I'm going around the side."

Crawford followed her along a rock path choked with a tangled mat of flowering groundcover. "If something doesn't feel right, you kick down the door. I love kicking down doors, just give me a reason."

"There's no sign that anybody is in imminent danger. I'm just being thorough, so keep your inner stud on a leash."

"After twenty years of marriage, I'm not sure I have an inner stud."

"Keep that information on a leash, too."

Nolan finally found a window with a half-opened blind that looked into a bedroom and saw a reason for Crawford to kick down the door. But he didn't have to—it was unlocked.

•

Unlocked door, a shattered vase paving the entry with jagged pieces of blue and white porcelain, an upturned table. A chef's knife lying in a pool of blood on the tiled kitchen floor, and red drag marks smearing the beige hallway carpet.

"She fought," Crawford mumbled.

Nolan felt the anger and depression rising, each negative emotion battling for dominance. She knew it would end in a miserable stalemate. "Home invasion?"

"How about her husband? She opens the door for him, but he's in a rage over the separation, maybe finances, maybe something else. She fights, she runs, but doesn't make it any farther than the kitchen."

"Sam Easton doesn't strike me as a rager type."

"What are the odds Traeger's boyfriend and Easton's wife were both killed in their homes within twenty-four hours of each other?"

Nolan didn't like it any more than Al. "Astronomical."

They carefully skirted the trail down the hall and followed it into the bedroom. A lamp had been knocked off the nightstand, and bloody feathers from a ruined pillow were scattered on the bed and floor. Yukiko Easton was lying on the bed. Without the violence, she might have been taking a nap. The front of her white shirt was sliced open and saturated with blood. She'd also been shot in the head with a large caliber gun.

"Different gun than the one that killed Gallagher. It's not impossible that there are two perps and two motives."

Crawford circled the bed, his eyes coursing the room. "There are no coincidences in homicide, Mags. And they're . . ."

"Almost always simple. I know, got it."

"Sam Easton is simple."

Chapter Thirty-nine

AFTER THE VISIT TO PINK'S AND another bizarre encounter with Rolf, Sam focused all his energy on purging his mind of all worldly sorrows. He lifted weights for an hour, ran ten miles without an episode of any kind, then got down to the business of cleaning the Mustang after her double outing this morning.

He sprayed and soaped and rinsed, then got to work with the chamois, buffing the body until the blue skin sparkled. Once he was satisfied, he moved on to the wheels, polishing the chrome to a blinding finish. The sun was high and hot on his shoulders and it felt good. Sweat dripped down his face like rain and his muscles were aching—sweet distractions from more saturnine thoughts, like the end of his marriage.

After a final inspection of his handiwork, Sam went inside to cool down. He looked out the front window as he drank a bottle of cold water, admiring the Shelby, all fluffed and buffed and sitting in the driveway, on rare display for all to see. Like he'd told Melody, you couldn't keep a race horse in a stall all its life. Maybe he would drive it more often.

His neighbor, a blond version of Katy Villa who had a rolled yoga mat slung over her shoulder like a weapon, gave it an appreciative double take as she walked to her Volvo. He knew nothing about her or her husband, even after living next to them for four years. Pretending your neighbors didn't exist was an unspoken canon of LA life. You had to deal with enough unpleasant people on any given day, why risk discovering that you might also live next door to some?

It suddenly occurred to him that in the eight years of their marriage, and even when they'd been dating, Yuki had never asked for a joy ride in the Mustang. She'd been an unenthusiastic passenger on occasion and had never been timid about her contempt for it. The engine was obnoxiously loud, the suspension too stiff, the odor of leaded gasoline nauseating. Maybe their relationship had been doomed from the start.

But now was not the time to dwell on Yuki because there was no definitive conclusion to be drawn until he spoke with her. Agonizing over it now was pointless. If the news was bad, he'd just be living through it twice. But it wasn't something he could easily shove aside into a mental pending file, and the hours between now and five o'clock spread out before him like an unnavigable sea.

Sam paced the house, frantic for some diversion. He took a shower, but even the mysterious Irish Spring had lost its ability to captivate. Pausing at a bookshelf, he considered the collection of photo albums filled with pictures from better times. No, not a good time for a trip down memory lane, he couldn't bear it now. He also averted his eyes from the framed photograph of him in Afghanistan with his men, more people gone from his life.

He went outside again and roamed the yard, but visual reminders of pain and loss weren't just in albums and frames, they were everywhere: Yuki's beloved persimmon tree, moribund from lack of care; her herb garden, now weed-choked; the empty shepherd's hooks where her baskets of flowers had hung not so long ago.

It bothered him that she'd taken the impermanent flowers, presumably because she had no faith he'd keep them watered, but hadn't even checked on her persimmon yesterday. If her intention was to return to him, to this house, she would have, and consequently excoriated him for destruction of precious property.

Sam abandoned the yard and slipped back into the house, feeling even more anxious and aimless. The bottle of rye was calling to him, promising escape, but succumbing to that weakness would be pure self-destruction. Drastic measures were required. He sank into the sofa, grabbed his backpack, and excavated Rolf's script—the ultimate act of desperation.

FADE IN:

EXT. DESERT—NIGHT

DYLAN WAGNER sits behind the wheel of a Mustang convertible under a sky dense with stars. The vast emptiness of the desert spreads before him. He hears the SOUNDS of crickets, owls, the furtive scratching of rodents. It's peaceful. Until . . . A siren WAILS in the distance. He starts the engine. Headlights pierce the darkness.

CLOSE ON

Dylan's face, illuminated by the dashboard lights. It's covered in blood.

Sam had never looked at a script before, knew nothing about them. As a reader of books, the format was alien and distracting. Still, this seemed like a pretty good start. He could envision the scene in his mind, and the bloody face was definitely a hook. And who didn't like a Mustang?

He kept reading.

INT. MOTEL ROOM—NIGHT

Weak, flickering neon from the DESERT DELIGHT INN sign infiltrates a dusty window partially covered by torn curtains. The light pulses on a YOUNG WOMAN splayed across a sagging bed. Her nightgown is bloody and one white arm reaches for something she'll never grasp, because she's dead.

The door CREAKS open and the shadow of a man falls across her body.

MALE VOICE O.S.
(agonized, full of remorse)
Bunny. Goddammit, Bunny, I told you not to do it.

Pretty decent noir so far, in the tradition of Papa Hesse. Maybe a little derivative, but still, it painted a picture, and he wanted to know what Bunny had done to get herself killed. He was pretty sure Dylan wasn't responsible. That would be too obvious, which set the story up for some twists and turns. Maybe Rolf had something going for him after all.

Sam was about to turn the page to find out what happened next when he heard car doors slam outside. Nolan and Crawford were walking up to the house, but their eyes were on the Mustang.

He laid down the script and went to the door. "Afternoon, Detectives. Melody isn't here, she's at work."

Detective Nolan's expression was grim. Grim was the only thing in her repertoire, at least from what he'd seen. "We're not here to see Melody."

"Oh. Here to arrest me, then?"

Nolan shook her head sadly. "I'm so sorry, Mr. Easton. Your wife Yukiko . . . she's been murdered."

Chapter Forty

SAM WAS DROWNING IN A VERY deep, cold pool. Every time he tried to surface, his fingers on the verge of breaking through the sunlit water, it turned to black sludge and dragged him down again. But somehow, he managed to speak and the three idiotic words didn't sound garbled, like they were coming from underwater. "Are you sure?"

Two somber nods.

"How?"

"She was stabbed and shot in her home, Mr. Easton."

Sam ran to the bathroom and discharged his Pink's dog violently. One minute, he was crouched in front of the toilet, the next, he was in his living room, sitting in the very same spot on the sofa he had been last night, looking at the very same people. Nolan's expression wasn't just grim anymore, it was concerned and pained. Crawford's was unreadable, but it felt chilly. His words sounded chilly, too, and Sam imagined cubes of ice floating from his mouth as he spoke.

"It's an understatement to say this is a terrible time, but we'd like to ask you some questions, Mr. Easton. What you tell us could help us find her killer."

Sam was numb, pretty much dead himself, but he knew it was important that he be present, at least as present as he possibly could be under the circumstances. He had to hold it together. *Had* to. For Yuki.

He wiped his brow, but it was cool and dry. No sweat. The sweat was all in his mind, which was partially back in an Afghan desert. Sweat, blood, it felt the same on your skin whether real or imagined. "Yeah. Of course."

Crawford leaned forward, braced his elbows on his knees. "We have several witnesses from our canvass that placed your car at your wife's residence early this morning. It's an unmistakable vehicle." Sam nodded, understanding how incredibly bad that looked, and he certainly couldn't deny it. "I was there. I have nightmares that seem real, and she was in one this morning. She was in trouble, and I had to make sure she was okay."

"What kind of trouble?"

"Someone was strangling her. And she was okay when I was there. I didn't kill her. Jesus Christ, I didn't kill her."

"Did you see her? Speak with her?"

"No, but a light went on in the house about the time she gets up for work. Around five forty-five."

"So you don't really know for certain if she was okay then."

"I do, and you do, too, if you have her phone. She called me later, around eight. We made plans to meet for dinner tonight."

Five o'clock at Sushi Roku. Goodbye, Sam.

"We haven't found her phone. We're waiting on the subpoena for the records."

"Was it a robbery, then? A home invasion?" God, he sounded so calm and rational and not remotely on the verge of a nervous breakdown. Way to go, Sam. Dr. Frolich would be so proud.

"We're looking into everything. We do know she never made it to work."

"She told me she had the morning off and planned to go in at noon."

Nolan and Crawford both made notes, building their timeline. They asked dozens of more questions but never mentioned a second victim, and maybe that was by design. A test. To the cops, a dead lover would paint a dream scenario implicating him. There would be no evidence to support it, but his fingerprints were probably still all over the house, he'd been there last week to help her move an armoire. He also didn't have an alibi for the two hours he'd spent lifting weights and running, something that pricked up Crawford's ears. It was all just enough to make his life a living hell, more than it already was.

The truth—something he was intent on evading lately—was the only hope they would have of finding Yuki's killer, and he really didn't give a shit about anything else. Funny, the detectives would be the only two people he'd told at least one whole truth to in several months.

He looked at the bottle of water he was holding and tried to find a memory of where it had come from. "Do you have any leads?"

"We're working on that."

"Was Yuki the only victim?"

Nolan frowned. "Yes. Why are you asking?"

"Then I think I know who killed her."

Chapter Forty-one

TEDDY WAS SCRUTINIZING THE LEMON TREES he'd finally finished pruning. According to The Plant Whisperer, it would set more and bigger fruit next crop thanks to his efforts, even if he lost some this time. The fig was next, but he still had some additional research to do before he tackled that.

Melody had left for work, but he was keeping a close eye on her place. He'd asked her about the cops and she'd dismissed the query casually, like it was no big deal. But something bad was brewing, he could feel it, as deep as he could feel the surf. He wasn't going let his guard down. He checked the street again for the black Jeep, then jiggled her doorknob to make sure it was locked. So far, so good.

He stretched his arms over his head and lifted his face to the sun. No wind today. Just as well, he was feeling a little beat up from his session at Zuma Beach yesterday. He settled into his lawn chair, put in earbuds, and cued up some Poke while he lit a sweet, chubby joint.

Melody had laughed at him when he'd asked her if she was Roxy Codone, but he knew better. He heard her playing riffs acoustically sometimes, saw her signature red Gibson SG propped in the corner of her living room. She was an underground LA treasure, and if some hodad came looking for her or tried to get into her place again, he'd take care of business.

He'd underestimated the potency of the Alaskan Thunder Fuck weed he'd recently procured because things got real fuzzy after that last, valiant thought, and then the fuzz turned to nothingness. When he finally jolted awake, he was still high. High as the sun in the sky.

He giggled at his inspired fragment of poetry, thinking it would be a great lyric for a new Poke song. And Roxy Codone would come up with a scalding riff to accompany it, a riff that would sear the paint off the walls. She knew about being high.

He let his head loll to the side, hearing angry, beautiful music bang inside his head, but when he saw Melody's door hanging wide open, he bolted out of his chair. He felt adrenaline sizzling through his veins, sweat popping on his forehead. Some goddamned sentinel he'd been.

"Mellie?" he called, creeping forward on rubbery legs. "Mellie?"

He reeled back and fell on his ass when a flash of blue burst out the door. "Jim," he said, his voice trembling. "You little shit." He pushed himself up. "Mellie? Are you home?"

No, she was at work. Which meant somebody else had been here. Might still be here. And then he heard laughter, or at least he thought he heard laughter, but he wasn't sure because he was so fucked up. He stared at the open door and dozens of slasher films stuttered through his mind. People were always getting ripped up as soon as they investigated something or went through a door.

But that was stupid. This wasn't a B-horror flick, and he wasn't a coward. Steeling himself, he walked into her apartment, bold as you please, no worries here. No boogey man, no guy in a hockey mask with a knife. Nothing seemed out of place except for the piles of empty peanut shells on the kitchen floor. Jim had been partying in an epic way. Rock on, dude.

There was no sign the door had been tampered with, but it had been locked. He was sure he'd checked it before he'd baked himself into a coma.

Are you sure?

Well, no, he wasn't entirely sure, but pretty sure. Teddy felt bad about searching the rest of the apartment without Melody here, but he was the caretaker, and what if something bad had happened when he'd been zoning out in his lawn chair? He walked quietly, cautiously, from room to room, terrified of what he might find behind the next door, but the place was empty and seemed untouched. In her bedroom were two dozen red roses in a clear vase, the ones somebody had snuck in to leave. Bad shit brewing here, no doubt.

He came back down the hall and saw the Gibson still in the corner, the only thing worth stealing. Not robbers. Who, then? Mellie needed a security system, like, right now, one with multiple cameras she could check from her phone. He was going to hook her up with one on the cheap. He knew a guy.

He ran to the window when he heard the screech of tires and saw a flash of black charging down Centinela. He hadn't gotten a good look, but he had a bad feeling it was the Jeep Rubicon. Of course, he was paranoid as hell, maybe it was just the Alaskan Thunder Fuck messing with his mind.

He fumbled for his phone and called Melody, but she didn't answer. Same with Sam. He thought about calling the cops, but he didn't know what kind of business Melody had with them already. Maybe cops at her place again was the last thing she needed. Besides, in his condition, they wouldn't take anything he said seriously.

But this was an emergency, wasn't it?

He looked up Pearl Club's number and called the main line. A woman who identified herself as Ashley answered. Before he could speak, he felt something hard come down on the back of his head. Stars blossomed behind his eyelids and then slowly faded.

Chapter Forty-two

SAM WAS STARING AT HIS COMPUTER monitor, feeling claustrophobic with Nolan and Crawford breathing down his neck. He was paging through the website of Deaton Graphics in Seattle, the place where Yuki's dream job was. Now it would become somebody else's dream job.

The employees all had professional head shots and brief bios under the About Us tab. The detectives had been intrigued by his idea that her dream job might also include a dream man, arguably the last person to see her alive, but they were getting impatient. At least Crawford was.

"Anything?" he asked.

"No, but there are a lot of employees."

"Are you sure you saw somebody, Mr. Easton? It was early and, personally, I don't think or see so straight at five forty-five myself. It was also dark."

Sam hesitated, thinking of the hallucinations, the paranoia, the dreams, the interactions between alcohol and medication that Dr. Frolich was always warning him about. "I'm positive, Detective Crawford," he finally said. "The porch light was on and I can identify him."

"You're focused on somebody out of Seattle, but the man you saw could have been anyone. Someone local makes more sense."

Sam ignored his subtle assaults on his mental competency and kept scrolling down the column of smiling faces that constituted one of the brightest young design firms in the country. "To you, maybe, but I knew her better than either of you. It was the way Yuki talked about the job and how she cried when she told me about it."

"So you suspected something at that time."

"No."

"Subconsciously, maybe? You just said her reaction was strange."

"I never suspected Yuki of infidelity, but I saw a man on her porch this morning, and now she's dead and I didn't do it."

Nolan spoke quietly to her partner. "Go check in, see where Crime Scene is at with things."

Crawford grunted and left the room, and Sam decided there was no better time to start asking more of his own questions now that he was alone with the good cop. But he couldn't look at her because she'd witness his pain, and that seemed unbearable. "I need to see her. When can I see her?"

"Let me speak with the medical examiner and see when he's planning the autopsy."

He closed his eyes. Of course there would be an autopsy. The thought sent bile crawling up his throat, but he had nothing left to vomit.

Identifying her body would make this real. Right now, he could cling to the faint hope that this was another nightmare and soon he would wake up. Another unhealthy delusion to add to the others accumulating like dust in the crawl space of his psyche. "Do you think Yuki's murder and Ryan's are connected?"

"Is there a reason they might be?"

"I can't think of one, but I'm a common denominator in both."

"By that line of reasoning, so is Ms. Traeger."

"Right. But I'm a terrific suspect in Yuki's murder, I have to be. I was her husband and I just found out she was unfaithful."

"You're a person of interest. Mr. Easton, this is a homicide investigation. Everybody is on our radar until they're not. We look at everything."

"Detective Crawford wants me for this, and maybe you do, too. It's fundamental logic, isn't it? Cheating wives get killed by their husbands. I know the statistics."

"Facts are the only things that matter."

"Why kill the person you love instead of the person who took them away from you?"

"That happens, too."

"I didn't kill my wife, Detective. After two tours in battle, I won't even kill a spider. But somebody else who doesn't have the same reverence for life I have murdered my wife. Find him. Please find him."

"We will find him."

Sam finally risked a glance at her. She was looking at him sympathetically but without pity, and it seemed strange to Sam that eyes so cold in color could impart emotion. "I've been in her house. I helped her move some furniture last week. My fingerprints are probably everywhere."

Nolan shifted on her feet. He noticed she was wearing very sensible shoes, just in case she had to chase after a fleeing suspect or scale the Hollywood sign in hot pursuit of a killer. "Let us focus on the details of the crime scene. You focus on this man you saw."

Sam nodded and returned his attention to his monitor, scrolling through unfamiliar faces on the Deaton website. The wall clock ticked away the passage of time. Nolan's busy phone occupied her. His finger froze on his mouse when he saw the headshot of Dawson Lightner. A pretty boy with an East Coast pedigree and education. Vice President of the Art Department and Chief Cuckold Maker. "That's him. That's the man I saw."

"You're sure?"

"I'm sure."

Nolan's demeanor changed from grave to anxious, eager to follow a new lead. She scrawled down some notes. "We'll check him out."

"Did you notify Yuki's mother yet?"

"We'll be going there next."

"She's her only living relative. In this country."

"Thanks for letting me know. Would you like to call her first?"

Sam thought about the charming Mrs. Saito, her husband long gone and now her only child. He didn't know her well. The language barrier had always been an impediment to forming any substantive bond. But she had respect for authority figures—maybe not a lot for him anymore because he'd come back from war all fucked up and made her daughter's life so impossible that she'd had to move out. "It's probably best you talk to her first. She'll have a lot of questions I can't answer. You probably can't answer them either, but . . . well, she'd appreciate an official visit from the police."

Nolan's face softened and she tipped her head in understanding. The sunlight from the living room window exposed streaks of brown in her right eye. "Of course. Do you have someone you can call, Mr. Easton, someone who can be here for you?"

Melody? His mother? Dr. Frolich? *Rolf?* He had a veritable rogue's gallery of support. "I do."

"Take care. We'll be in touch. You have my card. Contact me immediately if you think of anything else or just need to talk. Nobody should be alone at a time like this."

"Thank you."

"And please stay local for the time being."

"As in don't leave the state or the country?"

"Yes."

"That sounds incredibly ominous."

"It's not. This is an active investigation, and we'd like you to be available to answer any questions that may come up, that's all." She stood and walked toward the door, then turned back. "Mr. Easton, if you did have something to do with your wife's murder . . ."

"I didn't."

"Things would be better for you if you told me about it now."

"I did *not* kill my wife."

She fixed her gray eyes on him, then nodded and turned away. Sam accompanied her to the door, but she didn't linger this time, didn't even look back. The sun glanced off her hair, highlighting the strawberry in the blond.

He locked the door behind her, then went to the bedroom and opened the nightstand drawer—the Colt was lying there, just where he'd left it, an innocent piece of metal, meek and mild. Guns didn't kill people, people killed people.

He took a deep, shaking breath and picked it up. His hands were slimy with sweat as he raised the muzzle to his nose. No smell of cordite from a freshly fired weapon, just the pungent scent of gun oil. He collapsed on the bed, his thoughts circumnavigating the suppressed fear and uncertainty that had driven him to examine his firearm.

I did not *kill my wife.*

Chapter Forty-three

"CHRIST ON A CRUTCH, IT'S LIKE a kiln in here," Crawford grumbled as he cranked the sedan's air-conditioning on high. "You could have parked in the shade—under that tree with the camouflage bark would have been good."

Nolan looked at the pepper tree, its delicate silver leaves shimmying in the breeze. The branches draped and swayed gracefully, reminding her of ballerinas. With camouflage tights. "There was no shade when we got here, so stop grousing."

"Like it or not, we have a double homicide now, even if they're not connected in the end, and that's plenty of reason to grouse."

"Easton asked me if we thought they were."

"What did you say?"

"Nothing, I just asked him another question. Do you really think they're connected, Al?"

"They have to be. Things are looking pretty horseshit for Sam Easton right now. He's still not clear for Gallagher now that one of his alibis is dead, and the unfaithful wife's murder moves the needle in his direction big time."

Nolan thought about what they knew now. Easton had been watching his wife's house on the morning of her murder. He'd just discovered she was unfaithful, or maybe he'd known about it for a while. One of his witnesses for Gallagher's murder was dead, and he had no one to alibi him for the time he'd been lifting weights at home today. All circumstantial, useless without physical evidence to connect him to the crime. But Crawford was right, things looked horseshit for Easton. "We don't have any evidence on him yet, so it doesn't matter how it looks."

"Melody Traeger is supposedly his alibi for at least part of the morning." Crawford let out a half-grunt, half-wheeze, heralding an allergy attack. "Funny how people they love end up dead and they're each other's alibis."

"How is that funny?"

"Not funny, funny. Funny, convenient."

Nolan appreciated her partner's suspicious mind, but it also annoyed her sometimes. He could go from zero to full-blown conspiracy faster than a Formula One car, and she sometimes wondered if he did it intentionally, just to see if he could get her legendary ire up. *Long fuse, fast burn,* he called it. But she wasn't taking the bait this morning. "We'll see. Did you take something for your allergies?"

"No."

"You sound like a sick moose, take something."

"An LA girl like you knows moose sounds?"

"I watch nature shows when I can't sleep. You want a Benadryl? I have some in my purse."

Crawford sighed morosely. "Can't, it'll put me to sleep. I'm wondering about this mystery man, too, Mags."

"What are you wondering about him?"

"Like maybe he doesn't exist. You saw Easton pause when I pushed him on it. He could have made up a perfect suspect to deflect attention. While we chase down a cipher, he's going to bolt."

"You were pushing him to confess he suspected an affair to support your assumption of guilt—and now suddenly you think there was no affair, no lover, and he killed his wife for . . . what? Fun? Make up your mind."

"No, that's not what I'm saying. There was an affair, and I think he knew about it before this morning. But I'm not sure he saw anybody."

She tossed her notebook on his lap. "He says he saw this guy, Dawson Lightner, he ID'd him from the website. Check him out and we'll go from there."

Chapter Forty-four

DAWSON LIGHTNER WAS SLUMPED IN A chair in his hotel room at the Ritz Carlton in Marina del Rey, struggling to hold it together. Nolan was genuinely worried he was going to regurgitate his room service all over the nice carpet. From the looks of the remainders on the trolley, it had been salmon with some sort of vegetable medley, and she didn't want to see it twice.

He didn't have a criminal record, and a search of his social media revealed a man who was passionate about his work, sailing, and rock climbing. Unsaid in his various profiles, but just as obvious, was the fact that he was equally passionate about posting flattering shots of himself. Muscles, sweat, and blinding white smiles were the predominant features in all the photos. Another boring narcissist.

Lightner was in LA for a legitimate business trip and had checked into this glorious hotel last night. But he'd eschewed the luxury and boundless amenities for much simpler lodging at Yukiko Easton's rental cottage a mile away, which struck her. Affairs were almost always conducted in a neutral place, and who could resist a clandestine roll between satiny, million-thread-count sheets, followed by room service in the morning? Familiarity was one explanation. They hadn't been engaged in a capricious fling. It had been something more serious. There was history here. Maybe history Sam Easton knew about.

She thought about her most recent ex, something she rarely did. They'd spent plenty of mornings in her apartment or his, drinking coffee and reading the paper, and it had been comfortable, intimate, like playing house. On the one-year anniversary of their first date, he'd gotten a room at The Peninsula in Beverly Hills, an astounding act of sentimentality. As a detective, she should have immediately recognized it as suspicious.

Her hatred for her apartment had stemmed from that remarkable twenty hours in another world, another life. Her hatred for the ex had stemmed from his serial philandering, which she'd found out about a week later. The gesture hadn't been sentimental, it had been an act of contrition. And maybe Remy was the same kind of scoundrel, but she would never let things get far enough to find out. Just a drink with a colleague, no harm done. Right.

Lightner finally looked up, his handsome face diminished by the gray cast of his flesh, but he wasn't swallowing and licking his lips anymore, which was an encouraging sign that his nausea had passed.

"She told me she was getting a divorce."

Self-justification. Nolan loathed it as much as her apartment and her ex. It was another narcissistic trait, thinking your morality or lack thereof really mattered to outsiders. It really didn't, unless, of course, you were talking about murder. "Tell us again about this morning."

He folded his hands together and gazed down at them as if they were two unfamiliar objects that had suddenly ended up in his lap. "I left her house at eight and came here. I had a conference call, then went to the hotel gym, showered, and ordered room service. I've been here ever since, working on a proposal for tomorrow." He offered his phone. "Yukiko texted me at nine-thirty. She was still alive then."

Nolan took the phone, held it so Crawford could read, too.

Can't do tonight. Tomorrow? Romeo had texted back immediately. Meeting in Dana Point. Come with me. I love you. Juliet never responded. She either didn't reciprocate the sentiment or had been in the process of being killed.

"We haven't found her phone. Maybe she didn't send this text," Crawford said tonelessly.

Lightner's handsome face got a little ugly. "You think I killed her, took her phone, and then sent myself a text as an alibi?"

"You said it, not me."

"That's insane. I'm not your killer. I loved Yukiko. We were talking about her moving in with me when she got to Seattle."

Nolan didn't have a particular feeling about his guilt or innocence, but she was going to enjoy picking him apart like a crab. "Tell us about your relationship."

"I met Yukiko two years ago. Our firms frequently work together. We became friends. When she separated from her husband, we . . . well, we began seeing each other."

"When was that?"

"About four months ago."

Nolan cringed inwardly. Sam had been clueless, that much she now believed, even if Crawford didn't. "Do you know her husband, Sam Easton?"

"No, I don't. I know of him, but we've never met."

"She was going to have dinner with him tonight. Did you know about that?"

"No."

"Are you sure? Maybe you were jealous."

"I told you, I didn't know about it, and even if I had, I wouldn't have cared. In fact, I would have encouraged it. Closure is important."

Nolan hated the word closure and she was beginning to hate Lightner. "So it was your opinion the marriage was over?"

He swallowed and licked his lips again. Handsome or not, it reminded Nolan of a reptile. "She told me it was, otherwise I wouldn't have gotten involved with her."

"You said you didn't know Sam Easton, but knew of him. Did Ms. Easton talk about him to you?"

"Yes."

"And what did she say?"

"She never spoke ill of him, but she confided that he's struggling. He has severe PTSD, and she felt she had to move on before they destroyed one another. It had become a toxic environment." His eyes narrowed. "I know you have to question me, but I hope you're looking at him. I have tremendous respect for his service and sacrifice, but he's not well."

"Did Ms. Easton ever express fear of her husband or concern about her well-being?"

"Not to me." His brows lifted in revelation. "But at dinner last night, something was bothering her. She was quiet, distracted, very unlike herself. She wouldn't tell me what was wrong, but at the time I wondered if she and Sam hadn't been arguing."

"Did they argue often?"

"I couldn't really say, but I know their separation was difficult. For both of them."

"Where did you have dinner?"

"At the restaurant here."

Nolan closed her notebook. "But you two didn't spend the night here."

His mouth went slack, then he looked away and shifted in his seat. "That was the original plan."

"What happened to that original plan?"

He began twisting his hands together. "I brought up the subject of her moving in with me. I was excited about starting a future with her. She got upset and left." His shoulders slumped. "I should have known better than to press her."

Telling her husband she was leaving town had set her off, Sam Easton had said as much. "Were you angry?"

"No! Disappointed, but not angry."

"But you ended up at her house."

"We talked things through over the phone. I promised to take the subject off the table for the time being. She seemed calmer, more like herself, and invited me over."

Make-up sex. "Is there anyone here at the hotel who can confirm you've been here since the gym and room service?"

"I've been working in my room for the past four hours."

"So that's a no."

He suddenly withered like an underwatered plant and his eyes filled with tears. "I loved her. I would never kill her. I'm sure Sam loved her, too, but he's very unstable."

Lightner was emotionally immature and self-involved, which went hand in hand with jealousy. *If I can't have her, no one else will,* Nolan thought. It could apply to both the men in Yukiko Easton's life.

Chapter Forty-five

MELODY WASN'T SURPRISED WHEN ROLF WALKED into Pearl Club. Actually, it seemed inevitable. He was on a mission to cast Sam in his film, and he wasn't going to give up without a fight. But if he thought he'd find an ally in her, he was dead wrong.

He looked around, smiled when he spotted her, then headed to the bar. He carried a raggedy, canvas satchel that wouldn't have been out of place on Skid Row downtown. When he took a seat, she walked over and placed a coaster in front of him. "Hi, Rolf, long time no see. I don't suppose you're in here for lunch."

"Nope, just a drink."

"Uh-huh. You wouldn't happen to be following us, would you, trying to wear down Sam?"

He reared back and held his hands up. "Hey, no way, you got me all wrong."

Melody scowled at him. "Sam's not working today."

"No problem, I'll catch up with him another time. I just stopped by to drop off a script with you. Can I have an orange juice?"

"Ice?"

"Not if it's fresh."

"Of course it is, we couldn't charge seven bucks for it otherwise." Melody filled a glass with juice and passed it over.

"Thanks. So what do you think about being a part of my movie, Melody? You and Sam . . . it's picture-perfect in my mind."

"I told you, I'm not an actress."

"Everybody starts somewhere."

"Not interested. There's plenty of underused talent in this city, why are you so hung up on Sam?"

"Because he's made for the role. He's got an undercurrent, an edge, the kind of vibe that brings a character to life. And he's mysterious. So are you."

"I'm a bartender. Not much mystery there."

"You're more than that. So is Sam. He told me he got his scars in a farm accident."

It took great effort to stifle her laugh. Farm accident? What a smart-ass. "He doesn't like to talk about it."

Rolf took a sip of his juice, rolled it around in his mouth, and nodded approvingly. "So anyhow, I wanted to invite you two over to my place tonight if you're free—take a look at the storyboards, talk about my trip to the desert this weekend. I'm scouting locations and I want you and Sam to come along."

"You're a relentless pitchman."

"You also think I'm annoying, I can tell."

"What gave me away?"

"Your eyes. They're a really bitching green, by the way, they'd really pop on film." He frowned. "Do you have a black eye?"

"I got bumped with a surfboard. Rough water."

"I tried surfing once and the same thing happened to me. You did a good job covering it up, I almost didn't notice." He folded his hands on the bar in what Melody imagined was an attempt at supplication. "Look, I'm just fighting for something I believe in. You and me and Sam, we can all fight together. We can all share the dream."

"Is this when the mawkish music cues up and the heroes hug and walk off into the sunset?"

He gave her a sheepish smile. "Pure cheese ball, right? But I mean it. I offered Sam Guild rate, but I can probably do a little better than that for both of you."

Melody dipped some glasses into the wash sink. Rolf was weird, naïve, and immature, but he wasn't entirely unpleasant. And like it or not, she felt a connection with him. She knew what it was like to be creative and have a dream, knew what it was like when the dream fell apart. They also shared the journey of recovery from addiction, which said a lot about his strength and character, even if he was a little whack.

Still, she figured him for a spoiled Hollywood brat with delusions of grandeur and a bank account that opened doors in his world. Had anyone ever told him *no*? Would that two-letter word launch him into a tantrum? Part of her hoped so, it would be good entertainment on a slow day. "Thanks, but there's some stuff going on. Personal stuff."

"Yeah? I hope it's not bad."

"It's not a good time for Sam or for me."

He nodded in understanding. Disappointment. Both. "Okay. Doesn't hurt to ask, right?"

"For what it's worth, you made a good case."

He reached into his bag and laid a bound script on the bar. "This is my screenplay. It's called *Deep into the Dark*. I hope you have time to read it someday."

Melody glanced at the script, then stashed it in her bag beneath the bar. So much for a tantrum. "Thanks. I will."

"I did some rewrites last night. I'm pretty happy with them. Don't forget, storyboards tonight. You could even stay if you want. There are ten extra bedrooms—and Pops is out of town, so I have the whole place to myself. We could leave early tomorrow morning for the desert."

"Ten extra bedrooms?"

"Yeah. And a pool with a waterfall. Give me a call if you change your minds. Sam has my number. And you do, too, my card is in there." He finished his juice and hopped off his stool. "How long have you worked here?"

"A couple years."

"Do you like it?"

"I like it fine."

"Do you play guitar?"

"No."

"Too bad. The female lead plays guitar, but we could fudge that if you decided to take the role. I can teach you a few chords, and we won't light those scenes much." He laid a hundred-dollar bill on the bar. "Keep the change. I've gotta run, I'm picking up some lenses. Think about the trip to the desert. I've got a suite at Two Bunch Palms for the weekend, and I can always book another one for you and Sam. Hope to see you around."

Melody looked down at the hundred, wondering what it would be like to leave a ninety-three-dollar tip for a glass of orange juice or book a couple thousand-dollar suites at Two Bunch Palms without a second thought. She would probably never know, not unless she won the lottery. But in spite of Rolf's privilege, she had the sense that he was a lonely, lost soul, loitering on the outer perimeter of life, hoping to buy his way in.

"Mel?"

She looked up and saw Ashley slipping behind the bar, moving faster than her usual, wine-mellowed pace. She looked anxious. Maybe Langdon had finally figured out the white coffee situation. He was cool; but drinking on the job, along with personal cell phone use, was expressly verboten, grounds for immediate termination.

"Hey, Ash, what's wrong?"

"Your neighbor Teddy called the main line. He's been trying to reach you."

Maybe he'd seen the black Jeep. "What did he say?"

"Somebody broke into your apartment and he got knocked unconscious when he was sussing it out. He said he just came to and he sounds freaked out."

Melody felt the blood drain from her face, leaving it cold. The roses had been disturbing enough, but it had been easy to imagine Ryan as the perpetrator in spite of his denial. But Ryan wasn't in a position to mess with her head anymore. Teddy had been hurt, and what would have happened if she'd been home? "Ash, I need to go. Can someone cover for me?"

"I'll cover. Go, girl. And be careful."

Chapter Forty-six

MELODY RAN OUT THE BACK DOOR of Pearl Club and almost collided with Detectives Nolan and Crawford. She was panting, on the verge of hyperventilating, and she bent over and tried to catch her breath. It wasn't helping. She felt a gentle hand on her back.

"Cup your hands and put them over your mouth and nose," Nolan said calmly. "Try to breathe from your diaphragm slowly. Hold your breath for a few seconds if you can."

Melody obeyed and eventually felt her breathing slow. Sweat dripped from her face onto her sneakers. She tried to focus on the spreading circles of dampness on the yellow canvas.

"Okay?"

Melody rose slowly. "Thank you."

"What's wrong, Ms. Traeger?"

"Someone broke into my apartment and knocked out my neighbor."

Nolan held out her hand. "Give me your keys."

"Why?"

"I'm driving you home. I don't want you having a panic attack on the road. Detective Crawford will follow us there. Get in, please."

Melody obeyed, leaned back in the seat, and closed her eyes. She'd never been a passenger in her own car and it felt strange; almost as strange as her life suddenly turning into a gigantic maelstrom of shit.

"I have a stalker, don't I? Somebody's obsessed with me. Or somebody wants to ruin my life. Or kill me."

"It could have just been a break-in."

"You don't believe that and neither do I."

"You've had some time to think. Are you sure nobody comes to mind?"

She sighed heavily and opened her eyes. They were stuck at a light on La Cienega. Markus Ellenbeck was the only person who was aggressively flirtatious with her, but he didn't make her uncomfortable. No way—it couldn't be him. She'd known him for two years and he was a sweetheart, a solid citizen who was esteemed in music circles as a producer and for his drum work on some of the greatest rock albums of the past thirty years. Famous people didn't stalk bartenders.

But rabid fans sometimes stalked musicians.

"The only thing I can think of is that I was in a rock band a few years ago. We had a small following, very loyal. But nothing crazy ever happened back then, and I went by a pseudonym, so nobody knew who I really was. I didn't even know who I was, I was so messed up all the time."

"What band?"

"Poke."

Nolan nodded, giving no indication whether the name was familiar or not. "What was your stage name?"

"Roxy Codone," she said bitterly. "It seemed so funny back then."

"That's your past."

"My future's not looking so great right now, either."

"You're sober and smart. I'd say your future is wide open."

Melody fixed a brooding gaze at the dashboard. The last thing she'd expected from a homicide cop was optimism.

Nolan took a call, then shoved the phone in her blazer pocket. "Detective Crawford just arrived at your apartment. The police are already there. They'll get your neighbor's statement and then they'll speak with you."

Melody felt her eyes stinging and she turned toward the side window, furious that the fear was back. "I'm never going to feel safe there again. And that really pisses me off because I love my place."

"We'll make sure you feel safe there again."

Melody looked at Nolan. She was a pretty woman, she realized. Imposing, rigid, but pretty. She couldn't imagine her smiling, but of course she did. Everybody smiled, didn't they? "Why were you and Detective Crawford at Pearl? Do you know something about Ryan?"

"We're still investigating. But no, we don't have anything new to share with you."

"So why were you at Pearl?"

"To ask you some questions."

"Go ahead."

"We don't have to do this now."

"No. Please. It'll keep my mind occupied. I don't like where it's at right now."

"Were you with Sam Easton this morning?"

"Yes. Until about ten-thirty or so, and then I went home to get ready for work." Nascent coils of panic began to unfurl in her stomach. "Why?"

"How long have you known him?"

"Six months, I guess."

"And you're friends."

"Friends and coworkers, yes."

"Close friends?"

"We're not sleeping together, if that's what you mean," she said tartly.

"Did you know Mrs. Easton?"

"No."

"Did he ever mention anything about his wife being unfaithful?"

Melody's thoughts slammed to an abrupt halt. No wonder Nolan had been so anxious to chauffeur her to a B and E; she had a captive audience and a perfect environment for interrogation. For what reason, she wasn't sure, but she didn't like the direction the conversation was taking. "He found out this morning."

"Has he ever talked about someone named Dawson Lightner?"

"No. What is this about?"

Nolan kept her eyes on the road ahead. "Yukiko Easton was murdered."

The world seemed to fall away, and Melody was certain that if she hadn't been sitting down she would have passed out. "Oh my God. What the hell is happening?"

"We don't know yet."

"He didn't kill her. Yuki was his world. Poor Sam." Her voice cracked as she punched in a call to him that went to voice mail. "Take me there."

"We need to check out your apartment, and you need to file a report first."

"No. Detective, I'm worried about Sam. He's going through a hard time."

Nolan finally looked at her, but her eyes were covered with large sunglasses. Ray-Bans. "Are you concerned about his welfare?"

"Hell, yes, I'm concerned about his welfare. His wife was just murdered. If you won't take me there, I'll get out and walk."

Chapter Forty-seven

SAM WENT TO THE BATHROOM, TURNED on the faucet for background noise, and leaned against the vanity for a long time. It was a nice vanity, zebrawood with a marble top and basin. Yuki had designed it; a carpenter she knew had built it; and he'd installed it. Nice work all around.

The mirror he hadn't looked into for two years had been part of the upgrade, too, a vintage Hollywood Regency Yuki had proudly acquired for too much money. It was a sunburst monstrosity with wicked, writhing, gilt tongues manically licking an escape from an oval of silvered glass. He called it the Exploding Porcupine.

It was hanging directly in front of him, but his eyes were fixed on the sink and the water that swirled down the drain. *Down, down, down.* Where did it go? Where would it end up? Universal questions you could ask about everything and everyone.

He was a widower now. It struck him as odd that in a world where no sorry human condition was without classification or political currency, losing a spouse wasn't a category worth dissection or exploitation. Shouldn't there be a codified difference between being a widower whose spouse had died of natural causes versus a widower whose spouse had been murdered?

No. Dead was dead.

Sam turned off the faucet, took a deep breath, and finally looked into the mirror. It was a milestone, but it wasn't a heart-stopping moment, not even a significant one, which stunned him. Sleepless, violet puddles under amber eyes. A good nose. Flesh marbled with scar tissue on one side, smooth on the other. He wasn't looking at a monster, he was looking at a man. Just a man. A widower.

Sam ran his fingers along the scars. They were hard and gnarly and without sensation, a perfect analog to his cerebral state. Gnarly. He thought of Teddy, who probably said "gnarly" on a regular basis. Or maybe the slang was passé and surfers didn't use the term anymore. And why was he thinking stupid, irrelevant things?

Because you can't think of relevant things.

He wanted desperately to feel grief instead of deadness, but there was some indiscernible obstruction cocooning him. He could practically see grief seething all around, coagulating, pulsating, but it couldn't push its way in. Not yet.

He opened the medicine cabinet and stared at the orange bottles of different tranquilizers. He hadn't taken one in two months, but today was the day to snuggle up with an Ativan. Ease the anxiety, kill the pain. He shook one out, swallowed it, then stared at his face again. Why had he been avoiding his reflection all this time? It's not like it was the sole reminder of his past—it wasn't even the most significant one. Maybe this was a breakthrough on a day when he should be having a breakdown. Or maybe he was having a breakdown and this was what it was like.

His sluggish pulse sparked to life when his forehead suddenly misted with amorphic red. He pinched his eyes closed and took deep breaths, willing the Ativan to kick in, but it wasn't fast-acting. He should have taken a Xanax instead.

When he finally opened his eyes again, he watched in morbid fascination as letters slowly appeared: S . . . U . . . I . . . C . . . I . . . D . . .

He turned away and stumbled out of the bathroom. The hallway floor was warping and buckling beneath his feet, and brilliant, coruscating patterns flashed on the walls. He made it to the kitchen and confronted a large, translucent projection of himself, Colt in hand, rising slowly to his temple.

"No. No, no, no, no, no!"

The phantasm flashed, then disappeared—and along with it, his consciousness.

Chapter Forty-eight

A MAN WAS STANDING OVER SAM, offering a bony hand latticed with blue veins. Half of his face was obscured in the penumbra cast by an unknown occlusion, but the visible half looked familiar: a lantern jaw stippled with whiskers, a long nose that defied symmetry, a watchful hazel eye set in a deep, shadowy socket. Undulating, psychedelic colors splashed the walls behind him.

"Get up, Sam my man."

The voice. "Rondo?"

"You got it."

Sam ignored the hand and scrambled to his feet. "Stop visiting me, you're dead."

"Yeah. But you should be used to visitors from the other side by now," he cackled. "Ty, Shaggy, Wilson, they couldn't make it. Did I tell you last time they send their regards?"

Sam backed into a chair, knocked it over. "You're not real."

"I'm obviously real enough to you, and that's a good thing because I'm here to help you. Don't let me go. Can you do that?"

Sam grimaced and pressed hard against his pounding temples, against the specter of death, maybe an augury of his own. He pinched his eyes shut, but Rondo was still there when he finally opened them again, the visible half of his face wavering in and out of focus.

"Nice try, but closing your eyes won't work because you don't want me to go."

"Why are you here?"

"I just told you, I'm here to help."

The neon lights faded, and Sam felt his mental fog dissipate as he faced the same question he'd asked himself the last time Rondo had visited. When dreams bled into reality, was it a psychotic break? Oh, yes, he believed it was. Game over. Charon and the straightjacket and a one-way ticket downstairs.

But maybe Rondo *was* here to help. Sam had been fighting the dead for so long without results. What would happen if he played along this time, pretended this was real? His mind couldn't sustain that fantasy within a fantasy for long, and then Rondo might go away forever.

"How did you get in?"

"Ghosts can walk through walls." He let out his phlegmy cackle again. "I'm just shitting you, Sam, ghosts can't really walk through walls, I ought to know. Your door wasn't locked. I tried knocking and when you didn't answer, I looked in the window and saw you on the floor. I thought maybe they got you, thank God they didn't. You need to lock your door, Sam, at all times. Especially now."

He emerged from the shadows and Sam recoiled. He wasn't in bloody camo this time, and his face didn't belong to the man who'd died two years ago or the man who'd visited him last night. This time, it was chapped and sunken and smeared with grime. The deep eye sockets were bruise-purple. His mouth was slack, and dried spittle frosted the edges of his lips. He was wearing a tattered woolen coat that smelled like decay and should have been roasting him alive on this hot June day, but there was obviously something wrong with his thermostat.

Sam instantly understood. This version of Rondo was mentally ill, likely schizophrenic. Probably homeless, like so many veterans in LA. He'd seen enough of them to perfect the image.

Keep pretending Rondo is real. Challenge him.

"So you're alive?"

He batted his hand in the air, either fending off the question or an imaginary swarm of predatory insects. "You need to pay attention to the message, not the messenger. I came here to warn you, Sam. Fuck, we're in trouble. They're going to kill us. They've got operatives everywhere. *Everywhere.*" He started shuffling and fidgeting and his eyes were suddenly wild, searching for his imaginary tormenter.

A man on fire. A potentially dangerous man his own mind had conjured, and he was afraid of what Rondo might do to him because nightmares weren't always safe. This one didn't feel safe, not remotely.

Calm him down.

"Why don't you have a seat, Rondo? Can I get you some water?"

"Yeah, yeah, that would be great. Thanks."

He didn't sit down, but he seemed to relax a little. Sam backed into the kitchen, his eyes fixed on the disturbed dream visitor as he grabbed a bottle of water from the refrigerator.

Rondo snatched the bottle from his hand, ripped off the cap, and drank greedily, water spilling down his chin onto the front of his filthy coat. "Thanks, man."

"No problem. Where are you staying nowadays?"

He stared at him for a moment with empty, unfocused eyes, then looked around the room nervously. "Here and there. I've been on the move since Mexico, had to jump the border."

How far could this go?

"What happened in Mexico?"

He shook his head. "Gotta stay on the move, and you do, too. They almost got me a few times, they're shape-shifters, you've gotta watch out for that. I told you, they're trying to kill us."

"Who's trying to kill us?"

"You know who. The Army. Greer."

Sam didn't recognize the soft rasp that came from his own mouth. "Captain Greer?"

"Yeah."

"I don't think so. Why would he want to do that?"

Rondo slammed the bottle down on the coffee table and started pacing tight circles. "You know why!"

Sam had more than a passing acquaintance with mental illness, and he knew about delusions. They were flimsily constructed things, absent of logic, and held together solely by a sick mind—*his own* sick mind, he reminded himself. Inserting rationality into the discussion appeared to be a potent trigger for agitation, and the image of the Colt to his head terrified him.

"Have you talked to the colonel about this?"

Rondo's face contorted in an ugly sneer. "Colonel Doerr is in on it. My own father. My own fucking father!"

"Okay, Rondo, it's just me and you then. Tell me why you think Greer wants to kill us and we'll figure this out together. Come up with a plan."

"I was hoping you'd say that." He squatted down on his haunches and for a brief moment, Sam was afraid he was going to shit on his rug. But he just balanced there like a deranged yogi. "You remember what he did. We saw it."

What did you see? What do you remember?

Sam shook his head, dispelling the voice Dr. Frolich had told him to ignore. "I don't remember much these days, Rondo."

"The kids. The *kids,* the little boys! *Bacha bazi,* boy play. Christ, we could hear them screaming all night, you're goddamned lucky if you don't remember that." Rondo put his head in his hands and started sobbing. "Greer said we couldn't do anything about it."

A dark, malevolent veil settled over Sam, coming from nowhere and going nowhere. But he could hear a child screaming. "I don't understand."

Rondo looked up, his ravaged face illuminated by the afternoon sun that filtered in through the slats in the front window shades. His tears had drawn meandering runnels through the grime on his cheeks. Some of the grime looked rusty, like dried blood, and his flesh was pocked and scabbed, as if he'd been picking at it. "The Afghan commander, Raziq, that sick fuck, you remember him, you remember the kid he had chained up? His eight-year-old sex slave? Greer said to ignore it, the Army wouldn't touch it because he was on our side."

Sam shook his head. "I don't know what you're talking about—"

"But Greer did do something about it! He shot him and we saw it! And he saw us. Good for him, I say, kill a pedophile, the world's a better place. But he doesn't see it that way, no, he only sees a court martial and the death penalty or life in Leavenworth if one of us goes public. You think it's a coincidence that the next day, he put us on that unscheduled convoy and KABOOM!" Rondo screamed, jumping to his feet. "He had to shut us up. But we lived."

The tableau around Sam suddenly froze as incipient wakefulness and reality seeped into the fringes of his mind. With that single falsehood, the Rondo hologram split apart into meat and bone and blood, and the apparition melted away.

Sam jolted awake on the sofa, his shirt wringing wet, his heart flailing like it was trying to free itself from his chest. There was no bottle of water on the coffee table, no upturned chair, no lingering smell of decay. Another nightmare, as twisted as all his other ones and wholly possessed by death, but so much worse than last night because Melody hadn't been here to interrupt it.

The canker of PTSD was obviously accelerating its feast on his brain, and now it was planting false memories in his mind because he knew damn well Rondo was dead; Greer hadn't shot anybody or set up a roadside bomb attack to kill his own men; and Raziq never had children chained up in his barracks. Dr. Frolich had been right, warning him not to focus too much on the details of his dreams. Or maybe her warning had done just the opposite, planted the seed and he'd nurtured it during his blackout.

With a convulsive shiver, he recalled his hallucination of suicide, another warped mirage to add to his mounting catalog of psychotic symptoms. *He* was the man on fire. He was in trouble. And Yuki was still dead.

He fumbled his phone out of his pocket when it started buzzing and squinted at the caller ID. Dr. Frolich. What perfect timing. He took deep breaths in an attempt to calm his heart, but the effort was wasted. He answered anyhow.

"Hi, Doc."

"Sam? Are you all right? You sound . . . you don't sound like yourself."

"I'm really not myself."

"Listen, I just spoke with a police officer, a homicide detective Crawford. He was asking if you were at your appointment yesterday. Tell me what's happening."

She had no idea how much was happening, what had happened, but it was surprisingly easy to condense it down into a handful of simple, straightforward sentences. "I'm a person of interest in two murders I didn't commit. One of the victims was Yuki. She's dead. And I'm having blackouts and hallucinations like I did with Katy Villa, but they're escalating. They're bad. I'm in trouble."

No pause, no sharp intake of shocked breath. "Have you taken your meds today?"

Had he? "I'm not sure. I think so."

"I'll be there as soon as I can."

Sam listened to the fast beep-beep-beep of the disconnection. It was a steady, regular sound, unchanging and imperturbable. Preposterously, he wondered if his veteran's medical benefits would cover the house call.

Chapter Forty-nine

MELODY JUMPED OUT OF THE CAR the moment Nolan pulled up to the curb and jogged up Sam's front walk, but she checked herself before she mounted the steps to the porch. However bad her situation was, his was much, much worse, and he deserved a strong, calm, caring friend right now, not a hyperventilating basket case. And what was she thinking? That she'd find a blubbering pool of human jelly on the floor? That her very presence would transform Sam's collapsing life and save the day?

"Dumb ass," she mumbled, knocking on the door.

His brows lifted in surprise when he opened it. He was holding a glass of rye. "Melody. Why aren't you at work?"

"Because I heard about Yuki. I'm so sorry, Sam." She wanted to wrap her arms around him, but she resisted the urge because she sensed it would be exactly the wrong thing to do.

"How did you hear about . . ." He looked over her shoulder and frowned. "Nolan?"

"Yes."

"Why is she here?"

"It's a long story. Are you okay?"

"I don't really know, but Dr. Frolich is on her way here, so I'll be getting a professional opinion."

"Good." Melody chewed on her lower lip, one of many bad habits that resurfaced when she was anxious. She heard Nolan's shoes click on the sidewalk. "I have to go. The cops are at my place. Somebody broke in today and knocked Teddy out."

Sam braced an arm on the doorframe, once again glad it was there to hold him up. "Jesus. Is he okay?"

"Yeah, I think so."

"Come back here when you're finished. Stay here tonight."

"I will . . . or maybe we should stay someplace else. Something bad is happening, Sam. I don't know what, but I feel like we should be hiding. Is that stupid? Paranoid?"

"I'm the wrong person to ask about paranoia. You and Nolan came together?"

"Yeah."

"How is it possible you got a homicide detective with two hot cases to be your chauffeur in your own car?"

"I told you, it's a long story."

"She can be persuasive," Nolan said, mounting the porch steps. "How are you, Mr. Easton?"

"Pretty terrible. Did you speak with Dawson Lightner?"

"We did."

"And?"

"I'm sorry, Mr. Easton, but I'm not at liberty to say anything more."

"I can read between the lines."

"This is just the beginning of our investigation." She looked at Melody. "The police are waiting, Ms. Traeger."

Melody nodded, then searched Sam's face. He looked tired, stressed, and the scarred side of his face was blanched. Okay, but not, and her heart ached in empathy. She didn't know who Dawson Lightner was, but Sam obviously thought he had something to do with Yuki's murder and Nolan hadn't shared any good news on that front. "I'll see you later, Sam."

"Thanks for coming, Mel. Thanks for giving her a ride, Detective. I still don't know how you ended up driving her here in her own car, but I suppose I'll find out eventually." He broke eye contact for a moment and stared out at the street. "Did you speak with the medical examiner?"

She nodded. "He'll be performing the autopsy tonight. You can see her anytime tomorrow."

Melody was horrified, and from Sam's expression she knew it showed on her face. An autopsy. The thought of someone cutting up your dead loved one. Of course, they'd autopsied Ryan, she just hadn't thought of it. She reached out and touched his arm. "I'll come as soon as I can."

Nolan gave him a nod. "You take care, Mr. Easton."

Chapter Fifty

"THANK YOU FOR BRINGING ME HERE," Melody said as Nolan pulled away from the curb.

"No thanks required. You were concerned about your friend—that's plenty of reason to do a welfare check. That's a part of every cop's job, detective or not."

Melody gazed down at her hands. She'd picked or gnawed away almost all of her pink nail polish during the past twenty-four hours. It was a gaudy color, made more so by the remaining neon fragments stubbornly affixed to her fingernails. She would never ask for Cotton Candy Land again. "You see people's lives change forever, for the worse, every day, don't you?"

"That's part of the job. Helping them is another part of the job. The good part, the best part."

"Finding the bad guys."

"Finding justice. We owe it to the living and the dead."

"Justice doesn't bring the dead back. But you're doing the right thing for the right reason. I admire that."

Nolan looked at her curiously, then returned her attention to the road. "It's not everything, but it's something."

"Do you have any suspects in Ryan's or Yuki's murder yet?"

"You know I can't comment on that."

"Because we're persons of interest? Or is that people of interest?"

Nolan remained silent.

"Sam didn't kill anybody, certainly not his wife. Don't tell me you think he did."

"I'm sorry, Ms. Traeger, but I can't discuss active investigations."

Melody sighed impatiently. "Sam is kind and compassionate and strong even though he's been through hell and back. And things keep getting worse for him. It doesn't seem fair."

"Life rarely is, but that doesn't stop most people from fighting their way through it. It didn't stop you, and I doubt it will stop Mr. Easton."

"Do you believe in bad luck? Or good luck?"

"No. Luck is about choices and their consequences."

Melody gazed down at her shamrock tattoo. "I used to think that, too. But Ryan's and Yuki's murders had nothing to do with any choices Sam or I made. It had to do with somebody else's choices. So I'd say we're having some bad luck."

"Fair enough."

"Somebody asked me today if I liked my job. I said I liked it fine. I do, but it was a choice of necessity. I'm not going to be a bartender forever, it's just a means to an end."

"What is your end?"

"I finish college next year, and then I'll decide. Do you like your job, Detective?"

"I love my job."

"That's good. I want to be able to say that one day. What's going to happen? About the break-in, I mean."

"The police will investigate, take statements, and you'll have an active complaint on file."

"That's all?"

"It depends on what they find at your apartment. For instance, if there is a threatening note or something to that effect, the police would proceed differently."

"You mean they'd take it more seriously." Melody watched Nolan bristle. She always talked too much when she was anxious, didn't always think about what she was saying, and she'd offended her. But it was true, and the truth hurt sometimes. Most of the time.

"LAPD takes every case seriously," she finally said crisply, but Melody knew that was just a company line. There was triage in police work just like there was in the emergency room. There had to be; there weren't enough cops to cover every single person and complaint.

She sagged in her seat, deflated by reality. What was a break-in in LA? Nothing. And if there hadn't been a burglary, or a threat, it was double-nothing. Just another day in a big city. She would be a name in a forgotten file somewhere and that would be the end—unless her stalker ended up killing her, and then they'd have something to work with.

Chapter Fifty-one

TEDDY WAS SITTING ON THE BACK gate of an ambulance, holding a cold pack to his head. A medical tech was checking his eyes with a tiny flashlight while another one took his blood pressure. There were two squad cars parked on the curb, and beyond, uniforms were having a discussion with Detective Crawford in the courtyard.

Melody jumped out of the car while Nolan joined her brethren in blue. "How are you, Teddy?"

He gave her a pained smile. "I have a thick skull, good thing, too, the son of a bitch hit me hard. No concussion, right, ma'am?" he asked the pretty, pert brunette who'd been plumbing the depths of his bloodshot eyes.

The tech offered a splendid white smile and patted his arm fondly. "No concussion, just a big goose egg. Keep ice on it for a while and take Tylenol for the headache."

"Tylenol is lame."

"Pretty much, but it's better than nothing. You're good to go, sir."

Dismissed with a clean bill of health, Teddy got off his perch and pulled Melody aside. "I don't know what the cops think or what they can do about this crazy shit, but I've got a guy who's going to set you up with some security cameras. It's all wireless, and everything goes straight to your phone. Fifty bucks and we'll get this asshole."

"That's a great idea. You're the best, Teddy."

He tipped his head in the direction of the brunette, checking to see if she'd heard the glowing testimonial, but she'd already jumped into the ambulance cab. "This is some bad medicine, Mellie. What's going on? Tell me."

He had no idea how bad. But did he need to know? She finally decided he did, for his own safety. "I've been dating this guy . . ."

"He's the fuck who gave you the black eye?"

She nodded. "He was killed yesterday."

"Huh. Maybe he got what he deserved."

"Teddy!"

He shrugged unapologetically. "Sorry, but I have a real problem with assholes who hit women."

"Sam's wife was killed this morning, too."

Teddy's lanky body bowed back. "You're serious?"

"I'm serious."

"Did they catch anybody yet?"

"No, so stay sharp."

"Man. This is really messed up. Mellie, stay at Sam's until I get the security set up. And take your gun with you."

"I will."

"Ms. Traeger?" Detective Crawford was approaching on heavy feet, and he didn't look particularly happy to see her. "Come with me, the police would like your input."

The comment was meant to be sarcastic, she was sure of it. Maybe a little mean-spirited. He was pissed that he was cooling his heels at a B and E while two unsolved homicides were getting older by the minute. And his partner had hung him up, indulging someone who might be a killer or at least an accessory to murder. That was her assessment, anyhow.

The street part of her instantly formulated a sharp response, but the reformed Melody kept calm. Antagonizing him wouldn't do a thing except possibly confirm a bias that she didn't have control of her emotions and was therefore capable of a crime of passion. "Stalkers are deranged, aren't they? Mentally imbalanced?"

"That's a given."

"And they feel possessive about the object of their obsession. So it's not a stretch that they would harm anybody close to me, like Ryan and Sam. No telling what a stalker would do."

Crawford sighed. "A stalker might kill your boyfriend out of jealously, but if that's the case, he would have killed Sam, not his wife. What's your point?"

"I'm afraid all of this is connected somehow. I'm afraid of what might happen next."

His expression softened. "So are we. That's why we want your input. Come with me."

She followed him, walking the gauntlet of police to her open front door, and stepped inside for a surreal, guided tour of her own apartment. Had she remembered to put away her bras, or were they still hanging on the shower curtain rod to dry? As if the cops would care—it wouldn't even be worth a snicker.

No bras, no underwear. Her apartment was pristine and seemingly untouched. The gun was still stashed beneath her mattress. No eerie vibes that anybody had been in here. But they had been, Teddy was proof of that.

"Does anyone else have a key to your apartment?" one of the cops asked.

"No."

"Your caretaker said he didn't have keys, but what about your landlord?"

"I suppose she does, but she's eighty, senile, and I doubt she's a part of this equation."

"The front door lock wasn't compromised, but the kitchen windows were open. Did you leave them open?"

Hell no, not after her special delivery yesterday. "No. I definitely closed and locked them before I left for work."

"And your front door, are you sure that was locked?"

"I'm positive."

He gestured to the pile of empty peanut shells on the kitchen floor. "Somebody enjoyed some snacks while they were here."

"Jim."

"I thought you said nobody else has a key."

"Jim is a scrub jay that I feed. He doesn't need a key, he came in through the window that somebody pried open to get in here."

"The windows didn't seem to be damaged, but we'll check them again."

What was the point? she wanted to ask, but didn't. They already knew somebody had gotten in. Whether they'd adroitly picked her front lock or pried open the window, it didn't matter. No violent crime had taken place here and there was no imminent threat of one, so the investigation was as good as dead.

"Thanks," she offered insincerely, abandoning the hopeful detective-in-training to walk into the living room where Nolan and Crawford were speaking in hushed tones. Her eyes drifted to her precious Gibson propped in the corner, her touchstone of both joy and misery, and her throat closed tight. The detectives ceased their conversation and looked at her anxiously.

"What's wrong, Ms. Traeger?" Nolan asked.

It took a few moments to find her breath and her voice, and when she did, it came out in a muted little squeak. "That." She pointed at the guitar, at the white rose stuck in the fretboard, its stem secured by the strings. "The rose wasn't here when I left."

"Does it mean something to you?" Crawford asked.

Melody allowed her mind to drift back in time to her days with Poke, to the fans throwing roses on stage. White and red ones. The ritual was performed every time they played the violent squall of a song called "St. Valentine's Day Massacre."

Rose White, Rose Red, someone shot her in the head, Rose White, Rose Red, now she's bleeding on the bed . . .

She looked at Nolan. "It means somebody hasn't forgotten about Roxy Codone."

Chapter Fifty-two

SAM THOUGHT IT INCREDIBLY MUNIFICENT OF Dr. Frolich to reserve judgment on his drink of choice. She hadn't even given his tumbler of rye a second glance. Then again, after listening to his summary of the twenty-four hours since his office visit, a late afternoon cocktail was undoubtedly far down on the list of urgent concerns.

He'd told her *everything*, and hearing the oral account of his recent travails had a curious, twofold effect. It made him feel like he was on the cusp of irreversible personal calamity, yet he felt incredibly resilient because he wasn't on the floor in fetal position, foaming at the mouth. At least not yet.

It had also been liberating—he was no longer interested in propping up the false pretense of sure-footed stability—he was interested in solving problems.

Dr. Frolich took some time to absorb his doleful monologue before speaking. "I wish you'd called me earlier, Sam."

"I didn't exactly have time, things happened so fast. I haven't even had space to grieve. Maybe that's why I'm melting down, so I don't have to face it."

"I'm afraid it's more complicated than that. On top of PTSD, you're dealing with multiple stressors. The kinds that no one endures without significant emotional consequence. Infidelity, the murder of a spouse—those two alone are devastating events. It's no surprise your episodes are accelerating. Finding a way to curtail them is our goal. We can't affect the external causes, but we can find a way to deal with them, so that's what we need to focus on and that's where we'll start."

"So let's do it. By the way, it's not lost on me that 'Frolich' is the German word for happy, so I'm counting on you to make your Teutonic magic work."

She smiled, but it was a cheerless one that didn't inspire hope for an easy solution. "Your projection of suicide. That disturbs me a great deal."

"It disturbs me, too, because I'm not suicidal."

"But apparently your subconscious is. I trust you to be honest with me, Sam, but if suicide is something you've briefly entertained, even for just a millisecond, we need to discuss it."

"No. It's not something I would ever consider." He took a slug of rye and swallowed the lie down with it. "But I don't trust myself anymore."

"Tell me what you mean by that."

He dragged his hands down his face. "Do you know what I did when the detectives left today? I went to check my gun, smell it, count the load, just to make sure I didn't kill Yuki, even though I knew I didn't. And the waking nightmares about Rondo—those came from someplace dark and disturbed I didn't know was inside me. I'm concerned I'm breaking with reality."

Dr. Frolich stiffened in her chair, and her grandmotherly face was suddenly stern. "Do you recognize the distinction between your dreams and hallucinations versus reality?"

"When I'm awake I do."

"You're in crisis, Sam, but if you were breaking with reality, you wouldn't be able to recognize it. These waking nightmares, as you call them, they're new?"

"I would say they're more like a progression."

"Do they feature anyone beside Ronald Doerr?"

"No."

"Why do you think your subconscious is isolating him?"

"I don't know."

"Were you particularly close to him?"

"No, nobody was. He wasn't well-liked and could be a real jackass sometimes." Sam lowered his head. "Jesus, the guy got vaporized and I'm calling him a jackass."

"It's difficult to dislike a dead man. It makes perfect sense that he would become a singular focus for your survivor's guilt. You regret your feelings for him during his life because he's dead. But you have to remember those feelings were legitimate and separate from his death. It seems counterintuitive, but loss is easier when you cared for someone. There are no conflicts of the psyche. There is purity in that."

"So guilt and regret are my biggest enemies right now—is that what you're saying?"

"It's what I've always been saying." She studied his face carefully before continuing. "I'm going to ask you some questions, yes or no will do, but feel free to elaborate when answering."

"Hit me."

"Do you believe you have repressed memories from the time leading up to the explosion?"

"No. Everything I see or dream is a twisted fabrication. False narrative, like you said. They just keep getting more distorted. And more realistic."

"Don't dismiss the possibility. Even so-called normal dreams are distortions."

"Okay."

"Do you recognize the distinction between your dreams and hallucinations versus reality?"

"You already asked me that. Yes."

"I felt it was important to ask twice. Do you feel that you're a danger to yourself or others?"

"No."

"The suicide . . ."

"Another fabrication."

"But you checked your gun—that wasn't a fabrication."

"I never believed I killed Yuki. It was an obsessive-compulsive thing."

Dr. Happy, not looking particularly happy, folded her hands in her lap. "Let's discuss our next steps."

"Okay."

"I don't believe it would be useful or wise to change your medications or dosages at this point since you have reported some positive results. Palliative dosages of tranquilizers might be helpful in the short term, but it's not a long-term solution, and you've wisely expressed a fear of addiction."

"I took one today, after the cops left. Before Rondo showed up again."

"That's why you're so calm."

"Yes."

"Good. Right now, I don't think you should avoid them."

The presumed subtext being, the least of his worries right now was benzodiazepine addiction. Hell, that would probably be the best-case scenario, something he could definitively fix by going through treatment. Party time, bring on the rapturous fog of mother's little helper, swallow your cares away. But that pill hadn't done much for him when he'd really needed it. "Could the tranq have caused the last Rondo vision, or whatever you want to call it?"

"It's not impossible. Physiologically, tranquilizers suppress your central nervous system; and that may have opened up a playing field for other factors, psychiatric or neurological. But that's a secondary concern for now."

Sam had never thought of tranquilizers releasing other dubious creatures of the mind and body, but he was a little anxious about her hint of a more pressing, primary concern. "So what do we do?"

"Honestly, Sam, I would strongly recommend a short hospital stay to remove yourself from the things that are triggering your episodes, allow yourself and your brain to process and rest, and also to get some more tests. I spoke with Dr. Guzman at length yesterday and he concurs. He's very concerned that there might be some new neurological issues, and identifying them could help us form a better treatment plan."

Sam was nonplussed by his knee-jerk revulsion to the suggestion, which in all fairness did possess some logic. "I'm not going to check myself into the hospital."

"It would only be for a day or so."

"Voluntary commitment to the psych ward? I don't think so."

"Not a psych ward, a hospital, for testing and diagnostics. I can get you into UCLA tonight."

"The healing I need to do isn't going to happen in a hospital while I'm getting poked and prodded and shoved into machines."

"Or it could facilitate healing. You would have a team of doctors working on your behalf, myself included. As your psychiatrist, that's my recommendation. It's entirely your choice, Sam, but please consider it."

Chapter Fifty-three

MELODY TUCKED HER GUN AND AN extra clip deep into her suitcase beneath several changes of clothes. She'd tossed in a fresh Pearl Club tank and pair of shorts, too, just in case Teddy's security system solved the case of her stalker and she would be free to go out in public again, tending bar at Pearl without fear.

She sent Ashley a text and told her she couldn't come into work tomorrow. There had been a threat and the police were concerned about her safety. The threat part was speculative, but Nolan and Crawford had suggested she lay low, stay someplace else for the night, and she was damn well going to abide by their recommendation.

She had to sit on her overstuffed bag to zip it, then she went to the bedroom window and dumped out the remaining peanuts Jim had left after his binge so he had some fodder while she was gone. It was knee-jerk to check the lock after she'd closed it, as pointless as it was.

On the dresser next to the window were the red roses, even more spectacular today as their tight blooms unfurled. How sad that she would never enjoy the beauty of roses again. They would always represent fear to her now.

Melody rolled her suitcase into the hallway, got her guitar case from the closet there, and packed up her Gibson—Netta's Gibson—sans the rose. It was all she had left of her. She hadn't been lying when she'd told Sam she'd found it in a pawn shop. It took her six months to find it after she'd gotten clean, and it was no small miracle that it had come back to her. They'd been through a lot together and she wasn't going to leave it for some maniac.

She wondered why the maniac hadn't taken the guitar in the first place, but maybe that was the next phase of his plan. And maybe killing Sam was a part of the next phase, too, Yuki had just been a warning shot.

Why was someone after her now?

It was a good question, but since she'd been anonymous during her rocker days, maybe it had taken her tormenter all these years to track down Roxy Codone after she'd dropped off the face of the planet, lived on the streets, and finally reemerged as Melody Traeger, bartender and college student.

The cops had thought it was a good theory, but they'd also been fairly upfront about the hopelessness of pursuing it. In its heyday, Poke had enjoyed some devoted fans, but that was a long time ago. But the black Jeep had given them something to chew on, and maybe it would get them closer to an answer. Maybe it would be the answer.

The police assigned to the case were gone now, no doubt looking at vehicle registrations and hoping to find a violent former felon obsessed with Poke who drove a black Jeep Rubicon. Teddy had left on his heroic quest to acquire a security system. Only Nolan and Crawford remained. She paused when she heard them arguing about something outside and walked softly to the front door, hoping to eavesdrop. It was no problem. The walls were thin and she could hear everything they said.

"They found the weapon that killed Yukiko Easton in a dumpster half a mile away from her house, Mags, and it's registered to Sam Easton. His fingerprints are all over it, and all over her house."

"He told me his fingerprints would be all over the house. And he probably gave her the gun for self-protection when she moved out. Anybody could have used it, including Dawson Lightner. It's not enough to arrest him."

"It is if you consider the other factors, like the holes in his alibi for this morning, the cheating wife, his presence at her house, the fact that he's under psychiatric care, it's plenty. That's a solid case to argue for an arrest, but I'm not saying we should. Not yet."

"What's your plan, then?"

"Bring him in for questioning. If he's as unstable as Dawson Lightner said he was, we can crack him easy if he's good for his wife. And I'm liking him better and better for Gallagher's murder, too."

Melody shrank back from the door. Sam a killer? There was no way, they had something wrong. Didn't they?

"We never thought he was good for Gallagher. Don't make a case for convenience," Nolan countered.

"You never did, but I always thought his connection with Traeger made him a possible. Listen, I understand you've got a soft spot for Easton, you have some things in common, but don't make this about Max."

Max? Melody moved closer to the door again and pressed her ear against it.

"Fuck you, Al. This isn't personal. Sam Easton might be damaged, but he's not an insane, psychotic killer."

"Okay, I'll give you another option: Traeger. She kills her abusive boyfriend, then steals one of her lover's guns and gets rid of the wife."

"Put it back on the rails. Traeger's not our killer, but she might be the next person on a slab if we don't get our shit together."

"We need to make a move."

As Melody waited for Nolan's reply, she realized she was shaking so hard that her teeth were chattering. After a long silence, she finally heard the detective's voice.

"Okay, let's bring him in."

Melody slowly, carefully backed into the kitchen, trying not to make a sound. She jammed herself into the furthest space away from the front door and called Sam, praying he would answer. He did.

She spoke in a rushed whisper. "Nolan and Crawford are coming to take you in."

"For what?"

"They have evidence that links you to Yuki's murder."

"That's impossible. How do you know?"

"I overheard them talking. Crawford wants to arrest you, Nolan doesn't."

"Are they still there?"

"I think so. We need to talk."

"Can you come over now?"

"That was my plan, but they might get a head start."

"I'm leaving my house now. Pick me up in the alley behind that bakery by my house, will you do that?"

Melody kept her silence for a moment, revisiting her conversation with Nolan about her relationship with Sam: friends and colleagues for six months, never lovers. In truth, she really didn't know him that well, even though she felt like she did. And she definitely didn't know how deep his problems ran, maybe much deeper than the things he'd shared with her. There was compelling evidence against him, and he'd pointed out she was a poor judge of character.

Her uncertainties about him felt like a betrayal, but she had a strong survival instinct, too, which told her to push away from trouble. She'd had enough of that in her life. "You seriously want to run from the cops?" she finally said.

"Temporarily. Listen, Melody, don't do this if you're not comfortable with it. But I'm not a killer. I hope you believe that."

She did believe it. With all her heart. And if she was wrong . . . well, she just wouldn't worry about that right now. "I'll be there as soon as I can."

Chapter Fifty-four

IF YOU WANTED TO DISAPPEAR FOR a while, a city with millions of people was a good place to do it—unless you had a badly disfigured face. Los Angeles didn't have a lot of places that offered privacy, but Sam decided Will Rogers State Park in the Santa Monica Mountains was a decent choice. It had plenty of isolated spots along the hiking trails, and there had been times he'd gone running there and not seen another soul.

On the drive there, he and Melody exchanged information and when he heard about Poke and the white rose, something crystallized in his mind. Whatever was happening, things were coming to some kind of a head and they were both in danger. It wasn't paranoia, it was just common sense.

He'd been completely upfront with her about his blackouts and hallucinations—he owed her that. No more secrets at this stage of the game. Their lives might depend on mutual honesty. His story hadn't sounded any better the second time around. No wonder Dr. Frolich wanted him in the hospital, and maybe Melody did, too. It was a lot to take in all at once.

After a short hike, they found a secluded spot on the lip of a ravine that was sheltered by eucalyptus and live oak. Neither of them spoke as they watched the sun sink toward the mountains, a full moon rise.

"Why did you lie about the guitar earlier?" he finally broke the silence.

"It's part of my past. It's second nature to deny anything about it."

"Not all of it is bad. Especially not the guitar."

"I know, but it's hard for me to separate it from everything else."

"You can learn how to do it. I happen to know a good shrink who could help you."

She cocked a brow at him, the corner of her mouth twitching as she tried not to smile. "And what would your shrink say about the fact that we're fugitives from the law, sitting in the middle of a park, staring down at a scrubby ravine?"

"She would say it's a perfect metaphor for our situation. But all things considered, I think she'd understand after overanalyzing it." The brief detour into levity was a relief, a safety release valve during times of crisis or despair. But it wouldn't last. It couldn't. He took her hand. "Don't let the past take away something you love, Mel. I know a little about that and it sucks."

She squeezed back, then released him and hugged herself against the encroaching evening chill that was sweeping inland from the ocean. "I'm scared, Sam."

"I know. I am, too."

"Last night, you told me not to avoid the cops. Was that 'do as I say, not as I do'?"

"This is a different situation."

"But you said you didn't kill Yuki and I believe you. They'll figure that out."

"Crawford is after me. And they have my gun and my prints."

"You explained that to me, and it's exactly what Nolan told Crawford. She's on your side. Crawford said she has a soft spot for you, something about Max. Who is he?"

Sam looked at her, at the tight lines fanning from the corners of her eyes. Her bruise was starting to yellow around the edges. "Her brother. He was killed in Afghanistan. But that won't keep her from doing her job. Mel, if they bring me in, they have less reason to look for somebody else, which is what they need to be doing."

"The fact that you're hiding from them also gives them less reason to look for somebody else. It looks bad, Sam. Really bad."

"Having hallucinations or breaking down in custody would look bad, too. So would checking myself into the hospital. They already think I'm unstable. I'm screwed in all ways."

"What's our plan, then?"

Sam felt the glancing blow of another encroaching migraine behind his eyes. "I'm working on that."

"You can't just live in a park and wait for them to find the real killer. And you can't hide from them forever."

She was right about that. "Mel, I'm not just hiding from the cops, I'm hiding from the person who's after us. This is all connected, it has to be. Ryan first, then Yuki. The black Jeep at both our houses. It's too much of a coincidence."

She let out a shaky sigh. "It is connected, that's why I'm scared. But the cops are looking at that, too."

"This guy killed your boyfriend and my wife in twenty-four hours. I'm worried about who might be next. Look, I know this might sound irrational and paranoid, and you have every justification for questioning my sanity after everything I just told you. But look at it this way, even if the cops weren't planning to take me in, the fact remains that neither one of us has a safe place to stay tonight, at least not in my mind, and I'm guessing not in yours. The cops will understand that. And I'm going to be totally honest with you. I'm on shaky ground right now and I need a night to pull myself together. I can't do that in an interrogation room, and if I get pushed any further—into some kind of major break—I don't know if I could ever come back. That's what scares me most."

Her eyes filled. "Oh, Sam, I didn't even think of that. I'm sorry."

Somehow, he managed a smile and wiped a tear from her cheek. "No reason you would have, you just found out how crazy I was."

"You're not crazy."

"From your lips."

"But what are we going to do? Check into a hotel?"

"We can't use our credit cards, they'll be looking for that. And we definitely don't want to stay anywhere that takes cash."

"So I guess I'm homeless again."

"Melody, you don't have to do this. You can check into a hotel and maybe the cops will put an officer by your door."

"I don't want you to be alone."

"I don't want you to be alone, either. I have this macho fantasy that I can protect you better than anybody."

"I trust you more than the cops. If we can't stay anywhere, we'll just have to drive all night, take turns sleeping."

"The cops will be looking for our cars, too. I think we're stuck here until we can figure something out."

Melody dug in her bag and pulled out her buzzing phone. "Nolan again."

"They'll keep calling. Turn it off, they'll be watching those, too."

She let out a sigh of frustration. "So we're completely cut off."

"You said it, we're fugitives from the law."

"You're a good person to be a fugitive with, you think of everything."

"You learn a lot of helpful things in the Army."

Melody tipped her head to look at him and the shadows of eucalyptus branches filigreed her face. "You need to rest, Sam. In a bed. There's got to be something we can do. What about your mom?"

"I don't want her involved in this."

She shoved her phone back in her bag and noticed Rolf's script. She'd forgotten all about it. His visit to Pearl seemed like something that had happened decades ago.

If there was ever a time for a Hail Mary, this was it.

Chapter Fifty-five

"NO WAY, MEL. IF I'M NOT already over the edge, Rolf will put me there."

"Just hear me out. He invited us over to look at storyboards tonight and said we could stay if we wanted to. He also said he'd get us a suite at Two Bunch Palms if we go to the desert with him. We have no connection to him. It would buy us time to figure out what to do, and we could both rest without worrying about the cops or the bogeyman coming for us during the night. And we don't have to tell him anything."

Sam's headache was throbbing relentlessly now, pacing his heartbeat. How had he gotten to a place in life where the only person who could help him was a screwed up, self-involved kid?

"I know he's annoying, but we don't have any other choices unless you want to sleep out here tonight."

Sam didn't want to sleep outside with no gear, but he didn't know if there were enough tranquilizers in the world to make Rolf tolerable. "I don't know, Mel."

"You said you needed time to pull yourself together. You could beg off sick and I could keep him occupied. He doesn't bug me as much as he does you."

"He will, just give him time."

"He's a spoiled, socially impaired kid. It could be worse. If he stresses you out, you can go sit in the pool. It has a waterfall. That's bound to be good for your chakras, whatever they are."

"A waterfall?"

"That's what he told me."

"A pool with a waterfall might instantly heal me. Maybe Rolf could baptize me while we're at it."

She gave him a long-suffering look. "Now is not a great time for sarcasm, even though I'm generally a big fan of its curative properties. We have to decide something, Sam."

"I know, but if we do this, we still have problems. For one, we can't call him from our phones and we have no idea where he lives, or if the offer's still good."

"Of course the offer is still good, we just have to play it. And I'll borrow a phone. There are still people in the park."

"We can't drive your car to get there."

"We'll leave it here and I'll call for a ride after I talk to Rolf."

Sam considered carefully. It was a solution, the only solution he could see. "Get a cab so we can pay cash."

"Way ahead of you."

•

Chez Hesse wasn't in the Beverly Hills Flats but in the actual hills, where only the ultrawealthy of the wealthy 90210 denizens lived. A high, bougainvillea-covered fence and gate obscured the property from the street, but once Rolf had opened it from his control center somewhere up in Valhalla, Sam could see a long, climbing drive, elegantly lit and lined with cypress, flanked by a sloping, emerald green lawn.

As the taxi crested the hill, a monstrous Mediterranean Revival came into view, complete with multilevel stone terraces and loggias overlooking flowering gardens and a citrus grove. The air was fragranced with jasmine, rosemary, fennel, and orange blossoms. The whole tableau transported Sam back to his honeymoon in Tuscany. It was a perfect, beautiful memory, now excruciating to recall.

Melody brought him back to the present, whispering, "Wow, I guess *Dead to Rights* did okay."

"Looks like it did a little better than that."

The taxi dropped them in a circular courtyard with an Italianate fountain surrounded by rose shrubs. Moments later, the towering, carved front doors of the house burst open, disgorging an elated Rolf. He was wearing a Sex Pistols T-shirt and ripped black jeans, dispelling some of the magical *La Dolce Vita* vibe.

"Welcome to Pops's shack—so stoked you're here!" He bounced down the stone steps, gave Sam's hand an enthusiastic pump and Melody's a more delicate one. "What changed your minds?"

Flight from the law. Potential murder charges. Poor judgment stemming from prescription pills and mental incompetency. "Dead end jobs, a sense of adventure, those sorts of things."

Melody gave him a subtle elbow to the ribs. "We decided we want to be a part of your film. We think it will be an amazing opportunity."

Her suave, kiss-ass statement stimulated Sam's vomit reflex, but it seemed to hit Rolf's egotistical sweet spot dead center.

"Hell, yeah! We're going to make an awesome team. Let me take your bags, Melody." He cocked his head at the guitar case. "I thought you said you didn't play."

"I'm not that good. Actually, I'm terrible, so I'm a little shy about telling people."

He gave her a full-beam smile. "Hey, you don't have to be Eric Clapton to make it work. This is fantastic, now we won't have to cheat your scenes. Not that I would have minded, but it's going to be way more authentic now." He turned to Sam with an earnest expression. "The female lead plays guitar."

"Oh." Rolf's grammar indicated that in his mind, the film was now a fait accompli. Sam would stand by the Salton Sea watching floating toupees and diapers while Melody serenaded him with her guitar. Time to write the Oscar acceptance speech.

Rolf glanced at the departing taxi as it disappeared down the hill. "You cabbed it, huh? I was hoping you'd come in the Shelby."

"It's getting detailed." Sam was sometimes amazed by how effortlessly he could lie. His recent dalliances with honesty evidently hadn't diminished his nimble skills of prevarication.

"Right on, that beauty deserves all the TLC you can give her. Come in, I ordered a bunch of sushi, and I've got a couple bottles of champagne on ice. We have to celebrate."

They followed the manic, junior lord of the manse into a vast, echoing entry foyer that was appointed with artwork and furniture that Sam assumed were appropriate to the architectural style and historically significant. Hallways shot off in different directions like spokes of a massive wheel, and two curving staircases with ornate iron railings vaulted up on either side. "Do you ever get lost in here?"

Rolf laughed. "I used to, when I was a kid, but half the time it was on purpose. So, all the guest rooms are upstairs, you can take your pick. Pops has his suite on the lower level, but he's in Berlin. He pretty much lives there unless he's working on something here. I hang in the guest cottage, so you have the main house to yourself. Except for the maid. She has an apartment downstairs, and you can call her if you need anything."

A Beverly Hills mansion and staff at his disposal, seemingly unlimited funds, no parental supervision: a recipe for disaster. Privilege could be a double-edged sword. Sam had to give him credit for pulling his life together. Overall, he was feeling a lot more charitable toward Rolf, who was not only turning out to be a first-rate host but was saving their hides in a real pinch, even though he didn't know it. As profoundly distasteful as it was, indulging his film aspirations at least temporarily seemed like the very least he could do in return. "Thanks, this is really generous."

Rolf lifted a bony shoulder. "Hey, it's my pleasure to have you guys here. We're going to have a lot of fun."

"This is a spectacular place," Melody said, her eyes wide as she absorbed the grandeur that surrounded her. She'd never had exposure to anything resembling opulence in her life, and Sam could tell that she was dwelling in a lush fantasy right now. Hell, he was, too, and he'd grown up around money. But not conspicuous consumption like this, and it was mesmerizing.

"Thanks, it's pretty cool living here. Come on upstairs."

They followed him as he trundled Melody's bag and guitar up the left staircase to a broad hallway lined with movie posters and behind-the-scenes shots from the *Dead to Rights* films, a vanity gallery and subtle reminder to house guests that their host was *Hans Hesse,* just in case they'd forgotten.

"Take a look around and get settled, then come down and we'll eat and drink and take a look at the storyboards. If you haven't had a chance to read the script, they'll give you an idea of the feel and where it's going."

"I did read the first couple pages."

"Yeah? So what did you think, first impression?"

Sam grudgingly offered his praise in the interest of expediency. "I thought they were good, Rolf, really hooky. I want to know what Dylan's story is and why Bunny got killed."

Rolf smiled, showing all his nice teeth. "At the bottom of every page, you have to give the reader a reason to turn it." His smile faltered. "Why didn't you keep reading?"

"I would have, but I had a personal thing come up."

He seemed satisfied by the answer. "I'll go crack open the champagne."

Chapter Fifty-six

SAM TOOK THE FIRST GUEST ROOM because there was no point in perusing his choices. He knew they'd all be good. This one had a brocade settee facing a fireplace, a generously stocked wet bar, and a California king-sized bed with a canopy. French doors opened onto a broad stone balcony that had a view of the city from one angle, the ocean from another. The bathroom featured a steam shower and a stone soaking tub that could accommodate at least six people comfortably.

Everything he'd seen since arriving was so over the top, he wondered if the nice little starter home in Mar Vista he was so proud of was forevermore going to seem like a moldering cardboard box under the First Street Bridge.

The unbearable pain in his heart wasn't gone, and flashes of his life with Yuki and the hallucination of his own suicide still dominated his thoughts, but the tranquilizers smoothed the rough edges of them. He was going to keep a steady load on board for the time being. He was glad Dr. Frolich had given him carte blanche to keep himself sedated—without it, he was reasonably certain he'd be in the hospital, and not voluntarily, as she'd suggested.

He took the Colt out of his bag and regarded it with the detachment of a do-it-yourselfer, taking inventory of his tool chest to make sure he had the right equipment for the next job. But this wasn't a screwdriver or a wrench; it was an instrument of death you hoped you'd never have occasion to use on anybody, including yourself. It was a precaution—a nicely engineered piece of steel precaution, with minimal moving parts, weighing a little over three pounds.

No, it wasn't something you ever wanted to use. Was it?

He stashed it in the empty drawer of a bedside table, then turned at the soft tapping on the door. "Come in, Mel."

She'd worked on her makeup and it completely obscured her black eye. "This is crazy, isn't it? What would it be like to live in a place like this?"

"Lonely, if Rolf is any indication."

"You've been nice to him so far."

"I've always been nice to him. And now he's doing us a favor, so I'm being even nicer. At least I'm trying."

"I feel sorry for him."

"That's exactly what I thought when we came up the driveway. Poor Rolf, what a miserable existence."

Melody made a sour face. "I meant he's going to be really crushed when he finds out we're not interested in being in his movie. We're using him."

"I'm not sure that warrants a crisis of conscience. We're a means to an end for him, too."

"At least he's not deceiving us."

"You could be in his film if you wanted to be. I think you'd be a great actress. What's the harm in trying? Hell, maybe it would pay off, just don't guilt-trip yourself into it."

"He wants *you*. I'm secondary."

"We all want a lot of things we don't get. And we all get a lot of things we don't want. That's life and the quicker you learn that, the better off you are. We might be doing Rolf a favor."

Melody sighed and sank onto the bed. "So what's our plan?"

The question of the day. Sam felt like she'd asked him that a million times, and he was always vamping, looking for answers. It was disconcerting because there was never any improvisation in the Army, with the exception of the battlefield. And maybe that was exactly where he was right now. Get your mind right, soldier.

"We'll go downstairs, drink champagne with our host, take a look at the storyboards. We can chitchat about his cinematic visions or whatever, then I'll get a migraine and go to bed."

"I mean our *plan*. What are we going to do tomorrow?"

The battlefield. Decisive, split-second decisions. "I'm going to the cops in the morning and leaving you out of it. You told me you were going to your friend Rolf's house because you were afraid to stay at your apartment."

"They'll want to corroborate, and Rolf will tell him you were with me."

"No, he won't because I'll tell him the truth, then tell him to keep his mouth shut. He'll love it and probably put it in the script."

"What are you going to tell the cops?"

"I went somewhere to grieve in private."

"Where?"

"I'll think of something when I need to. I'm going to take a steam shower, then let's go down and get drunk on champagne, I'll bet it's the good stuff."

"But you just took a Xanax in the cab."

"It wouldn't be the first time I mixed drugs and alcohol. The way things are going, it probably won't be the last."

"Are you okay, Sam?"

"I honestly don't know."

"Things will get better. You just can't see it now. Knock on my door when you're out of the shower."

After she'd left, he went to the bedside table, got the Colt, and brought it into the bathroom with him. He didn't know why and didn't care. The universe didn't seem to be interested in logic right now, so why should he be?

•

Vivian Easton refilled her wine glass at the kitchen counter and tried Sam again. "Honey, get back to me as soon as you can, *please*. The police called and they're looking for you and they told me Yuki was killed, what's happening?" Hysteria was creeping into her voice, so she paused and took a generous sip of chardonnay. “I love you and I’m here for you. Please call me back.”

She hung up and looked down at her hands, trembling like they wanted to take flight. Panic was putting down roots in the pit of her stomach and scattering her thoughts. Why hadn’t Sam called to tell her about Yuki? Nobody should face something so awful alone, and in spite of his brave stoicism she knew how emotionally fragile he was. The separation had devastated him, cut him to the quick. How was he managing the terrible shock of her murder? And perhaps the most frightening question—why were the police looking for him?

If they thought Sam had anything to do with Yuki’s death, they were wrong, the notion was preposterous. Sam had loved her, been devoted to her. She’d never liked the woman, so cold, abrasive, and imperious; and when Yuki had deserted Sam in his greatest time of need, a genuine hatred for her and her disloyalty had flourished. But her son had never seen it like that, had never blamed her, only himself. She’d demonstrated herself to be a craven bitch, but she hadn’t deserved what she’d gotten.

Another sip of wine, then another and another until the glass was empty. She gazed out the patio doors. Light from a full moon wobbled on the surface of the pool, reminding her of Jack and the hours he’d spent out there, backstroking up and down, with the biggest smile on his face as he lost himself in the soft, warm embrace of the water. He said they were healing waters, a place to remember, a place to forget, a place to just be. He had always been the strong one, deep down, where it counted. She and Sam needed him now.

“Where are you, Sam?” she whispered, redialing his number again and listening to his outgoing message just to hear his voice. She felt the unfamiliar sensation of hot tears on her cheeks while the rest of her body suddenly turned cold as a winter grave.

Maybe Sam couldn’t handle Yuki’s death on top of everything else.

Panicked, she tried the phone one more time to call the one person she knew would answer. “Lee, I think Sam is in trouble.”

Chapter Fifty-seven

WHEN NOLAN GOT BACK TO THE office carrying two fresh coffees, she found Crawford hunched in front of his computer, wearing a scowl that reminded her of a scary Halloween mask. "What a face, Al."

"Just talked to the mother. She doesn't know where he is. She didn't even know the wife was dead. Traeger and Easton have both been off the grid for four hours, that's deviant behavior in this day and age. I told you he was guilty, and Traeger's in deep shit for aiding and abetting."

Nolan could have correctly pointed out that even in this era of digital obsession, four hours without using your phone or credit cards wasn't proof of guilt. But there was nothing to be gained from arguing. Crawford had made up his mind about Sam Easton, and she was still convinced he wasn't a killer. Dialectics about prima facie evidence weren't going to accomplish anything.

"The poor bastard could be sitting in a church grieving for his wife. We've got a car on his house, his phone and cards are flagged, and the BOLO is live. There's nothing else we can do on that end, so stop fixating on it, it's just pissing away time. We've got this morning's Caltrans traffic footage from Yukiko Easton's neighborhood to look at, lab results, and half a dozen more follow-up interviews."

"You really don't think he's guilty, do you?"

"It doesn't matter what I think. Same goes for you." Her eyes picked out Remy as he entered the homicide pen with two other task force detectives. He looked even worse than he had in the parking ramp; but his smile was nice when he noticed her, and as humiliating as it was, her heart quickened when he changed course to head toward her desk.

He gave Crawford a brotherly pat on the shoulder and sank into the metal folding chair situated directly across from her. "So you two caught a double, what's the short version and where does the black Jeep fit in?"

"Abusive boyfriend and unfaithful wife are dead and the chummy significant others disappeared before we could bring them in for questioning," Crawford opined. "Supposedly, there was a black Jeep hanging around both their places."

"Turner took another look, we got nothing for you, sorry."

"Thanks."

"Runners always get caught, don't look so depressed, Al." Remy cocked a quizzical brow at her. "You two aren't on the same page?"

"Why do you say that?"

"You've got a deadpan gaze, Maggie, but your cheeks are pink, like you're pissed about something. I'm guessing you think Al's got it all wrong."

Nolan cursed her fair coloring and felt her cheeks flame hotter. Apparently, her body wasn't quite finished betraying her. Thank God Remy had read it wrong. "I'm not pissed, and what Al said is exactly right. We just disagree about the culpability of the significant others. That's a longer story."

"Cases wouldn't get solved without a little lively discourse."

"Forget about us. What's the news on the bodies at the Rehbein Building?"

"There wasn't enough soft tissue left on the decomposed corpse, so the coroner can't say definitively that it was the work of the Monster, but the victim was female and the damage to her bones is consistent with the knife he uses. Same with Froggy's injuries."

"Do you think it's him?"

"Nothing about it synchs with the Monster's three confirmed kills. It makes more sense that it was the crazy hanging around the Rehbein, flashing a knife at prostitutes."

"What does your gut say?"

"It's him, even if it doesn't make sense."

"What next?"

"We got hits on a few prints from the trace there. No surprise and not earth-shattering—that place is a landing zone for felons—but we're chasing down the leads. Stupid to hope, but I keep thinking one of these days we'll track some prints to a guy who has a bloody KA-BAR sitting on his coffee table."

"That's what he uses?" Crawford asked.

"That's what the coroner says. Big, heavy knife, serrated. You both saw the damage."

"A military combat knife?" Crawford suggested pointedly.

Nolan shot him a cross look. "Or a hunting knife. Common as dirt, I have one myself, picked it up at a military surplus place downtown."

Remy pushed himself reluctantly out of his chair. "So do I, got it as a kid. Good for skinning things down on the bayou."

Nolan narrowed her eyes at him. "You grew up in the French Quarter."

"That doesn't preclude trips to the swamp on occasion."

She kept her expression stony and played along. "I suppose it doesn't, that was prejudicial of me to say. So what sorts of things did you skin down there in the swamp?"

He gave her a rakish smile. "Whatever got in my way. I know what they say, but gator doesn't taste like chicken at all."

Crawford snorted; Nolan rolled her eyes.

"Good luck, you two."

"Likewise."

After Remy left, Nolan buried herself in work, collating reports and cueing up the most recent traffic cam footage. Crawford was uncharacteristically silent and it disturbed her. She'd been prepared for a passionate indictment of Sam Easton, not only a wife and boyfriend killer but now the Monster of Miracle Mile.

After ten minutes, she couldn't stand it any longer. "I know what's percolating in your mind about Sam Easton."

"I'm not thinking about Easton, I'm thinking about whether or not you're really pissed at me."

"Why would you care?"

"I don't care, I'm just curious. Remy's the one who called it, you were blushing. Everybody knows your face gets red when you're on a warpath. And it's okay, you've got a temper and you don't sit on it. It's a fine quality."

"I'm not pissed."

"That's what I thought." He shrugged and leaned back in his chair, a smug smile lifting the corners of his mouth. "One of you will have to transfer, you know. You can't have a relationship with somebody in the same shop."

He'd aced her, and now she *was* pissed off—at herself, for walking into an obvious trap. She wanted to tip over her desk, but she wouldn't give him the satisfaction. A reaction was exactly what he wanted. "I don't have a relationship with Remy."

"Not yet."

"I don't date cops."

He gave her an uncharacteristically cheerful smile. "Then you have nothing to worry about."

"No, I don't, so mind your own business and stop being a shit." She returned her attention to the traffic cam footage, trying to block out Crawford and the juvenile taunts coming from a grown man, married twenty years. How did Corinne deal with his remedial, playground mentality?

The obvious answer, at least from the Freudian perspective of the id, the ego, and the superego, was that she didn't have to deal with it at all. Men in domestic situations were as docile as bunnies; but take them out of that vacuum, give them strength in numbers like they had at the precinct, and they all reverted to their puerile baseline. Their id. Short for idiot? Maybe.

Men are idiots. Remy is a man; therefore, he is an idiot.

Now Crawford had her thinking in syllogisms. This one mildly amused her, but as she toggled through the different street views of the traffic cam footage and saw a dark Jeep Rubicon parked two blocks down from Yukiko Easton's bungalow at ten-thirty a.m., Freud, personal dilemmas, and office politics vaporized into meaningless brain dust. She enlarged the screen, but it was a side view; the license plates weren't visible, and when she back-tracked she was frustrated by a gap in the film. Some kind of interference or temporary camera feed failure. It happened a lot, more than it should.

"Al, call the cops handling Traeger's break-in. See if they've got anything on a black Jeep yet."

"What do you have?"

"Maybe proof you're wrong about Sam Easton. Come here, I'll show you."

Crawford's brows pitched up when he looked at the frame. "Timing could work. Who parked it there?"

"Don't know. There's a gap in the film."

"Fast forward and let's see who gets in."

She did, jumping ahead, watching carefully as cars and people came and went. At two-thirty p.m., a Hispanic woman approached the Jeep casually, slipped behind the wheel, and drove away.

"I'm guessing that's not our killer. Or Melody Traeger's stalker."

"But it might be his vehicle. It's all we have right now, so check in with the cops anyhow. I'll see what other footage we can get from Caltrans."

Chapter Fifty-eight

SAM WIPED FOG AWAY FROM THE bathroom mirror and stared at his face again. He waited, but the red fizz didn't appear on his forehead. The Colt was sitting on the vanity, its surface dulled from condensation. Bad environment for a gun. It was stupid to have brought it in here. The reasons for it were dubious, but he had no compulsion to examine them.

Melody had been so sincere when she'd told him things would get better, and she was correct that he couldn't see it right now. For now, he chose to believe her. Things couldn't get much worse, and the good news was he was still here, elbowing for space on Earth so he would live to fight another day.

He took another palliative dose of Xanax, slipped back into his jeans and T-shirt, then decided to shrug on the button-down he'd grabbed on his hasty retreat from his house. It was the same one he'd worn for his last lunch with Yuki and it felt strange on his skin now, but he hadn't wanted to leave it behind.

Sam walked out into the hallway. Melody's door was closed, but he could hear her humming "The Owl and the Pussycat" again. Either the luxurious accommodations had put her in a good mood or it was something she did when she was nervous, like whistling past a graveyard.

Sam and his escort, Madame Xanax, weren't quite ready to face Rolf and his unbridled enthusiasm yet, so he decided to take a closer look at the vanity gallery. He recognized all the stills from the movies, especially Magda in her Jaguar. Under normal circumstances, he would have been pleased by a glimpse into this private museum of film history, but images of fictitious murders now seemed like a mockery of the real thing. He was sick of death in every incarnation.

He rapped on Melody's door and the humming stopped.

•

They went downstairs and wandered the house until they found Rolf in what could only be described as a living room, lacking any distinguishing features aside from acres of comfortable seating that faced the primary focal point of an enormous fireplace suitable for roasting an ox. Well, maybe not an ox, but definitely a large hog.

It was one of many rooms like it, although they all probably had special designations determined by their utility to avoid confusion, and nothing so lowbrow as "living room." The room with the animal heads would be the Safari Room; the one with the pool tables would be the Billiards Room; the one filled with musical instruments would be the Conservatory. This was the Hog-Roasting Room. There was probably a Crossword Puzzle Room and a Gift-Wrapping Room somewhere, too.

Rolf was standing behind a table laden with an elaborate sushi platter that rested on ice. He beamed at them and sloshed champagne into flutes. Maybe this was the Sushi and Champagne Room. He raised a remote into the air dramatically, clicked it, and a stuttering guitar track filled the room.

"Listen up, this is 'Telegram Sam,' the Bauhaus version!" He did a jerky bop, then started singing along in a raw, off-key voice. "Telegram Sam, you're my main man!" He passed them glasses and held up his own. "Cheers to new friends and the film we're going to make together. It's going to be genius."

Sam took a deep drink. It was excellent.

"Do you like your song?"

He didn't really, but Rolf craved validation. It was pretty clear he didn't get a lot of it anywhere else. It wouldn't kill him to be a gracious guest. "Yeah. I'll put it on my playlist. Hey, does this room have a name?"

Rolf cocked his head in bewilderment. "What do you mean?"

"There are a lot of rooms in your house, how do guests know where to go?"

"You found me, didn't you?"

"Eventually."

"This is the living room."

What a disappointment. Sam pointed at the cloth-covered easel in the corner. "The storyboards?"

"Yeah. Let's take a quick look before we eat." He hustled over, pulled off the cloth, and launched into a lengthy, passionate dissertation. Sam zoned out for the first five minutes, so easy to do when your central nervous system was on a beach somewhere far away. The only thing that brought him out of his anesthetized bliss was the gentle bump Melody gave him with her hip, reminding him to play along.

"So, these linear cells are chronological representations of the scenes in the film," Rolf was saying. "Some of them are hand-sketched, some are computer-generated images. It's like a comic book or graphic novel, and in this format we can move things around to work out the kinks before we commit to production."

Sam was anxious to end the charade as quickly as possible and retreat to his temporary aerie in the rarified skies of Beverly Hills, but the quality of the graphics impressed and intrigued him. "You did all this?"

"Yeah, I love storyboarding. See, this is Dylan in his car in the first scene, and the next one is Bunny dead in the motel room. Then we do a smash cut to the past when Dylan gets hit by a car and suffers a brain injury. That's when all his mental troubles start." He shuffled to the next board. "Here, he meets Bunny at a concert. She's a guitarist for a rock band and pretty messed up herself. They start a relationship and we follow them from there. Most of the film takes place in the past and tells the story of how he ends up in the desert with blood all over him, and why Bunny gets killed and who did it."

"So the beginning is the ending?" Melody asked.

"Yeah. It's meant to challenge the viewers' perceptions of reality through the characters, who are both unreliable narrators, so you don't know what's real or not. I could take you through the rest, but it would really be better if you read the script first. Maybe you can tonight, then you'd have a better sense of the tone and the visuals I'm looking for in the desert."

Melody looked stricken. "I'm Bunny?"

Rolf nodded, draining his champagne and refilling all their glasses.

"So I die."

"Yeah, but you're a main character throughout. Tons of lines."

"And I'm Dylan, the crazy guy?" Sam asked.

"You got it. But we don't really know if you're crazy until the end."

"I can't wait to find out."

"That's the idea. I haven't incorporated those visions you have of how people will die. I'm planning to work on them tonight, but I think it's a solid gold addition that will really add to the uncertainty and anxiety over Dylan's mental state."

Sam swallowed some more champagne, soft and silky, with bubbles as soft as mousse, but it went down hard. "Yeah, it really would."

"Let's grab some sushi and get to know each other a little better. Oh, hey," he grabbed a book off a credenza and presented it proudly. "*Deep into the Dark.* I pulled it from Pops's bookshelf today, I knew I'd seen it before. Lynette Frolich, she's your shrink?"

Sam took the book he saw several times a week on the shelf in her office. He'd only seen the spine, never the cover. It was glossy black with the title embossed in silver, each letter fading at the bottom until it was engulfed by darkness. A representation of dissolution and hopelessness, as depressing a cover as could ever be imagined given the subject matter. "Yes."

"I read it this afternoon. You should read it, too, it's a total mind fuck, all about PTSD. Did you get PTSD from your farm accident?"

"Yeah."

"Dr. Frolich is pretty famous, at least in shrink circles. I might want to incorporate a character like her in the film, too. What do you think?"

"I'm sure she'd be really flattered."

"Can you see now how integral you are to this movie? I mean, you're literally rewriting it."

Chapter Fifty-nine

REMY HAD TRACKED DOWN TWO OF the former felons who'd left their fingerprints on some truly repugnant items from the Rehbein, but they both came up zeroes. One had overdosed a month ago. The second had been thrown back in the can on drug charges and aggravated assault in March, before the Miracle Mile killings had even started. On to the next scumbag.

The third set of prints didn't belong to a scumbag, at least on paper. They hadn't popped because of a criminal history but because he'd served in the military. His name was Ronald Doerr, and his prints had been found on a scrap of paper near Froggy's body. It was the lined notebook variety with wobbly letters and numbers written in blue pen: 3312NVY. Did NVY stand for Navy? That didn't make a lot of sense, he'd been in the Army. A password? An address? A message? Maybe. Some serials liked to leave little notes and mess with investigators' heads.

He expanded his search on Ronald Doerr, and his dim optimism faded to black. He'd been killed in action two years ago, so whatever 3312NVY meant, it didn't matter because he definitely wasn't a suspect.

A dead man's prints at a recent crime scene. Curious, but not really such a mystery. Either Ronald Doerr had been in the building at some point and dropped a piece of paper or somebody who'd had contact with him had been.

He slurped his disgusting, cold, vending machine coffee while frustration festered. They had similar fibers from two scenes that were meaningless without a garment to match, and useless fingerprints. No witnesses, no suspects, no place to go—maybe not until the Monster killed again. But that was a really shitty, defeatist attitude that didn't cut it with the three, possibly four, butchered women who deserved justice, not to mention Froggy. You had to keep moving, keep groping for a thread, any thread. They were out there, you just had to find them.

Expecting nothing, he plugged 3312NVY into a search. Stranger things had broken cases. It yielded a house for sale on Navy Day Drive in Maryland. He refined his parameters to Los Angeles and instead of an address found articles on a Los Angeles-class fast attack submarine. He tweaked his search some more, and five minutes later he found 3312 Navy Street in Mar Vista. The owner's name sounded oddly familiar, so he did a search on the police database and it lit up his computer. There was a BOLO out on the homeowner, courtesy of Nolan and Crawford.

It was easier to call than to run back to the Homicide pen, and Maggie picked up on the first ring. It bothered him that he was thinking of her hair and long legs instead of the reason he was calling, but he pulled it together before he spoke. "Tell me about Sam Easton."

Hesitation. "His wife was murdered this morning."

"He's one of the runners Al mentioned."

"Yeah."

"And you don't think he did it?"

"No. Why are you asking about him?"

"Prints popped on a scrap of paper from the Rehbein, and it had cryptic letters and numbers written on it. I ran some searches and his address came up as a possible match. I just saw the BOLO on him and it seemed like weird coincidence."

"Who do the prints belong to?"

"Ronald Doerr, formerly U.S. Army. He was killed in action two years ago, so that doesn't go anywhere. But when you find Easton, I'd like to talk to him."

"Easton was Army, too. Maybe there's some kind of a connection that can help you."

"I'm hoping. Keep me in the loop, Maggie."

"I will." Nolan hung up and stared at the wall behind Crawford's head, where a spidery crack from the last earthquake was metastasizing, creeping down toward the floor.

"Who's asking about Easton?"

"Remy."

"No shit? What's up?"

"He said a weird coincidence."

"Nobody believes in coincidences, especially not Remy."

Chapter Sixty

UNLIKE ANY OTHER SPECIES ON THE planet, humans possessed the vexing capacity to dwell in the past or speculate about the future, which sometimes made life unreasonably difficult. Tonight, Sam was trying to embrace the gift of lesser creatures: the ability, the purest necessity, of living in the moment. Even in combat, your dense focus on survival was still influenced by your past and thoughts of the future; but if you were a mouse running from a cat, instinct was your only reality, your only tool. There was no past or present, and things became very simple.

He had become that mouse. Life was now and there was no cat, no hallucinations, no blackouts. His world was the drink in his hand, the numbness in his brain. He was being incredibly reckless; but the alcohol, tranquilizers, and the Shangri-La fantasy of the Hesse mansion dulled his mental anguish—the horror of Yuki's murder, his fears about confronting Nolan and Crawford, the real possibility that he might be losing his mind. If Rolf knew how close his script paralleled reality, he'd be dancing a jig.

Rolf had opened up an expansive, luxe room that served as a bar-slash-club, as well stocked and appointed, if not better, than Pearl Club's. Bauhaus was still droning, and Rolf was jerking around to the dark Goth music while he mixed drinks with exotic ingredients like crème de violette and Aperol. It seemed like every five minutes he was gustily pushing a new creation across the bar for their approval, particularly interested in Melody's opinion since she was a real bartender. He was spilling more than he was serving now, and his eyes were bleary and unfocused. Like Melody, his former heroin addiction didn't interfere with ardent alcohol use. Maybe it was a new trend in treatment.

In truth, they were all getting bombed, and Sam knew it was time to slip away. Things were starting to seem a little off-balance, more than a little surreal. And it was getting late, although he'd had no sense of time passing. He was going to be seriously hurting tomorrow morning.

He looked over at Melody, who was watching him with a concerned expression.

"Maybe you should go to bed," she whispered, which wasn't necessary because the music was so loud.

He nodded. Time for a day of horror and questionable decisions to end. "Hey, Rolf," he shouted to get his attention.

"What's up, Telegram Sam, do you need another drink?" he shouted back.

Sam looked up at the ceiling-mounted speakers and made a slashing gesture. Rolf cut the music. "I need to go to bed. If I don't, I'm going to regret it."

"Yeah, it's getting pretty late, and I still have some work to do on the script." He knocked back a shot of something green and licked his lips. "But man, we had fun, didn't we? That's nothing to regret."

"I think it might be. We'll see in the morning."

"Thanks for everything, Rolf," Melody said kindly, her words slurring slightly.

His face twisted in an impish smile. "Hey, before we all hit it, I want to show you something I'm considering using as a set piece in the film. It will really blow your mind."

Sam shook his head, a definitive no. He'd had enough of that action lately.

"The pool with the waterfall?" Melody asked.

"No, this is way better. It really gets the creative juices flowing. Come on, let me take you into Pops's office. It'll just take a second."

They reluctantly followed him down a broad, dim hallway that had a decidedly spooky, haunted mansion feel. He pushed open two double doors and gestured them into a relatively small room—only half the size of a football field—but it was dark and the only thing visible in the ambient light from the hall were book-lined shelves and a massive desk.

Rolf clicked on a switch and a spotlight illuminated a corner, revealing a grotesque, terrifying specter: a life-sized human body stripped down to bone, muscle, and sinew.

Melody screamed, and Sam felt a sudden, startling fury consume him. "What the fuck is wrong with you, taking us to see some fucked-up movie prop before we go to bed? You stupid son of a bitch!"

Rolf's face fell and he backed up a few steps. "It's not a prop, it's a real person. That's why it's so cool. That's why I thought you'd want to see it."

"It's . . . a real person?" Melody squeaked.

"Haven't you heard of Body Worlds? Gunther von Hagens? He's an anatomist who came up with this technique called 'plastination' that preserves bodies. He's really famous and has exhibitions all over the world."

"You think that's cool?" Sam asked in a shaky voice.

"It is cool. It's amazing. Educational. Inspiring. It helped me get off smack, seeing how delicate the body really is."

"This can't be legal."

"Sure it is. All the bodies are donated. This stuff is in *museums*. Pops was able to get one for his private collection because Gunther is a good friend of his."

Sam felt Melody's hand tugging on his arm. "We're going to go to bed now, Rolf. Good night."

He trotted after them. "Hey, look, I'm really sorry if I freaked you out, I just thought . . . people wait in line for hours and hours to see Body Worlds, and half of them don't ever get in. You might never get to see it, and I wanted to give you the chance. And I wanted to know your opinion about how it could work for the film."

Melody turned around. "If your film is a horror movie, it's perfect. I accept your apology, Rolf, but you don't spring things like that on people out of the blue."

"I wasn't thinking. I hope there are no hard feelings."

"We'll see you in the morning, Rolf."

A small woman in a maid's uniform came scurrying down the hall. "Señor, is everything okay? I thought I heard a scream."

"Everything's fine, Consuela, we just had a scare. These are my friends who are staying the night, Sam and Melody."

She looked at them both, and for a very brief moment an expression of horror or shock or both passed over her face. Then it was gone. "You sure you're okay, Miss?"

"I'm fine. Thank you."

She bobbed her head, then rushed away.

Sam knew the look; he'd seen it plenty of times before. Consuela probably felt the same way about seeing his face as he did about seeing a dead body in somebody's office. If you weren't prepared for either one, it was a shock.

"I'm sorry about Consuela, too," Rolf said, watching her retreat down the hall. "That was so rude, the way she looked at you. Normally she wouldn't do anything like that, but she hasn't been herself since she found one of her clients dead."

Chapter Sixty-one

MELODY SAT ON THE EDGE OF Sam's bed and put her head in her hands.

"God, that was so freaky." She looked up at him. Mascara made raccoon rings around her eyes. "I don't think I want to be here anymore."

Sam pulled two bottles of water out of the bar fridge and passed her one. "We can leave right now. I'll call Nolan. I'm sure she'd be happy to pick us up."

"Sam, you're drunk, too, and you don't want to tangle with the cops now."

"Why not? I wouldn't be the first person to get drunk after someone they loved was murdered. And it would explain why I dropped off the face of the earth."

"You can explain it tomorrow. Sleep it off, it will be better that way." She stood up and started pacing. "I was actually having fun until that . . . thing."

"Rolf is an idiot and he's drunk, which compounds the fundamental problem."

"I guess." Melody stepped out onto the balcony and Sam joined her. She pointed to the lights illuminating the windows of a stone cottage below, partially obscured by jacaranda trees. "That must be the guest house."

"Rolf's burning the midnight oil."

"Do you think he has talent?"

"I'm not the best judge, but yeah, I think he does. But he needs to work on his social skills."

"Dylan and Bunny." She shook her head. "We should try to get some sleep."

"Yeah."

"See you in the morning."

"Night, Mel. And if you don't want to be alone, you can always come in here. I'll sleep on the sofa."

"Thanks, I'm okay."

"Just knock if you change your mind."

After she'd left, Sam flopped onto the bed and stared up at the canopy. It made him feel claustrophobic, even in a room this large, and it made his head spin and his stomach roil. God, he'd fucked up, getting drunk. He'd fucked up coming here in the first place, and he had zero confidence in his ability to make rational decisions anymore. It was like that part of his brain had shriveled up and died.

He closed his eyes, which made the spinning and nausea worse. He thought about taking another pill, then decided against it and instead got another bottle of water from the bar and gulped it down. Hangovers were mainly dehydration; hopefully it would help.

There was a knock on the door, one he hadn't been expecting, at least not so soon. "Come in, Mel."

But it wasn't Mel. It was Consuela the maid and she looked upset. Uncertain. Apologetic. But she didn't seem to be horrified by his face anymore because she was looking straight at him with an unwavering, desperate gaze that made him wonder if she was here against her will and wanted help from a stranger to get her out. "Is something wrong? Do you need help?"

"No, no, I'm sorry to bother you . . ."

"You're not bothering me, it's okay."

"I . . . I need to show you something."

Great, somebody else in this madhouse wanted to show him something. "What?"

She looked out into the hall nervously, and Sam gestured her into the room with a reassuring look. "Come in, it's okay. Close the door and tell me."

She did, with obvious relief. "You a friend of Señor Rolf?"

"We just met. He wants me to be in his film. What do you want to show me?"

She started tangling her fingers together like she was trying to knit them. "A room downstairs. Señor Rolf uses many times, for many hours, then locks it, but he don't know I have a key." She scowled in frustration, trying to find words. "Señor Hans worries when he's gone. Señor Rolf had drug problem before, so he give me key to every room."

"So you can check on him, make sure he's not doing drugs?"

She nodded. "It's not normal, him in that room all the time when he has guest house. Acting very secret. I clean the guest house, I think maybe he uses room for bad things. So I go in one day when he isn't here. No drugs, but pictures. I think maybe for his film. But when I saw you tonight, I went back to the room after Señor Rolf went to bed . . ." Tears started rolling down her cheeks.

"Pictures of what?"

"Of you and your friend. There were pictures of Señor Gallagher, too, my client, he just died."

Chapter Sixty-two

WHILE NOLAN WAITED FOR CALTRANS TO get back to her about additional traffic cam footage, she kept rewinding the tape of the woman getting into the Jeep. It was a tiny, poor, low-resolution image. She wouldn't be able to recognize her if she walked into the office right now.

"What are you working on?" Crawford asked.

"I want to ID this woman, but the picture is shit."

"How is a better picture going to help with an ID?"

"It's LA, she could be famous."

"Or she could be one of the thousands of nobodies who drive black Jeeps."

"Could be, but I'm not going to sit on my ass, waiting for a miracle."

"Miracles happen, Reverend Bandy says so."

"Who's he?"

"A televangelist Corinne listens to on Sundays. Drives me nuts, but it makes her happy. She told me a cop's wife can't afford to be agnostic. Kind of ironic since this job is the fastest way I know to lose your faith."

"Nice to have someone praying for you."

"Yeah, it kind of is. Call Ike in Tech. Have him plug the footage into his enhancement software and run it through facial recognition. It might be your miracle."

Ike was still in his office. He was always in his office. Nolan wondered if he ever went home. She didn't know much about him, just that he didn't have a family, he liked to drink, and he kept a bottle of Jack Daniels in his desk. He also didn't say much, which she thought was an exemplary quality. In general, cops talked too much and criminals talked too much. His youthful face was drawn, and he hadn't shaved in a while. He looked like a man with demons, but she'd never know what they were. Another mystery that wasn't hers to solve.

"The facial recognition will take a while, but if you want to hang around for ten, fifteen minutes, I can work up the enhancement for you."

"Thanks, Ike, I appreciate it."

He got up from his desk and moved a stack of files to clear a chair for her. "Have a seat. Do you want a drink? A little Old No. 7?"

"I desperately want a shot of Jack, but I can't, it would put me under." She sat down and closed her eyes while she waited, trying to make sense of Easton's address on a scrap of paper in a shooting gallery where two murders had taken place. An addicted war buddy named Ronald Doerr in town before his final tour, hoping to score some drug money? No, that didn't make sense, the Army wouldn't have taken him back if he had a problem. Of course, he could have cleaned up, or maybe the cryptic note meant something else entirely and had nothing to do with Easton.

To her amazement, she dozed off, jerking awake when Ike waved a printout at her. "This is the best I can do. You should get some rest. You conked out about two seconds after you sat down."

"I'm eternally embarrassed." And she was, but she didn't think Ike would rat her out.

"Don't be, nobody can run on fumes forever, I've tried it."

She got up and took the paper. Ike hadn't had much to work with, but the enhancement was good enough that she instantly recognized the woman who'd gotten into the black Jeep. Consuela Ortiz, the housekeeper who'd found Ryan Gallagher dead.

Chapter Sixty-three

SAM HAD NEVER FELT COLDER, NOT even when he'd lost half of his blood on a dusty roadside in Afghanistan. The room Consuela showed him was filled with vases of white and red roses and plastered with Poke gig flyers and posters. There were countless other pictures of Melody, too: on stage, in her house, entering his house, behind the bar at Pearl, at a nail shop and a grocery store, in her bed sleeping. In some of the photos, she had short black hair and there was no shamrock tattoo on her bicep. Back before Sam knew her. Jesus Christ, Rolf had been following her for years.

And there were photos of him: at the Coffee Bean and Tea Leaf on La Cienega, jogging different streets, sitting beneath a coral tree on San Vicente (yesterday morning?), his official Army portrait; some photos of Dr. Frolich; and more of Yuki, with him, and also with Dawson Lightner—kissing in front of a hotel, tangled together in the bedroom of her bungalow. Photos of a dark-haired man with "Ryan Gallagher" scrawled in black marker at the bottom. There were *X*s over his eyes. There was also a huge whiteboard with addresses, names, phone numbers, life histories. He stumbled to a corner and vomited in a big ceramic vase.

Consuela was sobbing. "I didn't know what to do . . ."

Sam wiped his mouth and stood up. "Call the police, Consuela. I'm going to get my friend Melody, and then we're all going to leave, okay?"

She nodded. "Okay."

They both froze at the voice behind them.

"Nobody's leaving."

Consuela let out a sharp cry and cowered on the floor. Sam spun around and saw Rolf in the hallway, gun raised. But it wasn't a little pea shooter; it was a big military rifle, an M4, the kind Sam had killed a lot of people with overseas. If he pulled the trigger, they'd both be cut to ribbons.

Rolf gave him an odd smile. "I got this gun for you, Telegram Sam. You know how to use one so well, I thought it might come in handy for the film. Do you like my research? It's pretty exhaustive, that's why the script turned out so well. If you'd read the whole thing, you would have known that." He looked down at Consuela, who was grasping the cross at her neck, praying in Spanish. "You really shouldn't have done this, Consuela. This was for my eyes only. It could ruin everything."

She shrieked and curled into an even tighter ball in the corner. Rolf trained his gun on her.

"Put down the gun, Rolf."

"No can do, sorry."

Sam lurched for it, knocking the barrel away from Consuela, then dove when a jagged orange flower flared in the darkness, accompanied by the deafening sound of battle. That was all it took to bring him back to Afghanistan, and everything went dark. Deep into the dark.

•

A scream. Gunfire. Melody jerked up in bed, breathless, with ice in her veins. A drunken dream? A horrible dream, the kind Sam had sometimes? She lay perfectly still, listening. The house was silent.

She slid from beneath the covers, found her phone in her tote bag, and turned it on. She autofilled her password just in case she needed the phone, just in case the scream and the gunfire had been real. Password denied. And denied again and again until she was locked out. Her flesh tingled because this had never happened before. Had there been some operating system breakdown or, more likely, had she been hacked? She thought of the Wi-Fi at Pearl and how willingly and stupidly she'd accessed it and left herself wide open to any number of guests savvy enough to hack her and see what the pretty bartender was doing on her phone.

The thought made her stomach churn, and it also fueled fear—maybe her stalker knew where she was right now. She rummaged frantically in her rollaboard for her gun, buried beneath layers of clothes. When she retrieved it, it wobbled erratically in her shaking hand. At this point, she'd be lucky to hit a building two feet away; more likely, she'd shoot herself in the foot.

Gun in hand, she crawled to the door and listened some more. It was still silent. Part of her felt supremely stupid, another part of her felt a panic so deep that she was afraid it would paralyze her if she didn't move right now. What voice did she listen to this time?

She stood on weak, trembling legs, entered the hall, and tiptoed down to Sam's door. It was open slightly, a slice of light issuing through the crack, painting a warm gold line on the rug. She stood there for a moment, listening to her heavy breath echo in her ears. Hadn't he heard anything? "Sam?" she whispered.

Melody pushed the door open. The bed was empty.

Something was wrong.

That was the voice she was going to listen to, the voice Sam had wanted her to pay attention to. She gathered her strength and courage and moved very quietly out of the room to the staircase.

Chapter Sixty-four

SAM CAME TO SLOWLY, LIGHT AND colors and disjointed images of photos swirling before his eyes, a nauseating psychedelia of malformed input. As far as he could tell, he was still alive and still in Rolf's sick collage room, but his hands were fastened to the back of the chair he was sitting on, his ankles to the legs of the chair, with no memory of how he'd gotten there—just a memory of a loud and grimly colorful burst of automatic gunfire. He didn't feel any pain, no wooziness from blood loss, so he hadn't been hit. But he didn't know how Consuela had fared. He didn't even know if any of this was real.

He tried to yank his hands free, but the bonds held fast. That seemed pretty goddamned real to him, but Rondo had, too, so he still wasn't positive, and he hated and feared the feeling.

"Telegram Sam, welcome back."

Rolf's blurry face and his blurry gun moved into his line of sight and he tried to focus. "Are you real?"

"Flesh and blood real. You really do have some problems. I hope Dr. Frolich and Dr. Guzman can figure them out. I honestly do. You're a good guy. A great man, too."

His vision finally cleared, and so did Rolf, sitting in a sofa across from him, gun resting on his knee. There had been some small consolation in the uncertainty that everything might be a hallucination, a bad dream, like he'd been hoping for when he'd learned about Yuki's murder, but he knew this was reality now. He could see it sitting in front of him; he could smell it in the cordite of a freshly fired weapon that permeated the room. "Where's Consuela?"

"I locked her up in another room."

"The police are on their way, Rolf. Melody would have called them when she heard gunfire."

He giggled. "She can't, her phone is locked. I hacked into it a long time ago, just like I hacked into yours. So, what should we do now?"

The cops aren't *on their way. Bad situation. FUBAR.*

"You should let me go, and then we can talk about this."

"Sorry, but I can't take that risk. You're going to have to talk from where you're sitting. You have strength and skills I don't. It was just luck you blacked out like you did at The Leaf. Consuela helped me get you into the chair. You weigh a lot, but they say muscle weighs more than fat and you're in awesome shape. She's a nice lady. Just so you know, she didn't want to help me, but to paraphrase the Dead Kennedys from 'Holiday in Cambodia,' you'll do anything with a gun in your back."

"Where's Melody?"

"Upstairs sleeping. Passed out probably, so it's just me and you."

Sam felt an impossible weariness, even hopelessness, but beneath it his body was coiling and getting ready to strike; and his mind was sharpening even in desperate fatigue and disorientation, a combat phenomenon. He had a single purpose. If he couldn't snap Rolf in half, he would find a way to get into his head and fuck him up more than he already was. "What are you going to do, Rolf? We can't stay like this forever."

"I guess that's up to you."

Sam stared at him, employing the time-honored strategy of staying silent and letting the bad guy or the mental patient talk, and Rolf was both. He eventually did, it worked every time. Amazing.

"Let me give you a little backstory so you can make an informed decision. I wrote this script for Melody, but I wasn't entirely happy with it. So I rewrote it, but I still wasn't satisfied. It was missing something. The magic. And then you came into her life and everything fell into place. Everything was perfect. Three's a charm," he giggled. "There really wouldn't be much of a film without either of you. You two are special people and I want to tell your story. I need to tell your story. And we can still make it happen, Telegram Sam."

"At gunpoint?"

"I didn't want you to leave, I had to explain things." His eyes moved jerkily around the room. "This is research, and research is important for any film. I can see how it might give you the wrong idea."

"Very perceptive. Ryan Gallagher. Did you kill him?"

His brows lifted curiously. "You think I could actually kill somebody?"

"No. You're a coward, you don't have it in you. I just thought I'd ask."

He glowered and his expression shifted from conciliatory to something impossibly dark and ugly. "Ryan Gallagher was a scumbag who didn't deserve to breathe the same air as Melody. He treated her like dog shit on the bottom of his shoe. You saw what he did to her."

"So you did kill him."

Rolf was getting agitated, and furious red was creeping up his neck and spreading to his skeletal face. "No, I *exterminated vermin* and made the world a better, safer place. Just like you did overseas."

"Did you kill my wife?"

"She was a cheating whore. Another vermin, who didn't deserve to breathe the same air as *you*. But relationships are complicated, and I knew neither of you could do the right thing, so I did it for you. They were acts of compassion, acts of love. I love you both."

Oh my God, Rolf was totally insane. The confrontation with pure madness and corrupted reasoning left Sam so stunned, he couldn't even access any anger or hatred over what he'd done to Yuki, and he was temporarily mute. But the shock eventually wore off, the anger finally came flooding in to replace it, and he thrashed in his chair until he felt the gun pressed against his temple.

"Settle down."

"I will kill you. Don't doubt it."

"When you cool off, you'll realize it was the right thing."

Sam was incredulous. "You don't feel any remorse? Not even a speck?"

"I consider Aldous Huxley one of the great twentieth-century visionaries, and he said that chronic remorse is an undesirable sentiment. I happen to agree with him, so I live my life without it."

"Maybe yours is a better story," he spat. "Why don't you tell that one? Fucked up, sociopathic film student, stalker and murderer. How do you think it would end?"

"I like happy endings."

"Rolf, you're a fucking murderer. People like you don't get happy endings, you end up as somebody's wife in a supermax prison."

"I disagree." He wandered over to the photo of Ryan Gallagher. "This fuck, for instance," he jabbed the gun into the picture, tearing a hole in it. "That was a happy ending. We can still have a happy ending, too, one where I don't go to prison and the movie gets made."

"You're going to have to kill us for that to happen."

"In case you didn't notice, I'm rich, Telegram Sam. Do you know how much I have in my trust fund?"

"No."

"Around fifty million dollars. I could part with ten or so for now. When Pops dies, I'll get another couple hundred mil anyhow. It would be no big deal."

"You want to buy your way out of murder?"

"It's a fair price for all of us. You would be set up for life, and you deserve it. You got dealt a really shitty hand. Plus, I'd give you a percentage of the film for your contribution. Melody and I will get married eventually, so she doesn't need any of it. It's all yours."

"Keep talking."

"Nothing to talk about. I just gave you option A—take my offer, we're good. Option B is I can make the film without you or Melody. It's not ideal, but you both basically wrote the script already, and that's the most important part. If you can't get over your moral qualms, then it's going to be so tragic." He raised his hands in front of his face like he'd done at The Leaf, framing an imaginary movie screen. "Sam Easton, a screwed up vet with PTSD, goes nuts, kills his girlfriend, then turns the gun on himself. Stuff like that happens all the time, it's so cliché, I'd never put it in a movie."

Sam had seen a lot of things, but he'd never seen such a broken mind before. It made his own seem completely unexceptional. Rolf was a monster, there was no other way to describe it. The Monster of Miracle Mile? Why not? He loved to look at the eviscerated body in his father's office; it would be a rush to try it in real life. He was probably planning to write his next script about it. "So we either take your money and make the film or you kill us."

He smiled cordially. "Yeah, pretty much. Seems like an easy decision to me. But Melody definitely needs to be a part of the process."

"No, Rolf, leave her alone."

"She can make her own decision, she's a smart girl. She's getting straight As in her college courses. Did you know that?"

Chapter Sixty-five

MELODY WAS CRAWLING ALONG THE WALL, heading toward the muffled sound of voices—conversational, not confrontational. She felt like an idiot, and wouldn't Rolf and Sam be surprised if they walked out into the hall after a friendly nightcap and saw her on all fours with a gun in her hand? Laughs all around, some good-natured jibes. *Come on, Mel, you need to relax, let's get another drink.*

She stood up, but her legs wouldn't move, wouldn't carry her any further, which was sign enough that she needed to stay concealed for now. It didn't make sense, but it didn't have to. Suddenly a door opened and closed down the hall, and instinct took over.

She dropped again and crawled through a broad archway and into a dark room, then inched her way behind a large ottoman. Perspiration born of fear was running down her face, dripping onto the parquet floor, and a crazy voice in her head told her to *STOP SWEATING! SOMEBODY WILL HEAR IT!*

Muted footsteps were getting louder and she peered around the ottoman. There was a shadow, growing larger as it drew near, and it felt like her heart was climbing up into her throat. The shadow began whistling "Telegram Sam." A moment later, she saw Rolf sauntering down the hall. He was carrying a rifle. She covered her mouth to stifle a cry.

•

Crawford was staring at Ike's printout incredulously. "What the hell?"

"I don't know what the hell, Al, but I tried calling Ortiz multiple times and she doesn't answer. It's late. I'm sure her phone is turned off. Look up the address she gave us and let's go pay her a visit."

"Okay, but you're hanging a lot on a vehicle we can't ID as definitively being relevant to either case."

"It's all we have. Put everything together and it stinks. Sam Easton and Melody Traeger told us about one hanging around their places, then a black Jeep shows up near Yukiko Easton's place the morning she was killed. And then Ryan Gallagher's cleaning lady, the one who found him dead, gets in it and drives away."

"Ryan Gallagher's cleaning lady could have a black Jeep and a client who lives in the neighborhood."

Nolan gave him an icy look. "Possibly, but we're going to find out."

"It's a place to go, I suppose." He shrugged, jumped on his computer, and after a few minutes he looked up. "Ortiz lives up in the Hills. Beverly. A really ritzy address, too."

"She said she had room and board at a client's house. Property records, who owns the house?" Nolan started pacing small circles while she listened to Crawford tapping his keyboard.

"Hans Hesse."

"A big fish. I'll give Beverly Hills PD a courtesy call and let them know we're on the way."

•

Melody waited behind the ottoman until Rolf's whistling was almost inaudible, and then she crept out into the hall and jogged toward the door he'd exited. She froze for a moment, terrified of what she might find behind it. It creaked when she finally pushed it open, and she nearly collapsed when she saw Sam tied to a chair.

"Sam!" she whispered, running toward him, dropping to her knees, trying to untie the ropes. "What's happening?"

"Melody, listen to me. Rolf is in the house looking for you and he has a gun."

"I know, I saw it, what does he . . ." Her eyes drifted up to the walls, to the mad collection of photos. "Oh my God," she choked.

"Look at me. Look at me! Go. Get out of the house, run like hell, and don't stop. Flag down a car, find a phone, call the cops. Tell them about the gun."

"I'm not leaving you, Sam . . ."

"Go. *Now.* Please, Melody, go now. Don't let him see you. Don't let him find you."

Tears mingled with sweat splashed on Sam's face as she leaned in, kissed his mouth, then turned and ran.

Much too late, Sam realized he didn't tell her to close the door behind her.

Chapter Sixty-six

SAM FELT A SHUDDER RATCHET DOWN his spine when he heard Rolf's voice calling softly over and over, "Melody? Where are you? Sam and I want to talk to you about something."

Rolf eventually gave up and stalked into the room, looking panicky. "I can't find her. Where would she go?"

"How the hell would I know? She probably got lost on the way to the bathroom."

"The bathrooms are en suite."

"I was just making the point that it's a huge house. She's probably walking around, chilling out before bed."

He started pacing. "I'm going to go and try and find her again, we need her."

Sam concentrated, willing himself to find focus, to uncover some hidden serene spot in his rioting brain. What would Dr. Frolich tell him to do?

Stay calm. Try to keep him here as long as you can. Buy some time. Save Melody's life, save your life.

"Give her a few minutes, she'll turn up. She's probably looking for us."

Rolf wasn't entirely satisfied, but he stayed, hung in the doorway, scanning the hall. Then he stopped dead and turned to him with narrowed eyes that looked yellow in the light from the hall sconce. Goblin eyes. "This door was open when I came back."

Sam tried to slow his heart. "Yeah, so?"

"I closed it when I left."

"No, you didn't."

"I'm sure I did."

"Hey, I'm tied up here, facing the door with nothing to do but stare at it. I watched you leave. You pulled it shut behind you, but it didn't catch."

He looked uncertain, which could be a good or a bad thing. Good that he was off his game a little, doubting himself, bad that it might cause him to launch into a frothing, homicidal psychosis. But Rolf didn't seem like that kind of out-of-control crazy. He was a worse kind of crazy. "Rolf, why don't you untie me? I'm not going anywhere, not without Melody."

"Can't untie you. I'll give her a few more minutes. You seem like you mellowed out a little."

"I'm tired. I'm distraught. I'm drunk, and there's nothing I can do. Why waste my energy?"

"Is that something they teach you in the military?"

"Yeah." That was a lie, but Rolf wouldn't know. "While we wait, let's chat."

"I already told you, there's nothing to talk about, just a decision to be made and we can't make it without Melody."

"Not about that, about other things."

"Like what?"

"I'm curious and more than a little impressed. You're really smart and organized, you plan things out."

"Thanks. That means a lot, hearing it from you."

"So how did you get to Gallagher? The cops seemed pretty clueless when they came to talk to us about it."

His face lifted. "Easy. He was a coke whore, and I can get any drug you want, anytime. I still have connections. So I took a sublet in the same building, and that along with the drugs gave me the access I needed. Then I referred Consuela to him and duped her key."

He desperately regretted bring up the subject because it led to Yuki. He didn't want to know how that had played out. He didn't need to know, at least not now.

Rolf started pacing again, and Sam had a bad feeling he was running out of time. He'd never deeply contemplated his position on the existence of a higher being, but he was praying hard right now to anything or anybody that would listen. "Tell me about Body Worlds."

Rolf shook his head. "Later. I'm going to go find Melody."

Chapter Sixty-seven

MELODY COULDN'T CATCH HER BREATH. SHE felt like a landed fish, gasping for oxygen on shore. But hyperventilation was the least of her worries. Every door she'd tried so far was either locked or went into a room without egress, and she didn't dare backtrack to the front door. That hallway passed the room Sam was in. And Rolf wouldn't leave him in there alone for long.

Now she was hopelessly lost in a confusing warren of hallways and stairwells. With each failure to find an exit, her panic grew, taking away not just her air but her ability to think clearly. Her brain was like a scattered puzzle she had no hope of putting back together.

She thought about breaking a window, but that would give her position away. Besides, she could slash herself, maybe badly, and bleed out before she could run to get help. The faster the heart pumped, the faster the blood would come, and hers was already a relentless gong in her chest.

She saw a pair of swinging doors at the end of the hall and crept toward them and pushed carefully, wincing when a hinge squeaked. They opened onto a kitchen, surely not the main one; this was smaller. A catering kitchen? A maid's kitchen? At the far end of the room, there was a door that led outside. Hallelujah, she could see leaves fluttering outside the panes of glass. Freedom.

She hurried over to it, looking over her shoulder, listening. She was about to twist the lock and open it when she saw a steady, red eye staring at her from an alarm pad. Of course a place like this had an alarm system. And if she opened the door, it would set it off. She could run fast, especially on the smooth concrete drive, but it was at least a quarter mile long and well lit. Rolf would spot her out in the open before she made it to the street. And he'd stop her.

The alternate route was off-road, where trees would offer concealment; but the grove was dark even with the full moon, and the terrain hilly and uneven. Rolf knew the property. She didn't. Morton's Fork: two choices leading to equally bad conclusions. But there were no other options. She had to take the chance.

She placed her hand on the knob, then froze when she heard Rolf's voice, coming from her right, close, too close.

"Melody, Sam and I need your opinion on something . . ."

If she went now, she wouldn't even have a head start, so she bolted to the left into a smaller hallway, passed a pantry, then a bathroom, and paused to listen. His voice was getting closer.

•

Nolan parked in front of a high, ornate gate set into tiled stone posts. An even higher iron fence fronting the property was almost entirely concealed by lush bougainvillea. Like his neighbors with equally secretive street facades, Hans Hesse valued his privacy.

"Think there's castle with a moat on the other side?" Crawford asked.

"Probably a double-wide trailer."

He chuckled. "I hope we get to find out." He unclipped his seatbelt, got out, and pressed the call box button. Waited. Pressed it again and again. Waited some more, then got back in the car.

"Nobody's answering."

"I cleverly deduced that. Try the main house again."

"I called the whole drive here, which took fifteen minutes longer than it should have because of that asshole who rammed into a traffic light on Sunset. Come on, Mags, it's late, this is going to have to wait until morning."

She saw headlights in the rear view mirror. A few moments later, a Beverly Hills squad pulled up next to them and the window opened.

"Detectives?"

Nolan assessed the patrol's face, washed pale from the light of his dashboard. Thirty maybe, with bright, eager eyes. Hopeful for some action, something to break up a boring night shift in paradise, she decided. "Hi, Officer . . . ?"

"Bell. I've been trolling the neighborhood, waiting for you. What's the situation?"

"We have reason to believe a person of interest in at least one homicide is here."

"Dangerous?"

"No reason to think so, otherwise I would have been over that fence five minutes ago."

Half his mouth lifted, like he didn't want to fully commit to a smile. "I hear you. No one's responding at the house?"

"No. Anything happening around here?"

"So far, just a barking dog call."

It was Nolan's turn to half-smile. "We're going to stick around for a while and keep trying."

"Thanks for the heads-up and good luck. Shout if you need anything, I'll be around."

Nolan sighed and put her head on the steering wheel. "This is so damned frustrating. Ortiz is here, we just can't get to her."

"That's exactly why people have gates and why the Constitution has a Fourth Amendment. And you're talking about Ortiz like she's going to break the case."

"Maybe she will. Run her name. See if she owns a black Jeep."

"What's the point?"

"If the guys on Traeger's break-in finally come up with an ID and it matches . . ."

". . . it still wouldn't be exigent circumstances, so stop looking at the damn fence like you're going to jump it. We are not getting in there without permission or a warrant."

"Try the call box again."

•

Somehow, Melody had managed to put a little distance between herself and Rolf and she was huddled in a tight vestibule, pondering the door there. It was an interior door, but now she was so terrified of alarms that she was doubting everything. She finally squeezed her eyes shut, turned the knob, pushed, and a loud chime rang. And rang and rang.

Jesus Christ, she'd set off an alarm and now she was dead. She launched through the door because there was nowhere else to go, tripped down some steps, and landed on a concrete floor. Bright stars swam in her vision as a searing bolt of pain radiated from her ankle up her right leg, pulsing with each beat of her heart. She bit down hard on her lip, trying to keep the instinctive, almost irrepressible cry of pain inside; took deep breaths like you were supposed to do in yoga—and smelled gasoline. A garage?

The pain is the least of your worries. Ignore it. Get your bearings. Find a way out.

The chiming stopped and there were no other sounds. Not footsteps, not Rolf's voice. As her eyes adjusted to the gloom, she made out the hulking shapes of cars, dozens of them. On a far wall was a faint square of light—a window in a man-sized door.

She crawled under a car and waited for what seemed like years. If the chime had been an alarm, Rolf would have come running by now. Surely the alarm system would tell him which door had been opened. But there was nothing but silence. That gave her the courage to crawl out and toward the door.

Why are you crawling toward the door? If you open it and the real alarm goes off, you sure as hell aren't going to outrun Rolf with a jacked ankle. You couldn't even outrun a snail.

Tears burned her eyes as she sagged back against the tire of an SUV. An SUV that might have keys in it. She couldn't run, but she could drive.

Chapter Sixty-eight

SAM LET OUT A RAW SHOUT of frustrated rage that made his ears ring. He was powerless, surrounded by inconceivable sickness—by stolen, private images of himself and people he cared about: his dead wife, Melody, and even his doctor. Their eyes were accusing. They had every right to be.

You're a prisoner, in every way—in this room, in your head. Because you're weak. Damaged. Helpless. Pathetic. Useless. You blacked out instead of fighting. All your men died, war hero, *so why are you still here? What's the point?*

He had to get out of these goddamned ropes. That was his only mission. To be successful, he had to go to another place and block out everything else: the eyes, his own cruel, chiding voice, his fears, his past. His father had told him that sometimes you had to find peace where it didn't exist in order to get a job done. The peace didn't have to be enduring. It didn't even have to be real. You just had to believe it was. That's how you won the fight.

Sam focused fiercely, channeling all his energy to the ropes. His fingers burned, bitten by the rough hemp he was trying to untangle, but at some point he felt a knot start to give. The brief time Melody had spent working on it had loosened it, maybe just enough. In a minute, his right wrist would be free. He visualized it and he believed it. He was going to win this fight.

When the chime sounded in the quiet house, Sam leapt in his chair and almost toppled over. If it was an alarm, it wasn't like any he had ever heard. And it was erratic. A gate bell? Or was it a notification that a door had been breached? If that was the case, it meant Melody had gotten out, Rolf knew it, and he was after her right now.

He redoubled his efforts. Maybe he was beyond saving, but Melody wasn't.

Win the fight.

•

Melody braced herself against the SUV for balance and stood up on her good leg, then tested her ankle. Bad idea—high voltage pain shot through her body and made her vision swim. But she had to fight through it because she had a plan now. She wasn't going to die in this garage.

She pressed a cheek against the cool, black steel for comfort and waited for the throbbing to subside. With each breath, the sharp scent of gasoline burned her nose, reminding her of Aunt Netta's Thunderbird, of Sam's Shelby.

When the pain eased a little, she tested the door handle and it opened. A dome light clicked on, illuminating the interior. No keys in the ignition, no keys beneath the floor mat, no keys in the console. She climbed in and opened the glove box. No key there, either, just an owner's manual. For a 2020 Jeep Rubicon.

Melody scrambled out of the Jeep as if it was incubating some fatal, contagious disease. Things started coming together piece by ugly piece, filling in a nightmare that started with Rolf. How would it end?

She glanced at the man-sized door again. The answer was there. It had to be. She stared at it until her eyes ached, and then a tiny flame flickered in her mind. It was just a dim glow in her mental shadows at first, but it flared and grew brighter and suddenly she heard Aunt Netta.

There are two ways out of every trouble. The right way sometimes isn't the one you think of first.

The door *was* the answer. It had been all along, but she'd initially only seen it through the lens of a desperate, panicked person—as an escape, nothing else. But now she could see the right answer clearly. She would open the door and set off the alarm. Rolf would run to the source, see the open door, and chase after her. He'd never guess that she would be hiding under a car, watching his feet run past her, inches away.

It wasn't perfect, but it was all she had.

She hobbled to the door, took a deep breath, and pushed it open. In an instant, a deafening wail filled the garage and she slid beneath the Jeep.

•

"Okay, Mags, we're officially wasting time here. Get us out of here and stop somewhere for coffee."

Nolan was too tired to answer or argue, and really, why should she? Either nobody was home or they simply weren't answering. And he was probably right about the Ortiz angle not going anywhere. A woman getting in her car, big deal. She started to pull away just as the house alarm went off.

Crawford rolled his head to look at her. "I guess you just got your exigent circumstances. You think we can actually get over the fence?"

"Damn right we can. I've been studying it for the past hour."

•

. . . *death, on shadowy and relentless feet.*

That's what Melody thought of as she held her breath and watched a pair of purple Converse sneakers race past in the dim light, close enough to stir the air in front of her face. A poem she couldn't remember, a terror she wouldn't forget.

The alarm was silent now, so she could hear footfalls smacking the driveway. When they faded, she released her breath and scuttled out from under the Jeep. Her ankle was on fire now, and it certainly wouldn't bear very much weight, so she used the front bumper to push herself up off the floor. That's when she noticed the damage. The Jeep had hit something.

Or somebody.

Katy Villa had been killed by a black Jeep. By this one?

Melody stumbled backward and limped as quickly as she could into the house and down a hall she hoped would lead her to Sam.

Chapter Sixty-nine

SAM COVERED HIS HEAD AND DROPPED to the floor when the alarm started whooping. He couldn't forestall the reaction any more than he could stop breathing, and the thrill of freeing himself from the ropes contracted, making way for images of war.

The same thing had happened when Rolf shot the rifle, but this time he didn't black out. In fact, the images seemed to hit an obstacle and began to recede. He couldn't envision the obstacle, but he knew it was Melody. Amazing. He could fight for someone else, just not himself. Maybe that revelation would be important in the future, but it wasn't important now.

The alarm went quiet. Rolf had canceled it before the cops would be called and now he was outside with his gun, chasing down his quarry. Sam vaulted up off the floor, ran full speed down the long central corridor to the foyer, and vaulted up the stairs three at a time. He felt like he could fly.

He grabbed his Colt and extra clips, checked his phone—locked, as Rolf had promised—then raced back down the stairs to the front door. Rolf was a dead man. He might know his own property, but he didn't know shit about ambush tactics. He was going to surprise that little fucker and unload everything he had because Rolf was the enemy, and the enemy had to die . . .

"Sam!"

He spun around and saw Melody leaning against the wall, doubled over in pain, and his heart seized. "Mel, what happened, are you all right?"

"Twisted my ankle. Bad."

It was puffy and triple in size, turning purple. He scooped her up in his arms and carried her into the first room he came across: the Safari Room, with animal heads on the wall and a green velvet sofa. He stuffed what was probably a thousand-dollar pillow under her calf. "Keep your leg elevated. Is Rolf outside?"

She nodded and winced in pain. "I tricked him, but I don't know how long he'll look for me."

Sam gazed up at an antelope, its glass eyes fixed on him judgmentally. "Stay here, I'm going to go get him."

"No! You have no idea where he is, and he has more firepower."

"That doesn't mean shit."

Melody grabbed his hands and squeezed them hard. "It does to me, Sam. Stay inside and go find a phone. There have to be a million of them in here."

Sam was so jazzed for battle that it took a moment for the blood lust to clear his system. She was right. It would be easier to defend the house and it was his best chance to keep Melody safe. "Okay, but you're coming with me."

"I can't walk, I'll just slow you down."

"No you won't, you're going to be an extra pair of eyes. Hang on tight." He scooped her up again, cradled her like a baby against his chest, and ran from room to room in a dark, strange house, looking for a lifeline. He hadn't wanted to go back to the ugly place, but Sam reasoned that if Rolf spent so much time in it, there might be a phone.

He found a mobile in a box beneath a desk. He turned it on and the screen came to life, displaying a picture of him and Yuki mugging for the camera in Venice Beach, the day he'd bought her sunglasses. A waiter had taken it for them and it had been her home screen ever since.

Sam punched in her password, praying to God Rolf hadn't messed with her phone, too.

•

Nolan and Crawford were skirting the driveway, staying close to the tree line, their guns drawn. The alarm was silent now, and their ears were honed to the slightest sound. When they flushed a startled bird out of a cypress, they both dropped and aimed.

Nolan could finally see part of the house now, but there were still too many damn trees, too many places to hide. It was worse than a parking garage. She wasn't expecting to confront burglars. The alarm had been shut off promptly, which meant someone was inside; but that didn't take the edge off, nor should it. Always assume the worst, hope for the best.

She and Crawford froze when they heard a rustle in the trees. Not a bird, not even a coyote, something bigger. A twig snapped. Assume the worst.

"LAPD, freeze! Hands up! Come out from your cover!"

A skinny kid with terrified, buggy eyes moved slowly out of the woods, his hands up. "You scared the hell out of me," he said shakily.

"Who are you?"

"Rolf Hesse. I live here."

Nolan lowered her gun. "Do you have an ID?"

"Sure. It's in my back pocket, okay if I get it?"

Nolan nodded. "Go ahead."

He passed her a California driver's license that checked out. "I'm sorry we startled you, Mr. Hesse, we heard the alarm. Is everything okay?"

"Yeah, fine. The alarm was my fault. I was letting my cat in and forgot I'd already armed the system. It scared the bejesus out of poor Bunny, so I'm out here looking for her, I've got to get her in. Coyotes, you know? They've been bad this year." He looked at their clothing. "You're not cop-cops, you're detectives."

"Yes."

"Cool. Are you on a sting or something?"

"Just following up on some things in the neighborhood."

"Like a robbery ring? Drugs? Human trafficking?"

"We really can't say," Crawford put in, a touch of amusement in his voice.

He shrugged. "Yeah, I know. I ask a lot of questions, I'm a filmmaker, I get ideas everywhere. You never know what goes on behind closed doors, right?"

"No, you never do. Mr. Hesse, does Consuela Ortiz live here?"

"She's the housekeeper. God, she didn't do anything wrong, did she?"

"We'd just like to speak with her. Is she here now?"

"No, she went to visit family. In Ensenada, I think."

"When did she leave?"

"I don't really know, I've been busy working on a film. She asked me a couple days ago if she could have some time off and I told her yes."

"Sorry to bother you, Mr. Hesse. I hope you find Bunny."

"I will, I have to. She means everything to me."

•

Scaling the fence wasn't any easier on the way out, and once they were in the car, Crawford started complaining bitterly about a pulled muscle. "Goddammit, it's my adductor again."

"Again? What did you do to it the first time?"

"Waterskiing. I thought I'd be cool and drop off, skim right up to the dock. Instead, I did the Chinese splits and got a Lake Arrowhead enema."

"Ouch."

"There are no words. Do we have a cold pack?"

"There might be one in the kit. You want me to check?"

"Yeah. And grab me some ibuprofen. If there's anything stronger, bring that."

Nolan smirked as she rummaged through the medical kit in the trunk. Men were such babies. A cold or a pulled muscle and they were in bed for a month, whining like croupy infants. What she couldn't figure out is why, when they got shot or stabbed, they were damn near profiles in courage. Maybe she should spare Corinne and shoot Al in the leg.

She tossed him a cold pack and a bottle of baby aspirin.

"Baby aspirin? Are you kidding me?"

"Look at the bright side, you won't stroke out on the way to intensive care for your pulled muscle."

"Laugh all you want, but I have thorns in my ass, too. Rats nest in bougainvillea, I could have bubonic plague in my system right now."

"You're on your own with that one."

"Why are you wearing that weird, scrunchy face?"

"Just thinking."

"God help us."

Nolan draped her arms over the steering wheel and looked up at the fence. There was a lot of missing bougainvillea where they'd gone over; she didn't doubt Crawford had thorns in his ass, she'd gotten nipped herself. She wondered if the Hesses would sue the department for vandalism. In her experience, rich people got indignant over really petty things and were litigious about it. Probably because they could afford lawyers. "The house alarm is set. The place is locked up for the night, including the gate. We go moseying up the driveway, and Mr. Inquisitive never asked us how we got in."

"He knew how we got in, it was the only way."

"That would be worth a mention, wouldn't it? Like, 'Hey, how come you two detectives climbed my fence in the middle of the night? Kind of overkill for responding to a false alarm, don't you think?'"

"You'd better hope he doesn't ask that question. We're on pretty thin ice here."

"That doesn't raise a red flag for you?"

"Sure it does, but he's young. Kids his age, their brains haven't fully developed yet. And he's been drinking, we're lucky the fumes coming off him didn't ignite. Combine the two and you've got nothing but meat with eyes."

Nolan made a U-turn and headed back toward Sunset Boulevard. She slowed when her phone rang, then slammed on the brakes when she saw the caller ID.

"Jesus, take it easy, Mags, I'm not buckled in yet . . ."

"This is coming from Yukiko Easton's phone." She put it on speaker. "Detective Nolan."

"This is Sam Easton we're at Hans Hesse's house in Beverly Hills his son has an automatic rifle he killed Yuki and Ryan he's going to kill us . . ."

Nolan flinched at a whimper in the background, then heard Melody Traeger's voice: "Oh my God, Sam . . ."

The line went dead.

Chapter Seventy

MELODY'S FACE WAS GHASTLY WHITE, HER eyes foggy and unfocused. She looked shocky. "He killed Ryan and Yuki?"

"It's going to be okay, Mel, the cops will be here soon."

"Sirens," she mumbled. "They'll chase Rolf inside and I didn't lock the garage door behind him, Sam. Goddammit, I forgot to lock the door. That's the way he went out, that's the way he'll come back in."

Sam was positive Rolf would be able to get into his own house when he wanted to; he would have control of the security system through his phone. But he might not have his phone, so every locked door might be a temporary blockade until the police arrived. "Show me where."

"I don't remember, I was lost." Her voice was climbing up the panic scale.

Sam picked her up again. Her skin felt clammy against his. "The front façade of the house was visible when we drove up and there was no garage, so it must be in back." He started jogging in the general direction. "Concentrate, Mel. Tell me if something looks familiar."

"Everything was a blur," she said, her voice bouncing along with his gait. "But I went through swinging doors into a kitchen. A small kitchen, like a maid's kitchen. There's a hallway to the left of it. That's where I found the garage."

A pair of swinging doors in a vast maze. But a maid's kitchen would be in the back by the garage, so he was heading in the right direction. "Do you remember anything else? Artwork, furniture, something you noticed?"

"There was a room with a piano."

The Conservatory. Sam stopped when he came to a literal fork in the road. Three hallways shot off in different directions. Door number one? Door number two? Door number three? "Do you remember this?"

"No, but I'm left-handed, so I would have gone left."

Sam started jogging again, and Melody stiffened in his arms. "There! The room with the piano! From here, I went straight ahead."

The swinging doors became visible in the gloom, and he followed Melody's directions down a tight hall and into a vestibule.

"This is it, Sam!"

They both froze when they heard a door slam shut just beyond where they stood. Rolf was in the garage, coming inside. No time, no time at all. Sam could hide in the shadows and shoot him when he came in, but he didn't want to do it in front of Melody, couldn't do it in front of her. That left one option.

RUN.

Sam engaged the deadbolt of the interior door, then turned and flew down the hallway toward the front of the house, holding Melody tight against his chest. He heard Rolf thudding on the door—it was a loud, sharp sound, the sound of the rifle stock being used as a battering ram. And then a short burst of fire. The crack of splintering wood. Footsteps pounding behind them.

He was too close. If Sam took a wrong turn, just one, they would be trapped. And dead. At this point, Rolf wouldn't want to talk about their options. He'd want to silence them and stash their bodies before the cops arrived. And the Colt, even wielded with all the proficiency in the world, still wasn't a match for an M4; Melody had been right about that.

Speed was his only advantage, but he couldn't run any faster without using his arms. Melody seemed to sense this because she started to squirm.

"Hide me and get help," she whispered.

"No." He tightened his hold on her and pushed harder, almost stumbled when he saw the front door ahead. Thirty feet, twenty, ten . . .

He became a terrestrial rocket man, launching out into the starry, moonlit space of a warm night that smelled like a Tuscan honeymoon. He ran faster than he ever imagined he could, even without using his arms.

Chapter Seventy-one

NOLAN WAS CRAB-WALKING THE MARGIN OF the driveway, sweating under the weight of the tạc vest and rifle. When you heard automatic fire, you geared up for war. Max was with her, applauding her bravery, but conversely chastising her for being impulsive and not waiting for backup that was minutes away—and for her lousy form and clumsiness under tactical gear.

But his criticism was benevolent and joking because he'd always told her she was as good as anybody in the family who'd come before her. Fuck the people who said any different, she was just fighting a different kind of battle.

She froze when she heard another burst of gunfire, and an icy cold squishiness seized her gut. It was a totally unfamiliar sensation, but her heart knew it was the abject terror of realizing you were straddling the gossamer line between life and death. Every single movement from now on had to be deliberate and decisive. No room for error, no room at all.

A sob clutched her throat as she thought of Max again. He had felt this same way, over and over. She should have asked him about it, how he dealt with it, but she hadn't known enough back then, and now he was dead and she and Al and Melody and Sam might join him if she didn't . . .

"MOVE!" she hissed, waving Al forward. He flanked her right side and dropped to the grass. He was better at this than she was. Of course he was—he had ten years on her and outranked her by two grades. But he trusted her enough to let her take lead.

Please God, don't let me get us killed.

As she signaled him to stay back and cover her, a third staccato salvo shattered the serene Beverly Hills night, much closer now. Pure instinct took over and she charged mindlessly up the hill of the drive, praying she wasn't too late to make a difference for somebody. She hadn't been able to save her brother, but goddammit, she was going to save somebody tonight.

She almost fired when a man crested the hill and came racing toward her; but before she inched the trigger back, he entered a corona of light from one of the lamps that lined the driveway and she recognized Sam Easton, recognized the cargo he was carrying, held close to his chest: Melody Traeger.

And then more gunfire, white and orange star-shaped blooms, now visible in the dark. Sam dove into the cypress with Melody. Nolan aimed at the retinal memories of deadly flowers and emptied her weapon.

•

Sam crawled along the tree line opposite and parallel to Nolan and Crawford, head rotating, his body rigid. It had been a long time since he'd been battle-ready, honed for a firefight and intoxicated by adrenaline, that magical, life-saving hormone. He didn't know if it felt good, but it felt right.

But there would be no firefight tonight. At the top of the hill, they found Rolf sprawled on the driveway, pale and semiconscious, bleeding heavily from a ragged hole in his arm. It shone black and oily in the faint illumination of a landscaping light.

Sam knelt down and felt his neck, his thready pulse. He couldn't shoot him in front of the cops, didn't even know if he had the will to anymore, but he was going to keep this son of a bitch alive to face prison. He ripped a sleeve off his shirt, the last thing Yuki had touched before she'd left him, and staunched the wound. "Rolf? Rolf!"

Nolan crouched beside Sam and checked for other injuries. "I hit his leg, too. *Shit.* There's too much blood. Crawford, get that gate open for the ambulance! Pull the cotter pins, knock it down with the car, just get it open! Jesus Christ," she whispered, pressing down on the wound to his leg.

Sam patted his cheek lightly. "Rolf! Wake up!"

His eyelids fluttered, but didn't open. "Telegram Sam?"

"Yeah, Rolf. Hang in there, there's an ambulance on the way."

"This is going to be one bitching movie," his voice was weak and fading.

"Sssh, save your breath, Rolf."

"Where's Melody?"

"I'm right here, Rolf." Melody was hobbling toward them, tears running down her face.

Rolf opened his eyes and his mouth trembled. "I'm sorry . . . things . . . didn't work out . . ."

Melody knelt down. "Stay with us, Rolf."

His eyes closed again. "Will you hold my hand?"

"Stay with us," she repeated, looking away.

"Please."

After a long moment, she took his hand and squeezed it tight, held it until he shuddered and went still.

Chapter Seventy-two

IN THE BACK SEAT OF THE detectives' sedan, Melody leaned against Sam, her head on his chest, silently soaking his ruined shirt with warm tears. Of all the harrowing things she'd endured in the past few days, the reluctant communion with Rolf at his end would probably be the one that would haunt her the most.

He knew what it felt like to hold somebody's hand as their life departed. It was a shocking, devastating intimacy that stirred the deepest, most elemental sense of being, and of not being. You became small, utterly insignificant when you felt death settle, felt the crushing finality as it traveled from their fingers to yours. Mortality ceased to be an abstract concept, and what that person had been in life, good or bad, didn't affect the impact of that grim revelation.

Sam looked out the partially open side window. The night was splashed with stuttering rainbows of emergency lights, loud with voices and the crackle of transmissions emanating from shoulder units as people told other people what to do.

Countless law enforcement and crime scene personnel had overtaken the property, which was now festooned with yellow tape and guarded at intervals by grim-faced police officers. The entire neighborhood was probably out on the street, hoping for a glimpse of whatever misfortune had befallen one of their own, but the barricades had been set back so far that nobody would be seeing anything. News choppers were trolling the skies, but their view wouldn't be much better for all the trees sheltering the property. The sequestration wouldn't last, and neither would any semblance of privacy for anyone involved, no matter how carefully this was managed.

Sam wondered if the Berlin police had contacted Hans Hesse yet—and if he'd even had an inkling of what his son had really been. He'd been complicit in creating him, there was no exoneration for him in that regard. Still, he felt sorry for him and would until the day he decided to exploit a tragedy and make a movie about it. Hopefully, he wouldn't, although whether it was Hans Hesse himself or someone else, it seemed inevitable.

He saw Nolan duck beneath one of the plastic barriers and walk down the driveway, her expression flat and immutable as her face pulsed under the strobing lights. She engaged in brief conversations with some of the people on the ground, then walked through the gate and slipped into the driver's seat of the sedan.

"Consuela Ortiz is okay. We found her tied up in the wine cellar."

Sam let out a breath. "Thank God. I was afraid he killed her."

Three pairs of eyes followed the wrecker coming down the driveway with the Jeep. "The coroner found black paint chips on Katy Villa's body. We're guessing they're going to match."

"It will. Rolf was following me. You saw the photo from San Vicente. Katy Villa was an accident, a distracted driving accident," Sam said bitterly, pinching his eyes shut, trying not to think of the lives lost because of him.

Because of Rolf, not you.

Dr. Frolich's voice was loud and clear in his head, and she was right. Maybe she'd be able to talk him down from the ledge of survivor's guilt after all.

When he opened his eyes again, Nolan was watching him.

"Thank you both for taking us through the scene," she finally said. "I know it was difficult." Her gray eyes softened and she passed back a box of tissues. "How is your ankle, Ms. Traeger?"

Melody straightened and wiped her eyes. "Better. The cold pack is helping."

"You should get an x-ray."

"It's just a sprain."

"Maybe so, but you should still have it looked at. I can have somebody take you to the hospital now, or I can drop you off when we're finished here."

"Thank you."

"No problem."

"I mean thank you for saving us."

"From what you both told me, you saved each other. And what you did for Rolf? In your position, I'm not sure I could have done the same."

"You would have. He was a human being and he was dying, that's all he was when I took his hand."

"It was an act of grace, Ms. Traeger. And same for you, Mr. Easton."

"Trying to keep Rolf alive definitely wasn't an act of grace on my part."

She nodded her understanding.

"What happens now, Detective?"

"I have a couple more things to tie up, then Detective Crawford will stay to finish up here and pass it off to Crime Scene. We go back to the station for more details and statements. Sorry, but it's going to be a long night."

Sam leaned back and closed his eyes, stroking Melody's shoulder as much for his own solace as hers, like a child caressing a stuffed animal after a bad dream. "How did you get here so fast?"

"It was dumb luck. We'll get to that before the night is over."

Melody leaned forward confidentially and captured Nolan's gaze. "You told me you don't believe in luck, Detective."

"I'm reconsidering that statement."

Chapter Seventy-three

CRAWFORD WAS STIRRING SUGAR INTO HIS sludgy, Homicide-brewed coffee, shaking his head. "This is absolutely insane. A fucking screenplay started this. Christ, LA is messed up."

"An obsession started it, and that can happen anywhere."

"Whatever. If the kid had made it, he'd really have something to write about while he was doing life in Pelican Bay."

They'd brought Remy in to brief him on the possible Monster connection during their break and he was still in the room, intermittently tapping a pen on the edge of a table. "That's exactly what's going to happen, you know. Movie deals, book deals, offers nobody can refuse. Who's going to be the first to sell out?"

"It won't be anybody here," Nolan said more sharply than she'd intended.

"I know that. What about Easton and Traeger? A bartender and a bar back looking at life-changing money? I'd be tempted."

Crawford slurped his coffee and winced, either from the scalding temperature or the horror of how bad it was. "More power to them, I say. They went through hell, why not get something besides nightmares out of it?"

Nolan felt the familiar heat of blood rushing to her cheeks. "Easton and Traeger aren't going to take money for something that almost destroyed them, Al."

He met her eyes and the creases that had lately been eating up the real estate around his mouth softened and lifted with a small smile. "Yeah, I believe you, Mags. But the fallout is going to be nasty. Once everything comes out, they're not going to have any peace for a long time, and no way Easton will be able to lay low with his face. How is this going to affect him? He's already in tough shape."

"He'll get through it." She looked at Remy. "So what do you think about his Rolf Hesse as Monster theory?"

"It's a good one, I couldn't make up a better suspect. We're looking into it hard, but I don't think it will go anywhere."

Crawford rubbed the stubble on his jaw. "Why not? Hesse was a freak and a heroin addict. He'd been following Traeger for years, Easton for six months; he probably carried around Sam's address like some people carry rosary beads. It could explain the piece of paper from the Rehbein."

"But it doesn't explain why the dead guy's prints were on it. Ronald Doerr was killed way before Easton was on Rolf Hesse's radar, so there's zero connection there, but Doerr and Easton served together in the same unit, and that bugs the shit out of me. I still want to talk to Easton. Are you almost finished with him?"

Nolan nodded, then gathered her computer and a bundle of files. "I'll send him your way before I cut him loose."

Crawford pushed himself up, but she dismissed him with a wave. "It's just wrap-up, Al, I'll take it from here. Go home and bother Corinne, she might actually miss you by now. She'll change her mind if you start bitching about your adductor, so try to keep your mouth shut."

"Mags is going to be fine," he said after she'd left.

"I have no doubt about that." Remy's dark eyes cycled around the room absently, looking beyond the present, or maybe back into the past. He did that sometimes, and Crawford had always found it disconcerting, like he knew something nobody else did.

"She's tougher than anybody I know. And mean."

Remy laughed. "You think she has a mean streak?"

"Maybe you should partner with her and find out for yourself."

"And ruin the pleasure of listening to you two snipe at each other? I don't think so." His smile faded. "Still, it's a big thing, killing. Blood always runs red, and it's a color you don't forget."

"Spoken like a man who's shed some. Bayou wisdom?"

"Something like that."

Chapter Seventy-four

AFTER REGURGITATING EVERY DETAIL OF THE past twelve hours for Nolan and Crawford, and clarifying some things preceding the ignominious visit to the Hesse mansion, Melody was dozing restlessly on an unyielding vinyl sofa in the conference room. Sam was somehow still upright, sitting across the table from Nolan. Crawford hadn't returned after the last break, which gave him hope that things were coming to a close and he could go home soon.

He felt delirious, but not crazy, hallucinating, blackout delirious. He wasn't stupid or insane enough to believe that another trauma was the remedy to healing from a previous one, but he felt a little better in spite of everything, like he'd reclaimed a small piece of himself that had existed before a roadside bomb had shredded bone and flesh and his tether to this world. He'd made it through this nightmare without falling apart when it really mattered. He'd won the fight. Melody had saved him; he'd saved Melody; and in the end, Yuki and Nolan had saved them both.

For the first time in a long while, he wasn't worried about what would happen tomorrow. He was alive and that was good enough for now.

One day at a time.

He'd have a chat with Melody about that. She was incredibly resilient, incredibly strong, but nobody got through something like this unscathed.

Crawford had seemed a lot warmer now that he knew he wasn't staring down Public Enemy Number One, but either way, Sam had nothing but respect for him. He'd just been doing his job, providing a necessary counterpoint to Nolan, whose perception probably was skewed because of her brother.

In spite of Crawford's new affability, Nolan's presence through the questioning had been the sole comfort. Tombstone eyes, strawberry blond hair, and a chilly demeanor contrary to her compassion. Cold and warm, all at the same time. Like Yuki. Poor Yuki, alone in a morgue. "I need to see my wife, Detective. Would it be possible to do that when we're finished here?"

Nolan looked up from her computer. "Of course."

"Through all this, it's like she was forgotten."

"You didn't forget her, and neither did I. I never will."

"Do you remember every victim?"

"By the time an investigation wraps up, I know everything about them, sometimes much more than their own families. You form a bond with them, so you never forget. And they deserve to be remembered."

"That must be difficult."

"I owe it to them."

"What do you remember most about them, their lives or their deaths?"

The surprise registered conspicuously on her face. It was the first time Sam had been able to read her with any confidence.

"I've never thought of it that way. But life and death are equally significant parts of a single continuum, so I guess I remember both with the same clarity."

Sam thought that was a good way to look at things. "You still haven't told me how you pulled things together."

"Consuela Ortiz. I saw her on traffic cam footage getting into a Jeep Rubicon parked near your wife's house the day she was murdered. I followed a whim."

Sam tried to squeeze a cogent thought out of his weary brain. "How do you know her?"

"She cleaned for Ryan Gallagher. She was the one who found his body. We think Rolf drove the Jeep to your wife's neighborhood yesterday and left it there after he killed her, probably figuring we'd be looking at traffic film and paying close attention to any vehicles leaving the area around the time of her death."

"So he had Consuela pick it up for him later."

She nodded. "He made up a yarn about having some kind of emergency and told her to take a bus to Marina Del Rey to get the Jeep."

"He was smart, but you're smarter. That wasn't dumb luck."

"Things fell into place when we needed them to."

Her comment was terse and dismissive, and Sam knew it was an attempt to place some distance between herself and what had happened, just like he'd always done. No need to dwell, everything turned out peachy, no big deal. But the truth was, tonight had been a very big deal, more for Nolan than anybody else because she'd killed somebody.

"How are *you*, Detective?"

"I'm fine."

"You don't have to say that to me. I know. I understand."

She looked at him with sadness and maybe even a little trust. "Mr. Easton, before tonight, I'd never even discharged my weapon in the line of duty, let alone used deadly force. None of this seems real right now, but it will."

Sam nodded. "Yes, it will, and it's something you'll learn to live with because there's no other choice. You're intelligent and brave, Detective, and you made Max proud tonight."

Her cheeks colored and she looked down and started shuffling papers around on the table unnecessarily. "I think we're finished here, Mr. Easton. Just two more things before we go. My colleague Remy Beaudreau would like to speak with you. He's working the Miracle Mile cases."

"Sure. What's the other thing?"

She handed him her phone. "Call your mother, she just left a message."

Sam felt his stomach clench. Of course they'd been in contact with her while he was missing; it was the obvious thing to do. And she'd had no way to reach him. He should have thought of that earlier. Shit, he'd put the lovely Vivian Easton in yet another hellish holding pattern, waiting for news. He hoped she'd had some wine.

"Thank you, Detective Nolan, I'll call her right away."

"I'll give you some privacy." She stood and walked toward the door, then paused briefly and turned around. "And thank you, Mr. Easton, for what you said earlier. I hope Max is proud of me."

Chapter Seventy-five

SAM FELT SICK WITH GUILT AS he listened to his mother sob. He'd only seen her cry once, at his father's funeral, and it had been a very collected display of emotion because Vivian was a stoic, dignified woman. But now she seemed frantic, and when she finally calmed down enough to speak coherently, Sam understood.

"I thought something horrible had happened, Sam, with the shock of Yuki's murder. I thought you might have . . . I thought I might have lost you."

Sam closed his eyes. "Mom, I'd never do that to you. I'm so sorry you had to go through this. I'm okay."

"You're not in trouble?"

"No. I'll call you when I get home and explain. It's a long story." He thought of her alone in that big house. She'd gotten used to being a widow, but he knew she didn't like the solitude. "I'm going to be tied up here for a while longer, are you going to be alright?"

"Sam, I'm fine now, and I'm sorry I can't stop crying. I'm just so relieved. And Lee is here with me. I called him when I couldn't reach you."

"God bless him. Mom, I have to go, but I'll talk to you later. And I'll see you tomorrow."

"I'll cancel the dinner."

"Please don't. The company would be nice. Maybe just what I need."

"I love you, son."

"I love you, too."

•

Remy Beaudreau's eyes were almost black, and something about them seemed chaotic, like they were barely containing mayhem. He was suffused with a manic energy even though he was sitting perfectly still. Sam would never know what his deeper waters were, but he felt an instant kinship with him—they were two men riding a razor.

"You've been through an ordeal, Mr. Easton. I'm sorry for that, and very sorry about your wife."

"Thank you, I appreciate it."

"Thank you for the courtesy of stopping by. This is more curiosity than anything, so I won't keep you long."

"How can I help you?"

"I'm sure Maggie . . . Detective Nolan told you I'm working the Miracle Mile killings."

Maggie. So that's what her friends called her. "She did. You want to know about Rolf Hesse?"

"Actually, no."

"You don't think he's the Monster?"

"As of fifteen minutes ago, I'm sure he's not. We chased that down and he has solid alibis for all three murders."

Sam frowned. Rolf had seemed like a blue-ribbon candidate. "He was cunning, are you sure about that?"

"Positive. He was out of the country for the first two, visiting his father in Germany."

"What about the third?"

"He was at UCLA, filming and editing a webinar on storyboarding with several other students and two professors. Trust me, we wanted him to be good for it, too, but it's just not possible."

Sam felt slightly embarrassed for putting Rolf up on a pedestal of demonic, superhuman capability while at the same time impugning the competency of one of the country's most elite homicide divisions. "But if you're sure Rolf's not the Monster, then why am I here?"

"I'm interested in Ronald Doerr. You served with him."

Sam blinked at him, bewildered. "I did. He died two years ago, killed in action."

"I know."

"So why are you asking about him?"

"We found a piece of paper with your address and his fingerprints at a crime scene two nights ago."

"*Another* Monster crime scene?"

"Possibly. At the Rehbein Building."

"I read about that, but it sounded like a drug thing."

"It may have been."

"But you don't think so."

He shrugged.

"That's bizarre, but Ronald Doerr obviously isn't the Monster."

"No."

"So what are you thinking?"

"He was either there at some point carrying your address or he came in contact with a piece of paper somebody else dropped at the scene. Somebody who knew him. Maybe somebody who knows you, too."

"We didn't have any mutual acquaintances outside of our squad. Is there anything that ties the piece of paper directly to the Monster?"

Beaudreau looked down and leafed through the pages of a file. "No. But since his prints popped from his military service and there was a BOLO on you, it was something I had to follow. In Homicide, you chase every single thing down to the end, whether it makes any sense or not."

Sam shook his head in bafflement. "I can't explain it."

"Did he ever come to visit you here?"

"Never. Rondo and I served together—Rondo is what we called him—but we were never close. Not even friends really, I guess. You rely on people in that type of situation, but it doesn't necessarily make you buddies. The last time I remember seeing him was a few days before the blast. IED. They found his dog tags. That's how they identified the bodies, it was pretty much all that was left."

Beaudreau winced. "I'm sorry."

"I am, too."

"You survived. How?"

"I was on foot behind the vehicle when it was hit. Dumb luck," he said, thinking of Nolan.

Beaudreau fixed his tempest eyes on Sam's, then reached into his desk, withdrew a card, and wrote something on it before passing it over. "If you think of anything, give me a call. Use the number on the back, it's my private cell. Meantime, take care of yourself, go home, and get some rest."

"I will. I just have one more thing to do."

Chapter Seventy-six

THE SHARP SMELLS OF FORMALIN AND death and antiseptic. The chill of the room. The ominous sound of a metal drawer sliding out on its tracks. The crackle of a body bag, the ratchet of a zipper.

And his tiny, pale Yuki, a hideous black hole despoiling the left side of her forehead. She was motionless in this desolate place of sorrows, her flesh cold and stiff, far beyond the realm of the living and hopefully somewhere much better.

Sam's throat constricted. She was gone, truly gone. He touched her hair, still shiny in death—wasn't that strange that her hair should look so alive when the rest of her didn't?

The last time he'd seen her she'd been crying. Their last moments together shouldn't have been so sad. But yesterday they'd been two islands separated by turbulent water, privately despairing over the widening gap between them, the ugly end to a beautiful thing, and neither one of them had been able to confront it.

If they'd been truly honest with each other, maybe things would have turned out differently. For all of her insights, Dr. Frolich hadn't been able to tell him that very simple thing because he hadn't been honest with her either. He'd lied to everybody in order to support the lies he told himself. And Yuki had done exactly the same thing. Denial had been their shared flaw and it had been ruinous.

He thought about their lives together and their dreams for the future that hadn't included imminent funeral plans. Two entwined lives struggling with so much loss and yet always love. Even yesterday the love had been there—battered, different, but still there. It would always survive in him as long as he lived, and he wasn't going to let either life or love go.

Sam forgave her and he hoped that she would forgive him, if it was possible wherever she was. And maybe one day he'd be able to forgive himself.

He bent, kissed her cold forehead, and said goodbye.

•

The sun had risen by the time Nolan dropped Melody and Sam off at the parking lot of Will Rogers State Park. She got out with them and shook their hands, which seemed like a cold and perfunctory gesture considering everything they'd been through together. She was already calling them by their first names in her mind, but business was business and they weren't friends. It was just trauma bonding, and that would dissipate as soon as she left them.

"Take care, you two. I'll be on mandatory leave for a few days, but you have my private number, in case . . ."

In case what? You want to have coffee and keep alive a horrid episode we all want to forget?

". . . in case you think of something else pertinent in regard to what happened. The Monster is still out there, and although there doesn't appear to be a connection, things can change."

The three of them stood awkwardly for a moment, listening to the maniacal chuckling of a mockingbird, until Melody finally broke the stationary tableau by reaching out to give her a hug, which stunned her. Her arms stayed stiff at her sides for a moment, but eventually she returned the hug and felt a warmth that made her throat tighten. It was hard to know what Sam was thinking because only half of his face had expression, but they locked eyes for a moment before she left and again, she felt the strange sensation that he had brought Max closer.

As she drove to the station to give her own statement and tie up the details of her leave with the brass, she wondered how Sam and Melody would endure their next few days and weeks. Hopefully well. They had each other, and after overhearing part of Sam's conversation with his mother, she knew he had her, too.

She pulled into the parking ramp, which seemed much less ominous now that she'd killed somebody. Jaded, seasoned, whatever you wanted to call it, she possessed a dark knowledge that rendered an enclosed space with abundant hidey-holes for trolls thoroughly benign and inconsequential.

Her mobile rang and she glanced down at the caller ID. It was Remy. "Hello?"

"Maggie, how are you holding up?"

"I'm exhausted. I'm about to turn in my gun and shield, then I'm going to go home and sleep forever."

"How about breakfast at the Pantry before you go home and sleep forever?"

"You can't be serious."

"Why not? If you're going to hibernate, you should get some food in you first."

Nolan stared out the windshield at all those pylons and shadowy corners that had seemed so scary a couple days ago. Remy didn't seem so scary now, either. "Yeah, why the hell not?"

Chapter Seventy-seven

SAM DROVE MELODY'S BEAUTIFUL PEA-GREEN BOAT, sparing her ankle. Neither of them spoke until he pulled into his driveway.

"I can't imagine what seeing Yuki was like, Sam. I'm so sad for you."

"It was important. We were close again. One last time. Come in?"

"I need to go home. I need to sleep. So do you."

"Just for a minute. I want to talk to you. I'll make some bad coffee."

"Nothing could be as bad as what they gave us at the station."

"Your confidence might be misplaced." Sam wanted to see her smile but realized it might be a while before that happened. It would be a while before he smiled, too. "Does that mean you'll come in?"

"For a little bit."

The house looked the same, but it didn't feel the same as it had the last time he was here, just twenty hours ago? Twenty years ago? He was seeing it through different eyes, and he wasn't sure he liked the view. Everything reminded him that Yuki was gone. But there were good memories here, too, and maybe they would eventually usurp the bad, consoling him as time passed.

Mel sat down at the ugly, garage sale dinette table and unwrapped yesterday's pastries, still sitting on the table beneath a shroud of plastic film. "I'm starving, but I don't know if I can eat."

"Give it a try." The coffee maker finally croaked out the last dribbles and he brought over two mugs and sat down across from her.

"What did you want to talk about?" she asked, fiddling lethargically with a limp, sweating kolache.

"Trauma. You've just been through a major one. I know what that's like, I live through the aftermath every day."

"It was nothing like what you went through."

"Listen to me. Trauma is trauma, you can't compare experiences or assign designations of bad and worse. It's what it does to your mind that matters."

"It's messing with it."

"It's going to take some time, and you're going to feel a lot of things. Healing is hard and painful and scary and frustrating. Sometimes you don't know if you'll ever heal."

She took a sip of coffee, her eyes downcast. "That doesn't sound good."

"It's going to be different for you because you're not alone."

"You weren't alone, either."

"But I always felt that way because nobody around me understood. They were sympathetic, they were great, but they weren't in my headspace, thank God. They couldn't be. But we share this trauma, Mel. I'll help you get through this. We'll help each other get through this."

Her lip quivered. "I just want to go away."

"Where do you want to go?"

"Somewhere. Anywhere. I can't be here anymore. I was ready to leave before all this. Now I have to leave. I don't care where I go, I just need to be gone."

"This will always be with you, no matter where you go. Just like your past. Just like mine. Stay with me, Mel, just for a couple days. It's no time to be alone. You were so brave, and you're not going to tell yourself that every day, but I will."

She looked up at him. "You need your privacy. Time to work through things, time to grieve."

"I used to think that, but I don't anymore. When Yuki left me, I made myself believe it was a positive thing. I didn't think I had the right to ask her to stay because of what I put her through, and that was idiotic. It wasn't good, it just made things worse for both of us. I should have fought harder. Mel, I'm telling you this and asking you to stay a while because you're my friend and I'm yours and we can be there for each other in a way nobody else can. And this isn't about . . . it's not about . . ."

"I know that. I'm sorry I kissed you."

"I'm not."

"I was kissing you goodbye, Sam. Just in case." She covered her face, concealing whatever emotions were playing out there. "I didn't want to leave you."

"But you did. If you hadn't, we probably wouldn't be here." He leaned across the table and touched her hand. "You can have the bed, I'll sleep on the sofa."

"Sorry, but I like the sofa, you can't have it."

Sam took her into his arms. There was a brief resistance, then her body eased into his. He held her and felt a part of his heart tearing while another part mended. They'd gone deep into the dark together, but he could see a little light now and hoped she could, too.

Chapter Seventy-eight

SAM HAD NEVER EXPERIENCED A HOMECOMING like the one Mrs. Vivian Easton threw for him, not even after a year-long deployment overseas. She hadn't cried, just clung to him for the longest time.

She'd finally released him and stepped aside to let Lee and Andy welcome him. Lee was as robust and jovial as ever, and civilian life hadn't softened Andy one bit; he was as tanned and fit as he'd always been. There was strain in his face, though, and his eyes seemed hollow and haunted. War did that to you. But tonight, that grimness was temporarily suspended for everyone by a mother's love, good friends, drinks by the pool, delicious food, Cuban cigars.

Their continuous, serpentine conversation flowed from topic to topic: Yuki, the events at the Hesse mansion, politics, warm memories, amusing military anecdotes, and life in general. Mental health never came up, but golf did, along with the neighbor's Shih Tzu. It didn't quite feel normal; nothing would for a while, but it felt good.

After an obscenely abundant, poolside meal of grilled steaks, Santa Barbara spot prawns, and spiny lobster, Vivian excused herself to check on dessert, leaving them to their post-gluttony snifters of cognac and cigars. An old boys' club, enthusiastically sanctioned by a model military spouse who was undoubtedly sick to death of war stories.

"I'm goddamned sorry about Yukiko, son." Lee took a long draw off his stubby Churchill, blowing a stream of chocolate-scented smoke over the pool. The surface reflected undulating, hypnotic shards of sunlight into the glossy leaves of the camellia trees. Sam felt himself melting into his mother's sweet-smelling, garden dreamscape and the camaraderie and support of two men he loved and admired.

"And what you went through," Andy added. "A hell of a thing, beyond belief. Sometimes nothing makes sense in this life."

Sam sipped his cognac. "Here's to hoping I can maintain an existence of mind-numbing boredom from now on."

Lee put his hand on his shoulder. "I wish you peace, never boredom."

"Better yet. Andy, are you really going for Congress? That won't be peaceful or boring, but it will be frustrating as hell."

"Well, like I said, we're just forming an exploratory committee right now, but I'm passionate about my platform and policy ideas. First and foremost is the undeniable fact that some things need to change in Veterans Affairs. A lot of good men and women are being forgotten. The homeless crisis is unacceptable." He leaned forward, braced his muscular arms on the table. "Sam, you take care of business, do what you need to do, but if things look good in the first straw polls, know you have a job waiting for you whenever and if ever you want it. It would be an honor to have you on board. Besides, we need a pretty face."

"Then I'm your man." Sam raised his glass with a smile, then settled back into the plump pillows on his chair. "Seriously, Andy, I appreciate that. Give me some time."

"No question."

"Maybe I'll wait to see the polls, make sure I'm picking a winner."

Andy and Lee guffawed, then the general ditched the stub of his cigar in a broad, cut crystal ashtray Sam hadn't seen since his father's death. "I'm going to see if Vivian needs any help and let you two youngsters talk about the future. I've got an amazing meal under my very large belt, and I can't wait to see what she has planned for dessert."

Sam listened to his mother and Lee laughing in the kitchen. It was a nice, happy sound, and maybe an indication that the two of them . . . but that wasn't his business and not anything to think about unless a different kind of relationship between them formed, if it ever did. "Andy, I'm interested in the future, but I'm more interested in the past right now."

"The memory problems aren't improving?"

"Not really. I can't recall anything from the time around the blast, so I'm trying to sort some things out. Tell me about Ronald Doerr. I've been having some really disturbing dreams about him."

Andy cocked a brow at him and let out a loose wreath of smoke. "You really don't remember?"

What did you see? What do you remember?

"I don't remember shit, Andy. And the things I dream about, they're warped, bizarre, not real. I didn't want to say anything in front of Vivian, but my brain is scrambled and I don't know if I'll ever get it back, so you might want to rethink that job offer."

"I'm so sorry, Sam, I didn't know it was that bad. But the job offer stands."

"Fill in some blanks for me. All I know is that Rondo was killed in the convoy."

Andy took a deep breath and leaned back in his chair.

"What? He was killed in the convoy, right?"

"That's what his record says."

"But that's not what you say?"

"I know he's dead."

"It's not the same thing. Talk to me."

He let out a heavy, burdened sigh. "It's not a pretty story."

"I'm not used to pretty stories."

Chapter Seventy-nine

ANDY TWIRLED HIS CIGAR IN HIS fingers, then took a deep drink of cognac before he spoke. "Before the blast, Rondo was on his way to a psychiatric discharge."

"Seriously?"

"Seriously."

Hence the schizophrenic Rondo of his dream. Sam didn't remember him being particularly unstable, but his subconscious obviously had. "We all thought he was a jerk and a little squirrelly, but he was bad enough for a psych discharge?"

"At the end he was, he couldn't cope. But that didn't sit well with his father."

"Colonel Doerr."

"Right. But a loose cannon is a loose cannon, and they endanger everyone around them. We agreed to keep things quiet out of respect for the family, but the crazy son of a bitch lost it before it could go through."

"What did he do?"

"You really don't remember, ah, Jesus, I envy you that. He killed Raziq. The Afghan commander. Gutted him with his KA-BAR."

"*What?* Are you sure?"

"I'm sure, but there were no witnesses."

"Then why are you sure?"

"By the time the body was found, Rondo was AWOL. And he'd been coming to me regularly with complaints about Raziq. When his behavior got erratic and he started making threats against him, I put the discharge in motion."

"Why the hell would he want to kill Raziq?"

Andy's face darkened. "Because Raziq was raping little boys. He kept one chained to his bed. Maybe you remember this—in certain areas of the country, it's a mark of social status among powerful men. It even has a name."

Sam swallowed, and it felt like he'd just ingested one of his mother's golf balls. He'd blocked it out. No wonder. But it had surfaced in his dream, you couldn't hide forever. "*Bacha bazi.* Boy play."

"Right. We were told not to intervene. The justification spiel we got from the brass was that it was just a part of the culture, a matter of domestic Afghan criminal law, no requirement that U.S. military personnel report it, ad nauseam. But the real truth is, we needed him. There's always a reason to sleep with the devil in war, but it's an outrage, and it's going to be a part of my platform if I get that far. Might end up with a court martial, might end up with a medal, but I don't care. I'll be able to live with myself. Frankly, it's been hard."

Sam drained his glass, which did nothing to tamp down the swirling dizziness he was feeling as jagged pieces of fantasy and reality collided. He understood now that his waking nightmares of Rondo had been fantastic, bent versions of repressed memories, working themselves out like infected splinters just as Dr. Frolich had suggested. She was probably going to need therapy herself after she was finished unraveling his mind.

Andy tipped his head curiously. "Are you starting to remember things now?"

"No, but I'm starting to understand some things. So what happened after Rondo killed Raziq and went AWOL?"

"We went looking for him. That was the convoy that almost got you killed, and got the others killed. We figured he'd fallen into Taliban hands."

An unscheduled convoy, just like his dream Rondo and his buried memories had told him. "So he definitely wasn't on it."

"No."

"But you found his dog tags. And his file says KIA."

Andy lowered his eyes, looked into his nearly empty snifter, and gave it a few twirls as if the gesture would conjure a refill. "We're both civilians now. This is friend to friend. What I say to you stays with you, okay?"

"Of course, Andy."

"A lot of it is conjecture, and it's going to sound pretty crazy."

"Crazy *is* something I'm used to."

"The investigators found Rondo's dog tags. I never saw them. I'm sure you're wondering how they got there. Or if they were ever there in the first place."

"Christ, Andy, what are you saying?"

"I'm saying that maybe the blast was a convenient solution to a vexing problem. Colonel Doerr is an ambitious, connected man with a five-generation military pedigree, in line for a general's star. Better if your son is killed in action instead of being an AWOL psychiatric discharge who murdered an important military ally."

Sam was so staggered, he couldn't form any words for a moment. "Frame his own son's death and leave him in the desert to die? That's outrageous."

"It is, but you don't know Colonel Doerr. I do. He's a death over dishonor guy. Best case scenario, Rondo was looking at life in prison—the death penalty if defense couldn't argue a solid mental incompetency case. In my mind, it's within the realm of possibility."

"But the AWOL and the psych report were out there already, on record. Rondo was the obvious suspect for Raziq's murder."

"I filed my reports, truthful to the letter. After that, it went up the chain and was out of my hands. Along the way, things went missing. Like the AWOL and the psych report."

Sam shook his head in disbelief. "Nobody can bury a murder."

"Unless you have two interested parties with a lot at stake. A day after Raziq's murder, the Afghan military released a statement saying it was the result of a personal grudge, conducted by one of his lieutenants. They had things to hide, too, like his taste for children. On our end, everything leading up to it suddenly got classified at the highest level in the interest of national security. Same thing with the blast investigation, including the forensics that would prove Rondo wasn't on that convoy. I was gagged. Anybody who knew anything about it was, and frankly you and I are pretty much the only ones left alive who did."

"Jesus Christ." Sam pressed a palm against his forehead, trying to fend off the first serious headache he'd had since the night at Rolf's.

What do you see? What do you remember?

Was the unrelenting voice of his dreams another repressed memory? An informal interrogation that had occurred when he was half-dead and out of his mind on painkillers and God knew what else at Walter Reed? "I'm having trouble wrapping my mind around any conspiracy, Andy, let alone one of this magnitude. It can't be true, there's another explanation."

"Maybe I'm as crazy as Rondo was. The thing is, if you've been in-country long enough, you realize almost anything that happens there is a mirage—and if it's not, it will be. And everything you ever believed in goes to shit. After that, anything can ride."

"Were you threatened during the debriefing?"

He lowered his head. "If I'd pursued further action while serving, I would have been destroyed. They didn't have to threaten me."

Once again, Sam felt like the ground beneath his feet was crumbling away into a vast, bottomless chasm. "That's why you left. And why you're running for Congress."

He nodded absently. "This has been killing me, Sam. I had to find a way to do some good. I fucking hate politics, but it can serve a greater purpose."

"Does Lee know?"

"He's been in Washington a long time. Field incidents don't rise up to that high-water mark."

"If you're working with him, you need to tell him. He's a good man, Andy, he can help you."

"I don't know if anybody can help me. I could use another drink, how about you?"

Sam found the bottle of Courvoisier in the outdoor bar cabinet and refilled their glasses. "I've always had a lot of respect for you, Andy."

"Even now?"

"Even more now. You'll find a way to do what's right. I'm with you, and Lee will be, too, believe me on that. But tell me this, do you think Rondo could still be alive?"

"It's not possible, Sam. He was a head case who fled with no supplies into a desert wasteland. If the climate didn't kill him, the Taliban did. Kev, Shaggy, and Wilson—three good men—died for him, and you almost did, too. If I thought he was still alive, I'd hunt him down and kill him myself."

•

After peach tart and coffee, Sam joined his mother in the kitchen while Lee dosed out the last of the Courvoisier. "Drink up, Captain. We have reason to celebrate. Our boy is going to get through this, too. I can't say I'd be standing so tall."

Andy watched Vivian behind the glass patio doors, putting her kitchen back together. Sam was trying to help, but she kept shooing him away. "He's got good people behind him. Vivian is a force of nature, isn't she?"

Lee chuckled and clipped a fresh cigar. "Anybody in her orbit is lucky to be there. What did you and Sam talk about while I was helping get your desserts on the table? It looked like an intense discussion."

"He's trying to put things together from the time around the blast. His memory is still shot."

"That might not be such a bad thing."

"We all deserve the truth."

Lee fired a cigar. "The truth is a funny thing—we all want it, but we're not always ready to hear the answers."

Chapter Eighty

SAM PULLED THE SHELBY OVER TO the curb by Brookside Park near his childhood home and slid down in his seat, watching families and lovers, joggers and dog walkers pass by. Regular people with regular lives, but he knew they all had secrets, big or small, and he wondered what they were. He envied them because they knew their own secrets. Sam didn't, didn't even know if he had any. He hadn't for two years.

He might never know what had really happened back in the desolate, ruined country of Afghanistan or satisfactorily fill in the blanks in the vast swath of mental wasteland residing in his skull. But he knew Andy wasn't the violent, demented killer of Raziq that the schizophrenic Rondo specter had proclaimed him to be, and he trusted Andy more than his twisted dream.

Rondo was your subconscious. Why would your subconscious tell you Andy was Raziq's murderer?

"Because I'm FUCKED UP," he hissed, slamming his palms against the steering wheel. A few passers-by looked over their shoulders in alarm, and he sank deep into his seat, trying to disappear. He took deep breaths and wished he had that damned Maneki Neko cat sitting on his dashboard right now.

He tried to martial whatever remaining rational, cognitive brain cells he had, abandoning all psychoanalytical confusion. What if Rondo hadn't been a dream? What if he'd managed to survive the desert and the Taliban and somehow got himself back here under the radar by jumping the Mexican border? His mental derangement would never allow him to take responsibility for a murder, so he would project it onto someone else, an authority figure—somebody like Andy or his father—whom he'd also implicated as a villain. If Sam had learned anything in life, it was that you couldn't discount any possible truth, no matter how improbable it seemed.

After some time spent watching a rumble between several elementary school soccer foes, he found Remy Beaudreau's card in his wallet and called him. He answered on the second ring.

"Mr. Easton, how are you doing?"

"Surviving. It's my default position."

"And that of the entire human race, but ninety percent don't realize it. What can I do for you?"

"The first thing you can do is promise me we're not having this conversation."

"We're not having this conversation. The number you called is private."

Sam closed his eyes and leaned back in the seat of the Mustang. "Ronald Doerr might still be alive. I just found out there may have been a mistake in his military record."

"How do you know?"

"I can't tell you that. And please don't pursue that angle. Give me your word, or we're done here."

No hesitation. "You have my word. I want to find my killer, not stir up any military scuttlebutt. You're protecting a source, I get that and I'll honor that. So you have more to say?"

"I don't know if Doerr is the Monster, but it could make sense if he's still alive."

Silence, tapping on a keyboard. Finally: "Tell me how it could make sense."

"He's mentally ill. He probably gutted an Afghan official with a knife."

More keyboard tapping. "Do you have any other specifics? Because it's going to be hard to find somebody who's dead on the books."

Sam gritted his teeth. He didn't know if any of the specifics he had were real or true. But if Rondo was alive and killing women because he thought they were military assassins, Beaudreau needed to know everything, real or not. Throw it into his lap and let him sort it all out. "I'm going out on a limb here, Detective. I'm trusting you."

"Your trust isn't misplaced, I promise you that. Right now, I'm getting an anonymous tip. No idea where it came from. I'll never know."

"You *never* got an anonymous tip. If this pans out, you did it on your own. Do you understand?"

"Understood."

Sam released a breath. "This is all speculation."

"Most of my job is speculation. Go ahead."

"Ronald Doerr is likely a paranoid schizophrenic and highly delusional. He thinks the military is trying to kill him. He's on the run, probably homeless in Los Angeles. You might find him in one of the encampments."

"If he really is alive, which is still in question?"

"It is."

"You just gave me some pretty specific speculation."

"That's all it is. And if you do find him, tell him you're going to save him from the Army and he'll cooperate."

•

Remy hung up from the strange conversation, churning it over in his mind. Sam Easton had just exhibited extreme paranoia, and maybe he had a reason. But whether the information was legitimate or the product of PTSD, he had to act on it and protect him at the same time. Bringing it to the task force without solid justification would raise questions because they would rightly wonder why he was suddenly sending them off to Skid Row to look for a dead man. He needed a reasonable answer that would serve both parties.

He opened up the forensics report and eventually found one. The matching fibers from two of the scenes were extremely worn wool and teeming with every disgusting bacteria known to science, along with louse droppings. A heavily soiled, old garment. He'd glossed over it before because all the murders had occurred in places where that was the typical dress code. But maybe it mattered now.

He called Sweet Genevieve in the lab, who really wasn't. She was, however, great at her job.

"I'm busy, Remy, what the hell do you want now?" she answered genially.

"I'm sorry to hear you're busy because I have all this free time on my hands and I was hoping we could grab lunch sometime."

She either snuffled in amusement or snarled. It was hard to tell which. "What do you want?" she repeated.

"I want you to help me solve the Monster killings."

"I gave you everything I have." Her voice was a little less combative now.

"The fibers. They're dirty and old."

"They're disgusting, came from something out of a dumpster, mark my words."

"So they're not just dirty like clothes are when you don't wash them often?"

"No way."

"So in your highly esteemed, professional opinion, they could have come from the garment of somebody living on the streets?"

"What an ass kiss you are, stop talking like a schmuck. Of course they could have. In my *highly esteemed, professional opinion,* they did."

"Thanks, that's all I need."

"Are you getting closer?"

"Maybe."

"Good, because you've been a real pain in my ass lately. Call me for lunch when people stop killing other people in this city and I might say yes."

"People are never going to stop killing other people in this city. Or anywhere else, for that matter."

"So I guess lunch is off indefinitely. Your loss. Go catch this fuck."

Remy smiled at her abrupt disconnection and laid his phone on his desk. Genevieve's word was good enough.

Chapter Eighty-one

SAM SLEPT TEN HOURS AND DIDN'T have a single nightmare, not even a dream, which was a miracle after his deeply disturbing conversation with Andy last night. With the soundness of his mind still in question, he was reluctant to form an opinion, so he'd relegated it to one of his many cerebral compartments where he stored things not yet ready to be confronted and dealt with.

In the spirit of living one day at a time, he focused on the most pressing concern of the moment, which was the media, reporting on the Hesse tragedy obsessively and around the clock. There was plenty of glamour there, and an irresistible "dark side of Hollywood" angle to give it legs. Mental illness became part of the conversation, and there was increasing speculation about the possibility Rolf had been holding hostages. They didn't have the whole story, not even close, and they wouldn't listen to the LAPD spokeswoman tell them she had no further information for much longer.

Sam clicked off the bedroom TV and decided to put a moratorium on all news from any source for a while. He also decided it was time to get out of town.

Melody had left a note on the kitchen table saying she would be back by five with dinner. She'd also left a fresh box of pastries and a new bag of coffee, Tanzania Peaberry. He didn't know what that was, but it sounded awfully cute and he hoped it tasted good, too.

He ate a bear claw while the Peaberry brewed, opened his computer, and started looking for rentals up the coast. Big Sur was his first choice. Vivian and Jack had taken him up there for the first time the summer before he started kindergarten and many times after that. He'd taken Yuki there a few times, too. It was a place filled with happy memories and magical moments that spanned decades. It was expensive, especially this time of year, but after what he'd been through, the concept of frugality seemed laughable.

His phone chimed and he answered. "Good morning, doc."

"Good morning, Sam. I'm calling personally to confirm your appointment for tomorrow."

"Afraid I wouldn't show up?"

"No. Honestly, I just wanted to know how you're getting along."

"I'm alive, and it feels great. I'm meeting with the funeral director today to make arrangements for Yuki, that doesn't feel great. Mainly, I'm walking around in a haze. Things haven't caught up with me yet."

"I'm sure they haven't."

"After the funeral, I'm going to rent a place in Big Sur for a week or two to get away."

"That's a wonderful idea. I'd like to continue our regular sessions by Skype while you're there."

"I'd like that, too."

"Good. I look forward to seeing you tomorrow."

Sam was looking forward to it, too. He liked her and respected her; if he'd met her personally instead of professionally, they might even be friends. Somewhere down the road, he hoped they could have some cocktails together and reminisce about the time he'd almost lost his mind.

He wasn't sure if he should tell her about the *Deep into the Dark* connection or the fact that she'd been a secondary subject of Rolf's surveillance. It was disturbing, and wasn't really germane, but she might take a professional interest. Just because her specialty was trauma didn't mean she wouldn't end up writing a scholarly piece on stalkers at some point, especially since she'd been involved with one, even if indirectly.

He filled his coffee mug and found that Tanzanian Peaberry was a revelation, then began nibbling a croissant while he continued to scroll through rental listings. He'd narrowed it down to three possibilities when his phone rang again: Remy Beaudreau.

"Good morning, Detective."

"Mr. Easton. Thank you for your call last night. I know you were taking a risk. I honored your request for privacy and kept you out of things entirely."

"I appreciate that."

"Now, I'm asking the same of you. I think you said last night, 'We're not having this conversation'?"

"I did."

"Right now, we're not having this conversation."

"Understood."

He sighed. "We found Ronald Doerr recently deceased near the encampment under the First Street Bridge early this morning."

Sam closed his eyes, trying to keep his world on its fragile axis. Rondo had been real. He'd survived somehow, had been in Los Angeles, and right here in his house. Jesus. "How?"

"Knife wound to the gut. It's possible that it was self-inflicted, but we're waiting to hear what the coroner has to say."

A man on fire. Rondo, a tormented soul, living a life of horror from Afghanistan to here—and dying in squalor and madness, homeless and alone, under a fucking bridge in a heartless city that let the beautiful park that was the West Side VA rent out storage and laundry facilities. Rondo had finally ended the agony himself.

If I thought he was still alive, I'd hunt him down and kill him myself.

Oh, no, don't even go there. The days of fucked-up, paranoid fantasy were over, and he was never going back, even if he had to live on tranquilizers and rye whiskey for the rest of his life.

"Mr. Easton?"

"Yeah, sorry. It's just a shock. Do you think he was the Monster?"

"No question, but we're just starting to pull that together on our end. We're keeping things under wraps until we can build our case, so you're the only person outside the department who knows. Please keep it that way."

"You have my word."

"Things may get difficult for you and your source once this breaks. The media may or may not put together your connection to Doerr; but once they find out that you were involved with the Hesse incident—and they will once it becomes public record—they'll start poking into every aspect of your life. It will die down eventually, but I just wanted to give you a warning so you can be prepared."

"I figured as much. I'd planned to get out of town for a while anyhow."

"It's a good idea. You have my gratitude, Mr. Easton, and know you have a friend in the LAPD if you ever need anything."

Sam hung up and stared down at the oily swirls of cream on the surface of his coffee as if they held some absolute truth. Things were going to get ugly for the Army and for Colonel Doerr and his family. Or maybe this would all go away, too, explained away as a clerical error in the vast red tape of the military machine. But what would never go away was the knowledge that their son had been a serial killer. That was about as FUBAR as things could get.

EPILOGUE

THE BAR WAS RIOTOUS AND FILLED with cops and detectives celebrating the victorious Miracle Mile task force. Remy was in the center of a clamoring group of law enforcement revelers who were sloshing beers all over themselves and the floor as they toasted boisterously. Nolan thought he looked uncomfortable as the subject of all the attention, but he was smiling.

"I've never seen so many drunk cops in one place before," Al said, sipping the foam off his beer. "If something major happens tonight, Los Angeles is screwed."

"Catching a serial is a big deal."

"Damn right it is. I'm anxious to have a chat with Remy and find out how he did it. I mean, he had some fibers and a set of prints from a dead guy supposedly two years in the ground and ended up finding him freshly dead in a homeless encampment. That's some diligent, enlightened detecting."

"It is."

Al lifted a brow at her. "Maybe he had some help."

Nolan had wondered the very same thing, but all that mattered was that the Monster wouldn't kill again. "It's all leg work in the end, and catching a break."

"Yeah, I suppose you're right." Crawford's gaze drifted to the pool table where there was a fierce game of 8-ball in progress between Gang and Narcotics and Robbery Special Section. "I was wrong about Sam Easton. Makes me wonder what else I'm wrong about."

"You were wrong about him, but not about me."

"What do you mean?"

"I did have a soft spot for him. Because of Max. You were being a cop, I was being a cop and a sister."

"And you ended up being right. Mags, everything we do is colored by experience. I wanted Easton, you didn't—we had our own reasons and everything worked out because of it. You can fight it, but you can't ever entirely vanquish it. You shouldn't. That's instinct."

"Thanks, Al."

"It's the way it is. And instinct can take you to the right places sometimes, that I can tell you." He gestured with his beer. "My instinct says Remy's on his way over, he's been staring at you all night. I think I'll go use the can."

Remy *was* on his way over, there was no instinct about it, and the crowd parted deferentially as he passed through the bawdy temple that was his realm for the night. Al gave him a fist bump as he passed, then turned back and winked at her, which predictably made her cheeks bloom. She was going to kill him.

Remy was at her table now, looking down at her with a smile that hadn't dimmed all night. "Mind if I take a seat and get out of the fray for a little while?"

"Please do. Congratulations, Remy." She tapped his martini glass with her beer mug.

"I'm glad it's over."

"The whole city is. Are you going to take some time off?"

"I am. One thing about Homicide, you have guaranteed job security. There's always going to be a case waiting for you when you get back to the office."

"Depressing, but true."

"What are you doing to keep yourself occupied during your leave?"

"Trying to get the bird of paradise in my front yard to bloom."

"A noble endeavor."

She looked over his shoulder and saw his tipsy disciples moving as a single, beer-sloshing organism toward the table. "Looks like they're not finished with you."

His eyes sparked with humor. "They're relentless. Never squander an opportunity to act like a pack of frat boys and sorority sisters. Since we're both on vacation, it would be a great time to grab that celebratory drink you promised me."

"We're having one right now."

He leaned forward and pinned her to her seat with those wild onyx eyes. "That's not what I'm talking about, Maggie. You're one of the sharpest detectives the LAPD has, don't tell me you haven't figured it out yet."

•

Sam stood on the small lawn of the cliffside rental cottage in Big Sur, watching Melody watch the ocean. She was perched on a rock, staring down at the slender, tawny beach and the tumbling surf. He wondered if Teddy had ever been up here with his board and his weed.

She'd started playing guitar again and had brought her acoustic, but she said the sounds of the ocean were so much better than the twang of strings, so it sat neglected next to her. Melody was stronger than he'd ever imagined, and it wasn't just street toughness. A brush with death could tear you down, but it could also tap an inner strength, and she was in the process of an astonishing transformation.

He hadn't had any hallucinations or blackouts in two weeks, not since the night in the majestic house of horror in Beverly Hills. He still occasionally had combat dreams, but they were diluted, more like watercolors than vivid oils. Ty, Shaggy, Wilson, and Rondo were never a part of them now, and he hoped they'd finally been laid to rest.

Dr. Frolich conjectured that the lessening intensity was twofold: some of the blank spaces had been filled in, and he'd been able to absolve himself of some of his survivor's guilt by saving others. He and Melody were still here, and Rondo would never kill again. Nolan believed he was here for a reason. Maybe she was right.

More often than war, he dreamed of Yuki, but not her violent end or the slow, painful disintegration of their marriage. He was only visited by beautiful scenes: her black hair shining in the sun as she plucked persimmons from her tree; on Venice Beach with her oversized sunglasses; in Tuscany, walking along a sloping gravel road beside a vineyard and sampling a sour wine grape that made her mouth pucker.

He always woke up crying from these dreams, with an unbearable void in his core, but he cherished the time he spent with her in sleep. Maybe she did have the capacity to forgive him in an afterlife, and these dreams were her way of telling him that. Or more likely, he was finally learning to forgive himself.

He still had Rolf's script, even though he'd planned to douse it with gasoline and incinerate it. One day he might need to read it in order to put that unfinished business away for good, so he kept it stored in a box on the top shelf of a closet he never used. He didn't know if Melody still had hers. He'd ask her about it one day.

"How was your run?" Melody asked without turning around.

"Hilly." He walked over and sat next to her.

"You went on the trails?"

"Where else would I run?"

"There are cougars out there. There are warnings tacked up all over the place."

"I didn't see any cougars."

"Nobody ever does until it's too late."

"I'm completely unpalatable, I still have shrapnel inside me, and those cats have a sharp sense of smell. So what do you think of Big Sur?"

"I love it, I want to live here. Think there are any bartending jobs?"

"I'm sure you could find one."

She put her chin in her hands. "I'd probably get bored up here."

"Maybe you're not done with Los Angeles quite yet."

"You might be right. What's next for you, Sam?"

"Dinner. I'm starving."

"That's a very short-sighted goal."

"There is great wisdom in knowing that sometimes, those are the best kind to have."

She rolled her eyes, then opened her guitar case and pulled out a small, white bag. “For you, I saw it when I was shopping today. It’s not the Hope Diamond or anything, so don’t have any big expectations.”

Sam reached into the bag and withdrew a key ring with a green enameled shamrock dangling from it. Irish Spring and a tattoo all in one magnificent little parcel of kitsch.

She gave him her charming, crooked Melody smile for the first time in a while. “For luck. Who knows? Maybe talismans work after all. Like you said, we’re not dead and we’re not in jail. Life doesn’t get much better than that.”

Acknowledgments

Every author owes a huge debt of gratitude to the team supporting them. St. Martin's Minotaur took the leap with me as I explored new characters, a new setting, and a new series, and I am very blessed to be backed by such talent. Kelley Ragland, I am so thrilled to be finally working with you! Thank you for your enthusiasm and brilliant editorial guidance. Madeline Houpt, Hector DeJean, Danielle Prielipp, and many others—all of you, thank you for your extraordinary efforts in helping bring this book to life.

Ellen Geiger at Frances Goldin Literary Agency: my dear friend and agent for almost twenty years. Oh, the stories we could tell! And Matt McGowan—you are the best. How you keep track of things on my behalf, I'll never know. Thank you both for taking such good care of me.

To Christine Pepe—your friendship and support means the world.

A belated thank-you to Scott Wentzka, for his sculptural inspiration. Your piece helped me write a book, and when I can afford you, I'll add it to my collection.

To PJ, always. Love never dies.